Dear Mystery Reader:

The Black Death has left its mark. Graveyards are filled with the corpses of plague victims and hunger is the prevailing mood in town. This is Cambridge 1350, the setting for Susanna Gregory's AN UNHOLY ALLIANCE. A Cambridge fellow and former police officer, Gregory is more than familiar with the territory she covers in her latest novel.

Crime is on the rise in medieval Cambridge. Three harlots are found murdered, a friar meets a mysterious end, and the chancellor of the university vanishes without a trace. Master of Medicine, Matthew Bartholomew is summoned to investigate the strange goings-on. Add the help of monk Brother Michael, and the tangled web begins to unravel. Conspiracy, devil worship, and all of the other sordid offspring of these dark and deadly times are exhumed in the search for answers in this sinful town.

If you're a history fan, or just in search of an exciting whodunit, this is a book you'll want to pick up. AN UNHOLY ALLIANCE is an enlightening read on the darkest days in history.

Yours in crime,

Joe Veltre
Associate Editor
St. Martin's DEAD LETTER Paperback Mysteries

NIGHT HORROR

Carrying the candle, the figure left the orchard and began to move down the path that led to the back gate. Bartholomew saw it reach out to open the door. He thought of the women with their throats cut by a maniac, and made his decision: the intruder must not be allowed to escape!

He abandoned his hiding place and made for the gate at a run. The figure glanced round in shock, and began urgently to heave at the gate. It flung open just as Bartholomew reached it and grabbed him. The figure spun round with a cry of horror and drew a knife. Bartholomew knocked it from his hand, struggling to wrench the hood from his face.

At that moment the door was thrown inwards with great force. It burst into flames, and a gigantic figure swathed in black leapt through it with an unearthly howl.

Bartholomew was aware of yellow teeth and glittering eyes as the huge shape swept towards him. . . .

"A believable medieval Cambridge, with muddy graveyards, fortified universities, and town/student antipathies."
—*Library Journal*

an
Unholy
alliance

Susanna
Gregory

St. Martin's Paperbacks

AN UNHOLY ALLIANCE

First published in Great Britain by Little, Brown and Company

Copyright © 1996 by Susanna Gregory.
Excerpt from *A Bone of Contention* © 1997 by Susanna Gregory.

Library of Congress Catalog Card Number: 96-27965

ISBN: 0-312-96631-8

Printed in the United States of America

St. Martin's Press hardcover edition/December 1996
St. Martin's Paperbacks edition/October 1998

St. Martin's Paperbacks are published by St. Martin's Press, 175 Fifth Avenue, New York, NY 10010.

10 9 8 7 6 5 4 3 2 1

For Peter Sage

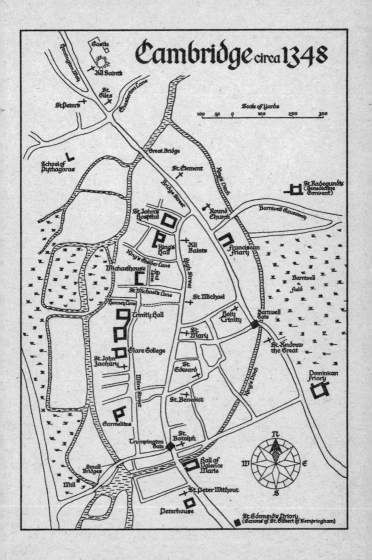

PROLOGUE

Cambridge, 1350

ISOBEL WATKINS GLANCED FEARFULLY BEHIND HER FOR AT least the fourth time since leaving the home of the wealthy merchant on Milne Street. She was sure she was being followed, but each time she stopped and looked behind her, she could hear and see nothing amiss. She slipped into a doorway and held her breath to control her trembling as she peered down the dark street behind her. There was nothing, not even a rat scurrying from the mounds of rubbish that lined both sides of the High Street.

She took a deep breath and leaned her head back against the door. She was imagining things, and the recent murder of two of her colleagues in the town had unnerved her. She had never been afraid of walking alone in the dark before: indeed, it was usually when she met her best customers. She poked her head out and looked down the street yet again. All was silence and darkness. In the distance she heard the bell of St Michael's chiming the hour: midnight.

Dismissing her fears, she slipped out of the doorway and began walking quickly up the High Street towards her home near the town gate. It was only a short walk, and the night-watchmen on duty at the gate would be within hailing distance soon. She grimaced. It would not be the first time she had been forced to give her night's earnings to the guards in order not to be arrested for breaking the curfew. She caught her breath again as she heard the faintest of sounds behind her, and decided she would be happy to part with an entire week's earnings just to be safely in her own bed.

1

She saw the pinprick of light coming from the gate, and broke into a run, almost crying in relief. She was totally unprepared for the attack that came from the side. She felt herself hurled to the ground as someone dived out of the small trees around St Botolph's Church. She tried to scream as she felt herself dragged into the churchyard, but no sound would come. She felt a sudden burning pain in her throat and then a hot, sticky sensation on her chest. As her world slowly went black, she cursed herself for being so convinced that she was being followed that she had failed to consider whether it was safe ahead.

A short distance away, a man wearing the habit of a Dominican friar knelt in the silence of the tower of St Mary's Church. In front of him stood the great iron-bound box that held the University's most precious documents – deeds of property, records of accounts, scrolls containing promises of money and goods, and a stack of loose pages recording important occurrences in the University, carefully documented by the University clerks.

The University chest. The friar rubbed his hands and, balancing the merest stub of a candle on the chest, began to work on one of the three great locks that kept the University's business from prying eyes. The only sounds in the tower were tiny clicks and metallic scrapes as he concentrated on his task. He felt safe. He had spent several days in the church, kneeling in different parts so he could become familiar with its layout and routine. That night he had hidden behind one of the pillars when the lay-brother had walked around the church, dousing candles and checking all the windows were secure. When the lay-brother had left, the friar had stood stock still behind his pillar for the best part of an hour to make certain that no one had followed him and was also hiding. Then he had spent another hour checking every last corner of the church to make doubly sure. He had climbed on benches to test that the locks on the window were secure and had taken the added precaution of slipping a thick bar across the door before climbing the spiral stairs to the tower.

He hummed to himself as he worked. The singing that evening had been spectacular, with boys' voices soaring like angels over the drone of the bass and tenor of the men. The friar had been unfamiliar with the music and had been told it had been written by a Franciscan called Simon Tunstede who was earning something of a reputation as a composer. He paused and stared into the darkness as he tried to recall how the Sanctus had gone. As it came back to him, he resumed his fiddling with the lock and sang a little louder.

The first lock snapped open, and the friar shuffled on his knees to the next one. Eventually, the second lock popped open and the friar moved onto the third. He stopped singing and small beads of sweat broke out on his head. He paused to rub an arm over his face and continued scraping and poking with his slivers of metal. Suddenly, the last lock snapped open, and the friar stood up stiffly.

He stretched his shoulders, cramped from hunching over his work, and carefully lifted the lid of the great box. It groaned softly, the leather hinges protesting at the weight. The friar knelt again and began to sort carefully through the documents that lay within. He had been working for only a few moments when a sound behind him made him leap to his feet. He held his breath in terror, and then relaxed when he realised it was only a bird in the bell chamber above. He turned back to the chest again, and continued to rifle through the scrolls and papers.

He suddenly felt a great lurching pain. He tried to stand up, but his legs failed him. He put both hands to his chest and moaned softly, leaning against the great box as he did so. He was aware that the light from the candle was growing dimmer as the pain in his chest increased. With the tiniest of sighs, the friar collapsed over the open chest and died.

CHAPTER 1

DAWN WAS COOL AND CLEAN AS MATTHEW BARTHOLOMEW and Brother Michael walked together across the College yard to the great iron-studded doors that led to Foul Lane. As Michael removed the stout wooden bar from the wicket gate and chided the rumpled porter for sleeping when he should have been alert, Bartholomew looked up at the dark blue sky and savoured the freshness of the air. When the sun became hot, the small town would begin to stink from the refuse and sewage that were dumped in the myriad of waterways, ditches, and streams. But now the air was cool and smelt of the sea.

Michael opened the gate, and Bartholomew followed him into the lane. The large Benedictine tripped over a mangy dog that was lying in the street outside, and swore as it yelped and ran away towards the wharves on the river bank.

'There are far too many stray dogs in Cambridge,' he grumbled. 'Ever since the plague. Stray dogs and stray cats, with no one left to keep the wretched things off the streets. Now the Fair is here, there are more than ever. And I am certain I saw a monkey in the High Street last night!'

Bartholomew smiled at the monk's litany of complaints and began to walk up the lane towards St Michael's Church. It was his and Michael's turn to open the church and prepare it for the first service of the day. Before the plague had swept through England, all the religious offices were recited in the church by the scholars of Michaelhouse, but the shortage of friars and priests to perform these duties meant that the College's religious practices were curtailed. Brother Michael would pray alone, while Bartholomew prepared the church for Prime,

5

which all the scholars would attend. After, they would go back to Michaelhouse for breakfast, and lectures would start at six.

The sky was beginning to lighten in the east, and although there were sounds – a dog barking, a bird singing in the distance, the clatter of an early cart to the market – the town was peaceful, and this was Bartholomew's favourite time of day. As Michael fumbled with the large church key, Bartholomew walked over the long grass of the churchyard to a small hump marked with a crude wooden cross. Bartholomew and Michael had buried Father Aelfrith here when, all over the city, others were being interred in huge pits at the height of the plague. He stared down at the cross, remembering the events of the winter of 1348, when the plague had raged and a murderer had struck at Michaelhouse.

Bartholomew had buried another colleague in the churchyard too. The smug Master Wilson lay in his temporary grave awaiting the day when Bartholomew fulfilled a deathbed promise and organised the construction of an extravagant tomb carved in black marble. Bartholomew felt a deep unease about the notion of removing Wilson's body from its grave in the churchyard to the church. Even after a year and a half of rethinking all he had learned, Bartholomew still did not understand how the plague spread, or why it struck some people and not others. Some physicians believed the stories from the East, that the pestilence had come because an earthquake had opened the graves of the dead. Bartholomew saw no evidence to prove this was true, but the plague was never far from his thoughts, and he was loathe to risk exhuming Wilson.

He heard Brother Michael begin to chant and dragged himself from his thoughts to go about his duty. Faint light filtered through the clear glass of the east window, although the church was still shades of grey and black. Later, when the sun rose, the light would fall on the vivid paintings on the walls that brought them alive with colour. Especially fine was the painting that depicted Judgement Day, showing souls being tossed into the pits of hell by a goat-devil. On the opposite side St Michael saved an occasional soul. Bartholomew often wondered what had driven the artist to clothe the Devil in a scholar's tabard.

As Michael continued to chant, Bartholomew opened the

small sanctuary cupboard, took out chalice and paten, and turned the pages of the huge Bible to the reading for the day. When he had finished, he walked around the church lighting candles and setting out stools for those of the small congregation who were unable to stand.

As he checked the level of holy water in the stoup, he grimaced with distaste at the film of scum that had accumulated. Glancing quickly down the aisle to make sure Michael was not watching, he siphoned the old water off into a jug, gave the stoup a quick wipe round, and refilled it. Keeping his back to Michael, Bartholomew poured the old water away in the piscina next to the altar, careful not to spill any. There were increasing rumours that witchcraft was on the increase in England because of the shortage of clergy after the plague, and there was a danger of holy water being stolen for use in black magic rituals. The piscina ensured that the water drained into the church foundations and could not be collected and sold. But Bartholomew, as a practising physician, as well as Michaelhouse's teacher of medicine, was more concerned that scholars would touch the filthy water to their lips and become ill.

Michael finished his prayers and Bartholomew saw him sneak a gulp of wine from the jug intended for the mass. The monk yawned hugely, and began to relate a tale of how a pardoner had tried to sell him some of the Archangel Gabriel's hair at the Fair the previous day. Michael, outraged, had demanded proof that the hair had indeed belonged to Gabriel and had been informed that the angel himself had presented it to the pardoner in a dream. Michael proudly announced that he had tipped the scoundrel and his fake hair into the King's Ditch. Bartholomew winced. The Ditch was a foul affair, running thick with all kinds of filth and waste, and Michael's righteous anger might well have caused the unfortunate pardoner to contract a veritable host of diseases.

Before he could respond, the doors were pushed open and sleepy-eyed scholars began to file silently into church. Michael and Bartholomew shot to the altar rail and knelt quickly in the hope that they had not been seen chattering when they should have been praying. Bartholomew watched the Michaelhouse scholars take their places in the choir: the Fellows in a line to the right headed by the Master, and the students and commoners behind. Cynric ap Huwydd, Bartholomew's book-bearer, rang the bell to announce that the service was about to begin. The scholars of Physwick Hostel, who had begged use of St Michael's Church from Michaelhouse because their own church had been closed since the plague, processed in and stood in a neat line opposite the Michaelhouse scholars. The arrangement was an uneasy one: Physwick resented being forced to rely on Michaelhouse's good graces, and Michaelhouse was nervous at sharing the church after twenty-five years. Bartholomew saw Physwick's Principal, Richard Harling, exchange a smile far from warm with Michaelhouse's Senior Fellow, Roger Alcote.

In the main body of the church a few parishioners drifted in, yawning and rubbing the sleep from their eyes, and Michael began the service, his rich baritone filling the church as he chanted. Out of the corner of his eye, Bartholomew saw something fly through the air towards the Michaelhouse students. It landed harmlessly, but a stain on the floor attested that it was a ball of mud. Bartholomew scanned the congregation, and identified the culprits in the form of the blacksmith's sons. They stood, hands clasped in front of them, eyes raised to the carved wooden roof, as though nothing had happened. Bartholomew frowned. The University had a stormy relationship with the town, and, although the University brought prosperity to a number of townsfolk, it also brought gangs of arrogant, noisy students who despised the people of the town and rioted at the least provocation. Bartholomew saw one of the Physwick students bow his head in laughter at the mud-ball. The University was not even at peace with itself: students from the south loathed scholars from the north and from Scotland; they all hated students from Wales and Ireland; and there was even fierce rivalry between the different religious orders, the mendicant friars and priests at loggerheads with the rich Benedictines and the Austin Canons who ran the Hospital of St John.

Bartholomew turned his attention away from the blacksmith's loutish sons, and back to the service. Michael had finished reading, and the scholars began to chant a Psalm. Bartholomew joined in the singing, relishing how the chanting echoed through the church. As the Psalm finished, Bartholomew stepped forward to read the designated tract from the Old Testament.

He faltered as the door was flung open, and a man walked quickly down the aisle, gesturing urgently that he wanted to speak to the Master, Thomas Kenyngham. Kenyngham was a gentle Gilbertine friar whose rule of the College was tolerant to the point of laxity. He smiled benignly and waved the messenger forward. The man whispered in his ear, and Bartholomew saw Roger Alcote surreptitiously lean to one side to try to overhear. The Master favoured Alcote with a seraphic smile until Alcote had the grace to move away. Out of the corner of his eye, Bartholomew saw that one of the clerk's frenzied gestures was directed towards him, and wondered which of his patients needed him so urgently that mass could be interrupted.

Kenyngham left his place and walked towards the altar, laying a hand on Bartholomew's arm to stop his reading.

'Gentlemen,' he began in his soft voice, 'there has been an incident in St Mary's Church. The Chancellor has requested that Brother Michael and Doctor Bartholomew attend as soon as possible. Father William and I will continue the mass.' Without further ado, he took up the reading where Bartholomew had stopped, leaving William to scramble to take his own place. Michael dropped his prayerful attitude with a speed that verged on the sacrilegious and made his way down the aisle, eyes gleaming with anticipation. Cynric followed, and Bartholomew went after them, aware of the curious looks from the other scholars. The Master of Physwick plucked at his sleeve as he passed.

'I am the University's Senior Proctor,' he said in a low whisper. 'If there has been an incident in the University church, I should come.'

Bartholomew shrugged, glancing briefly at him as he walked briskly down the aisle. He did not like Richard Harling, who, as the University's Senior Proctor, patrolled the streets at night looking for scholars who should be safely locked in their College or hostel, and fined them for unseemly or rowdy behaviour. Bartholomew sometimes needed to be out at night to see patients, and Harling had already fined him twice without even listening to his reasons. Harling had black hair that was always neatly slicked down with animal grease, and his scholar's tabard was immaculate.

The messenger was waiting for them outside. It was lighter than in the church, and Bartholomew recognised the neat, bearded features of the Chancellor's personal clerk, Gilbert.

'What has happened?' asked Michael, intrigued. 'What is so important that it could not wait until after mass?'

'A dead man has been found in the University chest,' Gilbert replied. Ignoring their looks of disbelief, he continued, 'The Chancellor ordered me to fetch Brother Michael, the Bishop's man, and Matthew Bartholomew, the physician.'

'Not the plague!' whispered Bartholomew in horror. He grabbed Gilbert's arm. 'How did this man die?'

Gilbert forced a smile. 'Not the plague. I do not know what killed him, but it was not the plague.'

Harling pursed his lips. 'This sounds like business for the Proctor.'

Gilbert raised his hands. 'The Junior Proctor is already there. He said you had been on duty last night, and you should not be disturbed until later.'

He turned, and set a lively pace towards St Mary's Church, so that the obese Michael was huffing and sweating within a few moments.

Bartholomew nudged the Benedictine monk in the ribs. ' "Brother Michael, the Bishop's man",' he repeated in an undertone. 'A fine reputation to have, my friend.'

Michael glowered at him. A year and a half before, he had agreed to become an agent of the Bishop of Ely, the churchman who had jurisdiction over the University since Cambridge had no cathedral of its own. Michael was to be alert to the interests of the Church in the town, and especially to the interests of the Benedictines, since Ely was a Benedictine monastery. There was a small hostel for Benedictines studying at the University, but the four monks that lived there were more concerned with their new-found freedom than the interests of their Order.

Bartholomew began to feel uncomfortable. The chest was where all the University's most important documents were stored, and the series of locks and bolts that protected it in the church tower was rumoured to be formidable. So who had broken through all that security? What sinister plot had the University embroiled itself in this time? And perhaps more to the point, how could Bartholomew prevent it from sucking him in, too?

The Church of St Mary the Great was an imposing building of creamy-white stone that dominated the High Street. Next to its delicate window tracery and soaring tower, St Michael's looked squat and grey. Yet, Bartholomew had heard that there were plans to rebuild the chancel and replace it with something grander and finer still.

Bartholomew had barely caught up with the clerk when they reached St Mary's. Standing to one side, wringing his hands and throwing fearful glances at the tower was St Mary's priest, Father Cuthbert, an enormously fat man whom Bartholomew treated for swollen ankles. A small group of clerks huddled around the door talking in low voices. The Chancellor, Richard de Wetherset, stood in the middle of them, a stocky man with iron-grey hair, who exuded an aura of power. He stepped forward as Bartholomew and Michael approached, allowing himself a brief smile at Michael's breathlessness.

'Thank you for being prompt, gentlemen.' He turned to Harling. 'Master Jonstan is already here, Richard. I was loathe to disturb you when you had been up all night.'

Harling inclined his head. 'But I am Senior Proctor, and should be present at a matter that sounds so grave.'

De Wetherset nodded his thanks, and beckoned Bartholomew, Michael, and Harling out of earshot of the gathered clerks. 'I am afraid someone has been murdered in the tower. Doctor, I would like you to tell me a little more about how and when he died, and you, Brother, must report this incident accurately to our Lord the Bishop.'

He began to walk through the churchyard, raising a hand to prevent the gaggle of clerks, and Cynric, from following them. Michael and Harling followed quickly, Father Cuthbert and Bartholomew a little more slowly. Bartholomew felt his stomach churn. At times, the University could be a seething pit of intrigue, and Bartholomew had no wish to become entangled in it. It would demand his time and his energies when he should be concentrating all his efforts on his teaching and his patients. The plague had left Cambridge depleted of physicians, and there was an urgent need to replace those who had died all over the country. Bartholomew considered the training of new physicians the most important duty in his life.

St Mary's was still dark inside, and the Chancellor took a torch from a sconce on the wall and led the way to the tower door at the back of the building. They followed him up the winding stairs into a small chamber about half-way up the tower. Bartholomew glanced around quickly, looking for the fabled chest, but the chamber was empty. Michael emerged from the stair-well, wheezing unhealthily, and Cuthbert's ponderous footsteps echoed until he too stood sweating and gasping in the chamber.

De Wetherset beckoned them close and shut the small wooden door so that they would not be overheard.

'I do not want the details of this incident to become common knowledge,' he said, 'and what I am about to tell you must remain a secret. You know that the University chest is kept in the tower here. To reach it, you must open three locked and bolted doors, and you must be able to open three locks on the chest itself. These locks were made in Italy and are, I am told, the finest locks in the world. Only I have the keys and either I, or my deputy, are always present when the chest is unlocked.'

He paused for a moment, and opened the door quickly to listen intently. He closed it again with a sigh and continued. 'You may consider all these precautions rather excessive to protect indentures and accounts, but the truth is that one of my best clerks, Nicholas of York, was writing a history of the University. He was quite frank, and recorded everything he uncovered, some of which could prove embarrassing if revealed in certain quarters. This book, you understand, will not be randomly distributed, but is intended to be a reliable, factual report of our doings and dealings. One day, people may be interested to know these things.'

He looked hard first at Michael and then at Bartholomew. 'The events of last year, when members of the University committed murder to make their fortunes, are recorded, along with your roles in the affair. And there are other incidents too, which need not concern you. The point is, a month ago Nicholas died of a fever, quite unexpectedly. I was uneasy at the suddenness of his death, and in the light of what has been discovered this morning, I am even more concerned.'

'What exactly has happened this morning?' asked Michael. Bartholomew began to feel increasingly uncomfortable as the Chancellor's revelations sank in.

'I came at first light this morning, as usual, to collect the documents from the chest I would need for the day's business. I was accompanied by my personal clerk, Gilbert. That group of scribes and secretaries you saw outside waited in the church below. Even in the half-light, we could see there was something wrong. The locks on the chest were askew and the lid was not closed properly. Gilbert opened the chest and inside was the body of a man.'

'Gilbert has already told us as much,' said Bartholomew. 'But how did the body come to be in the chest?'

The Chancellor gave the grimmest of smiles. 'That, gentlemen, is why I have asked you to come. I cannot imagine how anyone could have entered the tower, let alone open the locks on the chest. And I certainly have no idea how the corpse of a man could appear there.'

'Where is the chest?' asked Michael. 'Not up more stairs I hope.'

The Chancellor looked Michael up and down scathingly, and left the room. They heard his footsteps echoing further up the stairs, and Michael groaned.

The room on the next floor was more comfortable than the first. A table covered with writing equipment stood in the window, and several benches with cushions lined the walls. In the middle of the floor, standing on a once-splendid, but now shabby, woollen rug, was the University chest. It was a long box made of ancient black oak and strengthened with iron bands, darkened with age. It reminded Bartholomew of the elaborate coffin he had seen the Bishop of Peterborough buried in years before. Guarding the chest and the room was the Junior Proctor, Alric Jonstan, standing with his sword drawn and his saucer-like blue eyes round with horror. Bartholomew smiled at him as they waited for the others. Jonstan was far more popular than Harling, and was seemingly a kinder man who, although he took his duties seriously, did not enforce them with the same kind of inflexible rigour as did Harling.

De Wetherset stood to one side as Michael and Cuthbert finally arrived, and then indicated that Bartholomew should approach the chest. Bartholomew bent to inspect the wool rug, but there was nothing there, no blood or other marks. He walked around the chest looking for signs of tampering, but the stout leather hinges were pristine and well-oiled, and there was no indication that the lid had been prised open.

Taking a deep, but silent, breath, he lifted the lid. He looked down at the body of a man in a Dominican habit, lying face down on the University's precious documents and scrolls. Jonstan took a hissing breath and crossed himself.

'Poor man!' he muttered. 'It is a friar. Poor man!'

'Have you touched him?' asked Bartholomew of the Chancellor.

De Wetherset shook his head. 'We opened the chest, as I told you, but, when I saw what was inside, I lowered the lid and sent Gilbert to fetch you.'

Bartholomew knelt and put his hand on the man's neck. There was no life beat, and it was cold. He took the body by the shoulders while Michael grabbed the feet. Carefully, they lifted it out and laid it on the rug next to the chest. The Chancellor came to peer in at the documents. He heaved a sigh of relief.

'Well, at least they are not all covered in blood,' he announced fervently. He began searching among the papers and held up a sheaf triumphantly. 'The history! I think it is all here, although I will check, of course.' He began to rifle through the ream of parchments at the table in the window, muttering to himself.

Bartholomew turned his attention back to the body on the floor. It was a man in his fifties with a neatly cut tonsure. His friar's robe was threadbare and stained. Bartholomew began to try to establish why he had died. He could see no obvious signs, no blows to the head or stab wounds. He sat back perplexed. Had the man committed suicide somehow after lying in the chest?

'Do you know him?' he asked, looking around at the others.

Jonstan shook his head. 'No. We can check at the Friary, though. The poor devils were so decimated by the Death that one of their number missing will be very apparent.'

Bartholomew frowned. 'I do not think he was at the Friary,' he said. 'His appearance and robes are dirty, and the new Prior seems very particular about that. I think he may have been sleeping rough for a few days before he died.'

'Well, who is he then? And what did he want from the chest? And how did he die?' demanded the Chancellor from across the room.

Bartholomew shrugged. 'I have no idea. I need more time. Do you want me to examine him here or in the chapel? I will need to remove his robes.'

The Chancellor looked at Bartholomew in disgust. 'Will it make a mess?'

'No,' Bartholomew replied, startled. 'I do not believe so.'

'Then do it here, away from prying eyes. I will post Gilbert at the bottom of the stairs to make sure you are not disturbed. Father Cuthbert, perhaps you would assist him?' He turned to Bartholomew and Michael. 'If you have no objections, I will not stay to watch.' De Wetherset brandished the handful of documents. 'I must put these in another secure place.'

'*Another* secure place?' quizzed Michael under his breath to Bartholomew.

De Wetherset narrowed his eyes, detecting Michael's tone, if not his words. 'Please report to me the moment you have finished,' he said. He beckoned for Harling and Jonstan to follow him, and left, closing the door firmly behind him.

Bartholomew ran a hand through his unruly hair. 'Not again!' he said to Michael. 'I want to teach and to heal my patients. I do not want to become embroiled in University politics!'

Michael's face softened, and he patted his friend on the shoulder. 'You are the University's most senior physician since the Death. The fact that you have been asked here to help means no more than that. You are not being recruited into the University's secret service!'

'I should hope not,' said Bartholomew with feeling. 'If I thought that were the case, I would leave Cambridge immediately, and set up practice somewhere I would never be found. Come on. Help me get this over with. Then we can report to de Wetherset and that will be an end to it.'

He began to remove the dead man's robe. The stiffness meant that he was forced to cut it with a knife. Once the robe lay in a bundle on the floor, Bartholomew began to conduct a more rigorous examination of the body. There was no sign of violence, no bruises or cuts, and no puncture marks except for a cut on the left hand that was so small that Bartholomew almost missed it. He inspected the fingernails to see if there were any fibres trapped there, but there was only a layer of black dirt. The hands were soft, which implied that the man had been unused to physical labour, and a small ink-stain on his right thumb suggested that he could write. Bartholomew turned the hand to catch the light from the window, and the small callus on the thumb confirmed that the man had been a habitual scribe.

Bartholomew leaned close to the man's mouth and carefully smelled it, ignoring Michael's snort of disgust. There was nothing to suggest he had taken poison. He prised the man's mouth open and peered in, looking for discoloration of the tongue or gums, or other signs of damage. There was nothing. The man had several small ulcers on one side of his tongue, but Bartholomew thought that they were probably more likely caused by a period of poor nutrition than by any subtle poisons.

He turned his attention to the man's throat, but there was nothing to imply strangulation and no neck bones were broken. He looked at one of the man's hands again. If he had died because his heart had seized up, his fingernails, nose and mouth should show some blueness. The man's fingernails were an unhealthy waxy-white, but certainly not blue. His lips, too, were white.

Eventually, Bartholomew sat back on his heels. 'I have no idea why he died,' he said, perplexed. 'Perhaps he came here to steal and the excitement burst some vital organ. Perhaps he was already ill when he came here. Perhaps he was already dead.'

'What?' said Michael, his eyes wide with disbelief. 'Are you suggesting that someone brought a corpse up here in the middle of the night and left it?'

Bartholomew grinned at him. 'No. I am merely following the rules of the deceased Master Wilson and trying to solve the problem logically.'

'Well, that suggestion, my dear doctor, has less logic than Wilson's crumbling bones could present,' said Michael. 'How could someone smuggle a corpse into the church and leave it here? I can accept that someone might hide below and then sneak up here after all was secured for the night, but not someone carrying a corpse!'

'So, the friar hides in the church, picks three locks to reach this room, picks three locks to open the chest, lies face-down in it, and dies. Master Wilson would not have been impressed with your logic, either,' retorted Bartholomew.

'Perhaps the friar came up here as you suggested and died suddenly,' said Michael.

'And closed the lid afterwards?' asked Bartholomew, raising his eyebrows. 'De Wetherset said it was closed with the friar inside. I think it unlikely that he closed it himself.'

'You think another person was here?' asked Michael, gesturing round. 'What evidence do you have for such a claim?'

'None that I can see,' replied Bartholomew. He went to sit on one of the benches and Michael followed him, settling himself comfortably with his hands across his stomach.

'Let us think about what we do know,' the monk said. 'First. It is likely that this man hid in the church and then made his way up to the tower after the church had been secured. We can ask the sexton what his procedures are for locking up.'

'Second,' said Bartholomew, 'I think this man was a clerk or a friar, as he appears, and that he has been sleeping rough for a few nights as attested by his dirty clothes. Perhaps he had undertaken a journey of several days' duration, or perhaps he had spent some time watching the church in preparation for his burglary.'

'Third,' Michael continued, 'you say he appears to have suffered no violence. He may have died of natural causes, perhaps brought on by the stress of his nocturnal activities.'

Bartholomew nodded slowly. 'And fourth,' he concluded, 'the locks seem to have been picked with great skill.'

'But there are no tools,' said Michael. 'He must have needed a piece of wire at the very least to pick a lock.'

Bartholomew went to the chest and rummaged around, but there was nothing. 'So either he hid the tools before he died, or someone took them.'

'If there was another person here with him to take the tools and close the lid, that person could have killed him,' said Michael.

'But there is no evidence he was murdered,' said Bartholomew.

They sat in silence for a while, mulling over what they had deduced.

'And there is the question of the Chancellor's scribe, Nicholas of York,' said Bartholomew. 'De Wetherset says he is now suspicious of his death – a death that appeared to be natural, but now seems too timely. Two deaths that seem natural, connected with the University chest?' He frowned and drummed on the bench with his fingers.

Michael looked at him hard. 'What do you mean?' he said.

'Although I can find nothing that caused the death of this man, I am reluctant to say it was natural. I suppose it is possible he could have suffered a fatal seizure, fell in the chest, and the lid slammed shut. But what of the missing tools? And anyway, people who have such seizures usually show some evidence of it, and I can see no such evidence here.'

'So what you are saying,' said Michael, beginning to be frustrated, 'is that the friar does not seem to have been killed, but he did not die naturally. Marvellous! Where does that leave us?'

Bartholomew shrugged. 'I have just never seen a man die of natural causes and his body look like the friar's.'

'So what do we tell the Chancellor?' said Michael.

Bartholomew leaned his head back against the whitewashed wall and studied the ceiling. 'What we know,' he said. 'That the man was probably an itinerant friar, that he probably had some considerable skill as a picker of locks, that he died from causes unknown, and that there was probably another person here.'

'That will not satisfy de Wetherset,' said Michael, 'nor will it satisfy the Bishop.'

'Well, what would you have us do, Michael? Lie?' asked

Bartholomew, also beginning to be frustrated. He closed his eyes and racked his brain for causes of death that would turn a man's skin waxy white.

'Of course we should not lie!' said Michael crossly. 'But the explanation we have now is inadequate.'

'Then what do you suggest we do?' demanded Bartholomew. He watched Michael gnaw at his thumbnail as he turned the problem over in his mind. It gave him an idea, and he went to look at the tiny cut on the friar's thumb. He sat cross-legged on the floor and inspected it closely. It was little more than a scratch, but it broke the skin nevertheless. He let the hand fall and sat pondering the chest. It suddenly took on a sinister air as his attention was drawn to the locks.

He reached across the body to the middle lock. Protruding from the top of it was a minuscule blade, less than the length of his little fingernail. He took one of his surgical knives and pressed gently on it. Under the pressure, it began to slide back into the lock. When he moved his knife, the small blade sprang back up again.

Michael watched him curiously, and stretched out a hand to touch it.

'No!' Bartholomew slapped Michael's hand away. 'I think the lock has its own precaution against intruders,' he said, looking down at the dead friar. 'I think it bears a poison.'

The Chancellor looked in horror at the lock that lay on his table, the little blade coated with its deadly poison protruding from the top.

'A true Italian lock,' he said in hushed tones. He picked up a quill and poked the lock further away from him, as though he was afraid that it might poison him from where he sat, and exchanged a look of revulsion with his clerk, who stood behind him.

'Did you know that the lock had the capacity to kill?' asked Bartholomew. Michael gave him a warning elbow in the ribs. The head of the University was not a man of whom to ask such a question.

De Wetherset looked aghast. 'I most certainly did not!' he said, standing and walking to the opposite side of the room, still eyeing the lock with deep suspicion. 'I unlocked it myself many times!' The thought of a possible narrow escape suddenly dawned on him and he turned paler still.

'Are you sure that the lock has not been changed since you last saw it?' said Michael.

The Chancellor thought for a moment, his eyes involuntarily swinging back to the lock on the table. 'Not really,' he said. 'It is the same size, the same colour, and has the same general appearance, but in a court of law I could not swear that this lock was the one that was there yesterday. It probably was, but I could not be certain. What would you say, Gilbert?'

'It looks the same to me,' said his clerk, leaning down and examining it minutely.

'Father Cuthbert?' asked Bartholomew of the fat priest.

Cuthbert put up his hands defensively. 'I am priest only of the church. The tower is beyond my jurisdiction and belongs to the University. I know nothing of poisoned locks.'

'Who else might know?' said Bartholomew.

'My deputy, Evrard Buckley, is the only person other than me who is permitted access to the chest. Even Gilbert does not touch it,' said de Wetherset. 'And the only person other than me to have keys is the Bishop. He keeps a spare set in Ely Cathedral, but we have had no cause to use those for years.'

'Are you the only person actually to use the keys?' asked Bartholomew. 'Do you ever give them to a clerk or your deputy to open the locks?'

De Wetherset pulled on a cord tied around his neck. 'I keep my keys here and I only remove them when I hand them to Buckley to lock or unlock the chest. The keys are never out of my sight, and, outside the chamber where the chest is kept, I never remove them from round my neck.'

'Not even when you bathe?' pressed Bartholomew.

'Bathe? You mean swim in the river?' said the Chancellor with a look of horror.

'No, I mean take a bath,' said Bartholomew.

'A bath would mean that I had to remove all my clothes,' said the Chancellor distastefully, 'and I do not consider such an action healthy for a man in his fifties.' He held up a hand as if to quell any objection Bartholomew might make. 'I am aware of your odd beliefs in this area, Doctor,' he said, referring to Bartholomew's well-known insistence on cleanliness. 'I cannot think why Master Kenyngham allows you to entertain such peculiar notions, and while I suppose they may have a measure of success on the labourers you physic, I do not believe they will apply equally to me.'

'All men are equal before God, Chancellor,' said Bartholomew, taken aback by de Wetherset's statement. He ignored Michael's smirk. 'And all men are more likely to contract certain sicknesses if they do not keep themselves clean.'

De Wetherset looked sharply at him. 'Do not try to lure me into a debate on physic,' he said. 'The Bible does not say those who do not bathe will become ill. And it also does not recommend against drinking from God's rivers as I have heard you do. Now, we have more important matters to discuss.'

Bartholomew was startled into silence, wondering whether his teaching and practice were really as outlandish as many of his colleagues seemed to feel. Bartholomew had learned medicine at the University in Paris from an Arab doctor who had taught him that incidence of disease could be lessened by simple hygiene. Bartholomew fervently believed Ibn Ibrahim was right, a notion that brought him into conflict with many of his patients and colleagues. De Wetherset's arguments had tripped very lightly off his tongue, suggesting that he had debated this issue before. Michael, hiding his amusement, resumed the questioning of de Wetherset.

'So there is no time ever when you might remove the keys?'

'Never,' said de Wetherset. 'I even sleep with them.'

'What about Master Buckley?' said Michael. 'Where is he? We should really ask him the same questions.'

'He is unwell,' said de Wetherset. 'Did you not know that, Doctor? He is your patient.'

Master Buckley, the Vice-Chancellor, was a Fellow of King's Hall. He taught grammar, and, many years before, Bartholomew's older sister Edith had hired Master Buckley to coach him when the school at Peterborough Abbey broke for holidays. Bartholomew's knowledge of grammar had not improved, and Buckley's dull company had done a great deal to convince him that this subject made a very poor showing after arithmetic, geometry, and natural philosophy. Bartholomew had met Buckley again when he had been made Master of Medicine at Michaelhouse six years before, and had treated Buckley frequently for a skin complaint.

'Who usually opens the chest?' Bartholomew asked.

'Well, Master Buckley, actually,' said de Wetherset. 'Gilbert usually kindles the lamps, and I like to set out the table, ready to work on the documents locked in the chest.'

Bartholomew looked at Gilbert, who hastened to explain. 'Master de Wetherset hands Master Buckley his keys, he unlocks the chest and removes any documents we require, and then he locks it again immediately.' He looked down at the lock in renewed horror. 'You mean poor Master Buckley could have been killed like that poor friar just by unlocking the chest?'

Michael shrugged. 'Yes. Assuming the lock has not been changed.'

Bartholomew stood to leave. 'That is all we can tell you,' he said. 'I am sorry it is not more, but perhaps Masters Harling and Jonstan will uncover the truth when they begin to investigate.'

The Chancellor shook his head slowly, and indicated he should sit again. 'My Proctors cannot investigate this,' he said. 'They have their hands full trying to keep peace between students and the gangs of people gathered for the Stourbridge Fair. Also, there are scores of entertainers, mercenaries, and the Lord knows what manner of people wandering through the town gawking at our buildings and assessing our wealth. An increase in non-University folk around the town has always been a danger, but has been especially so since the Death, with lordless labourers strolling free.'

Bartholomew knew all this: the Fair was the largest in England, and merchants from all over England, France, and even Flanders came to trade. The Fair also attracted entertainers – singers, dancers, actors, fire-eaters, jongleurs, acrobats, and many more – and with the entertainers came pickpockets, thieves, rabble-rousers, and tricksters. The Proctors always struggled to keep the scholars out of trouble, but this year the situation was far more serious. The plague had taken landowners as well as those who worked for them, and many previously bonded men had found themselves free. A shortage of labour had forced wages up, and groups of people wandered the country selling their services to those that could pay the most. Compounding all this, the soldiers who had been fighting the King's wars in France had begun to return. It was easier to steal than to work, and robbers on the roads were increasingly common, especially given the number of carts that trundled along taking goods to and from the Fair. The Fair was only in its second week, but already there had been three deaths, and a riot had been only narrowly averted when a local tinker had stolen a student's purse.

'Because my Proctors are busy with the Fair,' the Chancellor continued, 'I will need to crave your indulgence a little longer, and ask that you might make some preliminary enquiries on my behalf. Of course, Harling and Jonstan will help wherever they can, but . . .'

'If you will forgive me, Master de Wetherset,' interrupted Bartholomew, 'I would rather not be a party to an extended investigation. I am a physician, and I think the events of two Christmases ago show clearly that I am not adept at this kind of thing. You would be better asking one of your clerks to do it. Perhaps Gilbert?'

'I require a physician to examine the body of my scribe Nicholas to see if he, too, was killed by this foul device,' said de Wetherset, gesturing to the lock on the table. 'Gilbert cannot tell me whether a man has been poisoned or not.'

'But Nicholas is buried!' said Michael, shocked. 'You said he died a month ago.'

'You mean to dig him up?' gasped Gilbert, his face white under his beard.

Cuthbert joined in. 'Nicholas has been laid to rest in hallowed ground! You cannot disturb him! It is contrary to the will of God!'

De Wetherset looked disapprovingly at them before addressing Michael and Bartholomew. 'Nicholas lies in the churchyard here. I will obtain the necessary permits from the Bishop and you will exhume the body this week. You will also report back to me regularly. I will speak with Master Kenyngham and ask that you be excused lectures if they interfere with your investigation.'

Bartholomew felt a flash of anger at de Wetherset's presumption, followed by a feeling of sick dread. He had no wish to investigate murders or delve into the University's sordid affairs.

'But my students have their disputations soon,' he protested. 'I cannot abandon them!'

'I need a physician to examine the corpse,' repeated the Chancellor. 'You underestimate your abilities, Doctor. You are honest and discreet, and for these reasons alone I trust you more than most of my clerks. I think you – both of you,' he added, looking at Michael, 'are perfectly equipped to get to the bottom of this matter. I know you would both rather teach than investigate University affairs, but I must ask you to indulge me for a day or so, and do my bidding. I know the Bishop will support me in this.'

'But if your clerk has been dead for a month, I will be able to tell you nothing about his death,' Bartholomew protested. 'Even if there were once a small cut on his hand, like the one on the friar, the flesh will be corrupted, and I doubt I will be able to see it.'

De Wetherset winced in distaste. 'Perhaps. But you will not know until you look, and I require that you try.' He leaned towards Bartholomew, his expression earnest. 'This is important. I must know whether Nicholas came to harm because of the book I ordered he write about the University.'

Bartholomew held his gaze. 'You must be aware of the stories that say the plague came from the graves of the dead,' he said. 'It is a risk . . .'

'Nonsense,' snapped de Wetherset. 'You do not believe that story, Doctor, any more than I do. The plague is over. It will not come again.'

'How do you know that?' demanded Bartholomew, irritated at the man's complacency. 'How do you know someone at the Fair is not sickening from the plague at this very moment?'

'It has passed us over,' said de Wetherset, his voice rising in reply. 'It has gone north.'

'There are people at the Fair who have come from the north,'

24

countered Bartholomew, becoming exasperated. 'How do you know they have not brought it back with them, in their clothes, or in the goods they hope to sell?'

'Well, which is it, Doctor?' said de Wetherset triumphantly, detecting a flaw in Bartholomew's argument. 'Is it carried by the living, or in the graves with the dead? You cannot have it both ways.'

'My point is that I do not know,' said Bartholomew, ignoring Michael's warning looks for arguing with the Chancellor. 'No one knows! How can we take such a risk by exhuming your clerk? Will you endanger the lives of the people of Cambridge, of England, over this?'

De Wetherset snorted impatiently. 'There is no risk! Nicholas died of a summer ague, not the plague. I saw his body in his coffin before he was buried. Your peculiar ideas about cleanliness are making you over-cautious. You will exhume the body in two or three days' time when I have the necessary licences. Now, what do you plan to do about this friar?'

Michael pulled thoughtfully at the thin whiskers on his flabby cheek, while Bartholomew threw up his hands in exasperation, and went to stand near the window to bring his anger under control.

'Can you test the lock to make certain it is poisoned?' Michael asked Bartholomew.

Bartholomew looked at him distastefully and stifled a sigh. 'Will one of your clerks do that?' he asked de Wetherset.

'How?' asked de Wetherset, looking at the lock in renewed revulsion.

'Test it on a rat or a bird. If the poison killed the friar through that tiny cut, then the poor animal, being considerably smaller, should die fairly quickly.'

Bartholomew felt a sudden, unreasonable anger towards the friar whose death was about to cause such upheaval in his life. What was the man doing in the tower anyway? He could only have been there to steal or to spy. Bartholomew watched de Wetherset issue instructions to Gilbert to test the lock on a rat, and gestured to Michael that they should go.

'Wait!' the Chancellor commanded, standing as they made to leave. 'I must ask that you observe utmost discretion over this business. That a man has died in the University chest cannot be denied, but I do not wish anyone to know about the University history that was being written.'

Michael nodded acquiescence, bowed, and walked out, while Bartholomew trailed after him, feeling dejected. He was going to become entangled in the unsavoury world of University politics a second time, and be forced to question the motives of his friends and family.

Outside, Michael rubbed his hands together and beamed. 'What shall we do first?' he asked, and Bartholomew realised that the fat monk was relishing their enforced duties. Michael had always loved University affairs, and thrived on the petty politics and plots that were a part of College life. He saw Bartholomew's doleful expression and clapped him on the shoulder.

'Come, Matt,' he said reassuringly. 'This is not like the other business. There are no threats to those we love, and your Philippa is safely away visiting her brother. This has nothing to do with Michaelhouse. It is just some minor intrigue that has gone wrong.'

Bartholomew was unconvinced. 'I should have gone with Philippa,' he said bitterly, 'or followed her brother's lead and moved away from this vile pit of lies and deception to London.'

'You would hate London,' Michael laughed. 'You make enough fuss about the filth and dirt here. In London it would be ten times worse, and they say that the River Thames is the dirtiest river in England. You would hate it,' he said again, drawing his morose friend away from the shadows of the church and into the bright sunlight to where Cynric waited for them.

They began to walk down the High Street towards King's Hall to visit Master Buckley. The streets were busier than usual because of the Fair, and houses that had stood empty since the plague were bursting at the seams with travellers. A baker passed them, his tray brimming with pies and pastries, while two beggars watched him with hungry eyes.

With an effort, Bartholomew brought his mind back to what Michael was saying about the dead friar. Michael, strolling next to him, began to run through the possibilities surrounding the friar's death, for Cynric's benefit. They turned suddenly as they heard a wail. A woman tore towards them, her long, fair hair streaming behind her like a banner. Bartholomew recognised her as Sybilla, the ditcher's daughter, and one of the town's prostitutes. Her mother, brothers, and sisters had died in the plague, and her father had allowed her to follow any path she chose, while he took his own comfort from the bottles of wine she brought him. Bartholomew caught her as she made to run past.

'What has happened?' he said, alarmed by her tear-streaked face and wild, frightened eyes.

'Isobel!' she sobbed. 'Isobel!'

'Where?' asked Bartholomew, looking down the street. 'Has she been hurt?'

He exchanged glances with Brother Michael. They were both aware of the murder of two of the town's prostitutes during the last few weeks. Bartholomew had seen the body of one of them, her eyes staring sightlessly at the sky and her throat cut.

Sybilla was unable to answer and Bartholomew let her go, watching as she fled up the High Street, her wailing drawing people from their houses to see what was happening. Bartholomew and Michael, concerned for Isobel, continued in the direction from which Sybilla had come, until they saw people gathering in St Botolph's churchyard.

Two women bent over someone lying on the ground, and Bartholomew and Michael approached, the monk stifling a cry of horror as he saw the blood-splattered figure. Bartholomew knelt next to Isobel's body and gently eased her onto her back. Her throat was a mess of congealed blood, dark and sticky where it had flooded down her chest.

Michael squatted down next to him, his eyes tightly closed so he would not have to look. He began to mutter prayers for the dead, while Bartholomew wrapped her in her cloak. Cynric disappeared to report the news to the Sheriff and to locate the dead woman's family. When Michael had finished, Bartholomew picked up the body and carried it into the church. A friar, who had been in the crowd outside, helped put her into the parish coffin and cover her with a sheet. While the friar went to clear the churchyard of ghoulish onlookers and to await Isobel's family,

Bartholomew looked again at the body, while Michael peered over his shoulder. The sheet was not long enough to cover the dead girl's feet and Bartholomew saw that someone had taken her shoes. Her feet were relatively clean, so she had not been walking barefoot. He looked a little more closely and caught his breath as he saw the small red circle painted in blood on her foot.

'What is wrong?' asked Michael, his face white in the dark church.

Bartholomew pointed to the dead girl's foot. 'That mark,' he said. 'I saw a circle like that on the foot of the last dead girl, Fritha. I thought it was just chance – there was so much blood – but Isobel has a mark that is identical.'

'Do you think it is the killer's personal signature?' asked Michael, with a shudder. 'I assume all three women were killed by the same person.'

Bartholomew frowned. 'Perhaps, yes, if there were a similar mark on the foot of the first victim. I did not see her body.'

'God's teeth, Matt,' said Michael, his voice unsteady. 'What monster would do this?' He clutched at one of the pillars, unable to tear his eyes away from the body in the coffin. He began to reel, and Bartholomew, fearing that the monk might faint, took him firmly by the arm and led him outside.

They sat together on one of the ancient tombstones in the shade of a yew tree. A woman's anguished cries suggested that Cynric had already found Isobel's family and that they were nearing the church. Next to Bartholomew, Michael was still shaking.

'Why, Matt?' he asked, looking to where a man led his wailing wife into the church, escorted solicitously by the friar.

Bartholomew stared across the churchyard at a row of young oak trees, their slender branches waving in the breeze. 'That is the third girl to be killed,' he said. 'Hilde, Fritha, and Isobel, and all of them murdered in churchyards.'

The Fair had resulted in a temporary increase in prostitution. The town burgesses had called for the Sheriff to rid the town of the women, but Bartholomew believed the prostitutes were providing a greater service to the town than the burgesses appreciated: as long as they were available, scholars and itinerant traders from the Fair did not pester the townsmen's wives and daughters. Bartholomew suspected Michael felt much the same, although such a position was hardly tenable publicly for a Benedictine Master of Theology.

They sat for a while until Michael regained some of his colour, and watched the crowd in the churchyard. When the Sheriff's men arrived, it became ominously silent.

Bartholomew frowned. 'What is all that about?'

They watched as the soldiers tried to disperse the crowd. 'There are rumours in the town that the Sheriff is not doing all he might to investigate the murders of Hilde and Fritha,' said Michael. 'As Sheriff, his duty is to try to prevent prostitution, and it is said that he considers the murderer to be doing him a favour by killing these women.'

'Oh, surely not, Brother!' said Bartholomew in disbelief. 'What Sheriff would want a killer in his town? It will do nothing to make it peaceful.'

'True enough,' said Michael. 'But it is said that the killer fled to St Mary's Church and claimed sanctuary. The Sheriff set a watch on the church, but the killer escaped, and now it looks as though he has struck again.'

'How is it known that this man was the killer?' asked Bartholomew curiously.

'He is supposed to have killed his wife before fleeing,' said Michael. 'It is rumoured that the Sheriff deliberately set a lax watch on the church so that the killer could continue his extermination of the prostitutes.'

'Do you think there is any truth in these stories?' asked Bartholomew, watching the soldiers, frustrated with the sullen crowd, draw their swords to threaten the people away.

'It is true that a man killed his wife and claimed sanctuary at St Mary's, and it is true that he escaped during the night despite the Sheriff's guards. Whether he is also the killer of Hilde, Fritha, and now Isobel, is open to debate.'

The crowd, faced with naked steel, reluctantly began to disperse, although there were dark mutterings. Bartholomew was surprised that the crowd was sympathetic to the prostitutes. There were those who claimed that the plague had come because of women like them, and they faced a constant and very real danger from attack.

'Come on, Brother,' Bartholomew said, rising to his feet. 'We must pay a visit to the ailing Master Buckley. Perhaps he will explain everything, and this University chest business will be over and done with before more time is wasted.'

Michael assented and they walked in silence up the High Street, each wrapped in his own thoughts. Michael could not stop thinking about the face of the dead girl, while Bartholomew, more inured to violent death, was still angry that he was being dragged into the sordid world of University politics and intrigue.

Towards King's Hall the houses were larger than those near St Botolph's, some with small walled gardens. Many homes had been abandoned after the plague, and the whitewash was dirty and grey. Others were well maintained, and had been given new coats of whitewash in honour of the Fair, some tinged with pigs' blood or ochre to make them pleasing shades of pink, yellow, and orange. But all were in use now that the Fair had arrived.

The street itself was hard-packed mud, dangerously pot-holed and rutted. Parallel drains ran down each side of it, intended to act as sewers to take waste from homes. By leaning out of the upper storeys of the houses, residents could throw their waste directly into the drains, but not everyone's aim was accurate, and accidents were inevitable. Scholars especially needed to take care when walking past townspeople's houses in the early mornings. On one side of the street, Bartholomew saw a group of ragged children prodding at a blockage with sticks, paddling barefoot in the filth. One splashed another, and screams of delight followed as the spray flew. The physician in him longed to tell them to play elsewhere; the pragmatist told him that they would find somewhere equally, if not more, unwholesome.

King's Hall was an elegant establishment that had been founded by Edward II more than thirty years before. The present King had continued the royal patronage, and it was now the largest of the Cambridge Colleges. The centre of King's Hall was a substantial house with gardens that swept down to the river. Bartholomew and Michael asked for the Warden, who listened gravely to Michael's news, and took them to Master Buckley's room himself.

'Many of the masters have a room to themselves now,' the Warden said as they walked. 'Before the Death, we were cramped, but since that terrible pestilence claimed more than half our number, we rattle around in this draughty building. I suppose time will heal and we will have more scholars in due course. Master Kenyngham tells me that Michaelhouse has just been sent six Franciscans from Lincoln, which must be a welcome boost to your numbers.'

Bartholomew smiled politely, although he was not so certain that the arrival of the Franciscans was welcome. So far, all they had done was to try to get the other scholars into debates about heresy and to criticise the Master's tolerant rule.

The Warden led them up some stairs at the rear of the Hall and knocked on a door on the upper floor. There was no answer.

'Poor Master Buckley was most unwell last night,' said the Warden in a whisper. 'I thought it might be wise to allow him to sleep this morning and recover his strength.'

'What was wrong with him?' asked Bartholomew, exchanging a quick glance of concern with Michael.

The Warden shrugged. 'You know him, Doctor. He is never very healthy and the summer heat has made him worse. Last night, we had eels for supper, and he always eats far more than his share, despite your warnings about his diet. None of us were surprised when he said he felt ill.' He knocked on the door again, a little louder.

With a growing fear of what he might find, Bartholomew grasped the handle of the door and pushed it open. The three men stood staring in astonishment. The room was completely bare. Not a stick of furniture, a wall hanging, or a scrap of parchment remained. And there was certainly no sign of Master Buckley.

chapter 2

AFTER THEY TOOK THEIR LEAVE OF THE BEWILDERED warden, Bartholomew and Michael walked back to Michaelhouse together.

'We still need to talk to the man who locked up the church,' said Bartholomew.

Michael pulled a face. 'Not until I have had something to eat,' he said. 'What a morning! We are dragged out of mass to look at a corpse in the University chest, we discover a nasty poisoning device, we see a murdered harlot, and we find that the Vice-Chancellor has run away carrying all his worldly goods and some of King's Hall's. And all before breakfast.'

'I am supposed to be teaching now,' said Bartholomew, glancing up at the sun, already high in the sky. 'These students will face their disputations soon and need all the teaching they can get, especially Robert Deynman.'

'They will have to wait a little longer,' said Michael, pointing across the yard to where the porter stood talking with a young woman. 'You have a patient.'

Seeing Bartholomew and Michael walk through the gate, the woman began to walk towards them, the porter's attentions forgotten. Bartholomew recognised her as Frances de Belem, the daughter of one of the wealthy merchants on Milne Street, who owned a house next to that of his brother-in-law Sir Oswald Stanmore. Years before, Stanmore and de Belem had started negotiations to marry Frances to Bartholomew, so that Stanmore's cloth trade could be linked to de Belem's dyeing business. At fourteen years of age, Bartholomew had no intentions of being married to a baby, nor of becoming a tradesman, and he had fled to study at Oxford. De Belem had promptly found another merchant's son, and Stanmore, fortunately for Bartholomew, was not a man to bear grudges when his errant kinsman returned fifteen years later to take up a position as Fellow of Medicine at Michaelhouse.

The rift between Stanmore and de Belem caused by Bartholomew's flight, however, had never completely healed, and Bartholomew was still occasionally subjected to doleful looks from his brother-in-law when de Belem overcharged him for dyes. But Frances bore Bartholomew no ill will and always seemed pleased to see him. Her marriage ended, as did many, when the plague took her husband the previous year.

As Bartholomew walked towards her, he noticed that her face was white and stained with tears. She almost broke into a run as he drew close, and was unable to prevent a huge sob as she clutched at his arm.

'Frances?' said Bartholomew gently. 'Whatever is the matter? Is your father ill?'

She shook her head miserably. 'I must talk to you, Doctor,' she said. 'I need help, and I do not know who else to ask.'

Bartholomew thought quickly. He could not take a woman back to his room, especially with the Franciscans undoubtedly already watching with disapproval the presence of a woman on Michaelhouse soil. He could not take her to the hall or the conclave because they would be in use for teaching, and he was reluctant to send her away when she obviously needed his help. The only possible place for a consultation was the kitchen, where the hefty laundress Agatha could act as chaperon and preserve Frances's reputation and his own.

He ushered her across the yard towards the main building. Michaelhouse comprised several buildings, joined in a three-sided structure around a courtyard. The south and north wings, where the scholars lived, were two-storeyed buildings. The hall linked the two wings and was a handsome house built by a merchant. The house had been bought in 1324 by Hervey de Stanton, Edward II's Chancellor of the Exchequer, when he founded Michaelhouse, and was dominated by the elegant porch topped with de Stanton's coat of arms. A spiral staircase led from the porch to the hall on the upper floor, while a door below led to the kitchen.

Frances in tow, Bartholomew made his way through the servants scurrying to prepare the main meal of the day, to the small room where Agatha kept her linen. She sat in a chair, legs splayed in front of her, snoring loudly in the sunlight that flooded the room. Agatha was a huge woman, almost as big as Brother Michael. Women were not usually allowed to work in the University's Colleges and hostels, but Agatha was exempted since she was unlikely to attract the amorous attentions of even the most desperate scholar. As Bartholomew entered, she awoke, and looked balefully at him, and then at Frances behind. It was not the first time Bartholomew had used her services when female patients had arrived unannounced, and she said nothing as she scrubbed at her eyes and heaved her bulk into a less inelegant position.

'You can trust Agatha to be discreet with anything you might say,' he said, as Frances looked nervously at Agatha's formidable form.

Agatha smiled, revealing an array of strong yellow teeth. 'Never mind me,' she said to Frances. 'I have things to be doing, and nothing you can say to the Doctor will shock me.'

'I am with child!' Frances blurted out. Agatha's jaw immediately dropped, and the hand that was reaching for some sewing was arrested in mid air. Bartholomew was startled. Her father, who had allowed Frances a free rein since the death of her husband, would be furious; especially so since Stanmore had told Bartholomew that arrangements were already in hand to remarry Frances to a landowner in Saffron Walden, a village south-east of Cambridge.

Bartholomew collected his tumbling thoughts when he saw Frances was waiting for an answer with desperate eyes. 'I cannot help you,' he said gently. 'You must seek out a midwife to advise you about the birth. Physicians do not become involved in childbirth unless there is danger to the child or the mother.' He smiled at her reassuringly. 'And I am sure that you need have no worries on that score. You are young and healthy.'

'But I do not want it!' cried Frances. 'It will ruin me!'

Agatha, seeing the girl's tears, gave her a motherly hug.

Bartholomew looked at them helplessly. 'I can do nothing to

help,' he said again. 'I can only advise you to see a midwife to secure the safe delivery of the child.'

'I want you to get rid of it for me,' said Frances, turning a tear-streaked face to Bartholomew. 'I do not want it.'

'I cannot do that,' said Bartholomew. 'Quite apart from the fact that I do not know how, it would be a terrible crime, and dangerous for you.'

'I care nothing for the danger,' cried Frances. 'My life will be worth nothing if I have it, so I have nothing to lose. You must be able to help me! I know there are medicines that can rid a woman of an unwanted child. Of all the physicians in the town, you are the one most likely to know them, since you learned your medicine in dark and distant lands from foreign teachers.'

Bartholomew wondered if that was how all his patients saw him, endowed with knowledge of mysterious cures alien to physicians who had studied in England. 'I do not know how to make potions for such purposes,' he said, looking away from Frances and out of the window, hoping that she would not see he was lying. He did know of such a potion, and it was indeed Ibn Ibrahim who had shown him writings by a woman physician called Trotula where such remedies could be found: equal portions of wormwood, betony, and pennyroyal, if taken early, might sometimes cause the foetus to abort. He had seen it used once, but that was because the mother was too exhausted from her last birthing to manage another. Even then, Bartholomew had been confused by the ethics of the case.

'You do know!' said Frances, desperation making her voice crack. 'You must.'

'Go to a midwife,' said Bartholomew gently. 'They understand, and will help with your baby.'

'Mistress Woodman killed Hilde's younger sister,' said Frances bitterly, meeting his eyes. 'Did you know that?'

'Hilde the prostitute?' asked Bartholomew. 'The one who was killed?'

Frances nodded. 'Her sister was three months with child, and she went to Mistress Woodman, the midwife, to rid herself of it. Mistress Woodman tried to pluck the child out with a piece of wire. Hilde's sister bled to death.'

Bartholomew knew such practices occurred – many dangerous poisons were used, and if these failed, operations were attempted that invariably left the mother either dead or suffering from infection. He turned away and looked out of the window. There was no disputing that it was wrong to kill, but what if Frances went to Mistress Woodman and died of her ministrations?

'What of the baby's father?' he asked. 'Will he marry you?'

Frances gave a short bark of laughter. 'He cannot,' she said, and would elaborate no further. Bartholomew assumed the father must already be married.

'Do you have money?' he asked. Frances nodded, hope flaring in her eyes, and she showed him a heavy purse. 'You have relatives in Lincoln. Tell your father you are going to stay with them. If you can trust them, have the baby there. If not, there are convents that will help you.'

The hope in Frances's eyes faded. 'You will not help?' she said.

Bartholomew swallowed. 'Think about going away to have the child. Come to talk to me again tomorrow, but do not go to Mistress Woodman for a solution.'

Frances sighed heavily, and turned to leave. 'I will give it thought,' she said, 'and I will come tomorrow. But my mind is already made up.'

As she left, Agatha sank down in her chair. 'Poor child,' she said. 'One rash act will cost her everything, while her paramour lives on to sully another.'

'That is not fair, Agatha,' said Bartholomew. 'Frances is twenty-four years old, and has been married. She is no green maiden taken unawares.'

'But the outcome is the same,' growled Agatha. 'The woman suffers, and may even die, while the man merely selects another for his attentions. Perhaps I will tell her how to rid herself of the baby.'

'How?' demanded Bartholomew disbelievingly. Agatha never ceased to amaze him with her assertions.

'You take two parts of wormwood to one part of crushed snails, add a generous pinch of red arsenic, and grind it into a poultice. You then insert the paste into the private regions, and the babe will sicken and die.'

'And so might the mother,' said Bartholomew, cringing. 'Where did you learn such a dangerous recipe?'

Agatha grinned suddenly and tapped the side of her nose. Bartholomew wondered whether she might have made it up, but the use of wormwood was common to effect cures of women's ailments, and crushed snails were also popular. The thought of medicines reminded him that he was supposed to be teaching. Thanking Agatha for her help, he walked quickly back through the kitchen, and up the wide spiral staircase that led to the hall on the upper floor. Father William, the dour Franciscan teacher of theology, was holding forth to a group of six or seven scholars on the doctrine of original sin, his voice booming through the hall to the distraction of the other Fellows who were also trying to teach there. Piers Hesselwell, Michaelhouse's Fellow of Law, was struggling valiantly to explain the basic principles of Gratian's *Decretum* to ten restless undergraduates, while Roger Alcote, probably tired of competing with William's voice, had ordered one of his scholars to read Aristotle's *Rhetoric* to his own class. As Bartholomew passed him on his way to the conclave at the far end of the hall, Alcote beckoned him over.

'What is the news?' he asked. 'Are these rumours true about dead friars in the chest?'

Bartholomew nodded, and tried to leave, reluctant to engage in gossip with the Senior Fellow. He was a tiny, bitter man who fussed like a hen and had a fanatical dislike of women that Bartholomew thought was abnormal.

'What House?' Alcote asked.

'Dominican,' answered Bartholomew, guessing what was coming next.

Alcote shot him a triumphant look. 'Dominican! A mendicant!' Bartholomew gave him a look of reproval. If the Fellows harboured such unyielding attitudes, what hope was there that the students would ever forget their differences and learn to study in peace? Alcote had recently taken major orders with the Cluniacs at Thetford, and had immediately engaged upon a bitter war of attrition with the mendicant Franciscans. Michaelhouse had been relatively free from inter-Order disputes until then; Brother Michael, the one Benedictine, picked no quarrel with the strong Franciscan contingent there, while those who had taken minor orders, like Bartholomew, had no quarrel with anyone.

Most scholars at the University took religious orders. This meant that they came under the jurisdiction of Church, rather than secular, law. This division between scholars and townspeople was yet another bone of contention, for secular law was notoriously harsher than Canon law: if Alcote or Bartholomew stole a sheep, they would be fined; if a townsman stole a sheep, he was likely to be hanged. Being in minor orders meant that Bartholomew had certain duties to perform, such as taking church services, but the protection it offered was indisputable. Other scholars, like William, Michael, and now Alcote, had taken major orders, which forbade marriage and relations with women.

Bartholomew left Alcote to his nasty musing, and made for the conclave. It was a pleasant room in the summer, when the light from the wide arched windows flooded in. The windows had no glass, and so a cool breeze wafted through them, tinged with the unmistakable aroma of river. The coolness was welcome in the summer, but in the winter, when the shutters had to be kept firmly closed against the weather, the conclave was dark and cold. The lime-washed walls were decorated with some fine wall-hangings, donated by a former student after a fire had damaged much of the hall two years before, and, at Bartholomew's insistence, there were always fresh rushes on the floor.

Bartholomew's students were engaged in a noisy dispute that he felt certain was not medical, and they quietened when he strode in. He settled himself in one of the chairs near the empty fireplace and smiled round at his students, noting which ones smiled back and which ones studiously avoided his eye because they had failed to prepare for the discussion he had planned. Sam Gray was one of the ones looking everywhere but at his teacher. He was a young man in his early twenties with a shock of unruly, light-brown hair. He looked tired and Bartholomew wondered what nocturnal activities he had been pursuing. He was certain they would not have had much to do with trepanation, cutting the skull open to relieve pressure on the brain, the subject of the day.

Bartholomew had been taught how to perform a number of basic operations by Ibn Ibrahim, and was considered something of an oddity in the town for knowing both surgery and medicine. He believed that medicine and surgery could complement each other, and wanted his students to have knowledge of both, despite the fact that most physicians looked down on surgical techniques as the responsibilities of barbers. Another problem he faced was that those students who had taken major orders were forbidden to practise incision and cautery by an edict passed by the Fourth Lateran Council in 1215.

'What is trepanation?' he asked. He had described the operation the previous term, but was curious to know who had remembered and who had not.

There was a rustle in the room as some students shuffled their feet, and one or two hands went up. Bartholomew noted that the first belonged to Thomas Bulbeck, who was his brightest student.

'Master Gray?' Bartholomew asked maliciously, knowing that Gray would not have the faintest idea what trepanation was because he had missed the previous lecture.

Gray looked startled. 'Trepidation,' he began, his usual confident manner asserting itself quickly, 'is a morbid fear of having your head sawed off.'

Bartholomew fought down the urge to laugh. If these young men were to be successful in their disputations, there was no room for levity. He saw one or two of the students nodding sagely, and marvelled at Gray's abilities to make the most outrageous claims with such conviction. Secretly, he envied the skill: such brazen self-assurance in certain situations might give a patient the encouragement needed to recover. Bartholomew was a poor liar, and his Arab master had often criticised him for not telling a patient what he wanted to hear when it might make the difference between life and death.

'Anyone else?' he asked, standing and pacing back and forth in front of the fireplace. Bulbeck's hand shot up. Bartholomew motioned for him to answer.

'Trepanation,' he said, casting a mischievous glance at Gray, 'is the surgical practice of removing a part of the skull to relieve pressure on the brain.'

'Surgery!' spat one of the Franciscans in disgust. 'A trades-man's job!'

Bartholomew wandered over to him. 'A patient comes to you with severe headaches, spells of unconsciousness, and uncoordinated movements. What do you do, Brother Boniface?'

'Bleed him with leeches,' Brother Boniface replied promptly.

Bartholomew thrust his hands in the folds of his tabard and suppressed a sigh of resignation. Wherever he went, people saw bleeding as a panacea for all manner of ailments, when other, far more effective but less dramatic, methods were to hand. He had lost many a patient to other physicians because of his refusal to leech on demand, and some had not lived to regret it. 'And what will that do?'

'It will relieve the patient of an excess of bad humours and reduce the pressure in the brain. Without the use of surgery,' he concluded smugly.

'And what if that does not work, and the patient becomes worse?' asked Bartholomew, sauntering to the window and sitting on one of the stone window seats, hands still firmly in his gown to prevent himself from grabbing the arrogant friar and trying to shake some sense into him.

'Then it is God's will that he dies, and I give him last rites,' said Boniface.

Bartholomew was impressed at this reasoning. Would that all his cases were so simple. 'But anyone who becomes ill and who is not given the correct treatment may die,' he said, 'and any of you who are unprepared to apply the cure that will save the patient should not become physicians.'

There was a sheepish silence. Bartholomew continued. 'Under certain circumstances there may be a surgical technique that can be used to save a patient's life. If it were God's will that these people should die, He would not have made it possible to use the technique in the first place. But the point is that many people who might have died have been saved because a surgeon has known how to do it. You need not perform the operation yourselves, but you should be prepared to hire the services of a barber-surgeon who will do it for you. Your first duty as a physician is always to save life, or to relieve painful symptoms.'

'My first duty is to God!' exclaimed Boniface, attempting piety, but betrayed by the malice that glittered in his eyes.

'Physicians serve God through their patients,' said Bartholomew immediately, having had this debate many times with Father William. 'God has given you the gift of healing through knowledge, and the way in which you use it is how you serve Him. If you choose to ignore the knowledge He has made available to you without good reason, then your service to Him is flawed.'

'Do you believe you serve God without using the leeches He saw fit to provide for that purpose?' asked Boniface blithely.

'I try to save my patients' lives with the most effective method,' replied Bartholomew. 'If I was certain leeching a patient would secure his recovery, I would leech him. But when my own experience dictates that there are other, more effective, cures for certain ailments than leeches, it would be wrong of me not to use them.'

'Does trepanation hurt the patient?' asked Robert Deynman suddenly, causing stifled laughter among the other students, and effectively ending Bartholomew's debate with Boniface. Deynman was Bartholomew's least able student, who had been accepted by Michaelhouse because his father was rich. Bartholomew eyed him closely, wondering if the question was intended to needle him, but a glance into the boy's guileless eyes told him that this was just another of his unbelievably stupid questions. Bartholomew felt sorry for him. He tried hard to keep up with the others, but study was entirely beyond him. The thought of Deynman let loose on patients made Bartholomew shudder, and he hoped he would never pass his disputations.

'Yes,' he answered slowly. 'It can be painful.' He wanted to ask how Deynman thought having a hole sawn in his head would feel, but did not want to embarrass the student in front of the others, especially the Franciscans. 'But there are things we can do to alleviate some of the discomfort. What are they?'

He stood up again and went back to the fireplace, kicking at the rushes as Bulbeck recited a list of the drugs and potions that might be used to dull the senses. 'What about laudanum?' he snapped. They had discussed Dioscorides' recommendations for doses of laudanum the previous day, and Bulbeck had already forgotten it.

Bulbeck faltered, and then added it to his list.

'How much would you give to a child you were going to operate on?' he demanded.

Bulbeck faltered again and the others looked away.

'Three measures,' said Deynman.

'For a child?' said Bartholomew incredulously, his resolution not to embarrass Deynman forgotten in his frustration. 'Well, you would certainly solve the problem of pressure on the brain. You would kill it! Master Gray? Come on! Think!'

'One measure,' guessed Gray wildly.

Bartholomew closed his eyes and tipped his head back and then looked at his students in resignation. 'You will kill your patients with ignorance,' he said quietly. 'I have told you at least twice now how much laudanum is safe to give children and you still do not know. Tomorrow we will discuss Dioscorides's *De Materia Medica* and the medicinal properties of opiates. Bulbeck will read it here this afternoon, and I want everyone to attend. Anyone who does not know correct dosages need not come tomorrow.'

He turned on his heel and stalked out of the conclave, hoping he had frightened them into learning. He was frustrated that they did not learn faster when there was such a dire need for physicians, but he would not make their disputations easier. Badly-taught physicians could be worse than none at all.

The bell began to ring for dinner and Bartholomew went to wash his hands. Michael was already speeding across to the hall so he could grab a few mouthfuls before the others arrived. The Franciscans gathered together before processing silently across the beaten-earth of the yard. Father William, the fanatic whom, rumour had it, had been dismissed from the inquisition for over-zealousness, was their acknowledged leader.

Bartholomew took his place next to Michael at the table that stood on a raised dais at the south end of the hall where the Fellows sat in a row. The large monk had tell-tale crumbs on his face and there were obvious gaps in the bread-basket. To Bartholomew's left sat Father Aidan, another Franciscan. Aidan was prematurely bald with two prominent front teeth and small blue eyes that never changed expression. Bartholomew had been told that he was an outstanding theologian, although his few attempts at conversation had been painful.

Aidan sat next to William, while next to him sat Kenyngham, his wispy white hair standing almost at right angles to his scalp. Next to the Master was Roger Alcote, and Piers Hesselwell sat on the end. Hesselwell taught law, and always wore fine clothes under his scholar's tabard. It had been difficult to find a Master of Law, for life in post-plague England was sunny indeed for lawyers. The plague took many individuals who had not made wills, while many wills that had been made were contested bitterly, and there was work aplenty for the lawyers. Few were willing to exchange potentially meteoric careers as practising lawyers for poorly paid positions as University teachers.

The last students slipped into place at the two long trestle tables that ran at right angles to the high table in the main body of the hall, and the buzz of conversation and shuffling died away. After the meal, the tables would be stored along the walls so that the hall could be used for teaching.

The Master said grace and announced that conversation would be allowed that day, but it was to be exclusively in Latin. This was because some students had disputations the following day, and the Master thought academic debate during meals would allow them more practice. The Franciscans frowned disapprovingly and maintained their own silence. It was the usual custom for a Bible scholar to read during the silence of meals for the scholars' spiritual edification, and the new Master's occasional breaks from this tradition were causing friction between the friars and the others.

For Bartholomew and Michael, this afforded an opportunity to discuss what they would ask the clerks at St Mary's that afternoon.

'How was your lecture?' asked Michael, leaning over Bartholomew to peer suspiciously at a dish of salted beef.

'Grim,' said Bartholomew. He looked down to where his students sat together at the far end of one of the tables. Gray shot him an unpleasant look, and Bartholomew knew his words had been taken seriously.

He picked up a piece of bread and inspected it dubiously. Since the plague, staple crops like barley, oats, and wheat had become scarce. College bread was made with whatever was cheapest and available, which sometimes included flour that was too old even for pig feed. Today, the bread was a grey colour and contained dark brown flecks. It tasted worse than it looked, ancient flour vying for dominance with rancid fat. The salted beef was hard and dry, and there was a large bowl containing lumps of something unidentifiable smeared with a blackish gravy.

Michael gulped down a large goblet of ale and crammed bread into his mouth. He gagged slightly, his eyes watering, and swallowed with difficulty.

'You will choke one day if you do not eat more slowly,' said Bartholomew, not for the first time during their friendship.

'You will be able to save me,' said Michael complacently, reaching for more meat.

Bartholomew chewed some of the hard College bread slowly. The ale, he noticed, was off again, and the salted beef should be thrown away before it poisoned everyone. The thought of poison brought his mind back to the business with the University chest. He had heard of such devices that were designed to kill unwanted meddlers, but never thought he would see one in action. He wondered who had put it there. A thought suddenly struck him and he almost choked on the bread in his eagerness to tell Michael.

Michael pounded on his back, and Bartholomew was reminded that the monk might look fat and unhealthy, but he was a physical force with which to be reckoned.

'It looks as if I will be the one to save you,' Michael said with malicious glee. 'Do not gobble your food, Doctor. You will choke.'

'Buckley,' gasped Bartholomew. 'His hands!'

Michael looked at him blankly. 'What about his hands?'

Bartholomew took a gulp of the bad ale, and resisted the urge to spit it out again. 'I treated Buckley for a skin complaint. He has weeping sores on his hands.'

'Please!' Michael looked disapproving at such matters mentioned at the table.

'He wears gloves, Michael! Not because the disease is infectious, but because the sores are unpleasant to see and he is embarrassed about them. Can you not see?' he cried, drawing the unwanted attention of the Franciscans. He lowered his voice. 'He probably wears his gloves when he unlocks the chest!'

Michael stared at him for a few moments, thinking. 'So,' he said slowly, 'we cannot be certain when this poisonous lock was placed on the chest, since de Wetherset says Buckley is the one who usually opened it, and he has been protected by his gloves. It may have been there for weeks or even months before it did its gruesome work. Buckley may even have put it there himself knowing that he would be safe from it if he wore gloves.'

Bartholomew thought for a moment. 'Possibly,' he said, 'although I do not think so. First, that was a very small cut on the friar's hand. He may not even have noticed it, which suggests a very concentrated form of poison. It would be a brave man who would risk touching such a lock, even wearing gloves. Second, perhaps the poison was meant for Buckley, if it were known that he was the one who regularly opened the chest, and not the Chancellor.'

Michael rubbed his clean-shaven chin thoughtfully. 'But that would mean that someone so wants Buckley dead that he has been to some trouble to plant that poisonous lock on the chest. I have never bought one of those things, but I warrant they are not cheap.'

'So perhaps Buckley has fled, not because he planted the lock and was responsible for the death of the friar, but because he was in fear of his life. Although,' Bartholomew added practically, 'most men fleeing in fear of their lives do not take tables and chairs with them.'

The conversation was cut short as the Master rose to say grace at the end of the meal, and the Fellows filed in silence from the hall. As soon as they were out, Michael winked at Bartholomew and headed off towards the kitchens to scavenge left-overs. The students clattered noisily down the stairs into the yard, followed by the commoners. There had been ten commoners at Michaelhouse before the plague, but the numbers were now down to four, all old men who had devoted their lives to teaching for the College and were rewarded with board and lodging for the remainder of their lives. Bartholomew went to pay his customary call on one of them, a Cistercian in his seventies called Brother Alban. Alban grinned toothlessly at Bartholomew as the physician rubbed warmed oil into his arthritic elbow, and began to talk in graphic terms about the murder of the prostitutes. As always, Bartholomew was amazed at how the old man managed to acquire his information. He never left the College, yet always seemed to be the first to hear any news from outside. Occasionally, Bartholomew found his love of gossip offensive, but tried to be tolerant since the poor man had little else to do. Although he could still read, Alban's elbow prevented him from producing the splendid illustrated texts for which he had once been famous. Bartholomew occasionally saw the old man leafing wistfully through some of his magnificent work, and felt sorry for him.

'There will be yet more murders,' Alban said with salacious enjoyment. 'Just you see. The Sheriff is less than worthless at tracking this criminal down.'

'And I suppose you know who the murderer is,' asked Bartholomew drily, finding the discussion distasteful. He poured more oil into the palm of his hand, and continued to massage it into the swollen joint.

Alban scowled at him. 'Cheeky beggar,' he muttered. 'No, I do not know who the murderer is, but if I were your age, I would find out!'

'And how would you do that?' said Bartholomew, more to side-track Brother Alban from his lurid and fanciful descriptions of the killer's victims than to solicit a sensible answer.

'I would go to the churches of St John Zachary or All Saints'-next-the-Castle, and I would find out,' said Alban, tipping his head back and fixing Bartholomew with alert black eyes.

'Why those churches?' said Bartholomew, nonplussed.

The old monk sighed heavily and looked at Bartholomew as he might an errant student. 'Because they have been decommissioned,' he said.

After the plague, the fall in the population meant that there were not enough people to make use of all existing churches, and many had been decommissioned. Some were pulled down, or used as a source of stone: others were locked up to await the day when they would be used again. Two such were St John Zachary and All Saints'-next-the-Castle. At the height of the plague, the entire population north of the river next to the Castle had died. Bartholomew had burned down the pathetic hovels there so that they would not become a continuing source of infection for the town. People claimed that the site of the settlement and All Saints' Church were haunted, and few people went there.

'So?' said Bartholomew, his attention to the conversation wavering as he concentrated on Alban's arm.

'Do you know nothing?' said Alban, more than a touch of gloating in his voice.

Bartholomew flexed the old man's elbow. 'I know that your arm is improving.' He was pleased. The old man could bend it further than he had been able to a week ago, and seemed to be in less pain. Typically, Alban was more interested in his gossip.

'There are works of the Devil performed in the churches,' he crowed, 'and I am willing to wager you will find out from them who is killing these whores.'

'Works of the Devil!' scoffed Bartholomew dismissively. 'Always the excuse for the crimes of people!'

'I mean witchcraft, Matthew,' said Alban primly. 'It goes on in those two churches, and a good many others too, I imagine. I do not need to tell you why. People are wondering why they should pray to a God that did not deliver them from the Death, and so they are turning to other sources of power. It is the same all over England. The murder of these harlots is symptomatic of a sickening society.'

Bartholomew finished his treatment of Alban's arm and left the old man's chatter with some relief. He had heard about the increase in witchcraft, but had given it little thought. Brother Michael had mentioned it once or twice, and it had sparked a fierce debate one night among the Franciscans, but Bartholomew had not imagined that it would occur in Cambridge. Perhaps Alban was right; he often was with his gossip. Bartholomew decided to ask whether Cynric knew anything about it, and, if he did, he would suggest to Sheriff Tulyet that he might consider asking questions about the murders in the churches of St John Zachary and All Saints'-next-the-Castle.

Michael was waiting for him in the yard and reluctantly Bartholomew followed him out of the gates to interview the clerks. The sun was hot and Bartholomew shed his black scholar's tabard and stuffed it in his bag. He knew he could be fined by the Proctors for not wearing it, but considered the comfort of wearing only leggings and a linen shirt worth the possible expense. Brother Michael watched enviously and pulled uncomfortably at the voluminous folds of his own heavy gown.

At St Mary's Church, they saw that the body of the dead friar had been laid out in the Lady Chapel. Bartholomew walked over to it and looked again at the small cut at the base of his thumb that had caused his death. Michael sought out the lay-brother who had locked the church the night before, a mouselike man with eyes that roved in different directions. He was clearly terrified. Bartholomew led him away to talk, but the man's eyes constantly strayed in the direction of the dead friar.

'What time did you lock the church last night?' asked Bartholomew gently.

The man audibly gulped and seemed unable to answer. Michael became impatient.

'Come on! We do not have all day!'

The man's knees gave out and he slid down the base of a pillar and crouched on the floor, casting petrified glances around him. Bartholomew knelt next to him.

'Please try to remember,' he said. 'It is important.'

The man reached out and grabbed his sleeve, pulling him close to whisper in his ear. 'At dusk,' he said, glancing up at the imposing figure of Michael with huge eyes. Michael raised his eyes heavenward, and went to gather together the other clerks with whom they would need to talk, leaving Bartholomew alone to question the lay-brother.

'At dusk,' the man repeated, watching Michael's retreating

back with some relief. 'I doused the candles and went to see that the catches on the windows were secure. I put the bar over the sanctuary door as usual, and checked that the tower door was locked.'

'How did you do that?' asked Bartholomew.

The lay-brother made a motion with his hands that indicated he had given it a good shake. 'Then I made sure the sanctuary light was burning and left. I locked the door behind me and gave the keys to Father Cuthbert.'

'Why did Father Cuthbert not lock the church himself?' asked Bartholomew.

'He does when he can. But he has pains in his ankles sometimes, so I lock up when he cannot walk.'

Bartholomew nodded. He had often treated Father Cuthbert for swollen ankles, partly caused by the great pressure put on them by his excess weight, and partly, Bartholomew suspected, caused by a serious affinity for fortified wines.

'Did you notice anything unusual?' he asked.

The man shook his head hesitantly, and Bartholomew was certain he was lying.

'It would be better if you told me what you know,' he said quietly. He saw sweat start to bead on the man's upper lip. Then, before he could do anything to stop him, the man dived out of Bartholomew's reach and scuttled out of the church. Bartholomew ran after him and saw him disappear into the bushes in the churchyard. He followed, ignoring the way the dense shrubs scratched at his arms. There seemed to be a small path through the undergrowth, faint from lack of use, but a distinct pathway nevertheless. Bartholomew crashed along it and suddenly found himself in one of the dismal alleys that lay between the church and the market-place, his feet skidding in the dust as he came to a halt.

This was one of the poorest areas of the town, a place where no one valuing his safety would consider entering after dark. The houses were no more than rows of wooden frames packed with dried mud. One or two of the better ones had ill-fitting doors to keep out the elements, but most only had a blanket or a piece of leather to serve as a door.

But it was not the homes that caught Bartholomew's eye. The

lay-brother had disappeared, but others stood in the alley, a group of scruffy men who moved towards him with a menace that left Bartholomew in no doubt that he was not welcome there. He swallowed and began to back towards the pathway in the bushes, but two of the men moved quickly to block his way.

The alley was silent except for the shuffling of the advancing men. There were at least eight of them, with more joining their ranks by the moment, rough men wearing jerkins of boiled leather and an odd assortment of leggings and shirts. Bartholomew wondered whether he would be able to force his way through them if he took off as fast as he could and made for the market square. A look at the naked hostility on the men's faces told him he would not succeed. These men meant business. Fear mingled with confusion as he wondered why his blundering into the alley had resulted in such instant antagonism.

They moved closer, hemming Bartholomew against one of the shacks. He clenched his fists so that they would not see his hands were shaking; he was nearly overwhelmed with the rank smell of unwashed bodies and breath laden with ale fumes. One of the men made a lunge for his arm and Bartholomew ducked and swung out with his fists blindly. In surrounding him so closely, the men had given themselves little room for movement. Blows were aimed, but lacked force, although judging from several grunts of pain, Bartholomew's own kicks and punches, wildly thrown, were more effective.

A leg hooked around the back of his knees and sent him sprawling backwards onto the ground, and he knew that it was all over. He twisted sideways to squirm out of the reach of a kick aimed at his head, but was unable to move fast enough to avoid the one to his stomach. The breath rushed out of him and his limbs turned to jelly so that he was unable to move.

'Stop!'

It was the deep voice of a woman that Bartholomew heard through a haze of dust and shuffling feet. The men moved back, and by the time Bartholomew had picked himself up and was steadying himself against a wall, the alleyway was deserted except for the woman.

He looked at her closely. She was dressed in a good quality, but old, woollen dress of faded blue, and her hair, as black as Bartholomew's own, fell in a luxurious shimmering sheet down her back and partly over her face. Her features were strong and bespoke of a formidable strength of character, and although she would not have been called pretty, there was a certain attraction in her clear eyes and steady gaze. As Bartholomew looked more closely, he saw two scars on each jaw, running parallel to each other. Not wishing to make her uncomfortable by staring, he looked away, wondering whether the scars marked her as a member of some religious sect. He had heard that self-mutilation had been common in Europe during the plague years, and it was possible that the scars had been made then.

'Who are you?' he asked.

She looked at him in disbelief and let out a burst of laughter. 'I save your life, and what do you say? "Thank you"? "I am grateful"? Oh, no! "Who are you?"!' She laughed again, although Bartholomew was too shaken to find the situation amusing. That she obviously held some sway over the band of louts who had just tried to kill him he found of little comfort.

'I am sorry,' he said, contrite. 'Thank you. May I know your name?'

She raised black eyebrows, her blue eyes dancing in merriment. 'All right, then,' she said. 'My name is Janetta of Lincoln. Who are you and what were you doing in our lane?'

'Your lane?' he asked, surprised. 'Since when did the streets of Cambridge become private property?'

The laughter went out of her face. 'You have a careless tongue for a man who has just been delivered from an unpleasant fate. And you did not answer my question. What are you doing here?'

Bartholomew wondered what he could tell her. He thought of the terrified face of the lay-brother and was reluctant to mention him to this curious woman. He also wondered why he had been so foolish as to chase the man when he easily could have found out his address from Father Cuthbert.

'I must have taken a wrong turning,' he said. He looked around him and saw that his bag had gone, containing not only all his medical instruments and some medicines, but his best scholar's tabard too.

Janetta stared at him, her hands on her hips. 'You are an ingrate,' she said. 'I stop them from killing you, and you repay me with rudeness and lies.'

Bartholomew knew that she was right and was sorry. But, despite the sunshine filtering down into the alley from the cloudless sky, Bartholomew felt something menacing and dark in the alley and longed to be gone. He straightened from where he had been leaning against the wall and took a deep breath.

'I saw a small path leading through the bushes in St Mary's churchyard,' he answered truthfully. 'I followed it and it finished here.'

She continued to stare at him for a few minutes. 'You were following it at quite a pace,' she said. 'I thought you were being pursued by the Devil himself.'

He grimaced and looked up and down the alley to see which way would be the best to leave. She followed his eyes.

'You will only be safe while you are with me,' she said. 'Would you like me to walk with you?'

Bartholomew ran a hand through his hair and gave her a crooked smile. 'Thank you,' he said. 'How is it that you seem to have so much control over these people?'

She gestured that he was to precede her down the alley. Although Bartholomew could see no one, he knew that they were being watched. The silence of the alley was a tangible thing. He glanced at Janetta walking behind him, striding purposefully.

She smiled at him, showing small, white teeth. 'I have taken it on myself to give them a community spirit, a sense of worth and belonging.'

Bartholomew was not sure he knew what she meant, but kept his silence. All he wanted to do was leave the filthy alley and go back to the relative peace and sanity of Michaelhouse. For some reason he could not place, the woman made him uncomfortable. He glanced behind them, and was alarmed to see that a crowd of people had gathered, and was following them down the alley, its silence far more menacing than words could ever be. Janetta also glanced round, but seemed amused.

'They wonder where you are taking me,' she said.

Then they were out of the alley and into the colour and cheerful cacophony of the market-place. Gaudy canopies sheltered the goods of the traders from the hot sun, and everywhere people were calling and shouting. Dogs barked and children howled with laughter at the antics of a juggler. Somewhere, a pig had escaped and was being chased by a number of people, its squeals and their yelling adding to the general chaos.

He turned to Janetta, who still smiled at him.

'Thank you,' he said again. 'And please tell whoever stole my bag that there are some medicines in it that might kill if given to the wrong person. If he or she does not want to give it back to me, the medicines would best be thrown into the river where they will do no harm.'

She nodded slowly, appraising him frankly. 'Do not come here uninvited again, Matthew Bartholomew,' she said.

Without waiting for a response, she turned and strode jauntily back down the alley, leaving Bartholomew staring after her, wondering how she had known his name when he had not told her.

'What happened to you?' exclaimed Michael in horror, looking at Bartholomew's torn and dirty clothes.

Bartholomew took his arm and led him back through the churchyard to the bushes where he had followed the lay-brother. But however hard he looked, he could not find the path. It simply was not there. He stood back, bewildered.

'What is going on, Matt?' asked Michael impatiently. 'What have you been doing? You look as though you have been in a fight.'

Bartholomew explained what had happened and sat on a tree-stump in the shade of the church while Michael conducted his own search of the bushes.

'Are you sure there was a path?' he asked doubtfully.

'Of course I am!' Bartholomew snapped. He leaned forward and rested his head in his hands. 'I am sorry, Michael. It was a nasty experience and it has made me irritable.'

Michael patted his shoulder. 'Tell me again about this woman.

Pretty, you say?' He perched on the tree-stump next to the physician.

Bartholomew regarded him through narrowed eyes and wondered, not for the first time, whether Michael was really the kind of man who should have been allowed to take a vow of chastity.

'Tell me what you discovered from the clerks,' he said, to change the subject.

'They said they had noticed the friar praying in the church for the last three days. Some of them spoke to him, and he said he was travelling from London to Huntingdon and had stopped here for a few days to rest and pray. They did not ask why he was travelling. They also do not know exactly where he came from in London. He seemed pleasant, friendly and polite, and none of them thought it strange that he should spend so much time in this church.'

'Is that all?' asked Bartholomew. Michael nodded. 'Then we are really no further forward. We still do not know who he was or why he was in the tower, except that he probably travelled some distance to be there. And that poor lay-brother was terrified of something, and I did not like the atmosphere in that shabby alleyway.'

'You should not frequent such places, then,' said Michael. 'Although I would have imagined you would be used to them by now.'

'I thought I was,' said Bartholomew. He thought he knew most of the poorest parts of town through his patients, but had not been called to the alleys behind the market square since the plague. Like the little settlement by the castle, the people who lived in the hovels near the Market Square had either died or moved to occupy better homes when others died.

He and Michael sat in companionable silence for a few moments and then Michael stood. 'Stay here,' he said. 'I will send Cynric back with your spare tabard. If Alcote sees you dirty and dishevelled, he will fine you on the spot, and now you need to buy a new tabard you cannot afford it.'

He ambled off, and Bartholomew leaned back wearily. Now that the excitement had worn off, he felt tired and sick. He wondered whether everything fitted together – the dead friar, the poisoned lock, the disappearing lay-brother and Vice-Chancellor, the murdered women, and the sinister alley – or whether they were all independent incidents that just happened to have involved him. He felt more than a little angry at the Chancellor. He wanted to teach and to practise medicine, not to become involved in some nasty plot where women and friars were killed, and that forced him to exhume dead clerks.

He squinted up and watched the leaves blowing in the breeze, making changing pools of light over the tombstones in the grave-yard. He could hear the distant racket from the market-place, while in the church some friars were chanting Terce.

'What are you thinking of, getting into all this trouble without me?' came a familiar voice. Bartholomew opened his eyes and smiled at the Welshman with Michael behind him. Cynric took a strange delight in the kind of cloak-and-dagger activity that Bartholomew deplored. He was more friend than servant, and had been with Bartholomew since he had been appointed to teach in Cambridge. As Bartholomew explained what had happened, Cynric made no attempt to conceal his disdain for Bartholomew's ineptitude in handling the situation.

While Bartholomew donned his tabard to hide his damaged clothes and Michael sat on the tree stump, Cynric went to see if he could find the path. After a few minutes, he came back to sit next to Michael, eyes narrowed against the sun.

'The path is there sure enough,' said Cynric. 'Small twigs are broken and the grass is bruised. Someone must have come up the alley and arranged the bushes so that the path is hidden. I will come back later and explore it.'

'No, you will not,' said Bartholomew firmly. 'Whoever hid it did so for a reason, and I am not sure I want to know why. I have a feeling the lay-brother made a grave error in using that path and I was probably lucky not to have been killed for following him. Let it be, Cynric.'

Cynric looked disappointed, but nodded his agreement. 'But next time you go out, boy, make sure I go with you. Old Cynric is far better at these things than you are.'

It would not be too difficult to be better at 'these things' than he was, Bartholomew thought wryly, but Cynric was right. He would never have blundered blindly into the alley as Bartholomew had done.

Michael stood and rubbed his hands together. 'We have had a difficult day,' he announced. 'I propose we go and enjoy ourselves at the Fair.'

Barnwell Causeway, the road that led from the town to the fields in which the Fair was held, was thronged with people. Men with huge trays of pastries and pies competed with each other for trade, while water-sellers left damp patches on the road as the river-water they carried in their buckets slopped over the sides. Beggars lined the route, sitting at the sides of the road and displaying sores and wounds to any who would look. Some were soldiers from the wars in France, once England's heroes, now quietly ignored. The Sheriff's men elbowed their way through the crowd, asking if anyone had witnessed the murder of a potter the night before.

Michael shook his head to the sergeant's enquiry. 'The roads are becoming more and more dangerous after dark,' he remarked, as the sergeant repeated his enquiry to a group of noisy apprentices walking behind them. 'Safe enough now with all these folk, but deadly to any foolish enough to wander at night.'

Cynric made a darting movement, and there was a yowl of pain from a scruffy man wearing a brown cloak.

'Not even safe in daylight,' said Cynric, handing Michael's purse back to him, and watching the pickpocket scamper away down the road clutching his arm.

Michael grimaced, and tucked the purse down the front of his habit. He brightened as the colourful canopies of the Fair booths came into sight, and stopped to look. War-horses pounded up and down a narrow strip near the river as their owners showed off their equestrian skills. Huge fires with whole pigs and sheep roasting over them sent delicious smells to mingle with the scent of manure and sweaty bodies. And everywhere there was noise: animals bleated and bellowed, vendors yelled about their wares, children shrieked and laughed, and musicians added their part to the general cacophony.

Bartholomew followed Michael and Cynric into the mêlée,

shaking off an insistent baker who was trying to sell him apple pastries crawling with flies. Bartholomew smiled at the people he knew – rich merchants in their finery, black-garbed scholars, and the poorest of his patients who eyed the wealth around them with jealous eyes. He saw the Junior Proctor, Alric Jonstan, and two of his beadles talking together near a stall displaying neatly-stacked fruit.

Jonstan hailed him pleasantly, and sent his beadles to disperse a rowdy group of scholars who were watching a mystery play nearby. He rubbed a hand across his face, and beckoned Bartholomew and Michael behind the fruit stall to a quieter part of the Fair. He sat on a wooden bench, and summoned a brewer to bring them some ale.

'This is the finest ale in England,' he said, closing his eyes and taking a long draught with obvious pleasure. The brewer smiled, gratified, and set the remaining tankards on the table.

Jonstan held up his hand. 'As a Proctor, I should not be setting the example of sitting in an ale tent, but I have been working since I left St Mary's this morning, and even the most dedicated of men needs sustenance.'

'Excellent ale,' said Michael appraisingly, raising his empty tankard to be refilled, and wiping foam from his mouth. 'And we are all well-enough hidden here, I think.'

'Master Harling would not think so,' said Jonstan with a wry smile. Bartholomew could well-believe it of the dour Physwick Hostel scholar. 'But what did you discover about this friar?'

Michael set his tankard down, and rubbed his sleeve across his mouth. 'Nothing other than what we told you this morning. But if you have been here all day, perhaps you do not know that Master Buckley seems to have disappeared.'

'Disappeared?' echoed Jonstan, stunned. 'But he is coming to dine with me and my mother this evening.'

'I doubt he will come,' said Michael. 'But if he does, you might mention that the Chancellor would like to see him, and the Warden of King's Hall would like his tables back.'

Jonstan stared at him and shook his head slowly as Michael described Buckley's empty room.

'Where will you start to sort out this mess?' he asked, looking from Michael to Bartholomew.

'I would rather not start at all,' said Bartholomew fervently. 'I would sooner teach.'

Jonstan pulled a sympathetic face. 'I can understand that,' he said. 'I taught law before I became a Proctor, but have done no teaching since. I moved out of Physwick Hostel and bought a house in Shoemaker Row, so that my mother could keep house for me to allow more time for my duties. I wish Harling and I could help you with this business, but I think we will be too busy with the Fair. Hot weather, cheap ale, and gangs of students are a lethal combination, and we will be hard-pressed to keep the peace as it is.'

He stood suddenly as a student reeled towards him, arm-in-arm with a golden-haired woman from one of the taverns. The student saw the Proctor, released the woman and fled, all signs of drunkenness disappearing as quickly as if Jonstan had dashed a bucket of cold water over him. The woman looked around, bewildered, and Jonstan sat again with a smile.

'I wish all my duties were as easy as that,' he said.

'There was another prostitute murder,' said Bartholomew.

'I heard about that,' said Jonstan. He frowned. 'Does it seem to you that there are more prostitutes now than before the Death?'

'Inevitably,' said Bartholomew, sipping the cool ale. 'Some women lost their families in the plague, and it is one way in which they can make enough money to live.'

'There are other ways, Doctor,' said Jonstan primly. 'They could sew or cook.'

'Possibly,' said Bartholomew, watching an argument develop into a fight between a buxom matron and a man selling rabbit furs. 'But all these travelling labourers mean that life as a prostitute is as well paid and secure as any occupation these days.'

'But it is sinful,' persisted Jonstan, his round blue eyes earnest. 'The plague was a sign from God that we should amend our wicked ways, and yet there are more prostitutes now than before. How can they fail to heed His warning?'

Bartholomew had heard these arguments before: the plague had been regarded as a punishment for all manner of wicked-ness – crime, the war with France, violation of the Sabbath, blasphemy, not fasting on Fridays, usury, adultery. Many people believed the plague was but a warning, and it was only a matter of time before it returned to kill all with evil in their hearts.

After a while, enjoying the ale and the warmth of the sun, he rose to leave. The others followed suit, and they parted from Jonstan. Moments later, Bartholomew felt a hand on his shoulder, and turned to see his brother-in-law, Oswald Stanmore, beaming at him.

Bartholomew returned his smile, and asked Stanmore how his business was faring.

'Excellent,' said Stanmore, his smile widening further still. 'I have sold almost all the cloth I had stored in my warehouse, and deposits have been made on the next shipment due to arrive within two days.'

'Has the Sheriff found the men who stole your cloth yet?' asked Bartholomew, referring to an incident in which two of Stanmore's carts were attacked and plundered on the London road.

Stanmore frowned. 'He has not. And I am unimpressed with what he is doing to get to the bottom of the matter.'

Bartholomew raised his eyebrows. Sheriffs were seldom popular, but Richard Tulyet had recently excelled at making himself an object of dislike. First the townspeople complained about his lack of progress on the murders of the women, and now Stanmore about his stolen cloth.

Stanmore sighed. 'I know Tulyet has his hands full with the whore murders,' he said, 'but the town will suffer if he does not look into the attack on my goods: merchants will not come here if the roads are dangerous.'

'There was another murder this morning,' said Bartholomew, to divert Stanmore from the lecture on the importance of safe travel and trade he was about to give.

Stanmore nodded. 'It was all the talk at the Fair today,' he said. 'Some womenfolk are thinking of leaving early because of it.' He leaned towards Bartholomew so that he would not be overheard. 'I heard a rumour today that one of the guilds might look into this prostitute business, since Tulyet will not.'

'Which guild?' asked Bartholomew, concerned. 'Witch-hunters who will accuse any man out alone after curfew?'

'No, no,' said Stanmore. 'They call themselves the Guild of the Holy Trinity, and there are priests and monks among their number. It is nothing sinister, but a group of honest men who are concerned that sin and crime have increased since the Death.'

Bartholomew looked dubious, and Stanmore shrugged. 'There are many who feel as they do,' he said. 'These are not religious fanatics sniffing out heresy, like your Father William, but plain folk who care about the changes that have occurred since the Death.' When Bartholomew failed to look convinced, Stanmore threw up his hands in despair. 'Look at the evidence in front of you! A tiny place like Cambridge, and we have a maniac who kills women in the dead of night, and it is not even safe for a cart of cloth to travel from London.'

'But the attack was miles away!' protested Bartholomew. 'You cannot blame Cambridge for what happened near London.'

'It was not near London, it was at Saffron Walden,' said Stanmore haughtily. 'A mere fifteen miles away.' He scratched at his chin. 'It is an odd business. I expected that the cloth would reappear at the Fair, sold by the thieves, but although I have had my apprentices scour the area, not so much as a thread of it has appeared.'

'Perhaps it was stolen for personal use,' said Bartholomew.

Stanmore looked impatient. 'This is finest quality worsted, Matt. You do not use such cloth to sew any old garment.'

Bartholomew shrugged. 'Perhaps the thieves anticipated you would look for it here, and plan to sell it elsewhere.'

'They must,' said Stanmore. 'But it is a wretched nuisance. I had to send that cloth to London to be dyed since de Belem's prices are so extortionate. So, not only do I lose the cloth, I have the expense of dyeing and transport. It is a bad time to be a merchant: labour prices are sky-high, fewer dyers and weavers mean that they can charge what they will because there is no competition, and, on top of all that, it is not safe to transport goods.'

'But most of that has always been true,' said Bartholomew, to placate the agitated draper.

'Not like this,' said Stanmore bitterly. 'English cloth and English wool are the finest in the world. But there are fewer shepherds to tend the sheep, less wool available for weaving, fewer weavers to weave it . . .'

'And fewer merchants to sell it,' interrupted Bartholomew, laughing. 'Come, Oswald! It is not all bad. You are not in the gutters yet!'

Stanmore smiled reluctantly. 'I suppose business at the Fair has been good,' he admitted. He turned to watch the antics of a small group of tumblers from Spain, who leapt, somersaulted, and cartwheeled in a flurry of red jackets and blue leggings. Bartholomew left him to admire the acrobats, and wandered off alone. He watched a troop of players perform the mystery play about Adam and Eve to a large and good-humoured crowd. Nearby, other players, with a far smaller audience, enacted scenes from the plague, claiming that the disease would come again unless wicked ways were mended. Bartholomew thought about the Guild of the Holy Trinity, and wondered if the few people watching and nodding sagely at the play's message were its members.

By the time Bartholomew met Michael and Cynric again, the daylight was fading, and traders were packing up. Many would stay, cooking stews on open fires, while others would leave an apprentice to guard their goods and walk back into Cambridge to sleep in taverns and brothels. The Fair was only half-way through, and already surrounding fields and coppices had been stripped of wood for the fires that provided warmth and hot food.

Bartholomew, Cynric, and Michael joined a group of exhausted traders to walk the short distance back to Cambridge. By mutual consent, they waited until there were about twenty people. Many traders carried the day's takings to be deposited with a money-lender, or hidden in a secure place, and robberies along the dark stretch of road were not uncommon during the Fair. Stanmore and his steward Hugh, armed with a crossbow, joined the group, and they set off, some singing a bawdy tavern song despite their weariness.

Stanmore continued his dismal analysis on the safety of roads, which had Bartholomew glancing nervously over his shoulder. But despite Stanmore's gloom, they arrived at Michaelhouse without mishap, where Michael went to the kitchen for something to eat, and Bartholomew went straight to bed.

Early the next morning, he was awoken by an insistent knocking on his door, and Eli, the bow-legged College steward, burst in.

'Doctor Bartholomew!' he gasped. 'You must come! There is a girl dying in our orchard.'

CHAPTER 3

ELI LED THE WAY TO THE ORCHARD THAT LAY BEHIND the kitchen. Agatha knelt in the long grass, leaning over someone lying on the ground. At a discreet distance, Master Kenyngham stood with Michael, Alcote, Cynric, and Piers Hesselwell.

As Bartholomew approached, he saw the bloodstained sheet that Agatha had used to cover the girl and knew what to expect. Yet another murder of a prostitute, except that this time the murder had not been in a churchyard, but on College property. As he knelt next to her, Agatha caught his wrist, her strong face unusually white. She glanced around to ensure she could not be overheard.

'Only you and I know about this, Matthew,' she said. 'We could keep it that way.'

He gazed at her, bewildered, but she would say no more, and Bartholomew turned his attention to the girl. He caught his breath in horror as he saw who lay beneath the sheet, and stared at Agatha in shock. She touched his arm and gestured at the figure on the ground, to bring his attention back to Frances de Belem. An attempt had been made to cut her throat, but, although there was a nasty wound there, it had failed to give her a quick death. Bartholomew had no idea how long she had been in the orchard in this condition. Her body was cold, but he could not tell whether it was from the loss of blood, or from lying in the wet grass. Her eyes were closed and blood bubbled through her white lips as she breathed.

Bartholomew sent Cynric to fetch a sense-dulling potion that he kept in a locked chest in the chamber adjacent to his own room. While Cynric was gone, Kenyngham gave last rites. When he had finished, Bartholomew dripped some of the powerful syrup between her teeth, but hoped that she would not regain consciousness to need it. Frances's breathing grew more laboured, and Michael and Alcote knelt, and began intoning prayers of the dying.

Just when Bartholomew thought she would slip away, she opened her eyes and looked at him. Agatha took her hand and crooned comfortingly, while Bartholomew motioned to the clerics to keep their voices down. He leaned close to her to hear what she was trying to whisper.

'I am sorry for what I asked you to do,' she said, her voice little more than a breath.

'No harm was done,' Bartholomew said. 'But who did this to you?'

'It was not a man,' she said in a low voice, her eyes filling with tears. Her hand fluttered to a silver cross she wore around her neck.

When Bartholomew looked from the cross to her face, she was dead. He felt for a life beat, put his cheek close to her mouth to see if he could detect breathing, and covered her with the sheet.

Agatha leaned towards him. 'Will you condemn her as a suicide? Or will you keep silent about what she told us yesterday?'

Before replying, Bartholomew pulled the sheet from her feet. She wore no shoes and there was the small circle on her left foot. Frances de Belem was too wealthy to go without shoes, so someone must have taken them. He covered her again, and glanced at Michael. Michael faltered in his prayers as he saw what Bartholomew was doing, and Bartholomew saw Piers Hesselwell look at them strangely as he noticed the exchange.

'She was no suicide, Agatha,' he said softly. 'She was murdered.'

'What?' queried Agatha loudly. 'Here in Michaelhouse? How do you know?'

'It is not easy to commit suicide by cutting your own throat,' said Bartholomew. And there were the circle on her foot and the missing shoes to consider, he thought.

Agatha hastily crossed herself. She let out a great sigh and muttered something about fetching the porters. Bartholomew watched her go, the usual aggressive buoyancy gone from her step. Kenyngham and the other Fellows came to form a circle around the dead girl.

'Does anyone know who she was?' Kenyngham asked.

'Frances de Belem,' said Bartholomew, looking up at him.

'The merchant's daughter?' queried Alcote, and then smirked. 'Ah, yes. I had forgotten how you would know that,' he added nastily.

The Master raised his eyebrows and Alcote continued, 'Matthew's sister married well, and her husband is Sir Oswald Stanmore, who owns the large building next to Sir Reginald's house. That is how Matthew knows the daughters of wealthy merchants.'

Bartholomew saw Alcote exchange smug looks with Hesselwell. Was Alcote trying to curry favour with the new Master to advance his own career? If so, his tale-telling had failed to impress Kenyngham, who smiled benignly at Bartholomew and touched him lightly on the head.

'Then I am afraid, Matthew, that you are probably the best man to tell her family what has happened,' he said. 'Does anyone know how she came to be here?'

Vacant looks answered his question until Eli spoke up. 'Mistress Agatha found her here when she came to hang out the washing. She called for me, and I fetched you and the others.'

Bartholomew looked around at the grass. A trail of blood leading to a spot some distance away indicated that Frances had dragged herself from one place to another, perhaps in the hope of reaching Michaelhouse for help. It had dried, suggesting that she had probably been in the orchard for several hours, and perhaps even since the night before.

'Thank you, Eli,' said Kenyngham, 'but that does not explain how she came to be here in the first place. I doubt that she could have entered through the College, which means that she must have come in through the door that leads out to the lane.'

Cynric had already looked. 'The gate is open,' he said. 'I bar it myself at dusk each night, and so someone inside must have opened it between dusk last night and now.'

'Well,' said the Master, looking round at his Fellows, 'has anyone used the back gate this morning?'

There was silence as the Fellows shook their heads and looked at each other blankly.

'I will ask the students,' said Kenyngham. 'Now, I suggest we return to our duties. Eli and Cynric, take Mistress de Belem to the church with the porters. Master Hesselwell, take Brother Michael to his room: he looks ill. Master Alcote, I would like you to inform the Sheriff and the Chancellor.' As they scurried to do his bidding, he turned to Bartholomew.

'Matthew, I do not envy you your task. Would you like me to come with you?'

Bartholomew thanked him, but felt it was a duty he should perform alone. On his way to Milne Street, he met Stanmore, already heading for the Fair with his apprentices. His good humour evaporated when he learned Bartholomew's news.

'Heaven help us,' he said softly. He grabbed Bartholomew's arm. 'Let me come with you. Reginald and I have had our differences, but he may need me now.'

It was a long time before Bartholomew felt he could leave de Belem's house. Sir Reginald was working in the dim morning light in his solar. He stood when Bartholomew and Stanmore were shown in and came to greet them, surprised but courteous. He was a man in his early fifties, powerfully built, with thick hair that showed no trace of grey. Bartholomew had been with his wife when she had died during the plague a little over a year before.

De Belem stared in disbelief when Bartholomew told him why they had come, and then shook his head firmly.

'The killer takes whores,' he said. 'Frances was not a whore. You are mistaken: it is not her.'

Bartholomew, feeling wretched, met his eyes. 'I am not mistaken,' he said gently.

'But she is not a whore!' protested de Belem.

'The murderer did not know that,' said Stanmore, with quiet reason. 'It was probably dark, and he saw a girl in the streets alone. He must have jumped to the wrong conclusion.'

'How was she killed?' de Belem demanded suddenly, looking at Bartholomew. 'You were with her when she died, you say?'

'With a knife,' said Bartholomew, reluctant to go into detail while de Belem still dealt with the shock of his news.

'Her throat cut?' persisted de Belem.

Bartholomew nodded. There was no point in denying it if de Belem already knew from local gossip.

'Did she say anything?' said de Belem, ashen-faced. 'Was she aware of what had happened to her?'

Bartholomew raised his hands in a gesture of uncertainty. 'What she said made no sense,' he said. 'I had given her some syrup to dull her senses and she was probably delirious.'

'What did she say?' asked de Belem, his voice unsteady.

'That whoever killed her was not a man,' said Bartholomew reluctantly.

De Belem looked bewildered and shook his head slowly, as if trying to clear it. 'What does that mean?' he said. 'What was it? An animal? A devil?'

Bartholomew could think of nothing to say. The wound on her throat had been inflicted by a knife, of that he was certain, and Frances's killer was unquestionably human. Was Brother Alban right, and were the murders of the women part of some satanic ritual?

'Do you have any ideas about why Frances may have been killed?' asked Bartholomew. 'Did she have any arguments with anyone recently?'

De Belem shook his head again, helplessly. 'We were not close,' he said, 'although I loved her dearly. Since my wife died, I have immersed myself in my work, and left her to her own devices. But I can think of no one who meant her harm.'

He paused and put his head in his hands. Stanmore reached out and patted his shoulder.

'Will you catch him for me?' de Belem asked suddenly, looking intently at Bartholomew. 'Will you catch the madman who killed my child?'

Bartholomew was startled. 'That is the Sheriff's duty,' he said.

De Belem stood abruptly and gazed down at him. 'The Sheriff is doing nothing to investigate the deaths of the other women. I know you are looking into the dead man found in the University chest. Give that up, and find out who murdered my Frances. I will pay you well.'

'I cannot,' said Bartholomew, disconcerted that his commission for the Chancellor seemed to be common knowledge. 'It is not only beyond my authority, it is beyond my capabilities.'

'You must,' said de Belem, seizing Bartholomew's shoulder with such force he winced. 'Or my daughter's death will go unavenged. The Sheriff will do nothing!'

'But how? It is not my affair!' protested Bartholomew.

'Please!' cried de Belem, grasping Bartholomew harder still. 'You and Brother Michael uncovered those murders last year. You will be my only hope!'

Bartholomew thought about Frances's unborn child, and was sorry that her last days had been tainted by unhappiness. She might have been his wife, had he not disobeyed Stanmore's wishes and chosen his own path.

'I will try,' he said finally. 'But anything I discover I will have to pass to the Sheriff.'

'No!' cried de Belem, virtually flinging Bartholomew away from him in his vehemence. 'Tell the Chancellor, or even the Bishop, if you must. But not the Sheriff! He would merely take your information and do nothing with it.'

Bartholomew made him sit down. 'There is no need to be arguing about whom we should inform when, as yet, we have nothing to tell,' he said soothingly.

De Belem relaxed a little, his hands dangling loosely between his knees.

'Why was Frances out alone?' said Bartholomew. 'She must have known that it is not safe at any time, but especially so with this killer at large.'

De Belem stared at him. 'She was a religious girl. She was probably going to mass.'

Bartholomew tried not to appear sceptical, and wondered if he had made a better job of it than Stanmore, who looked openly incredulous.

De Belem saw their expressions and sighed. 'She is gone,' he said to Stanmore. 'What good will come of questioning her actions now? Since her husband died, she has grown wild. I am too busy a man to be constantly chasing after an errant daughter.'

'Do you know why she might have been in Michaelhouse's grounds?' asked Bartholomew.

De Belem shook his head wearily. 'She must have been meeting someone.'

'Do you know who?' asked Bartholomew. He saw de Belem hesitate, but then seem to make up his mind.

'I do not want this to become common knowledge, but I think Frances had a lover. She did not stay out all night – even I could not countenance that – but she did leave early in the morning on occasions. Perhaps she had fallen for an apprentice somewhere, and joined him for his early morning chores.'

Or perhaps she had fallen in love with a scholar, thought Bartholomew, and met him as soon as the gates were opened to allow the academics out for church. He thought about the area where she died. There was Michaelhouse, of course, and opposite there was Physwick Hostel. King's Hall was a short distance to the north, while Garret Hostel, Clare College, Gonville Hall, and Trinity Hall were to the south. But Michaelhouse and Physwick Hostel were the closest.

It seemed de Belem could tell them no more, and they waited with him until the Sheriff's deputy arrived. De Belem agreed to speak to him only reluctantly. Bartholomew was nervous of leaving de Belem with the Sheriff's man in view of the merchant's evident contempt for the Sheriff's competence, but, as he pondered, de Belem's sister arrived full of concern and sympathy, and Bartholomew knew she would prevent any misunderstandings.

They stopped at Stanmore's business premises next door, before Stanmore left for the Fair and Bartholomew returned to his teaching duties at Michaelhouse. Stanmore ordered that a fire be built in the solar, for, despite the fact that it was summer, the day seemed chilly. He and Bartholomew sat in front of the flames and sipped some mulled ale.

'Have you heard about witchcraft being on the increase in Cambridge?' Bartholomew asked, partly to change the subject from Frances and partly for information. Stanmore had a network of informants who kept him up to date with the various happenings in the town.

'There have been rumours, yes,' said Stanmore. 'A religion where fornication, drunkenness, and violent acts are regarded as acceptable will have a certain appeal to people frustrated with being urged to practise moderation and told that the injustices of their lives are God's will.' He stared into the fire.

'What about in Cambridge?' Bartholomew tried to get comfortable on the wooden chair.

'I have heard that lights have been seen moving about All Saints' Church in the depths of the night. Many superstitious people think that part of the town is haunted. If you had not burned down those houses with the people still in them, the site of that settlement would not be so feared.'

'The people were dead, Oswald!' said Bartholomew, angry at the misrepresentation of fact. 'And no one wanted the task of taking the bodies to bury them in the plague pit! What would you have done? Left them there to rot and further infect the town?'

'Easy now,' said Stanmore, startled at his outburst. 'I am only telling you what people think, and you did ask. What is your interest in witchcraft?'

'None, really,' said Bartholomew, still annoyed. 'Old Brother Alban was rattling on about it and he thought it may have had something to do with the deaths of these women.'

Stanmore thought for a moment. 'It is possible, I suppose. I will ask my people to keep their ears open and will contact you if they hear anything.' He stood as Bartholomew rose to leave. 'Be careful, Matt. The rumours about these covens are unpleasant. In London, some fiend takes children from their cribs at night.'

'I am a little too old to be taken from my crib,' said Bartholomew, relenting from his irritation and laughing.

Stanmore laughed too. 'Your sister does not think so. You must visit her soon, Matt. She is lonely, and would like to see you.'

As Bartholomew walked back towards Michaelhouse, he thought about Frances. Was the father of her child the man who had killed her? And if so, did this mean that he was also the killer of the other women? Had they also been pregnant by him? He shook his head. That was absurd: the other women had been prostitutes who had probably known how to prevent pregnancy, as far as that was possible. Hilde's sister had not done very well, it seemed. But what had Frances's dying words – 'not a man' – meant? Was her death connected with the witchcraft that seemed to be on the increase all over the country? Why did so many people believe the Sheriff was reluctant to investigate? Bartholomew rubbed his chin thoughtfully. Was it possible he was involved in witchcraft too, and already knew the identity of the killer whom he had allowed to escape? Bartholomew ran a hand through his hair in frustration. The killer could be anyone! Hundreds of people had converged upon Cambridge for the Fair: any of them could be responsible. The more he thought about it, the more he realised he had set himself an impossible task by agreeing to help de Belem.

Bartholomew worked hard that morning, painstakingly discussing Dioscorides's text on opiates and how they might be used to ease a variety of ailments. After dinner he gave Gray and Bulbeck mock disputations to test their knowledge of Hippocrates and Galen, and then went to visit three different people who had contracted summer ague, a shivering fever that struck many people in the sweltering months of July and August. It was late by the time he had seen his last case, and the sun had already set.

He walked briskly through the dark streets towards Michaelhouse. Alcote, who had taken on unofficial duties as College policeman, saw to it that the gates were locked at dusk. Although Bartholomew had the Master's permission to answer summonses from patients after the curfew, he knew it was not an arrangement approved by the other Fellows, who considered that it set a bad example to the students. Bartholomew abused the privilege at times, despite knowing that it would take very little for the Fellows to exert sufficient pressure on Kenyngham to withdraw his limited freedom. Because of this, he usually used the back gate: if Cynric knew he was late, he left it unbarred.

As expected, the front gates were locked, and the porter on duty was the miserable Walter, who was paid a half-penny for every late scholar whose name he could report to Alcote. Bartholomew slipped off down the shadows in St Michael's Lane towards the back gate, to see if Cynric had left it open.

As he neared the gate, he saw a tiny movement, and instinctively melted further into the shadows at the side of the road. He strained his eyes in the darkness, trying to distinguish between the swaying of spindly bramble branches in the night breeze, and movements that might be more sinister.

A shadow glided silently from the shelter of one tree to another and he heard a soft, but unmistakable, cough. He pressed further into the shadows and cursed softly. The Master must have asked one of the Proctors to keep a watch on the gate. He stood for a moment and considered. He would have to retrace his steps, go along the High Street, and cut back through the Austin Canons' land that backed onto Michaelhouse. Cynric had shown him a portion of the wall that was in poor repair, where a desperate scholar might climb if both gates were locked.

Feeling absurd that he, a doctor of the University, should be sneaking around at night like some errant undergraduate, he made his way through the dark streets and prowled along the back of the College until he found the crumbling wall. He scrambled up it, wondering how many of his students had done the same, and hoping he would not meet any of them now.

Once on top of the wall, he walked along it until he came to a section where large compost heaps made the jump down the other side less hazardous. He crouched on the wall and let himself drop, landing in an undignified tumble that finished in a mound of cut grass. Swearing softly to himself, and trying in vain to brush the grass from his tabard, he made his way stealthily towards the kitchen door, keeping in the shadows as he had seen Cynric do. As he approached the bakery, he thought he saw something move. He froze and, for the second time that night, pressed further back into the shadows to watch.

Sure enough, someone was there. At first he thought it was Cynric, so soundlessly did the figure move, but it was a bigger person than Cynric. Bartholomew peered into the darkness, trying to gain some clue to the intruder's identity as he moved steadily towards the orchard to the place where

Frances de Belem had died. A tiny light flared as a candle was lit. Leaving the shadows of the bakery wall, Bartholomew crept carefully towards the laundry, a long wooden building that housed the servants on its upper floor. The intruder appeared to be searching for something. Bartholomew's stomach tightened. Could it be the murderer, the monster whom Frances had said was not a man, searching for some vital clue to his identity that he had mislaid or lost as he killed her?

He leapt with fright as a hand was clapped over his mouth and held there firmly to prevent him from calling out. He struggled violently, stopping only when he felt the sharp prick of a knife against his throat.

'Hush!' came Cynric's voice. Bartholomew twisted round in disbelief. 'Sorry, boy,' the Welshman whispered, holding up the dagger. 'It was the only way I could get you to stop struggling long enough to let you know it was me.' He slipped his knife back into his belt and poked his head round the corner to watch the figure with the candle.

As Cynric observed, Bartholomew sank onto the grass to try to regain his composure.

'Hsst!' Cynric was off, gesturing for Bartholomew to follow. Still carrying the candle, the figure left the orchard and began to move down the path that led to the back gate. Cynric motioned for Bartholomew to watch from the wall that ran down one side of the vegetable gardens, while he moved like a ghost through the bulrushes that fringed the fish-ponds on the other side.

Bartholomew saw the figure reach out to open the door. He thought of Frances de Belem and the others with their throats cut by a maniac, and made his decision: the person must not be allowed to escape! He abandoned his hiding place and made for the gate at a run. The figure glanced round in shock, and began urgently to heave at the gate. It flung open just as Bartholomew reached the intruder and grabbed him. The figure span round with a cry of horror and drew a knife. Bartholomew knocked it from his hand, struggling to wrench the hood from the intruder's face.

At that moment the door was thrown inwards with such force that Cynric, who was closing it to prevent the intruder's escape, was knocked off his feet. At the same time, it burst into flames and a gigantic figure swathed in black leapt through it with an unearthly howl.

Bartholomew was aware of yellow teeth and glittering eyes as the huge shape swept towards where he still held the first intruder. His hands were wrenched from his captive as the enormous shape pounced on him, swinging him round so that he lost his footing and went sprawling onto the ground. He saw the first intruder disappear through the door, and tried to scramble after him, his feet slipping and sliding on the wet grass. He felt himself grabbed, and a great weight dropped onto his chest as massive hands clawed for his throat. The burning door crackled and blazed, and Bartholomew saw, in the light from the flames, that his attacker wore a red hood with holes for eyes and mouth.

As the huge hands tightened around his throat, Bartholomew was seized by panic. He tried to ram the heel of his hand under the man's nose and was horrified to feel teeth take a grip on his fingers and bite down hard. He jerked upwards with his knees as hard as he could and heard the man grunt with pain, but his teeth were still firmly clamped on Bartholomew's hand.

He was vaguely aware of Cynric leaping onto the man's back and thought he heard urgent shouting from the lane. The man shook Cynric away and headed towards the gate. Bartholomew struggled to his feet, hoping at least for a glimpse of the first intruder's face. Seeing him follow, the huge man turned to fight. Bartholomew picked up a handful of dusty soil and flung it into the man's face. The giant bellowed with rage and turned to stumble blindly towards the lane. Bartholomew followed, but the big man turned and thrust him away with such force that Bartholomew went tumbling head over heels backwards into the raspberry canes.

By the time Bartholomew's head had stopped spinning, the breeze in the trees and a small crackle from the burned gate were the only sounds to be heard. Bartholomew tensed as he saw a dark shape moving towards him, and then relaxed again as he saw it was Cynric.

'Are you hurt?' he whispered. Cynric shook his head and went to look out of the still-smouldering gateway. After a few moments, he came back to sit with Bartholomew, who was trying to flex the fingers of his bitten hand.

'There is no one there, attacker or otherwise,' said Cynric unsteadily. 'What happened, exactly?'

'I am not sure,' Bartholomew replied, equally shaken. 'What were you doing in the orchard?'

'Coming to unbar the door for you. Then I heard you trampling like a herd of pigs along by the bakery and that figure in the orchard.'

Bartholomew ignored the unflattering reference to his attempt at stealth and Cynric continued. 'What was that thing that we fought? Did you see its face? It was bright red, like the Devil's.' He gripped Bartholomew's arm suddenly. 'Do you think it was the killer of Frances de Belem? She said the person who attacked her was not a man! Do you think it was the Devil?'

'Devil!' snorted Bartholomew. 'If that were the Devil, he would not have needed a gate to enter. That was a person, Cynric, wearing a red hood.'

'But how did a person make the gate burst into flames?'

'We will look tomorrow,' said Bartholomew, climbing wearily to his feet. 'It is too dark now. What shall we do about the gate?'

'I will slip out and inform the Proctor, and ask him to post a guard on the door.' Cynric looked at Bartholomew's hand. 'Did he bite you? Normal men do not bite, lad. That was no man. That was a fiend from hell itself!'

When Bartholomew awoke from a dream-filled sleep early the next morning, he was not surprised to find he was stiff and sore. As he was shaving and noting with annoyance a rip in a second shirt, Michael burst in.

'I was in the kitchen for something to eat before Lauds, and Cynric told me what happened last night!' he said excitedly. 'Why did you not come to wake me up? How will you explain what you were doing to the Master? How is your hand?'

Bartholomew went to the light of the window and inspected his hand where the man in the orchard had bitten him. There were clear teeth-marks but, oddly, while one row of teeth had scarcely made an impression, the others had made deep puncture marks surrounded by dark bruises.

'Do you think the man in the orchard was the murderer of Frances?' Michael asked. 'What about the man who bit you – Cynric's devil? Do you think he was the killer?'

'Why else would anyone be at the scene of a murder at that time of night with a candle?' Bartholomew asked with a shrug. 'Perhaps two people, rather than one, are responsible for the murders. It seemed to me that the smaller one was looking for something while the larger one kept watch outside. I saw and heard someone in the lane before I climbed over the wall. He came to his accomplice's rescue when I was on the very brink of pulling his mask away and revealing his face.'

'But what could they have been looking for?' asked Michael, frowning thoughtfully.

Bartholomew leaned back against the window-frame. 'Perhaps Frances struggled and tore something from his clothing that he only missed later.'

'That must be so,' said Michael, chewing on his lip. 'Why else would someone risk visiting the scene of a murder when, if he were caught, he would have much explaining to do? Do you think he found what they were looking for?'

Bartholomew thought carefully, tapping on the window-sill with his fingers. 'No. But I also think that what he was looking for was not there. Cynric and I did not frighten him into leaving: he had finished his search and was leaving anyway. I think he knew he would not find what he was looking for.'

Michael sat on Bartholomew's bed, his weight making the wood creak ominously. 'What was he like?' he asked. 'Was there anything familiar about him?'

Bartholomew shook his head. 'Nothing. He was swathed in a hooded gown. I think he was smaller than me, and he gave quite a yell when I seized him.'

'Could it have been a woman?' asked Michael.

'It sounded like a man's voice,' said Bartholomew. 'The large man was really enormous, but I could not see his face because of a red mask.'

'Well, someone of those dimensions should be easy to pick out in a crowd,' said Michael. 'What was the mask like?'

'Nothing more than a red hood, like an executioner's mask. Cynric thought he may have been what Frances saw when she said her killer was not a man.'

'He could well be right,' said Michael. 'I wish you had caught them, Matt. Now we have more information, but nothing tangible to lead us to the killer.'

Bartholomew looked around for his bag and remembered it had gone. 'Damn!'

'Father Aidan has a bag he never uses,' said Michael, guessing the cause of Bartholomew's annoyance. He glanced out of the window as he rose from the bed. 'Plenty of time before church,' he muttered. 'Come on.'

Bartholomew followed him across the yard, towards the orchard. The servants were already busy hauling water from the well, and starting fires in the kitchen. Bartholomew and Michael walked over the dew-laden grass to the back gate, and Michael whistled.

'Lord above,' he said. 'What a mess!'

Bartholomew pulled the door open so he could inspect it out of the shadows. He tugged at something and it gave way in his hand. He held it up to show Michael, who eyed it uncomprehendingly.

'The remains of a fire arrow,' Bartholomew explained. He rubbed his hand over the door and examined it closely. 'The Devil must be failing if he needs alchemy for his pyrotechnics.'

'I do not understand,' said Michael, taking the arrow from Bartholomew and examining it carefully. 'What alchemy?'

'The door was smeared with animal fat, soot, and something sticky. Some fats, when fermented, become volatile. I imagine it would not be safe to stand too close to ignite it, but an arrow dipped in pitch would burn. When the fire arrow hit the gate . . .' He raised his hands. 'Alchemy.'

'But why bother with all this?' asked Michael, scratching at the charred door with his fingernail. 'What was the point? They could have come and gone without us ever knowing they were there if they had not had the misfortune to run into you.'

'Perhaps it was intended for use at a later date, or perhaps it was meant as a warning to someone,' said Bartholomew.

He sighed, exasperated. 'You are right, Michael. The more information we gain, the less it all makes sense.'

He wandered out into the lane, where one of the Proctor's beadles lounged against the wall, picking his teeth with a knife. He stood up straight when he saw Bartholomew and Michael, and pulled his greasy jerkin down over his shirt. Bartholomew heard him telling Michael that he had been at the door since instructed to be so by the Proctor the night before.

Opposite the gate, Bartholomew kicked around in the weeds at the side of the lane where he had seen the shadow, and stooped to pick up another arrow that had apparently been lit, but not used. He rolled it between his fingers and looked thoughtfully at Michael.

'Do you realise what this means?' he asked. Michael looked blankly at him. 'The gate burst into flames at almost the precise moment that the large man came through it, while I still had the smaller man in my grasp. There must have been three of them, Brother, not two: the large man, the smaller one, and the one who fired the arrow.'

Michael shook his head slowly. 'Three men to kill a woman? Lord save us, Matt! What is going on?'

As they emerged from the church after Prime, one of Stanmore's apprentices was waiting with a message for Bartholomew to meet his master at Milne Street. Michael, uninvited, went too, knowing that breakfast at Stanmore's house was likely to be far better than breakfast at Michaelhouse.

The streets were beginning to come to life, with apprentices hurrying to prepare for the day's trading at the Fair. The great gates of Stanmore's business premises were still locked, and Bartholomew hammered until someone came to let him in. Inside, the yard was a hive of activity. Huge vats of oatmeal were being carried steaming from the kitchens to the hall, and apprentices darted around trying to complete their chores before breakfast. Two horses were being harnessed in carts ready to carry bales of cloth to the Fair, and a cook was busy chasing a squawking chicken around the yard for Stanmore's dinner.

Stanmore was waiting for them, and escorted them from the frenetic activity in the yard to the pleasant solar on the upper floor. Bartholomew had always liked this room. Its walls were hung with thick tapestries, and the floor was strewn with an assortment of rugs of varying quality, age, and colours. Several comfortable chairs were ranged around the stone fireplace, and bales of cloth were stacked along one wall. Although the house on Milne Street was luxurious, especially compared to Michaelhouse, Stanmore preferred to live with his wife, Bartholomew's sister, at his manor in Trumpington, a village two miles distant.

Stanmore had arranged for breakfast to be brought to them, and several pans were being kept warm by the fire. Before Bartholomew could stop him, Michael had grabbed a loaf of freshly baked bread and a pan of sizzling bacon, and had settled himself comfortably in Stanmore's favourite chair to enjoy his booty. Stanmore looked askance at the greedy monk and sat opposite him, while Bartholomew sipped at a cup of watered ale.

'I went to work on those questions you asked about witchcraft,' said Stanmore.

Bartholomew understood that his brother-in-law had contacts in the most unusual places, but knew better than to ask questions.

'Your old monk was right,' continued the merchant, reaching across to take a slice of bacon before Michael could eat it all. 'The churches of All Saints' and St John Zachary are used for purposes not altogether religious. There are two active, but separate, covens in Cambridge, each illicitly based at one of the churches. I am told that although both covens worship fallen angels, there is rivalry between them and they do not like each other. I am also told that at least one of the groups is known to be connected to a guild, although I do not know which one. It is not mine,' he added hastily.

There were many guilds in Cambridge. Some, like Stanmore's Guild of Drapers, were formed to ensure a solidarity between traders and to establish good standards and training for apprentices. Other guilds were formed for charitable or religious purposes. Bartholomew remembered the complaints when Sir Richard Tulyet, the Sheriff's father, was elected Mayor of Cambridge. He had been a member of the Guild of the Annunciation and he had seen that members of his Guild were elected as bailiffs, burgesses, and to other prestigious positions. The current Mayor, Robert Brigham, was a clerk, and members of his Guild of St Peter and St Paul seemed to be doing well, although not as flagrantly as had Tulyet's friends.

The three men talked for a while, discussing which guilds might be a front for a coven, but were unable to come up with any convincing proof. Michael thought a group of pardoners might be responsible, but Bartholomew knew that Michael loathed pardoners and their trade, which took advantage of the gullible and the desperate. Stanmore thought the Guild of Dyers might be a coven in disguise, but Stanmore had always hated the dyers, at whose mercy he was if he wanted to sell coloured cloths. Bartholomew considered suggesting the Franciscans, for he thought there was something diabolical in their refusal to accept some of his teaching for reasons that were founded in ignorance. Seeing they had merely reached a stage where they were fuelling each other's personal bigotries, Bartholomew stood, stretched, and suggested they should be about their business.

As Stanmore stood with them at the gate, a breathless messenger staggered towards him, mud-splattered, his eyes red-rimmed from weariness.

'It has all gone!' he wailed.

'What has gone?' said Stanmore, nonplussed. 'Pull yourself together, man!'

The messenger took a gulping breath. 'The yellow silk from London. We were ambushed . . .'

'What?' snapped Stanmore. 'That cannot be. That cart was part of a huge convoy.'

'The silk has gone!' insisted the messenger. 'It happened as we were making a camp for the night. We chose a spot near the middle of the convoy, as you said we should, and we were cooking our supper. Men armed with great long bows sprung from nowhere. Will Potter was shot as he reached for his sword, and so were two men who were guarding Master Morice's wines. The wolvesheads smashed the wine bottles, set fire to the silk, stole cheeses and dried meats, and escaped. Some of us gave chase, but the forests are dense, and what could we have done if we had caught them?'

'Damn!' said Stanmore, his lips pursed tightly together. He reached out and took the man by the shoulder. 'What of Will? Is he badly hurt?'

'He is dead,' said the messenger, shuffling his feet in the dust.

Stanmore paled. 'And the others? Where are they now? Are they injured?'

The messenger jerked his head back along Milne Street to where a dishevelled group of men shuffled towards them.

'Had you seen these outlaws before? Would you recognise them again?' Stanmore asked, taking a more secure hold on the man's arm as he reeled.

The messenger shook his head wearily, and Stanmore relented. 'Tell the others to get something to eat from the kitchens, and then come to my office,' he said. When the messenger had gone, Stanmore ordered an apprentice to take a message to the Castle, and sent for his steward to see to Will's body. He leaned against the door, and Bartholomew saw his hands were shaking. Bartholomew knew it was not only the loss of the valuable silk that distressed his brother-in-law; Stanmore was fond of the people who worked for him, and Will had been in his service for many years.

Michael looked grave. 'The roads are unsafe for decent people,' he said. 'We were even afraid to walk along Barnwell Causeway from the Fair the night before last, and you can virtually see the town from there.'

'But why bother to attack if not to steal?' asked Bartholomew.

'They stole,' said Stanmore tightly. 'They took cheese and meat, and food is a valuable commodity when there is so little of it about.'

'But attacking is dangerous,' persisted Bartholomew. 'Why take the time to burn your cart and to smash the wine bottles, when it would be better to seize the food, and flee as quickly as possible?'

Stanmore sighed impatiently. 'Only a scholar would reason like that,' he said dismissively. 'These are louts, Matt, who gain pleasure from the crimes they commit. They probably enjoyed the damage they caused. You credit them with more thought than they are capable of.'

'Well, I am sorry for your loss,' said Bartholomew. 'For Will, too.'

'Oh, damn all this!' Stanmore exclaimed. 'I had already promised that silk to a merchant in Norwich. De Belem's prices for dyeing silk have become ridiculous, and I would pay more to him for dyeing than I would be able to charge for it. His wife's death during the plague must have damaged his mind. His prices will have to come down, or he will ruin us all. And if we fall, so will he.'

He turned as his men came through the gates, limping and travel-stained. Stanmore ran towards them, counting them like a mother hen. Bartholomew went to help, and spent the next hour bandaging and dispensing salves for grazes and bruises. He and Michael took their leave as Stanmore's steward arrived bearing the body of Will Potter.

'The friar is to be buried today,' said Bartholomew as they walked away. 'We do not even know his name. De Wetherset will want to know what we have done, and we have done nothing. Tomorrow we had better exhume the body of his clerk. We should invite him to be present to make sure we have the right corpse.'

Michael gave a snort of derision. 'De Wetherset will have nothing to do with that! What shall we do about this guild business?'

'I am not sure,' said Bartholomew. 'We should hand the information to the Sheriff, since he is supposed to be looking for the murderer of these women.' He turned to Michael. 'Do you think the two are connected? The murder of the women and the murder of the friar?'

'On what grounds?' asked Michael, surprised. 'Four victims with slit throats and one poisoned by a lock on the University chest; four ladies of ill-repute and one mendicant friar? No, Matt, I cannot see that they are connected.'

'Frances de Belem was not a lady of ill-repute,' said Bartholomew. 'She was the daughter of a respectable merchant.' He stopped suddenly. 'I wonder if de Belem belongs to a guild.'

Michael waved a dismissive hand. 'Now you are grasping at straws. Of course he is a member of a guild. The Honourable Guild of Dyers, probably.'

'But he might also be a member of another guild unrelated to his trade. Oswald is and so is Roger Alcote.'

'Are they?' said Michael, surprised. 'Your brother-in-law did not mention that when we were talking just now. And Alcote? Scholars are forbidden to join guilds.'

'Oswald is a member of the Guild of the Annunciation. Why do you think he became a burgess when Tulyet was Mayor? And Oswald once told me Alcote is also a member. Membership of these organisations is supposed to be secret, but if I wanted to know who is involved, all I would need to do would be to watch who went into the church on the day of their services. It would not be difficult to ascertain who was a member and who was not.'

'Good lord!' said Michael, his eyes gleaming. 'All this intrigue going on that I knew nothing about. This makes it all far more interesting.'

'Perhaps, but it does not help with the dead friar. The only way forward I can see is to find that lay-brother and see if we can make him tell us what he knows,' said Bartholomew. 'I do not feel inclined to go back to that alley again, so I suggest we ask de Wetherset to tell his clerks to trace him.'

'Do you think the lay-brother knows something?' asked Michael.

Bartholomew nodded slowly. 'Oh yes. I am certain of it. And we do not have the faintest idea what happened to Evrard Buckley,' he continued. 'Why did he disappear? And why did he take all his furniture with him?'

Michael raised his eyebrows thoughtfully. 'It could not have been easy moving all those belongings in the middle of the night from King's Hall,' he said.

'Maybe,' said Bartholomew. 'Buckley has roomed alone since the plague carried off his colleagues, and his window opens directly onto the garden that runs down to the river. The window is large, and, unless he had some really enormous pieces of furniture, I think there would have been no problem in lowering them down to the ground by rope.'

'He must have had help,' said Michael. 'Or it would have taken an age to do.'

'We should have something to report to de Wetherset,' said Bartholomew, 'and doubtless your Bishop will be wanting some news. We should walk round the back of King's Hall to see if we can see anything.'

Michael was not impressed with the idea, but went anyway. Bartholomew was right in saying that the Bishop would want answers, and it would be Michael's responsibility to give him some. They walked down to the river and along the towpath. A barge was being docked at the wharves, three exhausted horses having dragged it through the night to be ready to trade its wares at the Fair. The smell by the river was powerful. Stale eels that had not been sold the previous day lay in grey-black heaps on the bank, being squabbled over by gulls. All along the river people were dumping night waste into the water, while further downstream a group of children splashed and played in the shallows.

Bartholomew saw one of Stanmore's apprentices bartering for threads, and a small group of women were admiring a collection of coloured ribbons. Walking past them, and heading in his direction, was Janetta of Lincoln. Bartholomew saw the sun glint on her blue-black hair, and memories of his experience in the alleyway came flooding back to him. For a reason he could not immediately identify, he decided he did not want to speak to her.

Bartholomew pulled at Michael's sleeve. 'Come on,' he said, 'we do not have all day.'

'What is the matter with you?' grumbled Michael, objecting to this increase in his pace when the air was already beginning to grow thick and humid with the promise of heat to come.

It was too late. Janetta had seen him and came forward with the enigmatic smile he remembered from the day before, showing under her cascade of black hair. Michael stopped dead in his tracks and eyed her suspiciously.

'So, Matthew Bartholomew. Good morning to you.'

Bartholomew nodded to her, hiding his bitten hand under his scholar's robe. He instinctively knew that she would ask him about it, and he did not want to tell her about the incident in the orchard. In fact, he did not want to tell her anything at all.

Janetta laughed at his cautious response. 'I trust I find you well?' she said, looking him up and down and appraising him coolly.

Did she know about his skirmish last night? Was she surprised to see him intact? Or was she merely thinking about her rescue of him from the alleyway?

'Very well. And you?' he asked guardedly.

'In fine health,' she said. 'And now, Doctor, I have a great many things to do, and I cannot stand around gossiping all day like a scholar!'

She sauntered away, walking slowly, as if she were in no particular hurry to get back to her 'great many things'.

'And we cannot stroll around idly like harlots,' retorted Michael, nettled by her comment. She evidently heard his remark, for she turned around and wagged a finger at him, smiling, although Bartholomew thought he detected a flash of anger in her eyes.

'Who was that?' Michael asked, staring after her.

'Janetta of Lincoln,' Bartholomew answered, embarrassed by Michael's retort.

'Ah, yes,' said Michael. 'You did not tell me she was a convicted felon.'

'What?' said Bartholomew, startled. 'How do you know that?'

'Did you not notice those scars on her face? There was a judge at Lincoln who liked to sentence prostitutes to that punishment. He reasoned that it would force them to turn from prostitution because they would be unable to secure clients. He was only in office a short time, but he made a name for himself locally because of the sentences he gave to petty offenders.'

'Petty offenders?' said Bartholomew. 'Then perhaps she was convicted of a crime other than prostitution.'

Michael shook his head. 'He only scarred women like that for the crime of harlotry. She was a whore, Matt, and was convicted and punished for it. You mark my words.'

'What happened to the judge?' asked Bartholomew.

'Killed in a brothel,' said Michael, laughing. 'Full of women with scarred faces, I expect! I would say your Janetta of Lincoln was almost certainly one of his victims.'

'That might explain why she left Lincoln. If this judge's punishments are not common knowledge, perhaps she thought she might be able to live here without her past being known,' mused Bartholomew.

'The only reason I know is because I saw similar scars on the face of a woman in a group of travelling singers,' said Michael. 'I asked her how she came by them, and she told me about the judge.'

Bartholomew looked doubtfully at him, wondering how the fat monk had managed to embark upon such an intimate conversation with a female travelling entertainer. Michael caught his glance and waggled his eyebrows before changing the subject. 'Let's go and look at this grass.'

As Bartholomew had predicted, the walls bore marks that Buckley's furniture had been passed out of the window. They also found the grass below it was trampled, and there were ruts made by a cart. But there was also something else.

'Michael, look,' said Bartholomew, bending to examine a small smear on the creamy stone.

'What is it?' asked Michael, looking, and not finding the brown mark especially enlightening.

'Blood,' said Bartholomew. He pointed to where the grass was less trampled to one side, and several blades of grass were stained. He straightened up and he and Michael exchanged a look of puzzlement.

'Well, at least we have something to report to the Chancellor.' said Michael.

chapter 4

THE CHANCELLOR WAS NOT IMPRESSED WITH THE INFORmation they had gleaned, and he agreed only reluctantly to send one of his clerks to bring the lay-brother to them so that he could be questioned. He was also unsympathetic about Bartholomew's experience in the alleyway behind the church and denied that there was a short cut there through the shrubs in the churchyard.

'Why would there be such a thing?' he snapped. 'None of those people would deign to set foot in a church.'

Bartholomew wanted to tell him that it might be a short cut to the river that just happened to be through the churchyard, but could see no advantage in antagonising the Chancellor.

'Gilbert stuck that blade on the poisoned lock into a rat,' said de Wetherset. 'It died in moments. I also sent him to the Dominican Friary, but you were correct in your assumption that the dead man was not one of them. The Prior came to look at the body and said he had never seen the man before.'

Bartholomew felt guilty that the Chancellor had more to report to them than they had to him. He wished he would have a sudden insight to tie all the loose threads together, so that they could be done with it all and he could concentrate on his students' disputations.

'What do you plan to do next?' de Wetherset asked, picking up a piece of vellum covered with minute writing and studying it. Bartholomew rose to leave. The Chancellor clearly was not interested in how they went about getting the information, only in what they discovered. Michael remained seated.

'I would like to read Nicholas's book,' he said.

The Chancellor was momentarily taken off-guard. 'What for?' he asked suspiciously.

'When we first saw the body of the friar, you were more concerned with the book than anything else in the chest. Therefore, it is likely that the friar wanted to read or steal it more than any other document. If I were to read it, I might gain a better notion of why someone might want to kill for it,' he said, folding his large arms across his chest.

'Very well,' said de Wetherset, after a moment's deliberation. 'You have until Sext. Then I have business at Barnwell Priory and I want the book locked in the chest before I leave.'

Michael inclined his head, and the Chancellor conducted them to the small chamber in the tower of the church, where he donned thick leather gloves and undid the locks on the chest. Bartholomew saw that the three locks gleamed bright and new: the Chancellor was taking no chances.

As the last lock sprang open, de Wetherset straightened, and Bartholomew saw his face was beaded with perspiration.

'Poisoned locks!' he muttered. 'Whatever next? A puff of poison in the rugs to kill those who trample on them? Arsenic soaked into the documents themselves?'

Michael's hand had been half in the chest after the mysterious book, but now he withdrew it hastily. The Chancellor gave an unpleasant smile and tossed him his gloves.

'I will return before Sext. Please bar the door after I leave. I do not want anyone else in the chamber. Should anyone knock, tell them to go away.'

Bartholomew shot a sturdy bar across the door after he had gone and wandered around the small chamber restlessly. Michael took the book from the chest and placed it on the table. The leaves of the text were thick and there was no problem turning them while wearing the gloves.

'Can you get the spare set of keys from the Bishop?' Bartholomew asked suddenly.

Michael looked surprised. 'I could ask him. Why?'

'Because then we could try them on the old locks. If they do not fit the poisoned one, we would know that not only must a new lock have been put on the chest, but that someone had exchanged de Wetherset's keys. Since de Wetherset said the keys are never out of his sight, it would mean that Buckley, the only other person with access to them, must have exchanged them by some sleight of hand when he undid the chest. If the key does fit, then we know that either the lock was tampered with and the poisonous blade fitted, or that it was there all the time.'

Michael nodded slowly. 'The keys will be of no use to the Bishop now there are new locks on the chest. I see no reason why he should not let me have them.'

Bartholomew went to the window and looked across the High Street. By leaning out, he could see Michaelhouse, and remembered his students. He left the window and went to a wall cupboard, opening the wooden doors to peer inside. Michael shot him an irritable glance as he closed the doors again noisily. Bartholomew bent down to look at the rug on which the friar must have knelt when he picked the locks, but there was nothing to see.

'I should be with my students. Some of them have already failed their disputations once,' he said. 'And I should visit Mistress Bocher's baby. It gets colic.'

'I will never get through this if you keep distracting me,' said Michael, exasperated. 'Go and see your students. Come back for me before Sext.'

Bartholomew was apprehensive about leaving Michael alone in a room where the friar had died by such sinister means, but could see no benefit in wasting the day in idleness. He waited until he was certain that Michael had barred the door from the inside and began to walk down the stairs. When he was almost at the bottom, he stopped as a thought occurred to him, and turned to climb them again.

He passed the chest room and continued upwards. As he climbed higher, the stairs became dirty and were covered in feathers and dry pigeon-droppings, and Bartholomew guessed they were seldom used. There was an unpleasant smell, too, and Bartholomew noted the decaying corpses of several birds that had flown in and had been unable to get out.

He reached the bell chamber and walked in. The bells stood silent among crooning pigeons and scraps of discarded rope and wood. The spiral stair ended, but a vertical wooden ladder led from the bell chamber to a trap-door in the ceiling above. Bartholomew tested it carefully, not trusting the cracked wood, nor the way in which the ladder leaned away from the wall as he prepared to climb.

The ladder was stronger than it looked, and he reached the trap-door without the rungs falling out or the ladder tearing away from the wall to deposit him on the bells below. He unbolted the trap-door and gingerly pushed it open, ducking as he disturbed a flurry of birds on the roof. The sunlight streamed down on his head, making him blink after the darkness of the tower. He hauled himself up and stood on the roof.

He surveyed the view in awe. The day was clear, not yet spoiled by the stinking mists that blew in from the Fens, and he thought he could see the distant towers of Ely Cathedral. He could certainly see the glitter of the maze of waterways snaking through the flat Fens, as they stretched off towards the sea. He leaned against one of the corner turrets and traced the silvery line of the river as far as he could, surprised that he could see a barge hauling in about two miles distant. He wondered that his brother-in-law did not post one of his informants on the roof permanently so he could have early warning of the arrival of trading vessels.

He peered directly down, intrigued at how the streets and buildings appeared from above. He saw the market stalls, looking brighter and prettier than they ever did in the market itself. Then he searched for the alley where he had been attacked the day before. He looked harder, leaning precariously over the edge as he screwed up his eyes to see. There was a gap between the rows of shacks, and following the line of it towards the church he saw a very distinct thinning of the undergrowth running towards the churchyard. There was his hidden pathway: he knew he would be able to see it from above!

He chose two prominent tombstones and a tree, quickly calculated angles and distances, and committed them to memory. He smiled grimly to himself. He would be able to find the entrance to it next time he looked, no matter how well hidden it was.

He stood for a few moments savouring the peace, and then made his way back down the ladder. As he was closing the trap-door, a tricky operation that involved wrapping one leg around the ladder and using both lands to heave the heavy wooden flap back into place, someone started to toll the bell for the friar's funeral. Bartholomew had heard that people were sent mad if they stayed too long in the chamber where bells were tolled, and that their ears would burst.

Another myth dispelled, he thought, as he climbed down the ladder. The bell's ringing was loud, but he did not feel it would send him mad or that his ears would burst. When he reached the bottom of the ladder, he put his hands over his ears to muffle the sound and watched the bell swing back and forth. His hands dropped to his side when he saw what had been concealed behind the bell, but what was exposed as the bell moved. He started towards it, but then stopped. While he did not believe the bell would damage his hearing within a short time, he did not relish the idea of being hit by the great mass of metal as it swept ponderously back and forth.

He went outside the chamber, closed the door, and sat on the stairs until the tolling had stopped. When the last vibrations had died away, and he could hear the first notes of the requiem mass drifting up the stairs, he opened the door again and edged his way towards the bell. There were four different-sized bells in the tower. It was the biggest one that had tolled for the friar and that concealed the body behind it. Even so, all that was visible was a white and bloated hand that dangled just below the bell frame.

The bells were supported in a wooden frame about three feet from the floor, and the easiest way to reach the body was to crawl on hands and knees beneath it. Bartholomew ignored the accumulated filth of decades and made his way to the other side of the chamber. Even as he neared the big bell, the sack that evidently held the body was all but invisible, and it was only the dead white hand that betrayed its presence. He used the bell to pull himself up onto the frame, and inspected the sack.

It had been jammed between the frame and the wall, quite deliberately positioned to hide it from prying eyes. Bartholomew, who had only spotted it when the bell was tolling, doubted if many people would choose to be in the chamber when the bells were ringing, and so the sack and its gruesome contents might have remained hidden for months or even years. He noted the debris that coated his clothes from his crawl across the filthy floor, and suspected that the cleaning of the bell chamber was not a high priority at St Mary's. He felt through the sack to the body inside. It was upside down: the legs were uppermost, while the head and torso were further down the bell frame.

He took a firm hold of the sack and pulled hard but it was securely wedged. He climbed further down the frame and tried to dislodge it sideways, but it was stuck fast. He leaned over to see if something was holding it in place and became aware of a rubbing sound behind him. For a moment, he could not imagine what it could be, and then he saw the great bell begin to tip. The requiem mass! Bartholomew could not believe his stupidity! When the mass was sung the bell ringer would chime the bell three times each for the Father, Son, and Holy Ghost. The ringer was beginning to haul on the bell rope, pulling hard to make the bell swing higher and higher until the clapper sounded against its side.

The bell swung upwards as Bartholomew flattened himself against the frame. It missed him by the merest fraction of an inch. The next time it swung up it would hit him. As soon as it began to drop, Bartholomew let himself fall to the floor, knowing that he would not have sufficient time to climb. He landed with a thump and flattened himself in the muck and feathers as the great mouth of the bell swished over him. He heard Brother Michael exclaim in the room below just before the bell spoke for the first time.

Bartholomew pressed his hands over his ears again, and tried to spit dusty old feathers from his mouth. The bell rang a second time and a third, and paused. Then came three more tolls and a pause, and then a final three and silence. Bartholomew did not wait for the last vibrations to fade before crawling away as fast as he could. He pounded on the door of the chest chamber.

'Go away!' shouted Michael, true to the Chancellor's instructions.

'Michael, it is me! Open the door!'

He fretted impatiently while Michael huffed noisily across the floor and fumbled with the bar. Bartholomew shot inside, leaving a trail of feathers and dried bird-droppings behind him. Michael looked at him, aghast.

'Have you been to that alley again?' he said, concern wrinkling his fat face.

'There is a body in a sack in the bell chamber,' said Bartholomew breathlessly. 'I tried to move it, but it is stuck fast.'

'I heard an almighty crash a minute ago. Was that you?' Michael stopped as the meaning of Bartholomew's words began to dawn on him. 'Who is the body?'

Bartholomew shook his head. 'I could not tell, but I saw the hand and it is that of an older man.' He ran an unsteady hand through his hair, oblivious to the feathers and cobwebs it deposited there. He looked at Michael. 'I have a terrible feeling we have just discovered the whereabouts of the Vice-Chancellor.'

Out of respect for the dead friar, they waited until he had been lowered into his grave in the cemetery before Michael approached the Chancellor and imparted the news. The Chancellor paled and gazed at Michael in shock.

'Another body in the tower? Do you know who it is?' he whispered.

'Not yet,' said Bartholomew. 'We will need help to get it out.'

De Wetherset closed his eyes and muttered something. When he opened them again, his eyes were hard and businesslike. He called for Gilbert and told him what had been discovered.

'What were you doing in the belfry to discover such a thing?' Gilbert asked, flashing the Chancellor a glance that indicated Bartholomew and Michael were not above suspicion themselves.

'Matt was looking to see if the friar had hidden his lock-picking tools there,' Michael lied easily.

Gilbert sighed. 'I should have thought of that myself,' he said. 'Although I would not have gone when the bells were ringing, and from what you say, I would probably not have seen this corpse.'

'We will recover the body ourselves before we spread the

news abroad,' said de Wetherset. 'Who knows what we might uncover? Gilbert, please arrange that we will not be disturbed while I fetch Father Cuthbert. Brother, Doctor, please wait for me in the tower.'

While Michael and Bartholomew waited, Bartholomew slit the sack and tied some pieces of discarded rope around the legs of the body inside. They tried a few preliminary hauls, but to no avail. De Wetherset arrived wearing an old gown, while Gilbert and Cuthbert hovered anxiously behind him. Bartholomew wondered whether the portly de Wetherset, the fat Cuthbert, and the slight Gilbert would make much difference to their efforts.

While Bartholomew lay on the floor and pushed, the others heaved on the legs from the bell frame. They began to despair of ever getting it out, and de Wetherset had started to talk ominously of the skills of some physicians with knives, when they felt the body budge.

'Once more,' cried de Wetherset. 'Pull!'

The body moved a little further, and Bartholomew joined Cuthbert to pull on one of the legs. With a puff of dust and a sharp crack from the bell frame, the body came loose, and Bartholomew and Michael hauled it across the bells and laid it on the floor by the door. De Wetherset, his face red from exertion, knelt next to it and slit the sack open with a knife. He gasped as the smell of putrefaction rose from the bundle, and then leapt up as the great swollen face looked out at him.

'God's teeth!' he whispered, staring at the face in horror. 'What is that? Is it a demon?'

'He has been hanging upside down for at least several days,' said Bartholomew gently. 'When that happens, the fluids of the body drain into the lowest part and cause the swelling you see here.'

'You were wrong, Matt. It is not Master Buckley,' said Michael, covering the lower half of his face with the sleeve of his gown.

Father Cuthbert coughed, his face pale. 'It is Marius Froissart,' he said. Bartholomew and Michael looked blankly at him and he explained. 'Froissart claimed sanctuary in the church about a week ago after he murdered his wife. You know it is the law that such criminals can claim sanctuary in a church, and he cannot be touched by officers of the law for forty days. The clerks locked him in that night, but by the next day he had escaped, despite the soldiers outside.'

'The whore killer whom the Sheriff was seeking!' exclaimed Michael. 'But dead himself!'

'But who killed him and put him here? And why?' asked de Wetherset, looking down at the body.

'Whoever hid his body here intended it to stay concealed for a long time,' said Bartholomew. He stretched out his hand to show the others what he had found. 'There was a reason it was so difficult to pull him free. He was nailed to the bell frame.'

De Wetherset stumbled down the stairs with his hand over his mouth. Gilbert followed him solicitously, while Bartholomew and Michael stayed with the dead man. Father Cuthbert hovered, uncertain whether to go or stay. When Bartholomew began to cut the sack to examine the body, Cuthbert looked away and gagged, and Bartholomew sent him with Michael to discover what de Wetherset wanted to do. He continued his examination alone. It looked as if Cuthbert's story of Marius Froissart's disappearance corresponded to the time that Bartholomew estimated him to have been dead. Which meant that Marius Froissart could not have killed Isobel or Frances.

Froissart's clothes were old, but neatly patched and mended. His beard and hair were unkempt, but, after a week in a sack, that was hardly surprising. Bartholomew tipped the head back and looked at the neck. Underneath the beard was a thin red line that circled his throat and was caked with blood. Bartholomew eased Froissart onto his back and inspected the dark marks at the nape of his neck. Garrotted. He felt the scalp under the matted hair, but there were no signs of a blow to the head. He prised the eyes and mouth open to look for signs of poison, and then looked at the rest of the body. There were no other injuries except for the marks on his shoulders and hips where he had been nailed to the bell frame.

Why would anyone go to such lengths? he wondered. He looked closely at the marks the nails had made. There was very little bruising and no bleeding at all. Some of the wounds were torn, but that had happened when he had been pulled out, and there was nothing to suggest that he had been alive when they were first made. Bartholomew walked around the chamber and looked at the great bell from as many angles as possible. When the bell was stationary, there was no earthly chance that the body would be seen. Even if someone had come to tend the bells, the body might remain hidden as long as the bells were still. And the smell? Bartholomew looked at the dead birds he had noted earlier. Anyone noticing a strong odour would assume that it came from the dead birds, as he had done.

In the confines of the narrow spiral staircase, the stench of putrefaction became too much even for him. He walked down to the chest chamber and took some deep breaths through the window. He winced. The sun was beating down like a furnace, and the ditches that criss-crossed Cambridge stank. Even from the tower he could see a haze of insects over the river.

He turned as he heard footsteps and de Wetherset and Michael entered. De Wetherset was as white as a sheet, and Michael was unusually sombre. De Wetherset listened at the door for a moment before closing it firmly.

'Gilbert and Cuthbert are downstairs to ensure that we are not disturbed,' he said. 'What can you tell me about this man's death?'

'Froissart was garrotted. If his hand had not slipped loose, I doubt he would have been found until someone decided to clean the bell chamber.'

De Wetherset pursed his lips. 'Father Cuthbert has problems getting anyone to ring the things, let alone to clean them,' he said. 'It appears that our murderer knew this, and the body was intended to remain undiscovered for a very long time indeed.'

Bartholomew walked to the window and rubbed his chin. 'Froissart's death must be connected to the dead friar,' he said.

'Logic dictates that is so,' said Michael. 'It is improbable that two sudden deaths in the same place within days of each other will be unrelated.'

'But Froissart must have been killed the night he claimed sanctuary,' Bartholomew pointed out. 'That was last Tuesday.

The clerks say the friar was here for about three days before he died. He was found dead the day before yesterday, and so he probably arrived here last Friday at the earliest, and Froissart had been dead for three days by then.' He picked up a quill from the table and examined it absently. 'The timing is such that Froissart and the friar could never have met.'

Michael sat on one of the benches and stretched his legs out in front of him. 'But perhaps the friar was here before. Perhaps he was in disguise and killed Froissart, and then came back to complete his business in the chest.'

Bartholomew thought for a moment and then shook his head. 'No. It does not ring true.' He saw the Chancellor wince at the mention of bells and continued quickly. 'The clerks were very observant about the friar. Had there been another person loitering in the church before him, they would have mentioned it. But more importantly, if the friar had been in disguise and had murdered Froissart, I think he would have been most unlikely to have returned to the church as himself, and there was nothing on the friar's body to suggest he was in disguise when he died.'

'But if he were responsible, what would he have to fear when he knew the body was so well hidden?' asked Michael.

Bartholomew thought for a moment. 'Master de Wetherset, you said Father Cuthbert has trouble finding people to ring the bells. Whoever put Froissart behind the bell frame knew that the chances of anyone going to the bell chamber to tend to the bells were remote. Why would the friar, a stranger to Cambridge, know that?'

De Wetherset grew exasperated. 'You two do not agree with each other,' he said. 'You, Brother, maintain that logic dictates that the two deaths are connected, while you, Doctor Bartholomew, confound any ideas we suggest to link them.'

Bartholomew smiled. 'Just because we cannot find the link here and now does not mean that it is not there. The evidence we have at the moment is just not sufficient to support any firm conclusions.'

De Wetherset sat heavily on the bench next to Michael and put his head in his hands. 'Tell me what we do have,' he said wearily.

Bartholomew sat on the chest before thinking better of it and moved to the window-seat. He quickly sorted out his jumbled thoughts and began to put them together.

'Last Tuesday, Froissart killed his wife and claimed sanctuary in the church. He was locked in Tuesday night, but had gone by Wednesday morning. It is most likely he was killed in the church on Tuesday night, and his body hidden at the same time. Three days later, on Friday, the itinerant friar arrived. He spent time, ostensibly praying and preparing himself to continue his journey, but more probably learning the routine of the church. Now that suggests to me that he had not been here before, and so was not the murderer of Froissart.'

De Wetherset nodded slowly. 'That is logical,' he said. 'Pray continue.'

Michael took up the analysis. 'We do not know why the friar was here, but we know he was a careful man. He spent three days watching and learning, and obviously possessed some skill in opening locks without keys. On Sunday night, he hid in the church while the lay-brother locked up, and then made his way to the tower. He picked the locks on the chest and began to go through its contents. The poison did not have an immediate effect, or he would not have been able to pick the third lock and open the lid. We do not know what happened next. He may have had a seizure brought on by the poison and fallen into the chest, closing the lid at the same time. Or he may have been put in the box by another person.'

'Perhaps the same person who killed Froissart,' said Bartholomew. 'I cannot imagine that the friar fell neatly into the chest and the lid closed of its own accord. I think it more likely that someone put him there.' He paused for a moment and continued. 'On the same night that the friar was preparing himself for his business in the tower, Evrard Buckley complained of stomach pains from a surfeit of eels, and retired early to bed. During the night, he removed the entire contents of his room through the window in King's Hall and loaded them onto a cart. At some point, he or another person, was wounded, perhaps fatally, as is attested by the blood on the ground outside his window.'

'We have forgotten Nicholas's book,' said Michael, gesturing to where the papers lay on the table near the window. 'He died a month ago, and no one thought much about it until the friar was found dead on top of his manuscript.'

'So, what we have left,' said de Wetherset somewhat testily, 'is a large number of unanswered questions. Who was the friar? What was he doing in the tower? Who put the poisoned lock on the chest? Was it intended to kill the friar or another? Who killed Froissart and why? Are the two deaths linked? Was Nicholas also murdered? Where is my Vice-Chancellor? And did he kill Nicholas, Froissart, and the friar?'

He stood with a sigh. 'I will have Froissart moved to the crypt. Gilbert will see to that. It might be most imprudent to let the murderer know his careful concealment has been uncovered, so I suggest we tell no one of this,' he said.

'But the Sheriff has a right to know,' said Bartholomew, startled. 'If Froissart is supposed to have murdered his wife, the Sheriff will be looking for him. We cannot keep such a matter to ourselves.'

'I said it would be most unwise to let the murderer know that we have discovered the body,' snapped de Wetherset. 'Supposing news of our discovery makes him kill again? The next victim might be one of us. The townspeople complain bitterly that the Sheriff is dragging his feet in tracking down the killer of the town prostitutes. There is little point in revealing this matter to such a man.'

'What if it were ever discovered that we kept such a matter secret?' said Bartholomew, unconvinced. 'The townspeople would have every right to be angry with the University, and relations between us and the town are strained as it is. There would be a riot!'

'The only way they would find out would be if you were to reveal it to them,' said de Wetherset coldly. 'And I am sure I need not worry on that score. Anyway, I imagine the killer would be more likely to strike at those who are seen to be investigating his crime if it were to become common knowledge Froissart has been found: you and Brother Michael.'

'Not if we turn the whole matter over to the Sheriff.' Bartholomew looked at Michael for support, but the monk looked studiously out of the window and would not meet his eye.

De Wetherset continued. 'I want you to question Froissart's family to see if they know anything, and I want you to examine Nicholas's body before dawn tomorrow. I have already obtained the necessary licences.'

He opened the door and left without another word. His footsteps were heavy and, despite his belligerence to Bartholomew, attested to his growing despondency about the events of the past few days. Bartholomew and Michael followed him, Bartholomew still angry, and they saw him giving instructions to Gilbert about the removal of Froissart.

'More lies and deceit,' said Bartholomew bitterly, watching de Wetherset walking away with an arm across Gilbert's shoulders. 'Why did you not come to my defence?'

'Because you were wrong,' said Michael. 'De Wetherset said that the Sheriff is conducting a less than competent investigation into the deaths of the women, and that is true. The townspeople are talking of little else. Why should we alert the murderer of Froissart that we have uncovered his carefully concealed victim by revealing it to the Sheriff? I do not see that it would do any good, and it might do a great deal of harm.'

'But perhaps one of the reasons the investigation is slow is because half the Sheriff's men are hunting Froissart, whom we know is dead. If we tell him that he need not look for Froissart, he will have more resources with which to hunt the killer of the prostitutes,' argued Bartholomew.

Michael shook his head. 'The Sheriff's problem is more deeply seated than manpower,' he said. He shook himself suddenly. 'Come, Matt! It is cold in here. You cannot reveal what you know to the Sheriff without contravening de Wetherset's orders, so do not even think about it. Let us put it from our minds and concentrate on the matter in hand.'

'So, what shall we do first?' said Bartholomew, walking with relief out of the cold church and into the hot sunshine outside. He brushed feathers from his gown and stretched stiffly.

'Back to College,' said Michael. 'You stink of that dead man, and it would not be tactful to question his family until you have changed. And anyway, I am hungry and you have students waiting for you.'

At Michaelhouse, Bartholomew washed and changed, giving his dirty clothes to the disapproving laundress.

'I cannot imagine what you have been up to these last few days,' Agatha grumbled. 'Filthy clothes, ripped shirts. You should know better at your age, Matthew.'

Bartholomew grinned at her as she pushed him out of the door. She watched him cross the yard towards the hall and allowed herself a rare smile. Agatha was fond of the physician, who had cured her of a painful foot that had been the bane of her life for years. She looked down at the dirty clothes and her smile faded: she hoped he was not doing anything dangerous.

She saw Gray and Deynman strolling across the yard and yelled at them in stentorian tones. 'Your master is waiting for you! He is a busy man and cannot be waiting around all day for you to wander into his lectures when you please!'

Gray and Deynman broke into a run and made for the conclave, where Bartholomew had already begun his lecture. He glanced at them, but said nothing as they hurriedly found seats and tried to bring their breathing under control. Bartholomew noted with satisfaction that the whole class was attentive, and when he sprung questions on them, they at least did not seem startled. Some even gave him the correct answers.

The time passed quickly, and soon the bell was ringing to announce lectures were over for the day. Bartholomew was surprised that the students listened to his final comments and did not immediately try to leave for the meal in the hall as they usually did. He stopped his pacing across the fireplace to address them.

'Tomorrow we must look again at diseases of the mouth. You may consider toothache to be an unimportant affliction, but it can make the patient's life a living hell. A toothache might be indicative of abscesses in the jaws, which can occasionally prove fatal to some people, by poisoning the blood. If I am late, I want you to consider dosages of different compounds that you might give to children who have painful swellings of the face, and what the possible causes of such swellings might be.'

He gave them an absent smile, his mind already busy making up such a list, and left. His students heaved a corporate sigh of relief.

'Another day survived!' said Gray, blowing out his cheeks and looking at the others.

'He is only trying to help us learn,' said Bulbeck defensively. 'He wants us to pass our disputations, and he wants us to become good physicians.'

Brother Boniface spat. 'He is teaching us contrary to the will of God. Why does he not teach us how to bleed patients? Why does he insist that we must always have a diagnosis? Some things are not meant to be known by man.'

'He does not believe that bleeding is beneficial,' said Gray. 'He told me that charlatans bleed patients when they do not know what else to do.'

Boniface snorted in derision. 'His teaching is heretical, and I do not like it. Give me a bottle of leeches and I could cure anything!'

Bulbeck laughed. 'Then tell Doctor Bartholomew that leeching is a cure for toothache in his lecture tomorrow,' he said.

Because Bartholomew had to see a patient, Michael went alone to hunt down the family of Marius Froissart. He asked the clerks in the church, but none of them knew where Froissart had lived. Somewhat irritably, he began to walk up Cambridge's only hill to the Castle to ask the Sheriff. The Sheriff had been called when Froissart had claimed sanctuary. Froissart could not, of course, be taken from the sanctuary of the church, but he had been questioned.

By the time Michael arrived, puffing and swearing at his enforced exercise, he was hot and crabby. He marched up to the Castle gate-house and pounded on the door. A lantern-jawed sergeant asked him his business, and Michael demanded an audience with the Sheriff. He was led across the bailey towards the round keep that stood on the motte. It was a grey, forbidding structure, and Michael felt hemmed in by the towering curtain walls and crenellated towers.

In the bailey a few soldiers practised sword-play in a

half-hearted manner, while a larger group were gathered in the shade of the gate-house to play dice. Before the plague, the bailey had always seemed full of soldiers, but there were distinctly fewer now. Michael followed the sergeant up wide spiral stairs to the second floor. As he took a seat in an antechamber, raised voices drifted from the Sheriff's office.

'But when?' roared a voice that Michael recognised as Stanmore's. The sergeant glanced uneasily at Michael but said nothing. There was a mumble from within as the Sheriff answered.

'But that is simply unacceptable!' responded Stanmore. Michael stood and ambled closer to the door in an attempt to overhear the Sheriff's part of the conversation, but was almost knocked off his feet as the door was flung open and Stanmore stormed out. He saw Michael but was too furious to speak as he left. Before the sergeant could stop him, Michael strolled nonchalantly through the door Stanmore had left open.

The Sheriff stood behind a table, breathing heavily and clenching his fists. He glared at Michael, who smiled back benevolently.

'Master Tulyet,' said Michael, sitting down. 'How is your father, the Mayor?'

'My father is no longer Mayor,' growled Tulyet. He was a small man with wispy fair hair and a beard that was so blond it was all but invisible.

'Then how are you? How is your investigation of the whore murders?' asked Michael, knowing instinctively he would touch a raw nerve.

'That is the King's business and none of yours,' Tulyet snapped. Michael saw the Sheriff's hands tremble when he picked up his cup to drink, and when he put it back down again, there were clammy fingerprints smeared on the pewter.

'Have you traced that other murderer yet? What was his name? Froissart,' probed Michael, leaning back in the creaking chair.

Tulyet glared at him. 'He escaped sanctuary,' he said through gritted teeth. 'I warned the guards that he might try, but they said they did not see him. I suppose they would not when they were asleep.'

'Who was it that he had killed?' asked Michael. 'A woman? And now a woman-killer stalks the night streets of Cambridge?'

'Marius Froissart is not the killer of the whores!' said Tulyet, exasperated. 'You believe that Froissart is the killer and that I lost him. Well, he is not the killer! Froissart did not even have the sense to confess to the murder of his wife, even though a witness saw him commit the crime! He could not have the intelligence to outwit me over the whore murders.'

'Oh? Who saw him commit the crime?' asked Michael with interest.

'His neighbour, a Mistress Janetta,' Tulyet said bitterly, 'although I am uncertain that her testimony is worth a great deal.'

Michael rose to leave. 'Thank you,' he said. 'You have been most helpful.'

Tulyet gaped at him. 'I have?' he said. 'You have not told me what you want.'

Michael beamed and clapped him on the shoulder. 'Keep up the good work,' he said, his comment designed to antagonise, and he swept out of the room and into the Castle bailey. He sauntered over to the soldiers playing dice.

'Gambling is a device of the Devil, my children,' he said cheerfully. 'Were you playing dice when you should have been watching St Mary's Church?'

The soldiers exchanged furtive glances. 'No,' one lied easily. 'Froissart did not leave. The only person to go in or out was the friar.'

'What friar?' asked Michael, feeling his interest quicken.

'The friar that visited Froissart in the church,' said the soldier with exaggerated patience.

'What time was this?' Michael asked.

The soldier squinted up at him. 'About an hour after the church was locked. It was dark by then, and we did not see him until he was almost on top of us.' He turned back to his game and threw his dice.

'Did you know him?'

The soldier shook his head, handing over a few pennies to one of his comrades, who laughed triumphantly. 'He said his name was Father Lucius, and when he shouted his name, Froissart opened the door and let him in.'

'What did he look like?'

The soldier shrugged. 'Like a friar! Mean-looking with a big nose, and a dirty grey robe with the cowl pulled up over his head.'

Michael nodded. If he were wearing a grey robe, he must have been a Franciscan. 'Did you see him leave?'

'Yes. After about an hour. He warned us about gambling, and left.' The soldier took the dice from his neighbour and threw them again. There was a series of catcalls as he lost a second time.

Michael sketched a quick benediction over them and strolled away. He had enjoyed making Tulyet give him the information he wanted by needling him into indiscretion. Michael had discovered not only where Froissart lived, but the identity of the neighbour who had witnessed his crime. From Tulyet's men, Michael had also discovered the identity of Froissart's murderer: the mysterious friar. He hummed a song from the taverns that he should not have known, and walked back down the hill a lot more happily than he had walked up it.

He saw Bartholomew talking to two Austin Canons outside the Hospital of St John the Evangelist as he turned from Bridge Street into the High Street. In fine humour he strolled across and greeted them. Bartholomew looked at him suspiciously and quickly concluded his conversation with the Canons.

'What have you been up to?' Bartholomew asked suspiciously. 'You are not usually so cheery after climbing Castle Hill.'

Michael told him, while Bartholomew listened thoughtfully. 'I know Richard Tulyet. He is not a bad man and, until recently, has been a good Sheriff. I hope you did not offend him. We might need his goodwill at some point.'

Michael hastily changed the subject to the Franciscan friar. 'How many do you know that are mean-looking and have big noses?' he said.

'Just about all of them,' said Bartholomew drily. 'We have at least five in Michaelhouse who match that description.'

Michael laughed. 'Shall we go and visit your Janetta, and Froissart's family?' he asked.

'We shall not!' said Bartholomew feelingly. 'It will be dark soon, and I have no desire to be there after curfew. De Wetherset's men can bring them to us tomorrow. I have had enough for today, and we have a very early start tomorrow when we exhume Nicholas.'

They began to walk back to Michaelhouse, stopping on the way for Michael to buy a large apple pie from a baker hastening to sell the last of his produce before trading ceased for the day. The sun was beginning to set, and weary tradesmen and apprentices were trailing in from the Fair.

'So Froissart knew his murderer,' said Michael, his mouth full.

'Possibly,' said Bartholomew. 'It is not absolutely certain that the Franciscan killed him. If Froissart allowed the Franciscan into the church, he may have let others in too while the soldiers were busy with their dice. And would one mean-looking friar have the strength to carry Froissart up to the tower and nail him to the bell frame?'

'I wonder whether Froissart fled up your path between the bushes from the scene of his crime to the church?' mused Michael. 'I wonder why Janetta of Lincoln went to such pains to hide it? Knowing what we do, I suspect that the only reason she intervened when the mob attacked you was because she is intelligent enough to know that two murders – yours and Froissart's wife – within a few days of each other might bring the unwanted attention of Tulyet's officers into her small domain. The death of Froissart's wife may have saved you, Matt.'

Bartholomew sighed. 'I want to read some Hippocrates tonight before the light fades completely. You could go to the Franciscan Friary and see if anyone there attended Froissart on the night of his death. The Franciscan's visit might be entirely innocent, and we should at least try to find out.'

Michael rubbed his hands. 'It is turning chilly,' he said, 'and not a red cloud to be seen. It will be raining when you dig up poor Nicholas tomorrow morning, Matt. You mark my words.'

chapter 5

THE PORTER WAS ASLEEP IN HIS SMALL OFFICE WHEN Bartholomew unbarred the wicket gate and stepped out into the lane long before dawn the following day. The night before, Kenyngham had enquired about the investigation concerning the body in the University chest, and Michael had given him a brief outline of what had happened, dutifully omitting any reference to Froissart and Nicholas's book. Kenyngham mentioned that the Chancellor had asked that they be relieved of teaching until further notice, a request of which he did not approve. It was relatively easy to find teachers of theology to take Michael's place, but there was no one who could teach medicine. Kenyngham instructed them to complete the business as soon as possible and to return to their obligations at the College.

'I am uncomfortable with the College becoming involved in this,' he had said. 'The relationship between town and University is unstable, and I do not want Michaelhouse to become a scapegoat. It is bad enough having to share St Michael's Church with Physwick Hostel – the Chancellor and both Proctors have connections there, and none but Jonstan are popular men.'

Bartholomew agreed. 'Perhaps relations may improve once the killer of these women is caught.'

'Ah, yes,' said Kenyngham. 'The man Tulyet allowed to escape.' Bartholomew and Michael exchanged a glance. 'That is not helping with University-town relations either. There is a rumour that he is being sheltered by one of the Colleges because the University does not approve of students visiting prostitutes.'

'That is an unreasonable assumption,' said Bartholomew. 'Women will always sell themselves so long as there is a demand.'

'I am not questioning the logic of the rumour, but of the damage it might do to us,' said Kenyngham, more impatiently than Bartholomew had heard him speak before. He must be concerned indeed, Bartholomew realised, for there was little that usually disturbed the gentle Gilbertine's equanimity.

Kenyngham continued. 'Michaelhouse is already the target for evil happenings. That business with the back gate worries me. We were lucky you and Cynric were to hand to save us all from being burned in our beds. Do you have any ideas as to why an attack should be aimed at us?'

Bartholomew and Michael shook their heads. 'It could only have been meant as some kind of warning,' said Michael. 'Perhaps it was not aimed at Michaelhouse at all, but at someone who uses the lane.'

'Really?' asked Kenyngham doubtfully. 'Like one of the merchants going to the wharves by the river?'

'It is possible,' said Michael. 'Such pyrotechnics need wood, and our gate is the only wood available.'

Kenyngham sighed. 'Well, I do not like it. I have asked that the Proctors set a beadle at the back gate until all this is resolved, and have stipulated that no one is allowed out of College after curfew for any reason except you two. The Bishop would not approve of me confining his best spy,' he said to Michael, 'and your work among the poor, Matthew, is very beneficial in maintaining good relations between us and the townspeople. So just remember that when you dispense some of your outlandish treatments. You might consider being more orthodox until this business is resolved.'

Bartholomew looked at him in bemusement, uncertain whether to be angry or amused that his work among the sick was being used as a political tool to placate the townspeople.

He mulled over Kenyngham's words as he waited for Michael and Cynric to join him, and glanced up at the low clouds that drenched the town with heavy rain. Michael's prediction had been right. Bartholomew pulled up the hood of his cloak and paced restlessly. The more he thought about what they were about to do, the more he felt it was terribly wrong. He was not averse to performing the exhumation in itself – he had seen far worse sights in his life – but he was afraid of the diseases the corpse might unleash. While he did not believe that supernatural powers opened the graves of the dead to bring the plague, he was reluctant to dismiss the rumour out of hand. When the consequences of an action might be as potentially devastating as a return of the plague, any risk, however small, was simply too great. He almost yelled out as a shadow glided up to him from behind.

'Easy, lad,' said Cynric, his teeth glinting white in a brief smile in the gloom.

'Do you have the lamp and rope?' Bartholomew asked, to hide his nervousness.

'And spades,' said Cynric. 'Stay here while I rouse that fat monk. He is probably still asleep.'

Bartholomew cursed softly as the first trickle of cold water coursed down the back of his neck. He closed his eyes against a sharp gust of wind that blew stinging rain into his face. What better conditions for an exhumation? he thought morosely. He remembered the murderer of the town prostitutes, the friar, and Froissart, and looked around uneasily. He hoped the night was sufficiently foul for murderers to want to be in their beds.

He almost cried out a second time as a heavy hand dropped onto his shoulder.

'Master Jonstan!' said Michael cheerfully, approaching and addressing the Junior Proctor who had given Bartholomew the fright. 'Were you told we have business tonight?'

Jonstan nodded. 'I have the licence here, signed by the Chancellor and the Bishop,' he said, waving a folded piece of vellum at them.

'Wonderful!' muttered Bartholomew irritably to Michael, his heart still thudding from the shock the Junior Proctor had given him. 'We may be about to risk the lives of hundreds of people by exhuming corpses, but all is well as long as we do so legally.'

'Believe me, Matt, I am as reluctant to do this as you are,' Michael replied. 'But the Chancellor has issued an order, and the Bishop's signature is confirmation that we have no alternative but to comply. Moaning about it will do no good at all.'

He took the bucket and a length of rope from Cynric, and set off up the lane towards St Mary's Church. Jonstan slipped away to instruct his beadles to stay at the College until he returned, while Bartholomew picked up a spade and trailed morosely after Michael, wishing the rain would stop. The single trickle of cold water down his back seemed to have developed into a deluge, and he was already shivering uncontrollably.

The others caught up with him, and they made their way silently to where St Mary's Church was a looming shadow against the dark sky. Father Cuthbert was waiting for them in the shelter of the porch, a huge black shape huddled up on a bench.

'Gilbert marked the grave with a rag on a stick,' he said, pulling a voluminous cloak around him against the cold. 'It is over there.'

'Are you certain it is the right one?' asked Bartholomew, aware of the priest's nervousness. He did not wish to dig up the wrong grave – especially since some of the first plague victims had been buried in the churchyard.

Cuthbert nodded quickly, and withdrew further into the shadows of the porch. He clearly had no intention of leaving his shelter to brave the elements, or to be directly involved in the unpleasant task that lay ahead. Bartholomew could not find it in his heart to condemn him for his attitude.

Cynric set up the lamp where it would be out of the rain, while Bartholomew took a spade and began to dig, grateful that Nicholas of York had not been considered important enough to have been given a tombstone that they would have had to move.

'No!' Father Cuthbert's voice was a hoarse cry. 'Not that one! The next one!'

Bartholomew peered at the mound Cuthbert indicated from the shelter of the porch. 'But this is the one that is marked.'

Cuthbert, reluctantly, left the porch, and came to stand next to the marker. 'It has been moved,' he said, surprised. 'Wretched children, I expect. I saw a group of them playing here late yesterday afternoon. That is the grave you need to dig, ńot this one.'

'How can you be sure?' asked Bartholomew, his resentment at the task imposed on him growing by the moment.

'Because when I said the funeral service for Nicholas, I stood under that tree, and water dripped down the back of my neck during the whole ceremony. I remember it clearly. I would not have stood so far away if he had been buried in this grave. I think this one is Mistress Archer's . . .'

'And she died of the plague,' Bartholomew finished for him, remembering her death vividly, one of the first he had witnessed. He shuddered. 'Really, Father, this affair is foolishness itself. Can we not merely assume the worst and say that Nicholas, too, was murdered? And then we can dispense with this distasteful business.'

Cuthbert gave a heavy sigh. 'Believe me, gentlemen, I tried as hard as you did to dissuade the Chancellor from this course of action, but he was immovable. I suspect the Bishop is behind it, and the Chancellor has little choice in the matter. Look,' he said, taking Bartholomew by the shoulder, 'you know what to expect, and you know how to avoid contamination. It is better that you do this than some of the beadles, who might well spread infection without realising what they are doing.'

Bartholomew nodded slowly. It was the first sense he had heard spoken since the business began. Cuthbert was right. Bartholomew had brought rags to wrap around their mouths and noses when they reached the coffin, and thick gloves to wear when he examined the body. Cynric had procured a bucket so that they could wash afterwards, and Bartholomew intended to burn any clothes that came in contact with the body. He doubted beadles would take such precautions.

He took up the spade a second time, and began to dig, while Cuthbert kicked around with his feet to hide the marks made on Mistress Archer's grave. Michael stood in the porch reading the licence, swearing to himself when he saw the ink had run in the rain, while Jonstan took the other spade and helped Bartholomew.

Despite the rain, digging was hard work. The last few weeks of hot, dry weather had baked the earth into a rock-like consistency. Bartholomew shed his cloak and tabard and dug in his shirt sleeves, grateful now for the rain that cooled him. Jonstan handed his spade to Cynric and went to sit in the porch next to Cuthbert to rest. When Bartholomew felt as though he had been digging for hours, the hole was still only thigh-deep. The rain sluiced down into the bottom of the grave as they worked, making their task even more difficult.

Michael relieved Bartholomew, who went to join Jonstan and Cuthbert in the porch. Cuthbert was telling Jonstan about the proposed rebuilding of the chancel, and both men were keen to discuss something other than the task in hand. Bartholomew glanced up at the sky. It was still dark, and dawn would come later because of the rain, but, even so, progress was slow. The law was quite clear that all exhumations should be carried out under cover of darkness, and they might have to come back the following night if they did not hurry.

Cynric looked exhausted, so Bartholomew went to take another turn. He bent to rest his hand on the ground and dropped lightly into the gaping hole. He was appalled to hear a loud splinter, and felt one foot break through wood. The water was too deep to see anything, and there was a horrified gasp from Jonstan, watching from above.

'I think we have reached the coffin,' Bartholomew said unnecessarily, looking up at the others. He poked and prodded with his spade and discovered that the coffin had been buried at an angle. When he dug further, he saw that a large boulder had blocked progress on one side, and so Nicholas of York's feet had been buried lower than his head. Bartholomew was able to clear the soil away from the top half of the coffin, and poked around under water until he felt the lower part was relatively free. Cynric dropped him a rope and he tied it around the crude wooden box.

Michael and Jonstan helped Bartholomew to climb out, and all five of them began to heave on the ropes. The coffin moved slightly, but it was immensely heavy. Bartholomew imagined it must be full of water.

After several minutes of straining and heaving to no avail, it became clear that they were not going to be able to get it out, and that Bartholomew would have to examine the body *in situ.* He tied one of the rags around his nose and mouth, donned the thick leather gloves and reluctantly climbed back into the grave, more carefully than he had the last time. The wood was slick in the rain, and it was difficult to stand upright. Until Cynric lay full length on the ground and held the lamp inside the grave, it was impossible to see what he was doing.

He inserted a chisel under the lid and tapped with a hammer. The lid eased up, and he got a good grip with his fingers and began to pull. The lid began to move with a great screech of wet wood, and came off so suddenly so that he almost fell backwards. He handed it up to Michael, and all five of them peered into the open coffin.

Bartholomew moved back, gagging, as the stench of putrefaction filled the confined space of the grave. His feet skidded and he scrabbled at the sides to try to prevent himself from falling over. Jonstan gave a cry of horror, and Cuthbert began to mutter prayers in an uneven, breathless whisper. Michael leaned down and grabbed at Bartholomew's shoulder, breathing through his mouth so as not to inhale the smell.

'Matt!' he gasped. 'Come out of there!'

He began to tug frantically at Bartholomew's shirt. Bartholomew needed no second bidding, and scrambled out of the grave with an agility that surprised even him. He sank to his knees and peered down at the thing in the coffin.

'What is it?' breathed Cynric.

Bartholomew cleared his throat to see if he could still speak, making Jonstan jump. 'It looks like a goat,' he said.

'A goat?' whispered Michael in disbelief. 'What is a goat doing there?'

Bartholomew swallowed hard. Two curved horns and a long pointed face stared up at him, dirty and stained from its weeks underground, but a goat's head nevertheless, atop a human body.

'Was Nicholas of York a devil?' breathed Jonstan. 'Was he not human, and reverted to his true form after death?' He raised his great round eyes to Cuthbert, who stared aghast down into the grave, his lips moving as he muttered his prayers.

'Men do not change into animals after they die,' said Michael, but his voice held no conviction, and Bartholomew saw Cuthbert and Jonstan exchange disbelieving glances.

'Perhaps he was not a man,' said Jonstan again, crossing himself.

'Nonsense,' said Bartholomew firmly, realising that if they did not get a grip on themselves soon, their imaginations would get the better of them. 'You knew Nicholas. Surely you would have noticed demonic qualities had he possessed them in life.'

He inhaled a deep breath of fresh air, thick with the scent of wet grass, took the lantern from Cynric, and leaned with it inside the grave. Shadows flickered eerily, but there was light enough to illuminate the peeling paint and the wood underneath.

'It is a mask!' he said, relief flooding through him. 'It is a wooden mask!'

'A mask? Why should Nicholas be wearing such a thing?' asked Cuthbert, his voice hoarse with horror.

For a few moments, no one said anything, and all five stared into the gaping hole at the strange figure below. Bartholomew pulled himself together, and slid back into the grave to complete his examination. Anxious to finish as quickly as possible, he reached for the right hand to look for a tiny cut that might suggest Nicholas had died from the poison on the lock. Puzzled, he peered closer. The hand he held was small and dainty, with paint on the nails, but was too decomposed for him to be able to see whether there had been a cut there or not. He straddled the coffin precariously, grabbed the mask by its horns and pulled as hard as he could. The mask came off with an unpleasant sucking sound to reveal the face underneath.

'What is this?' cried Cuthbert. 'That is not Nicholas!'

'He *was* a devil!' whispered Jonstan, crossing himself vigorously. 'He *did* change his form after his death.'

'You have the wrong grave!' said Michael accusingly, looking at Cuthbert.

Cuthbert stared at him, his face white with shock. 'I do not!' he whispered. 'This is Nicholas's grave without question. I am absolutely certain.'

Michael and Bartholomew exchanged a look of bewilderment. The body whose face had been hidden by the mask was that of a young woman. Her eyes were sunken deep into her face, and the lips had stretched back to reveal fine, even teeth. That explained the delicate hand and painted nails, Bartholomew thought. He suddenly felt a great wave of compassion for her. Not only had she been brutally murdered, attested by the stab wound in her throat, but her body had been desecrated with the mask. But what was she doing there anyway? And where was Nicholas of York? Bartholomew took a deep breath and quickly looked under the woman to make sure there was not another corpse in the grave.

He was angry at the callousness of it all, and his anger brought him out of the sense of shock that had been dulling his wits. He bent to look at the woman. Assuming that the coffin had not been changed after Nicholas's funeral, she had been dead for a month. The state of decay confirmed this to Bartholomew, taking into account the fact that she had died during warm weather and that the earth had been baked dry for several weeks. The grave was only flooded now because of the sudden downpour. He looked at her feet, but they were wet, and even if the rain-water had not washed her feet clean, he would not have been able to identify a circle painted in blood on her rotting skin. The lamp above him fluttered in the wind and went out. Cynric swore and cursed in Welsh as he tried to re-light it, but the rain was coming down harder than ever and the wick was sodden.

Bartholomew waited in the dark, the water lapping about his ankles. The smell was overpowering, and it was becoming more and more difficult to resist the urge to turn around and scramble out.

'I cannot light it,' said Cynric from above him, his voice unsteady.

'What shall we do, Father?' asked Bartholomew. 'There is no point in examining this woman when she is not Nicholas. Shall we rebury her and leave her in peace?'

'We must bring the body out,' said Cuthbert. 'If not, the Chancellor will order that you bring her out another night so that she can be identified and the whole matter investigated.'

'She cannot be identified now,' said Bartholomew. 'She has been underground too long. And I can tell you now that she died because she was stabbed in the throat. It does not take a physician to see that.'

'Bring her out, Matt,' said Michael. 'Father Cuthbert is right in that the Chancellor will demand an investigation, and I for one do not want to go through all this again tomorrow.'

Cynric handed Bartholomew a chisel. 'Make a hole in the bottom of the coffin to let the water drain,' he said. 'Then it will be easier to lift.'

Michael fetched the rope, and Bartholomew fumbled about trying to tie the knots in the darkness while Jonstan attempted to light a second lamp under the shelter of the porch. Eventually, Bartholomew thought the knots were secure, and Michael and Cynric began to pull. With a slurp of mud, the coffin came free, sending water everywhere. Bartholomew steadied it until the others were able to heave it up and onto the ground.

Bartholomew found that his arms were too tired to allow him to climb out again, and he had a moment's panic until Michael offered his hand and hauled so hard that Bartholomew shot from the grave like a cork from a bottle. Cynric had put the lid back over the coffin and was enlarging the hole in the bottom to allow any water still remaining to drain away. Jonstan watched.

'It was that mask,' he said with a shudder. 'If it had just been the woman, it would not have been so bad. But that thing looks like something from hell.' He crossed himself yet again and backed away.

'I will unlock the church and we can put the body in the crypt out of sight,' said Cuthbert, clearly the more practical of the two. 'The goat mask can go in the charnel house until the Chancellor has seen it. Who would do such a thing to a corpse?'

But more to the point, who was she? Bartholomew thought. And where was Nicholas? Was he alive or dead? He wanted to rub his eyes, but glimpsed his filthy hands and thought better of it. He and Michael had gained nothing from this grisly business. They had answered no questions, but had raised many more.

The sky was brightening noticeably by the time they had removed the woman's body and filled in the grave. Michael, white-faced, went with Jonstan to give a complete report to the Chancellor, while Cuthbert remained in the church to say prayers for the dead woman. Bartholomew looked down at his wet and muddy clothes despondently. The rain was easing off with the onset of dawn, but the day seemed cold and gloomy.

He and Cynric walked home, where they hauled buckets of water from the well to wash, and Bartholomew threw the gloves and his old clothes onto the ever-smouldering fires behind the kitchen. Bartholomew was down to his last shirt, and he hoped he would have an uneventful day in order to give Agatha time to do the laundry. Shivering, they went to the kitchen, where Cynric warmed some potage left over from the day before. When the bell chimed for Prime, Bartholomew was fast asleep in Agatha's chair next to the fireplace, and she did not waken him.

Michael returned later, having spoken to de Wetherset, and said he planned to continue his reading of Nicholas's book. Bartholomew spent the rest of the morning teaching, and was pleased with the way some of his students were learning, although he was finding Brother Boniface difficult. The friar seemed to have been talking to the fanatic Father William, for he was obsessed with the notion of heresy. Boniface proclaimed that Bartholomew teaching them surgery was heretical, and sparked a bitter argument, with Bulbeck and Gray defending Bartholomew's position, and Boniface and his fellow Franciscans opposing it. It was not an argument based on logic and reason, but on ignorance and bigotry on both sides. Bartholomew did not take part, and listened with a growing sense of weariness.

Ibn Ibrahim had warned him that some of the techniques and cures he had been taught would meet with hostility and suspicion, but he was unprepared for such reactions from his own students. He thought about the difference between Arab and Christian medicine, and wondered whether he had made the right decision in choosing the former. Naïvely, he had assumed that his greater success with diseases and wounds than his more traditional colleagues would speak for itself, and that in time people would come to accept his methods. But Boniface claimed that Bartholomew's success was because he used methods devised by the Devil, while Gray and Bulbeck claimed he was blessed by God with a gift of healing, as though his painstakingly acquired skills were nothing.

As he listened to Boniface's raving, Bartholomew considered

telling Kenyngham that he was impossible to teach. But all hostels and Colleges were finding it difficult to recruit students after the plague, with the exception of lawyers, and Michaelhouse could not afford to lose the Franciscans.

After the main meal of the day, eaten in silence, he went to St Mary's in search of Michael. The clerks told him they had been unable to find Janetta or Froissart's kinsmen. Bartholomew was relieved: he and Michael could not proceed until they had spoken to them, and the fact that they were unavailable would slow everything down and allow him to concentrate on his teaching duties.

He was about to return to Michaelhouse when he was hailed by de Wetherset, who wanted to know what could be discovered from the dead woman. Grimacing to register his reluctance, Bartholomew followed de Wetherset down into the small cellar under the altar. The door leading to the stairs was locked, and the Chancellor motioned the ever-solicitous Gilbert forward to open it and precede them down damp steps into the musty crypt. Gilbert held back, his eyes huge with fear. De Wetherset looked as though he would order Gilbert into the crypt, but he relented, and patted him on the shoulder.

'I have no taste for this either,' he said. 'Father Cuthbert!'

The priest waddled from where he had been scraping candle wax from the altar, took the keys from Gilbert, and puffed down the steps to the vault below. The crypt was little more than a passageway that ran under the altar from one side of the choir to the other. To the left was a small chamber protected by a stout door, where the church silver was kept. In the chamber, two coffins lay side by side on the ground: Froissart's and the woman's. Several large bowls of incense were dotted about, adding to the general overpowering odour.

'I am surprised you need to lock this,' said Bartholomew hoarsely, his eyes watering. 'I would think the smell alone would be deterrent enough.'

De Wetherset ignored him and pulled the sheet off the coffin in which the woman lay. Bartholomew was again filled with compassion for her. He made a cursory examination of the wound on her throat he had seen that morning, and looked again in vain for a circle on the sole of her foot. Lifting the simple gown of pale blue, he inspected her body for other wounds, but found nothing. Her dress, home-made and like a hundred others in the town, would not help to identify her, and her face meant nothing to Bartholomew. He suggested giving a description of her to Richard Tulyet to see whether he had been told of some person missing over the last month.

'This makes five,' said de Wetherset, dismissing his suggestion with a contemptuous wave of his hand. 'Five prostitutes dead.'

'We do not know she was a prostitute,' said Bartholomew. 'And Frances de Belem was not a prostitute either.'

De Wetherset made an impatient gesture. 'They were all killed by wounds to the throat, and she, like the others, is barefoot. How much of a coincidence is that?'

Father Cuthbert peered over Bartholomew's shoulder. 'What happened to her hair?'

Bartholomew looked at the wispy strands attached to the woman's head and shrugged. 'I suppose hair falls out when the skin rots. Or perhaps she had an illness which made her hair thin.'

'Then she will be easy for Tulyet to identify,' said de Wetherset. 'There cannot be many bald women in Cambridge.'

'I know some women who have used powerful caustics on their hair to dye it, and I have been called to treat the infections they cause,' said Bartholomew thoughtfully. 'Once the scalp has healed, the hair does not always grow again, and they need to wear veils and wimples.'

'Really?' queried de Wetherset with morbid fascination. 'How curious. The King's grandmother, Queen Isabella, always wears a wimple. I wonder if she is bald, too.'

Bartholomew stared at the woman in the coffin. Who was she? Had she been killed by the three men who had been in Michaelhouse's orchard two nights before? Or was there more than one group of maniacs in the town? Seven deaths – the five women, the friar and Froissart, plus Nicholas and Buckley missing. Were they dead too? Or were they the murderers?

'Did you see Nicholas dead?' asked Bartholomew.

De Wetherset looked momentarily taken aback by the question, and then understanding dawned in his eyes. 'Yes,' he said. 'I saw him here in the church, although I must confess

I did not poke and prod at his body as I have watched you do to corpses. A vigil was kept for him by the other clerks the day before his funeral. Then his coffin was sealed and left in the church overnight, and he was buried the following morning.' He turned to Cuthbert, who nodded his agreement with de Wetherset's account.

'So, he must have been taken from his coffin that night,' said Bartholomew, 'and replaced with the dead woman wearing the mask.'

De Wetherset swallowed hard. 'Do you think Nicholas may not have been dead after all?' he said. 'That he might have killed the woman and put her in the coffin that was intended for him?'

Bartholomew shrugged non-committally. 'It is possible,' he said. 'But how? You say the coffin was sealed the night before his funeral, so how did he get out to kill a woman and put her in his coffin? And why was she wearing the mask?'

'Perhaps she came to let him out,' said de Wetherset, 'and he killed her so that there would be a body in his coffin the next day when we came to bury it.'

'That seems unlikely,' said Bartholomew. 'Why would a woman take such a risk? Was your clerk the kind of man to conceive such an elaborate plot, and then kill?'

De Wetherset shook his head firmly. 'No. Nicholas was a good man. He would never commit murder.'

Bartholomew remained doubtful, knowing that extreme events might drive the meekest of men to the most violent of acts. Perhaps one of the covens had come to the church to perform some diabolical ceremony over Nicholas's body and had exchanged his body for hers, although Bartholomew could think of nothing that might be gained from such an action. He drew the sheet over her, covering her from sight. Cuthbert shuddered.

'Now will you look at the mask?' asked de Wetherset.

Bartholomew looked at him in surprise. 'What can I tell you about that? You can see as well as I what it is.'

'You are always thorough when you look at corpses,' said de Wetherset, 'and if you are as thorough with the mask, you might uncover some clue I have overlooked.'

Bartholomew trailed reluctantly after him into the small charnel house in the churchyard and looked down at the mask. In the bright light of day, it was a miserable thing, poorly carved and cheaply painted. But the horns and the top of the skull were real, which Bartholomew had not realised before.

'The horns probably came from the butchers' market,' he said. 'And as for the mask, I have seen nothing like it before, and I cannot tell you where it came from. It must belong to one of the covens.'

'Covens?' said de Wetherset suspiciously. 'What do you mean?'

Bartholomew repeated the information Stanmore had given him, while de Wetherset narrowed his eyes.

'So you know about that,' he said. Bartholomew shot him an irritable glance. De Wetherset was not surprised by the information because he had known all along. What else was he keeping from them? 'Do you know about the Guild of the Holy Trinity too?'

'That is not a coven, is it?' asked Bartholomew, confused.

'Indeed not,' said de Wetherset. 'It is a group of people who are dedicated to stamping out sin and evil lest the plague come again. They are the antithesis of the Guild of the Coming and the Guild of Purification, or whatever blasphemous names these covens have chosen for themselves.'

'Could the Guild of the Holy Trinity be responsible for the murders?' asked Bartholomew. 'People who believe that prostitution is one of the sins that brought the plague? Do you know who is a member? What about Master Jonstan? He seems opposed to prostitution.'

'So am I,' said de Wetherset. 'But I am not a member of the Guild of the Holy Trinity, and neither is Jonstan. But Cuthbert is, and so was Nicholas.'

Bartholomew chewed on his lip, trying to understand. 'So Nicholas was in a guild that is known for its antagonism to the prostitutes. A month ago he died, but in his coffin is found not Nicholas, but a murdered woman.'

'Yes,' said de Wetherset, studying Bartholomew intently. 'Curious, is it not? I can see you are thinking that Nicholas

123

might be the killer, freed from his coffin and stalking the town. But I am more inclined to believe that the disappearance of his body is the work of the covens, perhaps because he took an active stance against them. Perhaps they worked some sort of vile spell to bring him from his eternal rest.'

'I do not believe the dead can walk, Master de Wetherset,' said Bartholomew, 'and we should not allow that rumour to escape, or the town will revolt for certain if they think our dead clerks are killing their women. Perhaps Nicholas's body was stolen as you suggest. But the mask is the problem. Why go to the trouble of leaving this poor woman wearing the mask unless she was meant to be found – meant to be seen like this?'

De Wetherset looked appalled. 'Are you saying that someone knew we would exhume Nicholas?' he said.

Bartholomew spread his hands. 'Not necessarily. Perhaps the mask and the woman's body were meant to be found before he was buried, or even during the funeral service. I do not know. But why would anyone go to such trouble unless it was meant to be seen by others?'

'It could just be a person with a fevered brain,' said de Wetherset.

'Well, that goes without saying,' said Bartholomew drily, 'but I still think whoever did it intended his work to be found.'

De Wetherset shuddered again. 'I do not like being near this thing. Come with me back to my hostel and have something to eat. Have you ever been to Physwick Hostel?' Bartholomew shook his head and de Wetherset gave him a sidelong glance. 'I find it odd that Cambridge is small in some ways – one can never walk anywhere without seeing someone one knows – and yet you have never been inside Physwick, even though our gate lies almost opposite yours!'

Bartholomew smiled. It was not so odd. Hostels and Colleges were very competitive, and scholars were generally discouraged from wandering from one to the other. Less than a month before, students from one hostel had attacked those from another, and the result had been a violent fight. And only the previous week Alcote had tried to fine some unfortunate who had been caught dining in St Thomas's Hostel until the

Master had intervened. He thought the Chancellor must know this, but perhaps he was making desultory conversation to take his mind away from the unpleasant events of the day.

'I must wash my hands first,' Bartholomew said, thinking of his examination of the woman's decomposing body.

'What for?' asked de Wetherset, perturbed. 'They look clean enough to me. Wipe them off on your tabard.'

Bartholomew gave him a bemused glance. He knew his insistence on washing his hands after seeing every patient was regarded with amusement in the town, but surely, even someone as adverse to washing as the Chancellor could see that hands needed to be cleaned after touching corpses! He hoped the Chancellor's standards of hygiene did not extend to the Physwick Hostel kitchens.

They walked outside into the sunshine, and Bartholomew saw the Chancellor glance to where Nicholas of York's grave had been. As they walked past, de Wetherset stopped and peered at something.

'What is that?' he muttered, inching closer.

'My bag!' exclaimed Bartholomew in delight. 'The one that was stolen in the alley the other day.'

He picked it up and looked inside. It appeared to be exactly as it had been before it had been stolen. His tabard was there, rolled up and stuffed on top of his medicines and instruments. His notebooks were there too, containing records of patients he had seen and what dosages of various potions he had given them. Nervously, he looked in the side pouch where the strong medicines were, and heaved a sigh of relief that they appeared unmolested.

'You know what this means?' said de Wetherset in a low whisper, his face solemn. 'It means that whoever stole your bag also knows that something went on at this grave this morning. Why else would they leave it here to be found?'

Bartholomew's elation at getting his precious bag back evaporated at the implications of de Wetherset's comments. He was probably right. Janetta of Lincoln must be involved in all this. She was linked to Froissart, and she was present when Bartholomew's bag had been stolen. Did she watch them exhume the grave that morning from her secret path? There was too much coincidence for it to be mere chance.

'I would discard any potions in that bag,' said de Wetherset, eyeing it suspiciously. 'Who knows what they might have been exchanged for? You might end up killing one of your patients. Are there any locks on it that may now have poisoned devices?' he asked.

Bartholomew turned the bag over in his hands. It looked the same, and he was pleased to have it back. The one Father Aidan had lent him did not have the same feel to it, and Bartholomew could never find what he wanted. Nevertheless, de Wetherset was right, and he decided not only to discard the medicines, but to test some of them too.

He and de Wetherset strolled the short distance to Physwick Hostel, a small, half-timbered building opposite Michaelhouse. Bartholomew saw Alcote watching him enter, but assumed the Senior Fellow could not object to Bartholomew accepting an invitation from the University's Chancellor, even if he were from another College.

Bartholomew's insistence on washing his hands was met with some amusement by de Wetherset's colleagues, which Bartholomew accepted with weary resignation. He knew most of the men of Physwick from standing opposite them in church. Richard Harling nodded coolly towards him, and continued a debate on canon law with another lawyer. Alric Jonstan was there, and greeted Bartholomew warmly. He seemed to have recovered from his morning excursion, although he was pale and his eyes seemed red and tired.

The ale at Physwick was far superior to that at Michaelhouse, and was clear and fresh. The bread, however, was the same: grainy and made with inferior flour. There was some cheese too, but that had been left in the sun and was hard and dry, and sat in a rancid yellow puddle.

They discussed the advantages and failings of the Cambridge examination system for a while, and then Jonstan began to chat to Bartholomew about his duties as Junior Proctor. Next to him, de Wetherset and Harling talked about a guild meeting that was to be held the following day. Bartholomew listened to them while appearing to be paying close attention to

Jonstan's somewhat tedious account of the Proctor's statutory responsibilities. They were discussing a proposed meeting of the Guild of the Purification, and from what Harling was telling de Wetherset, trouble was expected.

'You recall what happened last time,' he said. 'The following day, St John Zachary's Church was full of spent torches and someone had drawn a sign on the altar in what looked to be blood.'

Bartholomew listened intently, strands of the mystery twining together in his mind. The goat mask on the woman in Nicholas's grave was clearly a demonic device, which might mean that the murders of the other women were also connected to witchcraft. The large man in the orchard who had bitten him had worn a red mask, obviously a satanic trapping.

Was this the clue he needed to tie it all together? Perhaps he would see whether Stanmore had learned anything else. Then they needed to find Froissart's family and Janetta of Lincoln. The reappearance of his bag told him that Janetta was most definitely in Cambridge, despite the claims of de Wetherset's clerks that they could not trace her. Should he try to seek for her himself? But she would know Bartholomew wanted to see her, and if she did not want to see him, nothing would be served by him risking his safety to go in search of her.

Of course, another thing he could do would be to talk to some of the friends of the women who had been killed. Some of them might have some indication of who the killer might be. Perhaps they were unwilling to talk to Tulyet, whose men were, after all, the ones who arrested them if they were caught touting for business on the town's streets. He decided he would ask Sybilla. She was the only prostitute he was aware he knew, and Sybilla had been the one to find Isobel.

And there was another thing: Frances de Belem had been killed in Michaelhouse grounds, but Physwick Hostel was a mere stone's throw away. He looked around at the men sitting with him at High Table – de Wetherset, Harling, and Jonstan. All high-ranking and well-respected University men, but was one of them the lover of Frances de Belem? Bartholomew reconsidered them: de Wetherset, stocky with pig-like features; Harling with his greased black hair and bad complexion; Jonstan with his odd tonsure and long teeth. Could she have fallen for any of these men? He would not have thought so, but Edith, his sister, frequently told him he did not understand women, and misjudged their likes and dislikes.

He became aware that Jonstan had asked him a question and was awaiting an answer, beaming affably, his large blue eyes curious. Bartholomew was embarrassed and reluctant to reveal to the pleasant Jonstan that he had not been listening to a word he had said.

'Oh, yes,' he said, smiling and hoping it was the expected response.

Jonstan looked puzzled, but shrugged. 'That is what my mother always told me,' he said, 'but I have never yet met a physician who agreed with her until now. I must encourage her to eat more of them.'

Oh lord! thought Bartholomew. I hope whatever it is does not make her sick!

After leaving Physwick Hostel, Bartholomew, on the Chancellor's orders, went to the Castle to talk to Richard Tulyet about discovering another victim of the killer. De Wetherset could not conceal two bodies from the Sheriff, and reluctantly conceded that he was obliged to tell him that the killer had claimed another. De Wetherset repeated his previous instruction that the death of Froissart should not be made known to the Sheriff, lest it should somehow lead the killer to strike again.

Bartholomew was shown into the same office in the keep that Michael had visited the previous day. At first, Tulyet refused to speak to Bartholomew, shouting angrily that he had better things to do than gossip with idle scholars. Bartholomew asked the sergeant to inform him that another victim had been found, and was escorted begrudgingly into Tulyet's office. Bartholomew could tell in an instant that Michael had antagonised Tulyet, and he was irritated with his friend. If the killer were to be tracked down, they would work a lot more efficiently by co-operating, than by bickering and playing power games.

He tried to begin the interview on a positive note by asking Tulyet about his wife and baby. When Tulyet's baby was born, it was a strange yellow colour. The midwife sniffed imperiously and announced that it suffered from an excess of yellow bile and should be bled to relieve it of a dangerous imbalance of humours. Bleeding was usually the province of barber-surgeons, but, since the plague, there was only the unsavoury Robin of Grantchester, and Bartholomew had been called in his place.

Bartholomew had declined to bleed the baby, and had prescribed a wet nurse and a mild concoction of feverfew, comfrey, and camomile to relieve its fever and bring healing sleep. Employing a wet nurse allowed the mother to rest, and both child and mother began to recover rapidly, despite the midwife's dire predictions. But when Bartholomew examined the mother afterwards, he found a wound from the birth that would mean she was unlikely to have another child. The last time he saw them, both had been happy and healthy, and Bartholomew saw with pleasure that neither required his services any longer.

Tulyet sat behind a large table, writing, and looked up with open hostility when Bartholomew asked after his child.

'By what right do you ask about my family?' Tulyet demanded belligerently.

Bartholomew was nonplussed. People usually expected him to ask them how they were, and he wondered if Tulyet had had an argument with his wife. He changed the subject and began to tell him about finding the dead woman that morning. Tulyet leapt to his feet in dismay.

'Another woman, you say? Dead, like the others, with her throat cut?'

Bartholomew nodded and waited for the Sheriff to calm himself before continuing.

'She must have been killed and placed in Nicholas's coffin about a month ago. The Chancellor and his clerks saw the body in the chapel the night before his funeral. Father Cuthbert says the coffin was sealed before the church was locked for the night, because Nicholas was to be buried the next morning. His body must have been removed and the woman's put there instead.'

'But why?' said Tulyet, shaking his head slowly. 'I do not understand why.'

'Nor I,' said Bartholomew. 'I cannot believe that whoever put her there could have anticipated that Nicholas would be exhumed at a later stage. I think her body was intended to be found before the burial for some reason.'

'The murderer intended her to be found in Nicholas's coffin?' Tulyet rubbed at the sparse beard on his chin. 'That makes sense. His other victims have been left in places where they would be found – including your College, Doctor.'

'There was something else,' said Bartholomew. 'There was a goat mask on the body.'

Tulyet gaped at him. 'A goat mask? Are you jesting with me?'

Bartholomew shook his head. Tulyet stared out of the door across to where his men were practising sword drills half-heartedly in the fading daylight.

'Well,' he said, standing abruptly. 'I can think of no reason for that. It is odd, I suppose. But stranger things have happened.'

Not much stranger, thought Bartholomew, surprised by Tulyet's dismissal of the desecration. He found himself wondering whether Tulyet was really as initially shocked by the revelation as he appeared to be. He changed the subject yet again.

'Have you noticed a common element to the deaths of these women?' he asked. 'Has a mark or a sign been left to identify their deaths as the work of one person?' He wanted to know whether the first victim, Hilde, had had a circle on her foot.

'Oh yes,' said Tulyet, bringing cold eyes to bear on him. 'Cut throats and no shoes. Signature enough, would you not say?'

'Have you noticed anything else?' persisted Bartholomew.

Tulyet regarded him suspiciously. 'What sort of thing did you have in mind, Doctor?' he asked softly, disconcerting Bartholomew with his icy stare.

'Nothing specific,' Bartholomew lied badly. He wished he had not attempted to question Tulyet. He should have left it to Michael, who was more skilled at investigative techniques than him. He recalled the rumours that Michael, de Belem and Stanmore had told him, that the Sheriff was not investigating the deaths as carefully as he might, and began to wonder whether there might be a more sinister reason for his inactivity.

Tulyet moved closer to him, fingering a small dagger he wore at his belt. 'Are you hiding information from us, Doctor?'

he asked menacingly. 'Have you learned something about this while you have been after the Chancellor's business?'

Bartholomew inwardly cursed both de Wetherset for sending him on this errand when the clerks seemed to have been spreading news of their investigation all over the town, and his own inabilities to mislead people convincingly. Michael would not be experiencing difficulties now, and neither would de Wetherset. He shook his head and rose to leave. Tulyet forced him to sit back down again. Bartholomew glanced out of the open door. He could overpower Tulyet as easily as he could a child, for the man was slight and Bartholomew was far stronger, but he would never be able to escape across the bailey and through the gate-house without being stopped by Tulyet's men. Tulyet had been watching him, and shouted for two guards to stand by the door.

'You are right, Doctor,' he said, drawing his dagger and playing with it. 'If you were to run, you would never leave the Castle alive. I could arrest you now and question you until you tell me what I want to know, or you can volunteer the information. Which is it to be?'

Bartholomew thought quickly. He had come to Tulyet with the intention of telling him the little he knew about the murders of the women – the circle on their feet and its possible link to the guilds, the link between the goat in the coffin and witchcraft, and the fact that the murders of the women might somehow be related to Nicholas of York. But now he had doubts. How could he be sure that Tulyet was not a member of one of the guilds that dabbled in black magic? His reaction to the goat had been odd, to say the least. Perhaps he already knew who the killer was, but his hands were tied because of his membership of a guild. From what Bartholomew understood of guilds, Tulyet would be unlikely and unwilling to arrest a fellow member.

'I know nothing more than what I have told you, except,' Bartholomew said, trying to quell his tumbling thoughts, 'that I wondered whether the other dead women might have been marked in some way. Perhaps with something from a goat, like the mask on the woman we found this morning.' He convinced himself he was telling Tulyet the truth. He knew very little, and was merely guessing at the tenuous links between the murders, witchcraft, the guilds, and the University.

'What nonsense are you speaking?' said Tulyet angrily. 'You saw four of the victims yourself! Did you notice a goat attached to them?'

'I did not say it would be a whole goat,' said Bartholomew testily, 'and you asked me what I knew, and I am telling you. I am only trying to ascertain whether there was something common to all victims that might give some clue as to the murderer's identity.'

'Well, your suggestion is ludicrous,' said Tulyet. He replaced his dagger in its sheath and leaned close to Bartholomew. 'I will let you go this time, Doctor. But you will report to me anything that you discover about the deaths of the whores while you investigate the body in the chest. If I think for a moment that you are withholding information from me, I will issue a warrant for your immediate arrest, and no amount of protesting and whining from your University will be able to help you.'

Bartholomew rose, not particularly unsettled by Tulyet's threat. The Sheriff was underestimating the combined power of the University and the Church. His arrest would be considered a flouting of the University's rights to be dealt with under Canon law, and the Sheriff would have no option but to release him once University and Church swung into operation. This protection was exactly the reason why most University scholars took minor orders.

Tulyet shadowed him out of the Castle, and Bartholomew was aware that he was watched until he was out of sight. He deliberately dawdled, stopping on the Great Bridge to see how much more of its stone had been stolen since the last time he looked. If the Sheriff had time to waste on trying to make him feel uncomfortable, let him waste it, he thought, leaning his elbows on the handrail and peering down at the swirling water below.

Later, back at Michaelhouse, he told Michael what had happened.

'I will tell de Wetherset and the Bishop,' said the fat monk. 'They will not countenance your arrest. Tulyet must either have a very inflated idea of his own powers, or what you said must have rattled him.'

'But why?' said Bartholomew. 'Is he connected? Is that why he has made so little progress in catching the killer?'

Michael thought for a while. 'It is possible,' he said, 'and I am even more prepared to think so because I do not like the man. I wonder why he reacted so oddly at the mention of the goat mask.'

'Perhaps he is a member of one of the guilds that is connected to witchcraft,' said Bartholomew. 'I have been told that the Devil is supposed to appear in the form of a goat.'

'Yes. Cloven feet and horns,' said Michael. 'Like the painting of the Devil devouring souls on the wall of our church.'

Bartholomew thought about the painting. Depictions of hell and purgatory were common in all the town's churches. No wonder people like Father Cuthbert and Nicholas joined guilds that denounced sin so vehemently, if they thought they would end up like some of the characters in the paintings. But equally, why would others risk that to become members of covens?

'I am going to Ely tomorrow,' said Michael. 'I want that spare set of keys, and I must report what we have discovered to my Lord the Bishop.'

'Ask him about witchcraft,' said Bartholomew.

Michael looked amused. 'Now why do you think a Benedictine bishop would know such things?' he said, humour twinkling in his green eyes.

'Because any Bishop that did not make himself familiar with potential threats to his peace would be a fool,' said Bartholomew. 'I am sure your Bishop will have clerks who will be able to furnish you with a good deal of information if you were to ask.'

Michael stood and cracked his knuckles. 'Time for something to eat before bed,' he said. 'I may be in Ely for several days, so be careful. I will warn de Wetherset of Tulyet's threat to you. You can talk to Froissart's family, or Janetta of Lincoln, if they deign to appear. Otherwise, do nothing until I return with orders from the Bishop.'

Bartholomew watched him amble across the courtyard to the kitchen. He heard an angry screech as he was evidently caught raiding by Agatha, and then the College was silent. Only the richest fellows and students of Michaelhouse could afford to buy candles in the summer, and so once the sun had set and the light became too poor for reading, most scholars usually slept or talked. Here and there groups of students sat or stood chatting in the dark, and the sound of raised voices from the conclave indicated that the Franciscans were engaged in one of their endless debates about the nature of heresy.

One of the groups outside comprised Gray, Bulbeck, and Deynman, and Bartholomew smiled as he heard Bulbeck, in exasperated tones, repeating the essence of Bartholomew's lecture on Dioscorides. Deynman mumbled outrageous answers to Bulbeck's testing questions, which made Gray laugh. The light was fading fast, and Bartholomew turned to go to his own room before it became too dark to see what he was doing. He undressed and lay on the hard bed, kicking off the rough woollen blanket because the night was humid.

He closed his eyes and then opened them again as he heard a sound outside the open shutters of his window. A lamp was shining through it, but it was the monstrous shape on the far wall that made him start from the bed with a cry of horror. A great horned head was silhouetted there: the head of a goat. He swallowed hard and crept to the window, trying not to look at the foul shadow on the wall as it swayed back and forth.

He stared in disbelief at the sight of Michael and Cynric kneeling on the ground shaking with suppressed mirth. Michael held a lamp, while Cynric made figures on the wall with his hands. They saw Bartholomew and stood up, roaring with laughter.

'Agatha showed us how to do it,' Michael said, gasping for breath. 'Oh, Matt! You should see your face!'

'Agatha told you to do that to me?' said Bartholomew incredulously.

'Oh, lord, no!' said Michael. 'She would rip our heads off if she thought we had dared to play a practical joke on her favourite Fellow. She has a fire lit to cook the potage for tomorrow's breakfast, and she was showing Cynric how to make the shapes of different animals with his hands. She showed him a goat, and I could not resist the temptation to try it on you,' he said.

Cynric grinned. 'It worked wonderfully, eh lad?' he said, beginning to laugh again.

Bartholomew leaned his elbows on the window-sill, and shook his head at them, beginning to see the humour of it, despite his still-pounding heart. 'That was a rotten thing to do,' he said, but without rancour. 'Now I will never get to sleep.'

Still chuckling, Cynric took the lamp back to the kitchen, watched curiously by Bartholomew's students still talking in the courtyard. Michael reached through the window and punched Bartholomew playfully before returning to his own room on the floor above. Bartholomew could hear his heavy footsteps moving about, and his voice as he related his prank to his two Benedictine room-mates. He heard them laugh and smiled despite himself. He would think of some way to pay Michael back, and Cynric too. He went to lie back down on his bed, and after a moment got up and closed the shutters, disregarding the stuffiness. Satisfied, he felt himself sliding off into sleep. At the fringes of his mind, he was aware that the meeting of the coven at St John Zachary was planned for that night and that he had intended to ask Stanmore about it. But it was late, Bartholomew's day had been a long and trying one, and he was already falling into a deep sleep.

CHAPTER 6

AFTER THE FRENZIED EVENTS OF THE LAST THREE DAYS, Bartholomew was grateful for a respite while Michael went to Ely. He drilled his students relentlessly, and when at noon on Friday the College bell chimed to indicate the end of lectures for the day, his students heaved a corporate sigh of relief and prepared to spend the rest of the day recuperating from the shock of being made to work so hard.

The porter had a message asking him to visit the miller at Newnham village half a mile away. He had a hasty meal of thin barley soup flavoured with bacon rinds and some unripe pears, and set off. He walked upstream along the river path, muddy and slippery from the rain of the day before. The river itself ran fast and grey-brown, and Bartholomew saw a drowned sheep that had obviously strayed too close to the edge and fallen in. He crossed the river at Small Bridges Street, paying a fee of one penny to use the two wooden bridges that spanned different branches of the meandering river. Once out of the town, peace prevailed. Larks twittered in the huge sky above him, and fields, neatly divided into ribbons, were rich with oats and barley. A man emerged from where he had been tending one field, and wielded a hoe at Bartholomew. Such was the shortage of crops that any farmer would need to guard his property well if he wished to feed his family or grow rich on the proceeds.

The miller and his family sat outside the mill sharing some baked fish. The three children – of ten – who had survived the plague looked thin and hungry, while their father's mill stood silent. There were three mills in Cambridge, and the one at Newnham was by far the smallest and the most isolated. Business was poor for all of them, for the lack of crops meant that there was little for mills to grind. Bartholomew had seen the miller at the Fair offering ridiculously low prices for his labour.

The family saw him coming and waved him over. The miller's wife held a child on her lap. Bartholomew, careful not to waken him, saw painfully thin limbs and a distended stomach that was full of nothing. The miller's wife said her milk had dried up, and the baby was unable to eat fish. She wanted him to bleed the baby, thinking that an excess of black bile might be making him sick from the fish, and offered him her last three pennies to do so.

Why people believed bleeding would cure so much was beyond Bartholomew's understanding. He sent one of the older children to buy bread and milk from a nearby farmer with the three pennies, and showed the mother how to feed the baby milk sops in small amounts so as not to make him sick. But what would happen when the bread and milk ran out next time? And what about the rest of the family, looking at the milk sops with envious eyes? Bartholomew vowed he would never complain about College bread again.

Since it was a pleasant evening for a walk, and he was not expected back at Michaelhouse, he decided to visit his sister in Trumpington. He walked slowly, enjoying the warmth of the sun and the fresh, clean air of the countryside. Birds flitted from tree to tree, and at one point a deer trotted from the undergrowth across the path. Bartholomew stood still and watched as it nibbled delicately at a patch of grass. It suddenly became aware of him and stared intently until, unconcerned, it took a final mouthful of grass and disappeared unhurriedly into the dark scrub to the side of the path.

As Bartholomew strolled through the gates to Edith's house, she came running to meet him, delighted at his unexpected visit. He followed her into the kitchen and sat at the great oak table while she fetched him cool ale and freshly baked pastries, which made him think guiltily of the miller's child. Oswald Stanmore heard his wife's greetings from where he had been working in the solar, and came to join them. The kitchen was full of delicious smells, as meats roasted on spits in the fireplace. Edith had been picking rhubarb, and great mounds of it sat at one end of the kitchen table ready to be bottled.

Edith, with many interludes for helpless laughter, told him about how the ploughman's geese had escaped and trapped the rector in his church for an entire afternoon. He told her about Michael's prank the night before, and she laughed until the tears rolled down her face.

'Oh, Matt! To think you were frightened by such a trick! I used to make those shadows for you when you were a boy. Do you not remember?'

Bartholomew had not told her about finding the goat mask in the coffin with the murdered woman, and was sure that she would not have been so dismissive of his gullibility had she known. She ruffled his hair as she had done when he was young and went to tend to her rhubarb, still smiling.

He played a game of chess with Stanmore, which Stanmore won easily because Bartholomew became impatient and failed to concentrate, and then he strummed Edith's lute in the solar until the daylight began to fade. Stanmore offered to walk part of the way back with him, and they set off as the shadows lay long and dark across the Cambridge road, and the last red glow of the sun disappeared beyond the horizon.

'Any news of who killed Will?' asked Bartholomew.

Stanmore shook his head angrily. 'Nothing! And Tulyet is worse than useless. I discovered that the attack was being discussed by men in the King's Head and, like a good citizen, I passed my information to Tulyet, who has refused to investigate.'

'Refused?' said Bartholomew. 'Or merely did not initiate enquiries.'

Stanmore shrugged. 'Pedant,' he said. 'He said he would consider the information, but my man in the King's Head said there have been no soldiers asking questions. For Will's sake, I regret bitterly sending the silk to London for dyeing. Now I have little choice but to use de Belem. Since his wife died of the plague, his work has become shoddy.'

'I suppose lately Master de Belem has had other things to worry about,' said Bartholomew.

'Has anything further been discovered about the killer of his daughter?' asked Stanmore, picking up a stone and tossing it at a tree stump that rose out of a boggy meadow at the side of the road.

Bartholomew told him about the dead woman in the grave of Nicholas of York, and that she had been wearing a mask depicting the head of a goat.

Stanmore looked appalled, and shook his head slowly. 'Since the Death ravaged the land, many have turned from God,' he said. 'Who knows what evil stalks the land!'

'I wish I knew why Frances was killed at Michaelhouse,' said Bartholomew.

'Did you follow up on that information I gave you about the guilds?'

'I am not sure I know where to begin,' said Bartholomew. He told his brother-in-law what he had overheard Harling telling de Wetherset. Stanmore frowned and pulled at his neat grey beard thoughtfully.

'I asked one of my men to make enquiries about which two covens were using the decommissioned churches that Brother Alban told you about. They are the Guild of Purification, which uses St John Zachary, and the Guild of the Coming, which uses All Saints'. "Purification" apparently means purification from God, rather than by Him, while the "Coming" refers to the coming of Lucifer, not the Messiah. The Guild of Purification met last night at St John Zachary's Church, as you heard Harling say it would, and my man posted a guard outside. As the guild members came out of the church, he saw each one make the sign of a small circle on the ground with their forefingers.'

'A circle?' said Bartholomew, staring at Stanmore and thinking of the feet of the dead girls.

Stanmore nodded. 'So, it does mean something to you. My man could not be absolutely certain because he, rather sensibly, had placed himself a good distance away. He also said that people wore black hoods, and did not linger to be recognised. What does the circle mean to you?'

Bartholomew rubbed a hand through his hair. 'A small circle was drawn on the sole of the foot of three of the dead women I saw. I do not know if Tulyet saw the marks or not. He reacted oddly when I tried to ask him whether there was a similar mark on the foot of the first victim.'

'What do you mean, "acted oddly"?'

'He became angry and then dismissive. It was after I mentioned the possibility of all the victims bearing a similar mark that he threatened to arrest me.'

'Arrest you?' said Stanmore, horrified. 'Be careful, Matt! Even though Richard Tulyet the elder is no longer Mayor, he is still an influential man. If you anger the son, you will also anger the father.'

'Do you think the older Tulyet is in a guild other than the Guild of the Annunciation?' asked Bartholomew.

'He is certainly in his trade guild, the Tailors,' answered Stanmore. 'I suppose it is possible that he could also be in one of these covens, although he would be hard pushed if ever his loyalty to one were tested over the others.'

'I think there could be some connection between the dead women and the Tulyets,' said Bartholomew, 'based on the Sheriff's reaction to me, and the fact that he seems to be doing nothing to investigate their deaths.'

Stanmore frowned. 'If there were, it would have to be through one of these covens. The Guild of the Coming probably has the edge over the Guild of Purification in terms of power. I suspect that some highly influential person might be a member of the Coming. It is possible that person could be one of the Tulyet clan.'

Bartholomew sighed. It was all becoming very complicated.

Stanmore slapped him on the back. 'I will put a man on it and see what I can find out for you.'

Bartholomew gave him a brief smile. 'Thank you. How many people were there at this coven at St John Zachary?' he asked.

'My man counted five people, but I suspect there are more members than this.'

'Do you know the name of anyone who is in one of these covens?'

Stanmore screwed up his face and looked away. 'Not for certain,' he said.

'Who?' persisted Bartholomew, studying Stanmore closely.

'I do not know for certain,' Stanmore repeated. He stared back at Bartholomew. 'But I think de Belem might be a member of the Guild of the Purification.'

'De Belem?' said Bartholomew incredulously. 'Reginald de Belem?'

Stanmore nodded, and grabbed Bartholomew by his tabard. 'I am not certain, so please be careful how you use that information. Sir Reginald has been through enough with the death of his daughter, and I would not want to be the cause of further grief should I be mistaken.'

Bartholomew looked away and stared down the darkening path, his mind working fast. If there was rivalry between the two covens as Stanmore suggested, did this mean that someone in the Guild of the Coming was killing the women and leaving the secret sign of the rival coven on the bodies as some kind of insult? Or was it simply the work of the Guild of Purification? He thought about the incident in the orchard where at least three people had trespassed in Michaelhouse. Was an entire guild involved? Was he taking on dozens of people in this business? Was de Belem's daughter killed by the Guild of the Coming and marked as a warning to him, or had she been murdered by his own guild as punishment for some perceived misdemeanour?

He chewed absently on a stalk of grass. The woman in Nicholas's tomb had been wearing the goat mask. Was a goat the symbol of the Guild of the Coming? He knew goats were associated with the Devil, as attested by the painting in the church. Was the woman killed by the Guild of the Coming and buried with a goat mask to claim the murder as their work? It seemed rather extreme. And how was Nicholas of York involved? Bartholomew thought about de Belem's insistence that he investigate Frances's murder. Did he suspect that Tulyet might be involved with the Guild of the Coming, his rival guild, and would therefore do nothing to help? And what of the third guild, the Guild of the Holy Trinity, which de Wetherset had told him about, and of which Nicholas was a member? Were they involved in this? Were they using the sacred symbol of one of the covens so that it would be blamed for the murders?

'Matt.' Stanmore's voice cut across his thoughts. 'I do not

like any of this, and I do not like the idea of you becoming involved in the doings of evil men. You must take care!'

Bartholomew turned to Stanmore and seized his arm. 'Do not bring Edith into the town until all this is over.'

'You can have no fear on that score,' said Stanmore fervently. 'And tomorrow I will bring my brother's widow and her children here, too. That will keep her safe and Edith busy.'

Bartholomew left Stanmore and began to walk home alone. He should not have spent so much time talking, for it was now dark and he began to feel uneasy. Walking along the Trumpington road to Cambridge alone in the dark was foolish in the extreme, especially carrying his medical bag. Anyone who did not know him would assume it was full of valuables, or even food, and he would be dead before they realised it contained little of worth to anyone but another physician. And perhaps not even then, he thought wryly, wondering how many physicians would be remotely interested in the surgical instruments he carried, or in some of the more exotic of his salves and potions.

He froze as something darted across his path, and forced himself to relax when he saw it was only a deer, perhaps even the same one that he had admired that afternoon. Somewhere behind him, a twig snapped, and he spun round scanning the pathway, but he saw only an owl swooping silently towards a frantically running rodent. He thought of how he had waited to join a large group of people before walking from the Fair into Cambridge at dusk, and now here he was, on a far more remote road, in the dark and totally alone. Something scrabbled in the bushes at the side of the road, and Bartholomew glimpsed two luminous eyes watching him balefully before slinking off into the undergrowth. A feral cat. He had had no idea there was so much wildlife on the Trumpington road at night which could frighten him out of his wits.

Swallowing hard, he took a few steps forward, wondering whether it would be better to go back to Stanmore and Edith for the night. Distantly, he heard the sound of hoof beats, no casual travellers, but moving quickly along the track. Were they outlaws bent on earning a quick fortune by raiding travellers on the road? Uneasily, he left the path to hide among the bushes until they passed.

The hoof beats grew nearer, coming from the Trumpington side. He pressed back further, feeling cold water from a boggy puddle seep into his shoes. Suddenly the horses were on him, and Bartholomew felt faint with relief as he recognised the ugly piebald war-horse that belonged to Stanmore. He left his hiding place and hailed him.

'Matt!' said Stanmore, looking as relieved as Bartholomew felt. 'It was only when I was home that I realised how dangerous it was for you to walk home alone. A man was almost killed here only last week.'

Bartholomew climbed clumsily onto the spare horse Stanmore had brought, still trying to quell his jangling nerves.

'Thank you,' he said. 'I was beginning to become nervous.'

'Looks scared half to death to me,' Bartholomew heard Stanmore's steward mutter, and one or two of the men with him laughed.

'We should all be cautious,' said Stanmore. 'Especially after what happened to Will and my cart,' he added, with a look that silenced all humour. 'We live in dangerous times,' Stanmore continued, 'when a man cannot walk the roads alone. People say the Death is over, and that it has passed us by. But perhaps the wrath of God is still with us in a different way: people falling into witchcraft, masterless bandits roaming the highways, starvation and poverty increasing, the strong taking from the weak because there is no one to stop them, prostitutes brazenly flaunting their wares, murders in the town and the Sheriff doing nothing . . .'

'We should be on our way, sir,' said Stanmore's steward politely.

Stanmore, his mouth still open to continue his diatribe, relented. 'Of course. Hugh and Ned will ride with you, Matt, and will spend the night in Milne Street. The rest of you, home with me.'

Bartholomew parted from Stanmore for the second time that night, and cantered towards Cambridge after Hugh and Ned. After an uneventful, but uncomfortable, ride along the rutted road, he arrived safely back at Michaelhouse and was allowed in by the surly Walter, who clearly disapproved of the privileges of free exit and entry afforded to Bartholomew by the Master. A few minutes later, Bartholomew saw the porter leave his post and slip across to Alcote's room to inform him that he had been late.

He crept up to Michael's room to see if he had returned from Ely but the monk's bed was still empty. His room-mates slumbered on and Bartholomew went to his own bed and fell asleep almost immediately.

He was wakened after what seemed to be only a few moments by someone roughly shaking his shoulder. He opened his eyes and blinked as he saw Michael hanging over him, holding a candle. He winced as hot wax fell on his arm, and pushed Michael away.

'What is the matter?' he said drowsily. 'What has happened?'

'I thought we were friends,' Michael hissed in the darkness. Bartholomew raised himself on one elbow, and looked at Michael in astonishment. The fat monk was agitated, and Bartholomew flinched a second time as Michael's shaking hands deposited more hot wax on his bare skin.

'Whatever is the matter with you?' he said, pushing Michael firmly away a second time and sitting up.

'I do not consider what you did was funny,' Michael said, his voice rising in anger.

'Shhh. You will wake the whole College. What are you talking about?'

Bartholomew jumped as Michael dropped something on his bed, and kicked it off in distaste.

'You left that in my bed,' said Michael in quiet fury. 'That is a far cry from shadows on the wall.'

Light began to dawn in Bartholomew's confused mind as he stared down at the severed head of a young goat that now lay on the floor. 'You found this in your bed?' he said, looking up at the furious monk.

'You put it there as revenge for my trick with the shadows,' stated Michael, his voice hard and accusing.

Bartholomew looked back down at the head. It had probably been taken from one of the butchers' stalls in Petty Cury.

Bartholomew knew that Agatha often bought heads cheaply from butchers to boil up for soups and broths. The head in itself was not an object for disgust; but the fact that it had been dumped on Michael while he slept gave it a sinister connotation.

'When did you get back?' he asked Michael.

'About an hour ago. You were already fast asleep, or at least pretending to be, when I called out to you. That thing was not in my bed when I went to sleep, so you must have sneaked upstairs and put it on top of me while I slept. The smell woke me.' Michael still glowered at him, the light flickering eerily in the room as the hand that held the candle shook.

Bartholomew glanced up at Michael and saw the hurt in his eyes. He caught his breath as the implications dawned on him. Since the College was locked and guarded, who but a Michaelhouse scholar could have put it there? 'Oh, no! Please do not tell me that the College is going to become mixed up in all this,' he groaned.

'Someone from the College did put it there,' said Michael angrily. 'You.'

'You should know me better than that, Brother,' said Bartholomew. 'Dead animals can carry disease. Do you honestly believe I would put something in your bed that might make you ill?'

'Are you telling me you did not do it?' said Michael, sinking down on Bartholomew's bed, his anger evaporating like a puff of smoke.

'Of course I did not,' said Bartholomew firmly. 'And I doubt that Cynric would either, before you think to blame him. I suspect that this bearer of gifts had something far more sinister in mind than practical jokes.'

Michael shuddered. 'So someone came into my room while I slept and put that thing on me?' he asked, his anger now horror.

Bartholomew nodded. 'So it would seem,' he said. 'I saw Walter slope off to Alcote's room to tell him I had returned late. I suppose if he did the same when you returned, it is possible that someone entered the College while he was away, and that the culprit need not necessarily be a member of College.'

'But how would whoever it was know which was my room?' asked Michael.

'Perhaps it was intended for someone else,' said Bartholomew. 'Perhaps there are secret members of those covens in Michaelhouse.'

He thought back to the conversation he had had with Stanmore earlier, and his assumption that while the circle was the symbol of the Guild of Purification, a goat might be the sign of the Guild of the Coming. He told Michael, and they regarded each other sombrely as they considered the possibilities.

'But what does it mean?' asked Michael, white-faced.

'Was there a note or a message with it?' Bartholomew asked.

Michael shrugged helplessly. 'Just the head. Do you think the Guild of the Coming is warning me to stay away from them?'

'It must be,' said Bartholomew, rubbing his chin thoughtfully. 'And their message is clear. If they can leave a dead animal on you in your own College in the middle of the night, they can harm you in other ways.' He stood and looked down at Michael. 'Perhaps they chose you and not me because it is you who went to see the Bishop, and you who is reading Nicholas's book.'

'The book!' exclaimed Michael, snapping his fingers. 'There must be something in the book! But the only person who knows I am reading it, other than you, is de Wetherset.'

He met Bartholomew's eyes, and they exchanged a look of horror.

'Surely not!' breathed Michael.

'Does this book record anything about these unholy guilds?' asked Bartholomew, refusing to dismiss too glibly the possibility that de Wetherset might be involved.

Michael shook his head. 'There is very little incriminating in any of it. I do not understand why de Wetherset was so relieved to discover it had not been stolen.'

'Unless he has not given all of it to you to read,' said Bartholomew.

Michael's green eyes were huge as he considered Bartholomew's words. 'Oh, lord, Matt! What have we been dragged into? You are right, of course. What I have read is nothing: de Wetherset had no reason to be concerned about the documents he has given me to read. He has only given me the parts he considers harmless! What a fool I have been! Do you think he is a member of a coven? Do you think he told them what I was doing?'

Bartholomew shook his head. 'If he knows you have access to only those parts of the book he considers innocuous, there is no reason for him to warn you away with dead animals. No, Brother. The warning is either from someone who has seen you at the church and who has guessed what you are reading, or it is unrelated to the book at all. I think de Wetherset has been less than honest with us, but I do not see why he would need to send you the head.'

Michael, appalled, stared at the head on the floor. 'I wish it had been you who left that thing on me after all,' he said fervently. 'If anyone had to dump dead animals on me in the night, I would rather it were you than anyone else! A practical joke, however vile, would be preferable to this sinister business.'

Bartholomew started to laugh and poked the monk with his elbow. 'Go back to bed,' he said. 'I will get rid of this thing. We can do no more tonight, and you should rest.'

Michael stood with a sigh. 'I am sorry, Matt,' he said. 'I was hasty in my accusation. Had I stopped to consider, I would have known that you, of all people, would do nothing that might endanger my health.' He left and went back to his own room while Bartholomew looked for a cloth in which to put the animal's head. He wrapped it up, and slipped out along the side of the north wing to the porch door. He unlatched it and went into the darkened building, first glancing across the courtyard to see if Walter were watching, but could see no moving shadows in the Porter's Lodge.

He walked through the kitchen to the gardens at the back. He tossed his grisly bundle, still in its cloth, onto the refuse fires that smouldered continuously behind the kitchen, and retraced his steps. He felt angry at Walter for being more interested in his half-pennies from Alcote for tale-telling than in doing his job of watching the College. He walked quickly around the courtyard to the small stone building that served as the Porter's Lodge, intending to berate him for being negligent in his duties.

He pushed open the door and called out. There was no

reply. Perhaps Walter was off checking some other part of the College. The small room where the porters usually sat was empty. Curious, Bartholomew went through to the back room where they ate their meals, relaxed and, occasionally, slept. Walter was sprawled out on the straw pallet that served as a makeshift bed. Bartholomew was about to shout at him, to wake him with the fright he deserved, when he saw the man's face was unusually white in the light from the open window.

Bartholomew knelt by him and felt a cold and clammy forehead. He put a hand against Walter's neck and felt the slow life beat. Walter moaned softly, and murmured something incomprehensible. On the table, Bartholomew saw the remains of a large pie, and some of it was on the floor. Walter had evidently been eating it when he was stricken.

'Poisoned!' muttered Bartholomew into the darkness. He grabbed Walter by the shoulders and hoisted him onto his knees, forcing fingers down his throat. Walter gagged painfully, and the remains of the pie came up. He began to cry softly. Bartholomew made him sick a second time. The porter slipped sideways and keeled onto the floor.

Bartholomew left him and raced to the room that Gray shared with Bulbeck and Deynman, snatching the startled student out of bed by his shirt collar.

'Fetch me some raw eggs mixed with vinegar and ground mustard,' he said urgently. 'As fast as you can!'

Gray scuttled off towards the kitchens, unquestioning, while Deynman and Bulbeck scrambled from their beds and followed Bartholomew. Walter lay where he had fallen, and Bartholomew heaved him into a sitting position, helped by Bulbeck, while Deynman watched with his mouth agape. Bulbeck kindled a lamp, while Bartholomew heaved the porter onto his feet and tried to force him to stand.

'What is wrong with him?' said Bulbeck, staring in shock at the ghastly white face of the porter as the room flared into light from the lamp.

'Poison,' said Bartholomew. 'We must force him to walk. If he loses consciousness he might die. Help me to hold him up.'

'But who poisoned him?' said Deynman, staring with wide eyes at Walter.

Bartholomew began gently slapping Walter's face. The porter looked at him blearily before his eyes began to close.

'Walter! Wake up!' Bartholomew shouted.

At that moment, Gray appeared with a large bowl of eggs and vinegar.

'I did not know how much mustard you wanted,' he said, 'so I brought it all.'

Bartholomew grabbed the small bottle and emptied the entire contents into the slippery egg-mixture. Gray and Bulbeck exchanged a look of disgust. Bartholomew shook Walter until his eyes opened and forced him to drink some. He was immediately sick again, sinking onto his knees. Remorselessly, Bartholomew forced more of the repulsive liquid down his throat until the entire bowl had been swallowed and regurgitated. Walter began to complain.

'No more!' he whispered. 'My stomach hurts, Doctor. Leave me be.'

Bartholomew grabbed his arm and dragged him out of the door. 'Walk with me,' he said. Bulbeck ran to grab Walter's other arm, and they began to march him around the courtyard.

'Will he die?' asked Bulbeck fearfully.

Bartholomew shook his head. 'I think most of the poison must be out of his stomach. We need to keep him awake for several hours, though, just to make sure.'

'I never sleep on duty,' muttered Walter thickly.

Bartholomew smiled. The porter was regaining his faculties. Bartholomew had arrived just in time. The poison he suspected had been used was a slow-acting one that was virtually tasteless, and could easily be concealed in food or drink. It brought on a slow unconsciousness, and Walter probably just felt pleasantly drowsy, until he fell into the sleep that might have been his last.

'Who did this to him?' asked Bulbeck. Bartholomew had been wondering the same thing. It stood to reason it was the same person who had put the kid's head on Michael's bed. The noise they were making began to wake the other scholars, and soon the courtyard was full of curious and sleepy students and Fellows. The Master arrived breathlessly, followed by Alcote, who exclaimed in horror when he saw the state of his informant.

Bartholomew quickly explained what had happened, and instructed Gray and Bulbeck to walk Walter around the courtyard until he could manage on his own. The students hurried to do his bidding, proud to be the centre of attention as the other students clustered round them with questions.

Kenyngham watched them with his lips pursed. 'Where are the beadles? They are supposed to be watching the gates.'

'They are watching the back gate, Master,' said Alcote. 'The front gate is locked after dark, and with a porter on duty is always secure. It is the back gate that is vulnerable.'

'Cynric.' Kenyngham looked around for the small Welshman whom he knew would not be far away. 'Find out where the beadles are, and then come back to me. Matthew? Have you any idea what prompted all this?'

Bartholomew told him about Michael finding the goat's head on his bed, while the other Fellows exclaimed in horror. Michael paled as he considered the implications of Walter's poisoning – that someone had wanted him to receive the goat's head sufficiently to kill for it.

Bartholomew went to examine Walter again, and came back satisfied that he was recovering. The Fellows stood in a small group around Kenyngham, confused and fearful. Father William muttered prayers to himself, while Father Aidan and Hesselwell looked on in shock.

Kenyngham ordered the students back to their rooms and Cynric returned from the back gate with Jonstan.

'I saw and heard nothing!' said Jonstan, appalled. 'I have been patrolling the lane and keeping a permanent watch on the back gate since dusk. We saw nothing!'

'Do not worry, Master Jonstan,' said Kenyngham, seeing the alarm in the jovial Proctor's face. 'You did your best. I suspect we are dealing with clever and committed people.'

'But I am committed,' said Jonstan, stung. 'I have been overseeing my men and ensuring that the lane is checked constantly since dark. I saw Doctor Bartholomew and Brother Michael return, and I am willing to wager that they did not see me!'

The surprise on Bartholomew and Michael's faces told the watching Fellows that Jonstan's claims were true.

'I set up a regular patrol once the night became quiet,' Jonstan continued.

'How regular?' asked Bartholomew.

'Every quarter of an hour,' said Jonstan, his eyes still wide with shock.

'Then that is probably why you did not see the intruder,' said Bartholomew. 'If you were working to an established pattern, it would not take much to work it out and slip into the College when you were furthest away.'

Jonstan's face fell. Kenyngham rubbed at his eyes wearily. 'This cannot go on,' he said. 'I will not have the lives of College members threatened, and poisoners breaking in. Come, Master Jonstan. We must discuss what more can be done.'

He held out his arm to indicate that Jonstan was to precede him to his room.

'Poor man,' said Hesselwell, watching the dejected Jonstan leave. 'He thought he was being rigorous by establishing a regular pattern in his checks, while all the time he was achieving quite the reverse.'

Bartholomew nodded absently. He watched Gray and Bulbeck with Walter, although the porter was now able to walk on his own. Bartholomew was pleased at his students' diligence, and knew they would remain with Walter until he gave them leave to stop.

'Who is doing this?' asked Aidan, his prominent front teeth gleaming in the candle-light. 'Why would anyone mean Michaelhouse harm?'

'I cannot imagine,' said Hesselwell. 'I wondered whether it might be a commoner, or perhaps one of the students, but that is unlikely. It must be an outsider.'

'What makes you so sure?' asked Bartholomew, surprised at Hesselwell's quick deduction.

'Because everyone in College knows that Walter sleeps all night when he should be on duty, and would know there would be no need to use poison in order to sneak unseen into the building.'

'But the gate is locked and barred,' said Bartholomew, gesturing to where the huge oak plank was firmly in place. 'Even if Walter were asleep, it would be difficult to break in.'

'There are places where the wall is easily breached, as you know very well, Bartholomew,' said Hesselwell. 'And before you ask me how I know, I occasionally have problems sleeping, and sometimes walk in the orchard at night. I have seen students using it, and I imagine you have used it yourself while out on your nocturnal ramblings.'

His tone was unpleasant, and Bartholomew resented the accusation in his voice. He had only ever climbed across the wall once, and would not need to do so again now he had the Master's permission to be out to visit patients. Alcote looked on with malicious enjoyment.

'And how would this intruder present Walter with the poison and be sure he took it?' Bartholomew demanded. 'Would you eat something that appeared miraculously in the middle of the night?'

Hesselwell smiled smugly. 'I would not. But Walter might. He is not intelligent, and his greed might well get the better of his suspicion.'

Bartholomew realised that Hesselwell was right, although it galled him to admit it. It did seem more likely that the person who poisoned Walter and left the grisly warning for Michael was from outside Michaelhouse, for exactly the reason Hesselwell suggested: that everyone inside knew Walter slept, and that it would not be necessary to kill him to move about the College unnoticed.

'Where is Deynman?' said Bartholomew suddenly, looking around him.

Gray and Bulbeck looked round briefly, and shrugged, more interested in Walter than in Deynman's absence. When Bartholomew had hauled Walter out into the yard, Deynman had stayed in the porters' lodge. Bartholomew began to walk across to the lodge, and then broke into a run. He shot into the small room, staggering as he slipped in the mess on the floor, and gazed at Deynman who was kneeling in front of the table, chopping the remains of the pie into ever smaller pieces. He grinned cheerfully at Bartholomew.

'I am looking for the poison,' he said.

Bartholomew leaned against the door in relief at seeing Deynman unharmed. He had been afraid that Deynman might have eaten the pie to see whether it had been poisoned. His eye was caught by a goblet on the table. He picked it up and looked at it before taking a cautious sip. It was slightly bitter and there was a grainy residue at the bottom of the vessel. He spat it out and looked at the bottle. It was not a kind that was kept in College. He inspected the chopped remains of Walter's pie: it was covered with some of Agatha's hard, heavy pastry and had, without doubt, been made in Michaelhouse.

'The poison was in the wine, Robert,' he said, and explained why. Deynman looked at the mess he had made, and his face fell as he realised that his initiative had failed.

Bartholomew relented at Deynman's crestfallen attitude. 'I will show you how to test for certain poisons,' he said, trying not to sound weary. 'But you are unlikely to find any of them by chopping something into tiny pieces. Go and help Sam and Thomas. I am trusting you to make sure that tonight Walter rests, but does not sleep. If he loses consciousness, fetch me immediately.'

Deynman's face brightened at being given such responsibility, and he scampered off to do as he was told.

'Is that wise?' asked Michael, looming in the doorway and watching him go. 'The boy is a half-wit.'

'Oh, hardly that,' said Bartholomew. 'He tries hard. I will give the others the same instructions before I retire. It is about time they had some practical training. With any luck it might put them off. They might choose a monkish vocation instead.'

'Heaven forbid!' said Michael. He became serious. 'Did you learn anything from Walter? Who poisoned him and when?'

Bartholomew rubbed a hand through his hair. Now the initial excitement had worn off, he felt exhausted. 'Walter had a close call. Whoever left that head was determined that you would get it.'

Michael shuddered. 'We should talk to Walter,' he said.

Out in the yard, Walter had recovered to the point of grumpiness. He glared at Bartholomew. 'My throat hurts,' he said aggressively, 'and I can still taste mustard.'

Bartholomew raised his eyebrows. 'Would you like some of that wine you were drinking in the lodge, to wash away the taste?'

Walter spat. 'I thought it had an odd taste about it. I should have known that no one gives gifts for nothing.'

'Who gave it to you?' asked Michael.

'The Master,' said Walter.

Michael and Bartholomew exchanged glances. 'How do you know it was from the Master?' asked Bartholomew. 'Did he give it to you in person?'

'He left it for me, and I knew it was from him, because who but the Master has fine wines to give away? You two do not,' he added rudely. 'Why should I question the Master when he was offering good wine?' He paused for a moment in thought. 'I should have done, though.'

'You should indeed,' said Michael.

Deynman hauled Walter away for another turn around the yard, and Bartholomew watched him thoughtfully. 'So, because it seemed a good wine, Walter assumed it was from the Master,' he said.

'Can we be sure it was not?' Michael asked.

Bartholomew shrugged. 'I doubt Kenyngham would leave poisoned wine for Walter when he would be such an obvious culprit,' he said. 'And anyway, Hesselwell is right. The poisoner must be an outsider, because Kenyngham would know Walter sleeps most of the night.'

They talked for a while longer, and went back to their beds. Bartholomew repeated his instructions that the students should wake him immediately if Walter went to sleep or became ill, and left the surly porter in their less than tender, but hawklike, care. He smiled, remembering that Walter had landed Gray in trouble two weeks ago when he had stayed out all night and Walter had informed Alcote. Now the student could have his revenge, and Walter would find himself walked off his feet by the morning.

As Bartholomew lay on his bed to sleep, questions tumbled endlessly through his tired brain. Who had left the goat for Michael? What was in the book that was so incriminating that the Chancellor had censored it? How were the guilds connected to the deaths of the friar and Froissart? Who had killed them, and was the killer also the murderer of the women? Was Frances de Belem killed because of her father's involvement with the Guild of Purification? He turned the questions over and over, searching for a common theme, but could think of nothing except the mysterious covens.

He lay on his bed, watching the clouds drift across the night sky through the open window shutters. Eventually he got up and closed them securely. He locked the door, too, something he had not felt obliged to do in Michaelhouse for a long time, and, when the bell chimed for Prime the following morning, he wondered whether he had slept at all.

Walter was back to his miserable self by dawn, complaining bitterly that his throat and stomach hurt from the enforced vomiting, and that his feet were sore from walking all night. Convinced that he was suffering no long-term ill-effects from his narrow escape, Bartholomew ordered that he rest, and he then returned to his teaching.

His students, having seen medical practice at work in their own College the night before, were full of questions, and Deynman proudly gave the class a description, reasonably accurate, of the treatment for a person with suspected poisoning. Bartholomew then described treatments for different kinds of poisons, and Deynman's face fell when he realised that, yet again, medicine was more complex that he had believed. Brother Boniface was sullen and uncooperative, refusing to answer questions, and Bartholomew wondered what was brewing behind the Franciscan's resentful eyes.

After the main meal, Bartholomew gave Gray and Bulbeck a mock disputation, and was pleased with their progress. He took them with him to treat Brother Alban's elbow. The old monk was delighted to have an audience of three whom he could regale with his gossip. He began talking about the increase in witchcraft in the town.

'More and more of the common people are flocking to evil ways,' he crowed gleefully.

'Oh, not you too,' said Gray disrespectfully. 'We have to listen to Boniface droning on about heresy and witchcraft all day.'

Bulbeck nodded in agreement. 'He sees heresy in everything,' he said. 'He thinks Doctor Bartholomew is a heretic for saving Walter last night. He says God called him and Doctor Bartholomew snatched him back.'

So that was it, thought Bartholomew. He was sure Walter would not agree with Brother Boniface's opinion, and wondered how Boniface proposed to be a physician with these odd ideas rattling around in his head.

Alban ignored them and chattered about the desecration of several churches in the town after one of the guild meetings two nights ago. He crossed himself frequently in horror, but his gleaming eyes made it obvious that he found the whole thing of great interest, and was eagerly waiting to hear what happened next.

'Have you found the killer of the whores yet?' he asked Bartholomew, beady black eyes glittering with malicious delight.

'They were not all whores,' said Bartholomew patiently, concentrating on his task.

'They were,' said Alban firmly. 'And you cannot try to defend that de Belem girl. She was worse than the rest.'

Bartholomew looked at him, startled, and seeing the pleasure in the old man's face at having surprised him, he shook his head and continued with his treatment. Alban really was a nasty old man, he thought, for taking such delight in the downfall of others.

'She was out in the dark seeing her man,' Alban continued. 'After her husband died in the Death, her father could not control her lust.'

'Who was her man?' asked Gray, interested.

The old monk beamed at him, pleased to have secured a positive reaction at last. He tapped the side of his nose. 'A scholar,' he said. 'That is all I can say.' He sat back, his lips pursed.

'That is enough, Brother,' said Bartholomew, standing up as the treatment was done. 'No good can come of such talk, and much harm.'

' "No good and much harm", ' mimicked Alban unpleasantly, beginning to sulk. Bartholomew was relieved to escape from the old man's gossip, although he could see that Gray would have been happy to stay longer.

When his bag had been returned to him the day before, Bartholomew had emptied all the potions and powders out, and exchanged them for new ones from his store. He did not want to harm any of his patients because someone had altered the labels, or substituted one compound for another. It would not be possible to tell whether some had been tampered with, and these he had carefully burned on the refuse fires behind the kitchen. But there were tests that could be performed on the others that would tell him whether they had been changed.

He left Gray, Deynmân, and Bulbeck in his small medical store carrying out the tests while he went to St John's Hospital to see a patient with a wasting disease. He stayed for a while talking to the Canons about the increase in cases of summer ague, and then went to the home of a pardoner with a broken arm on Bridge Street.

Since he was near the Castle, he decided to try to see Sybilla. She lived in a tiny wattle and daub house on the fertile land by the river. Although the land provided the families that lived on it ample reward in terms of rich crops of vegetables, their homes were vulnerable when the river flooded. It had burst its banks only a few weeks ago in the spring rains, and Sybilla and others had been forced to flee to the higher ground near the Castle for safety.

He knocked on the rough wooden door of Sybilla's house. There was a shuffle from within and the door was opened slowly. Sybilla, her face grey with strain, peered out at him. He was shocked at her appearance. There were dark smudges under her eyes, and her hair hung in greasy ropes around her face.

'Sybilla!' he exclaimed. 'Are you ill?'

She cast a terrified glance outside before reaching out a hand and hauling him into the house, slamming the door closed behind him. The inside of the house was suffering from the same lack of care as its owner. Dirty pots were strewn about the floor, and the large bed in the corner was piled with smelly blankets. Bartholomew had been told by Michael that Sybilla was renowned for offering a clean bed and a clean body to her clients, although how the monk came by such information Bartholomew did not care to ask.

He turned to her in concern. 'What is wrong? Do you have a fever? Are you in trouble?'

She rubbed a dirty hand over her face and tears began to

roll. He saw a half-empty bottle on a table in the middle of the room, and poured some of its contents into a drinking vessel that had not been washed for days. He handed it to her and then made her sit on one of the stools. He sat opposite, and patted her hand comfortingly, feeling ineffectual.

Eventually she looked up at him, her eyes swollen and red. 'I am sorry,' she sniffed.

'What is wrong?' Bartholomew said helplessly. 'Please tell me. I may be able to help.'

She shook her head. 'You are a kind man, Doctor,' she said, 'but there is nothing you can do to help me. I am doomed.'

Bartholomew was nonplussed. 'Doomed? But why?'

Sybilla sniffed loudly and scrubbed her nose across her arm. 'I saw him,' she said, her eyes full of terror, and began to cry again. Bartholomew waited until the new wave of sobbing had subsided, and made her drink more of the cheap wine from the clay goblet.

'Tell me what happened,' he said. 'And then we will decide what to do.'

She looked at him, her eyes burning with a sudden hope in her white face. Just then, the door swung open and a woman entered. Bartholomew rose politely to his feet. She stopped dead as she saw him, and looked from him to Sybilla, her face breaking into a wide smile.

'Oh, Sybilla!' she said. 'I am glad you have decided to go back to work. I told you it would do you good. You look better already. I will leave you in peace.'

She turned to leave. Bartholomew was half embarrassed and half amused at her assumption.

'You misunderstand, Mistress,' he said. 'I am only a physician.'

The woman beamed at Sybilla. 'Better than that stonemason you had! You are doing well.'

Sybilla rose unsteadily and grasped the woman's arm. 'He is not a customer,' she said.

The other's attitude changed. 'Well, what do you want then?' she demanded of Bartholomew. 'Can you not see she is unwell?'

'Yes, I can,' said Bartholomew. 'That is why I am trying to help.'

'Help?' asked the woman suspiciously. 'How do you think you can help?'

'I cannot know that,' said Bartholomew, his patience fraying slightly, 'until I know what ails her. She was about to tell me when you came in.'

'Have you told him?' she asked Sybilla. Sybilla shook her head. 'Then do not. How do you know this is not him, or someone sent by him to find out what you know?'

Sybilla shrank back against the wall, and more tears began to roll down her face.

'If I were "him",' said Bartholomew testily, 'you have just told me that Sybilla knows something, and you have put her life in danger.'

The woman looked at him aghast. 'God's blood,' she swore in horror. She turned her gaze on Sybilla. 'What have I done?' She pulled herself together suddenly, seized a rusty knife from the table, and brandished it at Bartholomew. 'Who are you, and what do you want from us?' she demanded, steel in her voice.

Bartholomew calmly took the knife from her hands, and placed it back on the table. The woman glanced at Sybilla, stricken.

'I am no one who means Sybilla any harm,' he said calmly. 'My name is Matthew Bartholomew, and I came because I saw her running from St Botolph's churchyard the day that Isobel died.'

The woman gazed at him. 'You are the University physician?' she said.

'One of them,' he said, sitting down on the stool and gesturing for the women also to sit. Sybilla sank down gratefully, but the other woman was wary. Bartholomew studied her. She was tall, graceful, and wore a simple dress of blue that accentuated her slender figure. But it was her voice that most intrigued Bartholomew; she did not have a local accent, but one that bespoke of some education. Her mannerisms, too, suggested that she had not learned them in the town's brothels, as Sybilla had done.

Her eyes met his even gaze, and she stared back. 'Agatha told me about you,' she said.

Bartholomew was not surprised. Agatha had so many relatives and friends in the town that he could go nowhere where she had no links.

'My name is Matilde,' said the woman.

Bartholomew smiled. So that explained her accent. 'Agatha has told me about you, too,' he said.

Matilde inclined her head, accepting without false modesty that she might be an appropriate topic of conversation in the town. Agatha had told him about a year ago that one of her innumerable cousins had taken a lodger who was said to have been a lady-in-waiting to the wife of the Earl of Oxford. Rumour had it that this woman had been caught once too often entertaining men of the court in her private quarters, and had been dismissed. She had come to Cambridge to ply her trade in peace and was known locally as 'Lady Matilde' for her gentle manners and refined speech.

'Matilde is my friend,' Sybilla blurted out. 'She has been bringing me food since . . .' She trailed off miserably and gazed unseeingly at her bitten fingernails.

'Since Isobel was murdered,' finished Matilde, looking coolly at Bartholomew.

'Tell me what you saw,' said Bartholomew to Sybilla. 'Do you know the man who killed Isobel?'

Sybilla shook her head. 'I did not recognise him, but I saw him,' she whispered.

Matilde seized Bartholomew's wrist with surprising strength. 'Now you know, you carry a secret that could bring about her death,' she said, her eyes holding his.

Bartholomew gazed back, his black eyes as unwavering as her blue ones. 'I know that,' he said, firmly pulling his wrist away. 'But so might anyone else who saw her run screaming from Isobel's body on Monday.'

Matilde winced, and looked at Sybilla, who hung her head. 'I was so frightened, I do not remember what I did,' she said, beginning to weep again. Matilde took matters in hand.

'You must pull yourself together,' she said firmly to Sybilla. 'You told me no one knew that you had seen Isobel's killer.

Now it looks as though half the town might know. I think it would be best if you told the doctor what you saw. He might be able to use his influence to catch this evil monster who is killing our sisters, since the Sheriff is unwilling to act.'

Sybilla took a great shuddering breath and controlled herself with difficulty. 'I was just finishing with one of the baker's apprentices in St Botolph's churchyard, when we heard the University Proctor and his patrol going past. The apprentice was able to slip off the other way, but I had to hide until they had gone. The Proctor's men usually leave us alone unless we are with scholars, but it is always best to avoid being seen when you can. It looks bad if you are seen about too often after the curfew.

'I decided to stay where I was, hidden in the bushes. The Proctor and his beadles were discussing that fight between two hostels last month, arguing about whether it could have been stopped if they had arrived earlier. I must have fallen asleep. When I woke, the Proctor and his men had gone. I was about to climb out of the bush when I heard a noise. At first I thought it was just a rat or a bird, but then I saw him.'

She stopped and turned great fearful eyes on Bartholomew. 'Go on,' prompted Matilde.

Sybilla swallowed loudly, wiped her nose on the hem of her dress and continued. 'He was skulking about in the bushes by the road. Then I saw Isobel coming back from one of her regulars. She kept looking behind her, and I saw that horrible black cat that the Austin Canons feed. It was following her, and she kept looking round as if she could hear it. If that vile cat had not been distracting her and making her look behind, she might have seen the monster in the bushes waiting for her. I wanted to call out, but I was too frightened.'

She stopped again and Matilde took one of her hands to encourage her to finish. 'He leapt at her, and I saw the flash of his knife as he cut her throat. I think I must have fainted,' she said, and was silent for a moment. 'When I came round, Isobel was lying on the ground and the man had gone. I stayed in the bush for ages, trying to bring myself to go to her. When I did finally, she was covered in blood, and I ran. I do not remember going home. I only remember Matilde talking to me later.'

Her story finished, she wiped away fresh tears and blew her nose on a rag that Matilde handed her.

'You saw only one man?' asked Bartholomew, thinking about the three he had encountered in the orchard. 'Are you sure there were not others?'

'There was only him,' said Sybilla firmly. 'I am certain of that. Had there been others, I would have seen them. There was only him.'

'I was worried,' said Matilde. 'I usually see Sybilla at the market. I thought she might be ill, and so came to see her. She has not left her home since then. I bring her food, but she cannot stay like this for ever.'

'Did you see his face?' asked Bartholomew.

Sybilla rubbed her sore, red eyes. 'It was dark, and I was quite a distance away. I did not see his face long enough to recognise him. He was wearing a dark cloak or gown, and he had the hood pulled up. All I can say is that he was not young: he was a man and not a youth. He had no beard or moustache, and he was just average.'

'Average?' said Bartholomew, not understanding.

'Just like anyone else,' Sybilla said. 'Just average. Not tall, not short, not fat, not thin. He had two arms, he did not limp. He did not have great scars on him, or teeth that stick out. He was just normal.'

'Would you recognise him if you saw him again?' asked Bartholomew.

Sybilla swallowed. 'I do not think so, which is why I am frightened to leave the house.'

Bartholomew stood and went to look out of the hole in the wall that served as a window. The sky had clouded over and a light drizzle had begun to fall. He watched the river flowing past a few feet away, all kinds of refuse bobbing and turning slowly in the currents.

What should he do now? He was aware of the two women waiting for him to come up with an answer that would solve their problems. Sybilla was right to be frightened, he thought. If the killer had any inclination she had seen him murder Isobel, he would be foolish not to come to ensure her silence. But Sybilla had provided little to elucidate the muddle of information that

Bartholomew had acquired over the past few days. All she could tell him was that the man was average. He could be anyone.

She could not stay in her home, that much was clear. It was probably only a matter of time before the killer heard that Sybilla had run screaming from the scene of Isobel's murder, and had refused to leave her home ever since, before he took action to ensure his identity could never be revealed. Even if he remained unaware that Sybilla had seen him, she had to be moved. She would become seriously ill if left by herself much longer.

He could not take her to Michaelhouse. Even for the best reasons, the Master would not allow him to bring a young prostitute to the College. He could give her money to find other lodgings in the town, but Cambridge was a small town and it was almost impossible to hide in it.

There was only one thing for it. He would have to impose upon Oswald Stanmore. He had done it before, when Rachel Atkin's son had been killed in a town riot, and Stanmore had benefited by gaining a very talented seamstress. However, Bartholomew thought wryly, Stanmore would not benefit from Sybilla unless he intended to open a brothel.

He told Sybilla to gather up what she would need for a stay at Stanmore's premises, and went outside to wait. Matilde followed him to the river bank, oblivious to the drizzle that fell like gauze upon her luxurious hair.

'It is kind of you to do this,' she said.

'I need not tell you that you must inform no one where she is,' he said. 'And you must not visit her until the killer is found, lest he follow you there. And do not cóme back here yourself. The killer may mistake you for Sybilla if he comes.'

Matilde gave him a smile. 'Agatha said you were a good man. There are not many who would take such trouble over a couple of whores,' she said. He looked away, embarrassed.

'There are quite a number of women like us,' she continued, 'and we talk a lot. It is imperative that we do: we need to know who might be rough, who might refuse to pay, who might be diseased. We hear other things, too, through our lines of communication. I heard that you blundered into Primrose Alley a few days ago.'

'Primrose Alley?' Bartholomew had never heard of it.

'Behind St Mary's,' said Matilde. 'Not an appropriate name for such a place, but I imagine that is why it got it. Anyway, I heard that you were escorted out by Janetta of Lincoln.'

Bartholomew was amazed. He seemed to be the only person in Cambridge without vast arrays of informants to tap into when he needed to know something. Stanmore had his own legion of spies; the Chancellor and the Bishop seemed to do well for information when they needed it; and even the town prostitutes appeared to know his every move.

Matilde touched his arm, seeing his reaction. 'It was Janetta we were interested in, not you,' she said. 'She arrived in Cambridge about a month ago and immediately assumed a good deal of influence in Primrose Alley with the rough men who have lived there since the Death. We did not know how much power she had accrued, until we heard that she was able to call off the louts that were attacking you, with a single word. We believe she was one of us in Lincoln, but she denies it to any who ask, and does not practise here. We do not usually share our information with outsiders, but you are helping us, and I would like to help you with a warning: have nothing to do with that woman.'

'I need to talk to her,' Bartholomew said. 'She may be able to give me information that might lead to the killer.'

'I would not trust any information gained from her,' said Matilde, 'although it would not surprise me to know that she had some to give. Who is she to have such command over those rough men within a month? She is a living lie from her fake smile to her false hair.'

'False hair?' said Bartholomew, surprised, thinking of Janetta's thick cascade of raven black hair.

'Yes,' said Matilde firmly. 'That black hair that you doubtless admired is none of her own. Perhaps she is grey and wants to retain the appearance of youth. Who knows her reason? But I know a wig when I see one.'

Bartholomew lent Sybilla his tabard and cloak, and pulled the hood up over her head to hide her face. He gave her his bag to carry, hoping that in the failing light she would pass for one of his students.

She trailed behind him, giving an occasional sniff. Matilde had already slipped away after giving him a final warning about Janetta of Lincoln. Bartholomew thought about her advice. He had thought it odd at the time that Janetta had such control over what seemed to be an unruly gang of men. She had arrived a month ago. Nicholas of York had died or disappeared a month ago, and the unknown woman buried in his place. The woman with no hair. He frowned. Had the woman's hair fallen out after she died, had she worn a wig like Janetta, or did Janetta's wig belong to the woman in Nicholas's coffin?

Bartholomew concentrated, barely aware of Sybilla behind him. Were the events related? Was the arrival of Janetta connected to the death, or disappearance, of the man who was writing the controversial book? He rethought Sybilla's story and Matilde's warning, but, try as he might, he could make no sense of them, nor tie them in with the information he already had.

When they arrived at Stanmore's business premises, most of the buildings were already in darkness and Stanmore had returned to Trumpington. Bartholomew bundled Sybilla into the small chambers behind the main storerooms, the place where Rachel Atkin worked, before anyone could see her. As he burst in unannounced, he stopped in astonishment. Cynric stood up, from where he had been sitting by Rachel on the hearth. He put down his goblet of wine and grinned sheepishly, caught in the act of his courting. It was late, and the other women had gone home, leaving Cynric to enjoy the company of Rachel alone.

Bartholomew was ashamed of himself for not knocking and giving the poor woman a chance to compose herself, but Rachel was unabashed. She looked curiously at Sybilla, still wearing Bartholomew's gown. Bartholomew found his tongue.

'Can Sybilla stay with you for a few days?' he asked, suddenly feeling awkward. 'I promise I will clear it with Oswald as soon as I can see him.'

'As you please,' Rachel said in her pleasant low voice. She helped Sybilla remove the heavy tabard and cloak. 'It appears Sybilla is in trouble, and she will not be turned away.'

At the kindness in her voice, Sybilla began to weep again, and Bartholomew took the opportunity to leave. Sybilla could tell Rachel her story and Rachel would have the sense and the discretion to deal with her accordingly. Bartholomew felt Cynric slip up behind him as he left.

'Sorry, Cynric. I should have knocked,' he said.

Cynric grinned at him. 'No matter, lad. We were just talking.' He became serious. 'Your brother-in-law saw me as I was going to Rachel's room, and told me to tell you that the Guild of the Coming are meeting tomorrow night at All Saints'.' He rubbed his hands gleefully, oblivious to Bartholomew's expression of dismay. 'Another night expedition, eh boy? You and I will get to the bottom of all this yet.'

chapter 7

AWN THE NEXT DAY WAS DULL AND GREY, THE HOT weather of the past few weeks replaced by a chill dampness. It was the turn of the Franciscan Fellows, William and Aidan, to prepare the church, and Bartholomew was able to stay in bed longer than he had the previous week. He thought about Sybilla, hidden away in fear of her life, and the dead women, especially Frances de Belem, and he felt depressed by the fact that he even had a witness to one murder, but was still no further forward with uncovering the killer's identity. He considered de Wetherset too, concealing documents from Michael that might help them to reason out some of the jumble of information that they had accumulated.

When he heard the Benedictines moving about in the room above, he reluctantly climbed out of bed to wash and shave in the cold water left for him by Cynric the night before, hopping about on the stone floor in his bare feet. He groped around in the gloom for his shirt, shivering in the cool air. The bell was already ringing by the time he was ready, and he had to run to catch up with the others. Michael told him in an undertone that they had been asked to meet with the Chancellor that morning. Bartholomew groaned, his scanty morning humour evaporating.

Michael jangled some keys at him. 'We can try these out,' he said. 'The Bishop gave them to me yesterday.'

Bartholomew took them from him. There were three large keys and three small ones, all on a rusting metal ring. 'Why are there six keys?' he asked. 'There are only three locks.'

Michael shrugged. 'The Bishop said they had been deposited with his predecessor. There is another University chest at the

Carmelite Friary containing duplicates of all documents. Did you know that? I thought not. I suspect that is a secret few other than de Wetherset know. Anyway, the scroll with the keys was dated November 1331. They have lain untouched at the bottom of one of the Abbey strong-boxes for almost twenty years! Can you believe that?'

Bartholomew wondered whether they were the right keys.

No such doubts assailed Michael, who cracked his knuckles cheerfully. 'Now we will get some answers. If they fit, it means that the lock was tampered with and the poison device installed recently; if they do not fit, it means the lock was changed completely.'

'And what does that tell us?' grumbled Bartholomew.

Michael shrugged. 'We will know whether someone planted that device deliberately to kill.'

'But if it were changed, it tells us only that it was done at some point between November 1331 and last Monday,' said Bartholomew, ignoring warning glowers from Alcote for talking in the procession. 'And that provides us with little information that will be of use.'

'It was your idea to check the Bishop's keys,' said Michael, crestfallen by Bartholomew's negative attitude. 'And if the lock has been changed, it must mean that de Wetherset's key must also have been changed – the key that only leaves the chain around his neck when it is given to the mysteriously absent Buckley.'

'So de Wetherset says,' said Bartholomew. 'But how do we prove that the poisoned blade was not put onto the lock only the day before the friar was killed?'

'Because Buckley locked the chest and the tower at dusk just a few minutes before the lay-brother locked the church. If the device was put there during the day, then Buckley would have been poisoned by it.'

'He wore gloves, remember?' said Bartholomew. He shook his head. 'Have you noticed that everyone we want to talk to, who might be able to help us, has disappeared? The lay-brother, Janetta, Froissart's family, Master Buckley. Even Nicholas, and he is supposed to be dead!'

Michael studied him in the gloom. 'What is wrong, Matt?' he

asked. 'You are not usually so morose. Are you worried about de Wetherset?'

'No. I expect he is merely trying to safeguard the University's secrets by deceiving you over the book. But I am fed up with all this. The more I try to fathom it all out, the less I understand. It is something to do with those damn covens, I am sure. One of them is meeting tonight, and Cynric thinks I am going with him to spy. Meanwhile this killer is still free, and Tulyet seems to be doing nothing to catch him.'

Michael sighed. 'One thing at a time, Matt. We will go to see the Chancellor, and then we will try to reason all this out. We are supposed to have some of the finest minds in the country. We must be able to solve this riddle.'

Bartholomew was not so sure. He tried to put it out of his mind during Prime, but found he could not. He thought about Sybilla and wondered if she would be safe at Stanmore's premises. He found himself looking at the wall painting where the goat-devil tossed people into the burning pit, and wondered whether Wilson's tomb, when he finally had it built, would hide it.

Father William was noted for the speed of his masses, but he was not matched by Aidan, who stammered and stuttered, and lost his place as he read. At one point he knocked the paten off the altar and the pieces of bread intended for communion scattered over the floor. Bartholomew saw Gray and Deynman start to laugh, making Alcote look at them sharply. As William and Aidan scrabbled to recover the bread, Bartholomew saw that Hesselwell was asleep. He watched, fascinated, as the lawyer slipped further and further down his seat until it tipped with a loud bang that echoed like thunder through the church.

Hesselwell looked startled, but returned the Master's deprecating look with a guileless smile that made it look as if the clatter had been caused by someone else. Gray and Deynman were having serious trouble in containing their laughter, and Bartholomew could see that if they did not control themselves, Alcote would fine them. Opposite, Harling watched in icy disapproval, making it clear that he regarded the students' behaviour as typical of Michaelhouse scholars. Kenyngham was blissfully oblivious to it all, his hands clasped in the sleeves of his monastic gown and his eyes fixed on the ceiling as he chanted.

Jonstan, standing next to Harling, looked from the students to Kenyngham, and smothered a smile.

Finally, order was restored and mass continued, but it was late by the time they finished. Since it was Sunday, there were no lectures, and the scholars were expected to read or spend time in silent contemplation. Bartholomew saw no reason why his students should not read something medical. He hailed Gray and Bulbeck and told them to read specific sections of Galen's *Prognostica* until midday, at which point they were free to spend their time as they pleased. He gave Gray the keys so that he could unlock the valuable tome from where it was chained to a wall in Bartholomew's storeroom, and read it aloud to the others in a corner of the hall.

Boniface regarded him aghast. 'It is the Lord's day!' he exclaimed. 'We cannot work!'

'Reading is permitted,' said Bartholomew. 'But no one is obliged to attend if they feel themselves unable.'

'Working on the Lord's day is a sin!' said Boniface, looking down his long nose at his teacher. 'It is because of evil men like you that the Death was visited upon us.'

'That is true, Doctor.' Bartholomew turned to see Father William standing behind him, tall, immovable, and with a fanatical gleam in his eye that forewarned Bartholomew he was spoiling for a good theological debate.

'Perhaps it is,' said Bartholomew. 'But I do not consider listening to medical texts work.'

'But you hold a book, you turn its pages, and you use your voice to speak the words,' said William. 'That is work.'

'In which case you are working now,' said Bartholomew. 'You are trying to engage me in a theological debate – and theology is your trade, quite apart from your vocation, since you are paid to teach it – and you are using your voice to speak the words.'

William nodded, appreciating the logic. 'True,' he countered. 'Yet I do not consider it work.'

'And I do not consider reading medical texts work,' said Bartholomew. 'So we have reached a stalemate.'

Before William could respond, Bartholomew gave a small bow and began to walk away. Boniface ran after him and seized his sleeve.

'I will not read your heretical texts,' he hissed. 'And I will not commit the sin of working on the Sabbath. I will go to the conclave and listen to readings from the Bible with Father Aidan.'

'Do so, Brother,' said Bartholomew wearily. He had neither the energy nor the inclination to ask Boniface what he thought the difference was in listening to one text or another. He disengaged himself from his obnoxious student, and made for his room. This time he was accosted by Gray and Bulbeck.

'All those potions we tested yesterday seemed to be what you said they should be,' said Gray. 'Except for the white arsenic. That was sugar.'

'Sugar? How did you know it was sugar?' asked Bartholomew, startled. 'I gave you no tests to prove that!'

'Deynman ate it,' said Gray.

'He what?' cried Bartholomew, looking in horror at Deynman skulking nearby, waiting for his friends. He grinned nervously at Bartholomew.

'We thought the arsenic looked like that fine white sugar that we had at the feast last year. Deynman ate it, and said it was indeed sugar.'

Bartholomew put his hand over his eyes. He wondered what he had done to deserve students like Boniface and Deynman, one unable to see past the dogma of his vocation, and the other unable to see much of anything. 'Deynman!' he yelled suddenly, making the others jump and several scholars look over to see what was happening. He strode to where the student stood and grabbed him by the front of his tabard.

'What are you thinking of?' he said fiercely. Deynman shrugged and tried to wriggle free. Bartholomew held him tighter. 'You might have been poisoned – like Walter!'

'Sam and Thomas would have fetched eggs and vinegar to make me sick!' Deynman protested, struggling feebly. 'Like Walter.'

'The chances that eggs and vinegar would have saved you from arsenic poisoning are remote,' said Bartholomew. 'It would have been a horrible death, and I doubt I would have been able to help you.' He released Deynman, and stood looking down at him, torn between wonder and anger at the young man's ineptitude.

'But it was not arsenic, it was sugar,' protested Deynman. 'The poison that made Walter ill must have been stolen from your bag and replaced with sugar.'

'Oh, Rob!' exclaimed Bartholomew in despair. 'How can that be possible? I have just told you that arsenic produces a violent death, not a peaceful slipping away into sleep like Walter. Walter was poisoned with a strong opiate used for dulling pain. The arsenic missing from my bag was not the poison used on Walter.'

'But who would exchange arsenic for sugar?' cried Deynman, confused.

'I do not know,' said Bartholomew. 'And anyway,' he added severely, 'that is none of your concern. But if you ever taste any of my medicines again without asking me first, I will make sure that you are sent home the same day. Do I make myself clear?'

Deynman nodded, frightened by his teacher's rare display of anger. Bartholomew gave him a long hard look and sent him off before Alcote, hurrying across the courtyard towards them, could catch him. Alcote watched Deynman run to Bartholomew's storeroom to fetch the book with Gray and Bulbeck.

'What was all that about?' he asked.

'Alchemy!' snapped Bartholomew, still angry at Deynman's stupidity, but reluctant to tell the nosy Alcote anything that would get him into more trouble.

'Your students are a disgrace,' sniffed Alcote. 'When I catch them, I will fine them for laughing in church.'

He headed towards Bartholomew's store, head tilted to one side, looking more like a hen than ever. As he entered, Bartholomew saw the shutters fly open and the students clamber out of the window. Alcote emerged to see them running across to the hall with the book tucked under Gray's arm. Bartholomew laughed despite himself, and wondered how long they could keep a step ahead of the vindictive Senior Fellow.

He went to close the shutters, wondering why Janetta's friends had exchanged sugar for white arsenic. Arsenic was an unusual item for a physician to carry, but Bartholomew found it useful for eliminating some of the vermin that he believed spread diseases to some of his poorer patients. Despite his words to Deynman,

Bartholomew did not carry enough of the white powder to kill a person, and he was not unduly worried about the amount that was stolen.

Michael was waiting for him by the porter's lodge, and together they walked to see the Chancellor.

'Why were you yelling at Deynman?' Michael asked curiously. He had seldom seen the physician angry enough to shout.

Bartholomew did not want to think about it, and avoided Michael's question. Cynric had already been dispatched to ask de Wetherset if they could try the keys on the locks, and when they arrived at his office, the Chancellor and Harling, recently promoted from Senior Proctor to Vice Chancellor to replace Buckley, were waiting for them. De Wetherset reported that his clerks had still been unable to trace Froissart's family, and suggested he be buried in St Mary's churchyard as soon as possible.

'I have made some enquiries,' said Harling. 'One of the two covens in Cambridge, the Guild of the Coming, uses goats in its rituals. I can only conclude that members of this guild must have left the head on Brother Michael's bed, perhaps as a warning?'

'A warning of what?' demanded Bartholomew. 'We cannot be a danger to them. We have made little headway in our investigation: we do not know who the friar was, or what he wanted from the chest, and we do not know who killed Froissart.' He stood abruptly and began to pace.

'We know that the Guild of the Coming must be connected to the woman in Nicholas's grave,' said Harling, trying to be placatory.

'Why?' snapped Bartholomew. 'How do you know it was not one coven trying to desecrate the sacred symbol of its rivals, or trying to implicate it in a murder of which it is innocent? And what of the Guild of the Holy Trinity? That may be leaving satanic symbols to bring the covens into disrepute.'

Harling spread his hands. 'The Guild of the Holy Trinity is dedicated to stamping out sin, not to committing murder and desecration. But regardless, how would anyone guess that Nicholas's grave would be exhumed and we would find the mask?'

'As I said to Master de Wetherset,' said Bartholomew, still pacing, 'I suspect Nicholas's coffin was meant to be opened before his burial, not after.'

De Wetherset sighed. 'You are right – we know nothing to be a danger to anyone. Unless we know something that may seem unimportant to us that means a great deal to them.'

He had a point, and Bartholomew stopped wandering for a moment to consider it. After a few moments, he resumed his pacing, frustrated.

'I can think of nothing,' he said. 'The only way forward that I can see is to look into the murders of the town women. We know their deaths involve the University now that we have discovered the woman's body in Nicholas's coffin. There are no witnesses that can identify the killer. Rumours are spreading that the murderer is Froissart, but we know that cannot be so.'

De Wetherset watched Bartholomew pace, and turned to Michael. 'I understand you visited Ely,' he said. 'Do you have the keys?'

Michael produced them and de Wetherset fetched the old locks from a cupboard in the wall. He carried them carefully and placed them on the table on top of a piece of cloth. Michael selected a key, donned the heavy gloves, carefully inserted it into the lock, and waggled it about.

'It always was a bit sticky,' said the Chancellor, watching from a distance.

Michael jiggled the key a little more, and stepped back in alarm as the tiny blade popped further out, revealing jagged edges. Michael, his hands a little unsteady, took a grip on the key again and twisted it back and forth, but nothing happened. 'It does not fit,' he said. 'The lock must have been exchanged.'

'Wait!' said Bartholomew, moving towards the table from the window-seat where he had been watching. The others looked at him. 'How do you know it was sticky?' he asked de Wetherset. 'You said Buckley usually opened it.'

'Well, he did, usually,' said de Wetherset. 'But he was sometimes ill, so I would open it. I always struggled with the damn thing, although Buckley never had a problem.'

'When was the last time you opened it personally?' asked Bartholomew.

De Wetherset blew out his cheeks. 'Heavens,' he said. 'I cannot recall . . . perhaps during spring. Why do you ask?'

Bartholomew's mind began to whirl. 'Open it now,' he demanded.

'Why?' said de Wetherset. 'Brother Michael has already shown the key does not fit.'

Bartholomew snatched the key from the table and handed it to de Wetherset. 'You try.'

The Chancellor looked puzzled, but donned the gloves and inserted the key in the lock gingerly. Unlike Michael, de Wetherset steadied the lock with his other hand, and after a few moments of jiggling, there was a loud snap and the lock sprung open.

De Wetherset and Harling stared at it, while Michael looked at Bartholomew, a sardonic smile tugging the corners of his mouth.

'Tell us what flash of inspiration suddenly occurred to make you suggest that,' he said.

Bartholomew sat on a stool next to the table and peered at the lock. 'It is old,' he said, 'and the tower is damp. I suspect that the lock's insides are rusty. Buckley opened it almost every day, and was probably used to the way it sticks; so familiar, in fact, that he did not need to fiddle like you did just now, Master de Wetherset. Similarly, you know better how to manipulate the thing than Michael, who was unable to open it at all. I think the small blade that killed the friar has been hidden in the lock for years. Over time, the mechanism has become faulty and rusty. I suspect it would have killed you, Master de Wetherset, had you opened it more recently.'

Harling looked puzzled. 'So you are saying that this nasty device has been in place since the locks were bought from Italy twenty years ago, and that it has become faulty over the last few months because it has become worn.'

De Wetherset looked at the lock in horror. 'Are you telling me that if Buckley had not been available to unlock the chest recently with his gloved hands and his familiarity with the thing, I might have suffered the same fate as the friar?'

Bartholomew nodded. 'That is exactly what I am telling you,' he said. 'And I think if you were to show a locksmith the other two locks, you would find similar mechanisms not far behind this one in terms of increasing unreliability.'

De Wetherset looked sick, but went to the door and called for Gilbert whom he dispatched to send for Haralda the Dane, the town's leading locksmith.

Harling tried to stop him. 'I must caution you to keep this matter a secret. Bartholomew's explanation seems a plausible one. Why can we not leave it at that? And anyway, it is Sunday, and you cannot encourage the locksmith to work on the Lord's day.'

'I want to be certain,' said de Wetherset. 'If Matthew is wrong, we may draw the wrong conclusions from this wretched business and a murderer may walk free. I am quite sure the Lord will overlook Haralda's sin if it is to prevent the more heinous crime of murder.'

Harling opened his mouth to argue, but de Wetherset eyed him coldly, and nothing was said. Harling turned away in anger, and went to the window. Bartholomew was surprised at Harling's objections. So what if the town got to know the University had discovered three poisoned locks? It might act as a deterrent to anyone considering burgling the chest a second time. It seemed to Bartholomew that Harling's other objection – that Haralda would be working on the Sabbath – was a second thought grasped at in desperation. After all, by his very presence in his office on a Sunday, it might be considered that Harling was working, too. Perhaps he had other reasons for wanting the presence of the poisoned locks kept a secret.

While they waited for Haralda, Bartholomew sat on the damp cushions in the window-seat and watched Harling more closely. He was certainly agitated, and paced up and down as Bartholomew had done earlier. Bartholomew saw Michael observing too, and knew that he was not the only one to note Harling's tension.

It was not long before Gilbert ushered the tall Dane into the Chancellor's office. Haralda's eyes immediately lit on the locks on the table, and he let out an exclamation of delight.

'Ah! Padua locks!' he said. 'I have not seen one of these in many a year. May I?'

'They are poisoned!' cried Michael, springing forward to stop him from touching them.

Haralda looked at him pityingly. 'Of course they are poisoned,' he said. 'They are Padua locks. Clever devices. I assume these are the reasons you have invited me here?'

De Wetherset nodded, while Harling began to gnaw on his fingernails. Bartholomew was impressed at the Dane's command of English. When he had arrived six or seven years ago, he had conducted his business almost exclusively in French. Now, he not only spoke perfect English, but had acquired a gentleman's accent, not a local one. Bartholomew commented on it as he watched the locksmith work.

'I was taught by a lady,' he said proudly.

Bartholomew was puzzled, unable to imagine what kind of lady would be willing to coach a rough man like Haralda the Dane. Then the answer came to him. 'The Lady Matilde?' he asked.

The Dane grinned at him conspiratorially. 'The very same,' he said.

Cambridge was indeed a small town, thought Bartholomew. De Wetherset apparently did not agree.

'Lady Matilde?' he said, frowning as he thought. 'I do not believe I know her. Is she the wife of one of the knights at the Castle?'

'She does not live at the Castle,' said Bartholomew, and changed the subject before it got him into trouble. 'What can you tell us about the locks, Master Haralda?'

'They are old,' said the Dane. He slipped on a pair of thin but strong gloves and unrolled a piece of cloth containing some tiny tools. He carefully picked up one of the locks in his paw-like hands. 'Yes, this one is broken, see?' He pointed to the blade and waggled it with his finger, laughing at the exclamations of horror from Gilbert and de Wetherset.

He selected a minute pair of tweezers and removed the blade completely. It was a third of the length of Bartholomew's little finger and yet it had already killed one man. Haralda deftly unscrewed the lock to reveal its innards. Bartholomew peered over his shoulder.

Haralda tutted and shook his head. 'You do not know how

to treat a lock, my lords,' he said reprovingly. 'This poor thing has not seen a drop of oil since the day it was made. You are lucky it has not killed someone.'

Harling glared at Bartholomew and Michael in turn, daring them to say anything. Haralda did not notice.

'This is an especially fine model,' he said. 'It became popular in Italy about twenty or thirty years ago, although few are made these days. It was one of the best locks ever to be produced. They are expensive, but worth the cost if you have something worth protecting.'

He looked up, and Harling eyed him coldly. 'Just documents,' he said. 'Nothing that would interest a thief.'

Haralda picked up the second lock and poked at it. 'Yes. This one is different. The blade comes through the back, not the top. It is in better condition than the other one, but not by much.'

He turned his attention to the third one, and wagged its finger at it as it gave a sharp click when he started prodding. 'Look at that! You are lucky, my lords. If any of you had tried to open this, you would be dead. The mechanism is so worn, it is almost smooth. I would say it would have released its blade within three attempts at opening it at most. You were right to have called me.'

'I do not understand why they have suddenly become so unreliable,' said de Wetherset. 'We have been using them for years without trouble.'

'But you have not cared for them as you should have done. They are rusty, and they have become dangerous. You could have had many years' service from them if you had treated them properly, but now I would recommend that you dispense with them.'

'How has the poison stayed for so long in so potent a form?' asked Bartholomew.

Haralda beamed at him, pleased that someone was expressing an interest, rather than disgust, at the locks. 'The blade has its own chamber here, see? It is sealed with lead, so no poison can leak and cause damage. If I were to open this chamber, which I would only do under the special conditions at my workshop, you would find the poison mixed with various mixtures, including quicksilver, to keep it fluid. Thus the poison is always ready. I saw a lock like this kill a dog in under ten minutes in Rome, although I would think perhaps, judging from the age of this lock, that the poison may have lost some of its potency. If you meant business, you would need to change the poison regularly to ensure its continued efficacy.'

Bartholomew nodded, staring down at the rusting insides of the three locks on the table. He picked up Michael's keys and played with them idly. Haralda took them from him.

'These smaller keys,' he said, holding them up, 'are to turn the poison mechanism on and off. In this way, the lock can be used normally.'

He inserted the smaller key into one of the parallel vertical slits on the back of one of the locks to show them. Bartholomew studied it closely and admired its ingenuity. The slit did not look like another keyhole, and anyone who did not know what it was, would never guess.

'I would assume,' said Haralda, 'that whoever last knew about this left the mechanism turned off. Once again, I say you are very lucky none of them slipped on while you were using them.'

'Which is why Buckley was safe, even without his gloves,' murmured Michael to Bartholomew. 'It must have broken as the friar poked about with it in a way that Buckley never had.'

Haralda stood up. 'Dispense with these, my lords. They are no longer safe.'

'Will you take them?' asked de Wetherset. 'I would feel more secure knowing that a professional man had disposed of them in a proper manner.'

Haralda bowed to him, flattered, and collected the pieces of the locks in the cloth. De Wetherset went to see him out of the church. Harling paced restlessly.

'It was a mistake bringing in another,' he said. 'He told us nothing we did not know or could not guess.'

'But now we are certain,' said Michael. 'We know the lock was not changed by Buckley, or by someone wanting to kill members of the University. We know that the locks are just old and worn, and that the friar was not murdered. I suppose it could be called accidental death.'

'But we still do not know what he wanted in the chest,'

said Bartholomew. 'In fact, we are not much further forward at all.'

'Yes, we are,' said Michael. 'We are no longer looking for the murderer of the friar.'

'But we still want the murderer of Froissart,' said Harling. He chewed nervously at his fingers. 'If you will excuse me, gentlemen, I have much to be doing.'

He bowed and left the room. Bartholomew leaned out of the window, and saw de Wetherset still talking to Haralda below.

'Harling was unaccountably nervous,' said Michael, opening one of de Wetherset's wall cupboards and peering inside. 'Even if it is a Sunday, I feel he had another reason why he did not want us to fetch the locksmith.'

Bartholomew sighed and made for the door. 'Come on, Brother. Harling is not the only one with much to be doing,' he said.

They stepped outside and began to walk home. There was a flicker in the sky, followed by a low rumble, and then rain began to fall heavily. Bartholomew and Michael joined several others who ran to St Mary's Church to wait the thunderstorm out. Inside, the church was dark from the grey clouds that hung low overhead, lit brilliantly by occasional flashes of lightning. Bartholomew had never been in a church during a thunderstorm before, and the way the wall-paintings suddenly lit up reminded him of passages from Revelations about the end of the world.

He wandered around aimlessly, listening to the rain drumming on the roof. The tombs in the choir reminded him of his promise to Master Wilson to attend to the building of his sepulchre. Some tombs were plain, while others were vulgar. A plain one in black marble would not be too bad, thought Bartholomew, but, in his heart of hearts, he knew that Wilson would have wanted a vulgar one. Not for the first time, Bartholomew was disgusted. Wilson should have arranged to be buried in a fairground with the kind of tomb he had had in mind, not a church!

A sharp tug on his sleeve pulled him from his thoughts. One of the clerks was there, hiding behind a pillar. He looked frightened, and Bartholomew pretended to be reading an inscription on a nearby tomb, so that no one watching him would know he was speaking with a man in the shadows.

The lightning flickered again, making the man wince and press further back, but the storm was moving away.

'The day after the friar's death,' said the clerk, glancing furtively around him, 'I saw that the bar on the front door had been moved.'

'What does that imply?' asked Bartholomew softly, rubbing the brass on the tomb with his sleeve and pretending to look closer.

'Everyone here thinks that the friar hid in the church before it was locked up. He then went upstairs and died. But the bar on the door was in a different place in the morning than it was the night before,' whispered the clerk hoarsely. 'What I am saying is that I think the friar barred the door after the church was locked, which means that someone must have unbarred it from the inside, or we would not have been able to get in the next morning.'

Bartholomew's heart sank. He had just proved, rather ingeniously he thought, that the poisoned lock had been a cruel twist of fate that had killed the friar, and now this clerk was telling him the friar had not been alone in the church on the night of his death, which threw the whole thing back under suspicion.

'Are you certain?' he asked heavily, still careful not to look at the man and give him away.

The clerk nodded quickly. 'I think I may be putting myself at risk by talking to you, but if I do not tell you what I know, how will you be able to solve this mystery and let us get back to normal?'

Bartholomew was taken aback by the man's confidence in his abilities as a detective, and not particularly pleased at the pressure he felt it put on him to draw this matter to an acceptable conclusion. 'Do you know anything else?' he asked. 'Like the whereabouts of the man who locked the church that night?'

The man huddled further back behind his pillar. 'He has not been seen since you chased him. He has not been home, and his family have had no word from him.'

'Did you know Nicholas of York?' Bartholomew whispered,

watching as a second clerk walked past him, carrying a pile of dirty-white tallow candles.

He felt the man's confusion. 'Yes. He died more than a month ago,' he said.

'Did you see his body or attend his funeral? Did you notice anything untoward?'

The clerk looked at him as though he were insane. 'I saw his body in his coffin the night before we buried him, but I fail to see why you ask.' He sank back into the shadows as the other clerk returned from depositing his candles. 'The friar died a few days ago, and Nicholas has been in his grave for weeks.'

Bartholomew sighed. 'Then do you know anything about the Guild of the Coming or the Guild of the Purification?'

The man crossed himself so violently that Bartholomew could hear his hand thumping hollowly against his ribs. 'You should not speak those names in this holy church!' he hissed. 'And do not try to find out about them. They are powerful and would kill you like a fly if they thought you were asking questions.'

'But they are small organisations with only a few members,' said Bartholomew, quoting Stanmore's information, and trying to allay the clerk's fears.

'But they have the power of the Devil behind them! They do his work as we do God's.'

Bartholomew already knew the two guilds might harm him or Michael if they thought they were coming too close to their secrets. When he glanced up again, the man had melted away into the shadows. He thought about what the clerk had said. Either two people were locked in the church that night, or the friar had let someone else in. But what was even more apparent was that the second person must have had a set of keys to the church, or how would the doors have been locked the following morning?

Bartholomew rubbed his chin thoughtfully. Buckley had to be involved. Perhaps he had not murdered the friar, as Bartholomew had considered possible, but did he lock the doors to the tower after the friar had died and he had put him in the chest? And then did he leave the church, lock it behind him, and flee the town with all his property? And was he also responsible for putting the murdered woman in Nicholas of York's coffin? In which case, he might also be the killer of the other women.

Even stranger was the case of Nicholas of York. The clerk and de Wetherset claimed they had seen Nicholas dead, which implied that someone must have made off with his body, first replacing it with the woman's. But what reason might anyone, even a coven, have for such an action? Bartholomew closed his eyes and leaned back against the tomb. But what if Nicholas were not dead? Perhaps he had feigned death, spending the day lying in his coffin while his colleagues kept vigil, and then broke out during the night. Perhaps the woman had helped him. Had Nicholas then repaid her by killing her and putting her in his place? Had she come to snatch his body away for some diabolical purpose and been foiled in the attempt? Perhaps Nicholas was the killer, a man assumed to be dead, and so not an obvious suspect.

And what of Tulyet's role in all this? The townspeople believed Froissart was the killer, but deaths had occurred after he was murdered and hidden in the belfry. Perhaps Tulyet was the murderer. He had reacted oddly to the mention of goats, and was doing nothing to catch the killer, although he could not know Froissart was dead. Perhaps it had been Tulyet who had snatched Nicholas's body for some satanic ritual.

Bartholomew opened his eyes and saw that the rain had eased. Michael was singing a Kyrie with another monk, their voices echoing through the church, Michael's rich baritone a complement to the monk's tenor. Bartholomew let their music wash over him, savouring the way their voices rose and fell together, growing louder and then softer in perfect harmony with each other. The faint smell of wet earth began to drift in through the open windows, momentarily masking the all-pervasive aroma of river. All was peace and stillness until a cart broke a wheel outside, and angry voices began to intrude.

'I am hungry,' announced Michael as they walked back to College in the light rain following the thunderstorm. 'Cynric foolishly told Agatha about that trick we played on you with the shadows, and she is refusing to allow me into the kitchen.

We could sit in the garden behind the Brazen George and have something to eat while we talk.'

Bartholomew looked askance. 'What are you thinking of, monk? First, it is a Sunday, and second, you are well aware that scholars are not permitted in the town taverns.'

'What better day than a Sunday to celebrate the Lord's gift of excellent wine?' asked Michael cheerily. 'And I did not suggest entering a tavern, physician, merely the garden.'

'Michael, it is raining,' said Bartholomew, laughing. 'We cannot sit in a tavern garden in the rain. People would think we had had too much to drink! And the Brazen George will be closed because it is Sunday.'

'Not true,' said Michael. 'The town has given a special dispensation for the taverns to open on Sundays during the Fair. Otherwise what do you think all these visiting merchants, traders, and itinerants will do, wandering the streets with nowhere to go? If the taverns were closed, they would form gangs and roam the streets looking for trouble. The town council was wise when it ignored the pious whinings of the clerics and granted licences for the taverns to open on Sundays until the Fair is over.'

Bartholomew glanced up and saw a figure coming towards them, his head bowed against the spitting rain. Michael saw him too, and hailed him.

'Master de Belem!'

The merchant looked up, his eyes glazed and his face sallow. His thick, dark hair was straggly and he looked thinner and older than when Bartholomew had last seen him. He glanced up and down the street carefully, and then back at the scholars.

'I must talk to you, but not here. Where can we meet?'

'The garden at the rear of the Brazen George,' said Michael before Bartholomew could stop him. 'It is secluded and the landlord will respect our privacy.'

The merchant nodded quickly. 'Go there now and I will follow in a few minutes. I do not want anyone to know that we have been together.'

Michael gave Bartholomew a triumphant look and led the way to the tavern. He stopped at the small stable next door to it, pretending to admire the horses. When he was certain no beadles were watching, he shot down a small passageway and let himself into a tiny garden. The bower would be pleasant on a sunny day: it had high lime-washed walls over which vines crept, and two or three small tables were set among rambling roses. But it was raining, and as the wind blew, great drops of water splattered down from the leaves.

Bartholomew sighed and pulled his hood further over his head, looking for a spot that might be more sheltered.

Within moments, the landlord came out, wiping his hands on a stained apron, and not at all surprised to see them.

'Brother Michael! Welcome! What can I fetch for you?'

'Two goblets of your excellent French wine, some chicken, some of that fine white bread, cinnamon toast, and the use of your garden for some private business.'

The landlord spread his hands. 'If only I could, Brother, but white flour is not to be had at any cost, and we have no bread. But there is chicken and wine, and you are welcome to the garden for your private business.'

Michael looked disappointed, but nodded his agreement. The landlord hurried away to do his bidding. Bartholomew was surprised that the monk would break the University's rules so flagrantly. 'From that, I assume this is not your first visit?'

Michael beamed and led him over to a table under some trees where they were at least sheltered from the wind, if not the rain. De Belem slipped through the door, latching it carefully behind him.

'I am sorry for the secrecy, but it is for your own safety. I am a marked man, and it would do you no good to be seen with me,' he said, as he came to join them at the wet table.

'Marked by whom?' asked Bartholomew.

'I do not know,' he said, putting his elbows on the table and resting his face in his hands. 'But they have already killed my daughter.'

'How do you know that?' asked Bartholomew curiously.

De Belem raised his head. 'Allow me to explain. After my wife was taken by the Death, I lost my faith. Half the monks and priests in the land were taken, and I thought if God would not protect His own, why would He bother with me? I said as much to one of my colleagues, and a few days later I received an invitation to attend a meeting of the Guild of Purification.

I did not know what it entailed, but I went because I was disillusioned and lonely. The Honourable Guild of Dyers was full of bickering because of a shift in the balance of power after the plague, and I felt I would have nothing to lose by joining another organisation.'

He paused and looked up into the swaying branches above. Bartholomew said nothing. Stanmore had already told him that de Belem was a member of the Guild of Purification.

'The guild pays allegiance to Satan,' de Belem continued. 'You are scholars, so you know Lucifer's story. He was an angel and was cast out of Heaven. His halo fell to his feet, and so our symbol is a circle – his fallen halo.'

Michael pursed his lips, and the three men were silent while the landlord brought the chicken and wine. De Belem huddled inside his hood. Discreetly, the landlord kept his eyes fixed on the food, and did not attempt to look at de Belem, leaving Bartholomew to wonder how many other such meetings Michael had conducted on his premises.

De Belem continued when the landlord had left. 'The religious, or,' he said, casting a rueful glance at Michael, 'the irreligious side of it held little appeal for me. But these people were united in a common bond of friendship and belief. It is difficult to explain, but I felt a fellowship with them that I had not felt since before the Death. I was even made the Grand Master.'

'You are the Grand Master of the Guild of Purification?' said Bartholomew, stunned. Michael looked at him with round, doleful eyes, as though he found the mere mention of satanic dealings offensive to his vocation.

'I was,' continued de Belem. 'Not now. In fact, I am no longer even a member, although it is too late to make a difference.'

He paused before continuing.

'I imagine you might think that someone from the Guild of Purification might have killed Frances, but I know that it is not so. Whatever you might believe about us, we do not kill or make sacrifices of living things. Like any other guilds, we join together for fellowship. The difference, perhaps, is that we speak as we feel, and have no priests to warn us of the fires of hell and to look ever for heresy.'

Bartholomew thought about the Franciscans at Michaelhouse, and their obsession with heresy, and did not wonder that some people were attracted to such an organisation. Michael appeared shocked.

De Belem continued. 'We met in disused churches, but did them no harm. The Guild of the Coming is perhaps a little more ritualistic than the Guild of Purification, but we do not kill: the deaths of those women and Frances were nothing to do with us. Someone else is responsible.'

'Like who?' asked Michael.

'Like the fanatics in the Guild of the Holy Trinity,' said de Belem. 'They are always railing about how the Death was brought by sinners like prostitutes and greedy merchants.'

'What makes you think they killed Frances?' asked Bartholomew.

'Because I was sent a note telling me that Frances would be murdered because I was a member of a coven,' said de Belem in a whisper.

'Do you still have it?' asked Michael.

De Belem shook his head. 'It so distressed me, I threw it in the fire. I was foolish. If I had kept it, we might have been able to glean clues as to the identity of her killer.'

'But why did you not tell me of this note before?' asked Bartholomew. 'Such as when you asked me to investigate Frances's murder.'

De Belem closed his eyes. 'I simply did not think of it until after you left. You must recall you had brought devastating news, and I was not thinking clearly.'

'Do you think notes were sent to the families of the other women?' asked Bartholomew. He had been assuming that the murders of the women were random killings, but de Belem's information suggested there might be a pattern to them. If there were a pattern, they might yet be able to solve the mystery.

'I do not know. Frances and Isobel were the only ones who meant something to me.'

'Isobel?' said Michael, through a mouthful of chicken. 'The whore?'

Bartholomew kicked him under the table. De Belem turned sad eyes on Michael. 'A whore, yes, if you would. She came to my house twice every week and left before first light so Frances would not know. I should have insisted that she stayed until it was light that day. Isobel's life should have been worth more to me than my reputation with a wild daughter.'

Bartholomew leaned his folded arms on the table and studied the wet wood, thinking about what de Belem had told them. He was saying that at least two of the murders had been attacks against the satanists, deliberate assassinations intended to strike at specific people. He thought back to what Stanmore had told him the night he had gone to Trumpington: that he thought Richard Tulyet the elder might be a member of the Guild of the Coming.

'Did you tell the Sheriff about the note you received?' he asked.

De Belem nodded. 'He said he would look into it, but of course he found nothing.'

'Will you tell us the names of the other members of the guild so we might question them?'

A faint smile crossed de Belem's face. 'I cannot. It might put them at risk. The two guilds are innocent of the murders, and this maniac must be brought to justice. Tulyet is worthless, and you are my only hope of seeing Frances and Isobel avenged. If the guilds were the murderers, Frances and Isobel would be here now, and we would not be talking.'

The rain became heavier, and de Belem glanced up at the iron-grey clouds.

'I must go. I have been here too long already.' He stood slowly, rain dripping from his hair where it was not covered by his hood. He knelt quickly and awkwardly for Michael's benediction, slipped across the tiny garden, unlatched the gate, and was gone.

'Oh, Lord, Michael,' said Bartholomew, when the door had been closed again. 'Now what? Do you believe him?'

Michael, who had been sufficiently interested by de Belem's words to stop eating, wiped the grease from his mouth with his sleeve. 'His claims are possible,' he answered. 'I am inclined to believe de Belem that his guild is not responsible. After all, he lost his daughter and his woman.'

'But who was in the orchard the night after Frances's murder?' asked Bartholomew.

Michael scratched his head. 'It all makes little sense,' he said.

'Unless,' said Bartholomew, watching a bird swoop onto the table to peck up crumbs from Michael's food, 'de Belem speaks only for the Guild of Purification, of which he was a member. Oswald told me the two guilds were rivals. I think de Belem is underestimating the power of the Guild of the Coming, especially if the Tulyets are involved. I also think his grief might be influencing his reasoning. Perhaps he feels guilty that his loved ones have died because he is a satanist, and is trying to convince himself it is not his fault. If the Guild of the Holy Trinity is antagonistic enough towards satanism to murder, they would not be leaving satanic regalia on people's beds. I still believe the Guild of the Coming left the goat mask in Nicholas's coffin and the head for you.'

Michael rubbed some crumbs across the table idly as he thought. 'You could be right,' he said. 'It would be too easy to dismiss the covens from our enquiries. And de Belem can only have knowledge of his own guild, not that of his rivals. I suggest we treat Master de Belem's information with scepticism.'

He turned back to the remains of his meal, and Bartholomew, chewing on a bacon rind that flavoured the chicken, began to mull over the evidence yet again.

If Isobel made regular visits to de Belem at night, it would have been simple for the murderer to lie in wait for her. Did Frances also have a regular time when she slipped out of the house to meet her lover? But why Michaelhouse? Was she meeting her lover there, the scholar, as Brother Alban had claimed? Perhaps it was her lover who had killed her.

And what had Frances meant when she had said her killer was not a man? He drew circles on the wet table with his finger, lost in thought. She must have glimpsed her killer wearing a mask – either a red hood like the man in the orchard, or one of a goat's head like the dead woman in Nicholas's coffin. He wondered whether the killer was from Michaelhouse, but reasoned that was unlikely. The three people he had seen in the orchard were leaving after their search, not returning to their rooms, and he and Michael had already established that an insider would not have needed to drug Walter to go about his business at night because he would have known Walter slept on duty. What had the murderer lost in the orchard? If it were the Guild of the Coming who were committing the murders, then it must have been they who had attacked him and set the College gate afire. But Sybilla was certain that one man had killed Isobel.

And was Nicholas of York still alive somewhere as the mastermind behind all this? It was odd that the first murder coincided with his death. Was it he who left the goat's head in Michael's room to warn him away? And what of the friar? Was he a member of the Guild of Purification killed by the Guild of the Coming, or perhaps a member of the fanatic Guild of the Holy Trinity rifling through the University history seeking out details of the covens? But Bartholomew and Michael had already shown that he was a stranger to the town and was unfamiliar with the daily rituals of St Mary's Church. Perhaps they should go back to the chest, and see whether there were any other documents there that related to these guilds which might explain why the deaths in St Mary's Church seemed to be connected to the murders of the women.

And where was Buckley? And why had Janetta and Froissart's family gone to ground? Bartholomew felt his head begin to reel. As soon as he felt he was beginning to make some progress, he merely raised more questions. He wondered suddenly how his students were proceeding. He should be with them, helping to train them to be good physicians, not sitting in beer gardens in the rain being warned against becoming involved in something that seemed to grow more sinister with each passing moment. He stood abruptly.

'I can see only one way forward,' said Michael, following him out. 'We must spy on the Guild of the Coming at All Saints' tonight and see what we can discover.'

Bartholomew turned his face to the falling rain, feeling it cool his face. 'I am tempted to go to the Chancellor and turn everything over to him. We are scholars, not witch-hunters. And anyway,' he added wryly, 'it is Sunday.'

Michael looked sharply at him. 'Are you giving up? Are you going to let evil men tell us what we can and cannot do in our own town?'

Bartholomew closed his eyes. 'How did we become embroiled

in all this, Michael?' he asked softly. 'I can make no sense at all of the information we have, and the more we learn, the less clear everything becomes. I do not mind telling you that I find the whole business frightening.'

'I share your fears, but I also think that we will be in danger whether we continue to investigate or not. Everything we do will be held suspect from now on, and whoever left the head for me knows what we are doing. I believe the only way we will ever be safe is to unravel this mystery and unmask its villains. And you owe it to Frances de Belem, who might have been your wife had you not chosen another path.' Michael saw his friend's hesitation and added firmly, 'Tonight we will go to watch this coven meet at All Saints'.'

'Is there no other way?' groaned Bartholomew, shifting uncomfortably in his sopping cloak. 'Perhaps we should just go straight to Tulyet.'

'And say what?' demanded Michael. 'Ask him which member of his guild is murdering the town's whores? Is it his father or just one of his friends? Come on, Matt! We would get nowhere there, and the last time we took him on, I ended up in bed with a dead animal, and you were threatened with imprisonment in the Castle dungeons.'

'Will you tell de Wetherset what we intend to do?' said Bartholomew. 'Then at least someone will know the truth if we are caught and disappear, like Buckley and Nicholas. And ask him if Master Jonstan will come too. This is more in his line of duty than ours.'

'We will not be caught,' said Michael. 'Not with Cynric with us. Asking for Jonstan is a good idea, although I think I will request that the Chancellor does not reveal his plans to Harling. I do not trust that man.'

As Bartholomew and Michael walked home together, the rain became harder, the wind blowing it horizontally in hazy sheets. Bartholomew shivered and pulled his cloak closer round him. The High Street became a river of mud, and water oozed out of the drains and collected in the pot-holes and ruts. The streets were deserted, everyone either at home or in the noisy taverns. Passing St Mary's churchyard, Bartholomew saw something move out of the corner of his eye. He stopped and peered forward, clutching at Michael's sleeve.

'There is someone at Nicholas's grave,' he whispered. Michael stiffened, and together they crept forward.

'Who is it?' breathed Michael. Bartholomew peered through the rain. It was a man of medium height dressed in a priest's robe that was too large. As they inched forward, the man spun round, and seeing them coming, turned and fled. Bartholomew tore after him, leaping over the tombstones and mounds of grass. The man skidded in the mud and almost fell. Bartholomew lunged forward and grabbed a handful of his gown, but lost his balance as the man knocked his hand away. As he scrabbled to regain his footing, the man rushed past him, heading diagonally away from where Michael stood.

As Bartholomew scrambled to his feet, he saw Michael dive full-length towards the fleeing man and gain a hold on the hem of his gown. The man was stopped dead in mid-stride. In an effort made great by terror, he tried to run again, tearing free from Michael. Bartholomew saw him reach the High Street and turn left towards the Trumpington Gate.

Robes billowing, the man began to gain speed down the empty street, Bartholomew in hot pursuit. Bartholomew began to gain on him. And then disaster struck. A heavy cart carrying kegs of beer pulled ponderously out of Bene't Street. The man skipped to one side, skidded in the mud, regained his balance and ran on. But Bartholomew collided heavily with the cart. The horse, panicked by the sudden movement, reared and kicked. One of the kegs fell from the cart and smashed, and Bartholomew went sprawling into the mud.

He covered his head with his hands, hearing the horse's hooves thudding into the ground next to him, and tried to scramble away, but the mud was too slippery. Just as he was certain his head would be smashed by the horse's flailing hooves, one of his arms was seized, and he was hauled away with such force that he thought it had been yanked from its socket. Hooves pounded the spot where he had been moments earlier.

Next to him, Michael leaned up against the wall of a house and gasped for breath, while the carter began to regain control of his horse. Bartholomew sat shakily on the ground and watched the man he had been chasing disappear up the High Street.

'Why don't you watch where you are going!' the carter shouted furiously at Bartholomew.

Michael raised himself up to his full height and pointed a meaty finger at the carter. 'You should not be trading on a Sunday!' he admonished severely. 'You are committing a grave sin.'

The carter was sheepish but unrepentant. 'Well, why was he in such a hurry on a Sunday?' he countered, pointing at Bartholomew.

'He is a physician,' said Michael. 'Physicians attend patients all days of the week.'

'But they do not usually chase them!' the carter retorted, tossing his head in the direction the man had fled. Michael took a step towards him, and the carter, wary of the formidable strength he had witnessed when the monk hauled his colleague from under the horse, backed down. He raised his hand in a rude gesture and urged his horse to move on, yelling abuse when he felt he was far enough away to be safe.

'Thank you,' said Bartholomew, climbing unsteadily to his feet and rubbing his shoulder. He looked at the fat monk and wondered where his strength came from. He seldom took exercise and ate far more than was healthy, but the fat monk's strength of arm was prodigious.

Michael nodded absently. 'A pity you did not catch him,' he said. 'You would have done had that wretched carter not been in the way.'

Bartholomew flexed his arm to ensure it was still attached. 'I had him in my grasp in the churchyard, and so did you.'

Michael shook his head slowly. 'A great pity,' he said again. 'That man could have answered many questions. That was Nicholas of York.'

ChAPTER 8

I T WAS STILL RAINING WHEN DARKNESS FELL THAT NIGHT and Bartholomew was more reluctant to go out than ever. He waited in the kitchen with Cynric and Michael until Michaelhouse grew silent, and followed them resentfully through the orchard to the back gate. He saw shadows flit across the lane as he eased open the new gate and Jonstan materialised out of the darkness, flanked by two heavy-set beadles.

'Two of my best men,' he whispered. 'We will station them within hailing distance of All Saints' as a safeguard, although the Chancellor has advised that we do nothing but watch.'

'I have a bad feeling about this, Brother,' muttered Bartholomew to Michael. 'We should not be sneaking off in the night to spy on satanic rituals.'

'According to Brother Boniface, most of the medicine you teach him involves satanic rituals,' Michael whispered back with a chuckle.

'He said that?' said Bartholomew loudly, and dropped his voice as the others glared at him. 'Did he tell you that?'

Michael nodded, still laughing under his breath. Cynric was elbowing him so he could close the door and Bartholomew was forced to let the matter drop. They made their way up the High Street and into Bridge Street. Once they met a group of beadles, but were allowed past without question when Jonstan spoke. They tried to keep out of sight as they neared the Great Bridge, lest any members of the guild were keeping a watch on it. Three soldiers guarded the bridge, talking in low voices. Bartholomew caught the glint of metal and saw that they were armed. Jonstan stopped to consider.

'It is likely that these satanists will cross the bridge,' he whispered, 'and must have done so for previous meetings. Therefore they must have bribed the guards. If we cross the bridge, the guards might tell them that others have already crossed.'

Cynric glanced at the river. 'We can wade across,' he whispered.

Bartholomew eyed the black, swirling waters dubiously. 'But the rain has swollen it,' he said. 'And besides, it is filthy.'

'You will not notice the filth in the dark,' whispered Jonstan consolingly.

Bartholomew stared at him in the dim light cast by the soldiers' lamps. 'Just because we cannot see it does not mean that it cannot do us harm,' he began.

The others made impatient sounds, and Michael pushed him towards the river bank. 'Now is not the time for a lecture on hygiene, Matt,' he hissed. 'Do not be so fastidious!'

Cynric led the way along the bank, well away from the bridge, and entered the water without a sound. The others followed more noisily, causing the Welshman to glare at them. Jonstan's amiable face was taut with concentration as he waded carefully through the water, swearing to himself when he slipped on the slick river bed. Jonstan was taking his duties seriously. Bartholomew gritted his teeth against the aching cold of the water that lapped around his knees, and then suddenly reached his waist. He tried not to think of Trinity Hall, Gonville Hall, Clare College, Michaelhouse, the Carmelite Friary, and St John's Hospital, all of which discharged their waste directly into the river upstream from where they were crossing. Next to him, Michael hoisted his habit higher and higher as the water rose, displaying startlingly white, fat legs.

They kept to one side of the road as they neared All Saints' Church. Overgrown land marked where a pathetic line of shacks had been burned to the ground during the plague. Few people ventured near the charred posts protruding from the tangle of weeds now: most claimed the area was haunted. While Bartholomew did not believe it was haunted, he felt it held an undeniable atmosphere of desolation. The Guild of the Coming had indeed chosen an apt spot for its demonic meetings.

The church itself was little more than four stone walls with gaping holes for windows. Although it had been decommissioned, it had not been made secure like the others. A wind was picking up, and it made a low hissing sound through the aisle. Cautiously, Bartholomew pushed open the door and stepped inside, while Cynric and Jonstan checked the churchyard, and Michael tried to wring water out of his sodden habit. Bartholomew looked down the small aisle with its peeling wall-paintings and stone altar. He had wondered whether it would hold an evil aura from the demonic ceremonies performed there, but All Saints' Church felt just like any other old and abandoned building: it smelled of damp wood, and a carpet of saturated leaves and a litter of twigs and moss was soft under his feet. He heard the distant chime of a bell. Not long to go now, if the Guild of the Coming intended to begin their unholy antics at midnight.

Jonstan returned to say that there was nothing untoward at the church or the grounds, and that Cynric had already secured himself a good vantage point in a tree. He suggested that Michael hid in the bushes to watch the entrance. Michael's habit was black and he was virtually invisible once he had secreted himself and the leaves had stopped rustling and twitching.

'I imagine that most of their ceremony will take place at the altar-end of the church,' said Jonstan to Bartholomew. 'We can either look through a window as Cynric is doing, or climb into the roof.'

'It will be rotten,' said Bartholomew, looking doubtfully at the roof timbers. 'We might fall through.'

'We stand a far greater chance of being discovered down here,' reasoned Jonstan.

Bartholomew peered up at the roof. He could see sky in patches, and a decaying piece of wood swung back and forth in the wind with a creaking sound.

'We could try,' he said, without conviction. Jonstan smiled and slapped him on the back. At the back of the church, a small spiral stair led up to the bell that had once hung there. The steps were crumbling, slick with wet leaves, and uneven, and Bartholomew was forced to steady himself by bracing both hands against walls that ran with green slime. Ahead of him, Jonstan suddenly lost his footing as a step gave way under his weight. Flailing with his arms, he tumbled backwards, falling heavily against Bartholomew. Both men were saved from falling further only because Bartholomew's cloak snagged on a jagged piece of metal that protruded from the wall.

'Are you all right?' whispered Bartholomew, when he had regained his balance.

'I think I have twisted my ankle,' replied Jonstan, sinking down onto the stairs and rubbing his foot, his face grey with pain. Bartholomew removed the Proctor's shoe and inspected the joint. In the dark, he could not tell whether it was broken or not, but at the very least, it was sprained. It already felt hot under his gently probing fingers.

'We should abandon this business,' he said. 'We should go home while we still can. It was a stupid idea to come here.'

'No!' Jonstan's grip on his arm was strong. 'We must get to the bottom of all this, or more people will die. We cannot leave now!'

'But you should rest your foot,' protested Bartholomew. 'It is already beginning to swell.'

'I will find somewhere I can take the weight off it,' said Jonstan. 'Putting an end to this evil is more important.'

Bartholomew looked up the stairs spiralling away into darkness. 'I suppose you might find somewhere to sit. But you will be in trouble if we need to run.'

'My mother is always telling me I am too old for things like this,' said Jonstan, trying to make light of their predicament. He stood unsteadily, and gave Bartholomew a weak smile. 'Perhaps I should take her advice and become a clerk!'

Bartholomew helped him hop up the stairs until they reached a doorway that afforded access to the inside of the roof. It was lit only by the gaps where the roof was open to the sky, and, looking down, Bartholomew could see that entire sections had fallen into the aisle below. But the main rafters seemed to be sound enough, and if he did not step on the weaker timbers to the side, he should be relatively safe.

'I think I will be able to see from over there,' said Jonstan, pointing. To one side, a large part of the roof had fallen, but there were sturdy timbers on which Jonstan would be able to lean. Bartholomew helped him move, and, although the timbers creaked ominously under their weight, they held. Jonstan wedged himself between two posts where he could take the weight off his ankle and still be able to look down.

Bartholomew made his way back, and looked through the rafters at the floor a long way below. He wondered how he had let himself become involved in such business, but a picture of Frances de Belem came into his mind, so he gritted his teeth and moved forward. At one point, his foot went through a particularly rotten part, shedding shards of flaky wood into the darkness beneath. Bartholomew closed his eyes and clutched a post until he had recovered his nerve. He edged forward again, feeling as though at any moment the whole roof would give way, and he would be sent crashing to the floor.

After what seemed like an age, he reached the end, and looked for a place from which to watch. There was a crown post just above the altar with strong timbers, but Bartholomew knew he would see only the tops of people's heads. He climbed to the far side, and found that, by lying full length along one wide timber, he could see the altar and most of the choir.

Once the fear of being so high up had receded, Bartholomew found he was quite comfortable on his timber, and was sheltered from the wind and rain. Although his legs were wet from wading through the river, the rest of him was dry, and his position was infinitely preferable to those of Michael and Cynric watching from outside. He pulled his cloak tighter round him for warmth, and felt his eyes close. The church below was in darkness and the only sound was the soft patter of rain on the broken roof above him. He heard the gentle hiss of trees in the wind, and, despite his misgivings about their mission, began to feel drowsy.

He awoke with a start wondering where he was, gripping the timber desperately as he felt himself tip. He took a deep, shuddering breath and raised his head to see if he could see Jonstan. The Proctor was almost beside himself, virtually out of his hiding place and gesturing frantically. Even at that distance, Jonstan's face was pale with tension. Bartholomew looked to where he was pointing, and almost fell off the timber in fright.

A few feet from him, another person was climbing over the rafters as he had done. He felt his heart begin to pound. Now they would be uncovered! He glanced at Jonstan, but the Proctor had slipped back into his shadows. Bartholomew did not know what to do. Should he stay where he was and hope he was not seen? Should he attack the person crawling towards him before he was attacked himself? But then they would both fall through the roof, and Bartholomew had no weapon in any case.

As the person inched closer, Bartholomew held his breath and huddled into his cloak. He tried to quell his panic by telling himself that if someone was not expecting him to be there, he was hidden well enough. He was wrapped from head to foot in a black cloak and underneath he wore his black scholar's tabard. As long as he kept his face covered and the person carried no lamp, there was every chance Bartholomew might remain undetected. The person reached the crown post and turned to wave. Bartholomew felt sick as he saw a second man begin to make his way along the rafters.

Meanwhile, in the church itself, people were starting to gather. At first, there were just black shapes moving around in silence. Then pitch torches were lit and the church flared into light. The people wore black gowns with hoods that came over their heads and hid their faces. Bartholomew counted. Twelve standing around the altar, plus the two in the roof. Fourteen. Bartholomew looked down, watching their movements. Each time someone spoke, the others jumped, and several looked around them anxiously. One man was shaking so badly he could barely stand, while another gnawed agitatedly at his fingernails. For an evening in pleasant company, which was how de Belem had described them, the congregation appeared unaccountably nervous.

The second person had reached the first, and was watching the people below. He carried a large bundle that the first man began to unwrap. Bartholomew cringed as the beam on which he lay gave a creak, causing the smaller of the two men to look up. He held his breath, expecting at any moment to feel a dagger at his throat, or the beam tipped so he would fall to his death. But nothing happened, and after a few agonising moments, Bartholomew risked a glance up. The attention of the two men was again fixed on the scene below, for the ceremony was beginning.

The voices were low at first, but began to rise as a figure standing at the altar climbed on top of it. Bartholomew recoiled in shock as he saw a red mask. The chanting continued as the man began to speak. Bartholomew, keeping a wary eye on the two people in the roof, strained to hear his words, but the language was unfamiliar to him. But one word kept occurring – *caper* – the Latin for a male goat.

The chanting grew louder, and one or two people dropped to their knees, while the high priest began to dance in time with the chanting. He suddenly stopped and gave a great yell, throwing up his hands and raising his face to look straight at Bartholomew. Bartholomew felt his stomach turn over and tightened his grip on the rafters in anticipation of being revealed. But nothing of the sort happened, and although Bartholomew saw the glint of the high priest's eyes through the red mask, he apparently was not seen.

One of the two people in the roof moved, and Bartholomew saw a great black crow swoop down towards the altar. It circled twice and then flapped out of one of the windows, cawing loudly. Several of the worshippers screamed and covered their faces, while others shakily resumed their chanting and the high priest began dancing again. It took Bartholomew a moment to realise that the bird had been released by the person in the roof. So, that was why they were there: they were part of an act! He could well understand that to the people standing below the black bird would have appeared to have materialised out of thin air.

The whole process was repeated again with more urgency, the high priest drumming his feet wildly on the stone. When the chanting reached fever pitch, the high priest flung himself onto the floor and began to writhe. Bartholomew saw immediately it was to attract attention away from the roof, and watched closely. It took both people this time to lever something through the hole. The chanting faltered as the church filled with swooping silent bats. There must have been at least seven of them, enormous ones, bundled in the sack ready to be released. They soared uncertainly before fluttering out of the windows into the dark night beyond. One of the worshippers screamed and tried to run away, but was prevented by the others.

The high priest lurched to his feet and began the chanting again. The ceremony was apparently reaching its climax for the high priest cavorted and writhed, uttering the most incomprehensible gibberish. The worshippers edged closer together, casting terrified looks around them. As the chanting grew faster, one of them dropped to his knees and put his forehead to the ground. One by one the others followed. While all heads were conveniently averted, the two in the roof became busy again, and the head of a goat was lowered through the hole on a thin rope.

The high priest, still gibbering, quickly untied the knot so the rope could be pulled back up. That done, he gave a monstrous shriek and hurled himself backwards. The church became silent. Nervously, the worshippers began to look up. The high priest hauled himself to his feet and lifted the head into the air by the horns. His people cowered in front of him.

'Our lord has spoken to me in the language of the dark angels,' he began in English. Several of the worshippers began to whimper. 'He says you, his children, should obey your high priest in all things. Before the new moon, he will claim another for his own, as a sign that he is near.'

He lowered the head to the altar, bowed to it and covered it reverently with a black cloth. The ceremony was over. Or so Bartholomew thought. The two people in the roof were busy, and as the worshippers began to leave, they found themselves splattered with blood that rained through the broken roof above the altar. Bartholomew saw the upturned face of the older Richard Tulyet before he fled, wailing as he went. One old lady stood frozen with fright, her eyes fixed on the black cloth. It was Mistress Tulyet, abandoned by her husband and left to fend for herself. The high priest helped her from the church, where she fled with the rest of her unholy brethren.

Bartholomew watched as the two people in the roof gathered their belongings, and crawled back along the rafters. They were thorough: the smaller of the two even braved a treacherous section of the roof to retrieve a black feather. Jonstan was invisible, and the two left the roof in silence.

The high priest was waiting for them, and he and the smaller man stood for a moment talking in low voices, while the other kept a respectful distance. Bartholomew strained to see their faces, but they wore gowns with deep cowls and were taking no chances that one of the others might come back and recognise them. The high priest ushered them out and began to tidy up. After what seemed like hours, he doused the last torch, and removed his mask, dropping it into a bag with his other belongings. He drew his hood over his head and left. Bartholomew swore softly. He had not been able to see his face, and hoped one of the others had.

Stiffly, Bartholomew eased himself up and stretched. He had no idea how long the ceremony had taken, but his shoulders ached with tension. As he made the treacherous journey back across the rotten rafters he glimpsed the aisle floor a long way down. For an instant he felt dizzy, and had to stand still until the feeling passed.

Jonstan was waiting for him by the stairs, a sheen of sweat on his white face.

'Hell's teeth, Matthew!' he said. 'I have never been so frightened in my life! We must get away from this foul place as quickly as possible!'

Bartholomew helped him down the stairs. Jonstan started violently as Cynric materialised behind him, and clutched at his chest.

'They have all gone,' said Cynric in a low voice. 'I tried to follow the last one, but he was away over the Fens before I could get close enough.' He refused to meet Bartholomew's eye, and Bartholomew wondered whether he had been as assiduous in his trailing as usual.

Michael joined them, his flabby face pallid. 'We should not stay here,' he said and grabbed Bartholomew's arm. 'De Belem was wrong. This was nothing harmless: it was evil and terrifying. I have no doubt those vile people are behind much that is wrong in the town.'

Cynric led the way, scouting ahead to make certain none of the worshippers still lurked. Bartholomew and Michael followed, almost carrying Jonstan between them. They forded the river as before, wading waist-deep through the cold water. Jonstan leaned on them heavily, making their progress slower than Bartholomew would have wished. It was with considerable relief that they finally reached the back gate at Michaelhouse and slipped through the orchard to the kitchen. While Cynric went to explain to Jonstan's beadles that he had sprained his ankle, Bartholomew kindled a fire. It was cold for summer, and while he and Jonstan had stayed relatively dry, Michael and Cynric were soaked to the skin.

He set some wine to mull and inspected Jonstan's foot. It was twice its normal size, and already turning dark with bruising. Deftly, he wrapped it in wet bandages and placed it on a stool, cushioned with his cloak. He looked around at the others. They were all pale and subdued, and Michael was shivering uncontrollably. Bartholomew poured the wine and Michael gulped his and Bartholomew's down at an impressive rate, even for him, and held his cup out for more.

Jonstan took a deep breath. 'Did anyone see the face of that cavorting leader?'

The others shook their heads. 'Damn,' said Bartholomew. 'I thought you might, Michael.'

Michael shook his head. 'He was too far away, and he had his hood pulled over his head. I am surprised he could see where he was walking. I saw Richard Tulyet, though.'

'The Sheriff?' gasped Jonstan.

'No, his father, the merchant. Perhaps the Sheriff was there, but I did not see him.'

'I saw his mother,' said Bartholomew. 'Her husband abandoned her when the blood started raining down.'

'That was disgusting,' said Cynric with a shudder. 'I thought it was just some dye at first, but I had a good look and it really was blood.'

'Probably from the goat,' said Bartholomew.

'Of course,' said Jonstan, looking relieved. 'From the goat.'

'I was scared out of my wits,' said Michael in a low voice. 'Did you see that bird appear out of nowhere? And that head just lowered itself from the sky. I will never again mock powers I do not understand.'

Cynric nodded vigorously, while Jonstan closed his eyes and crossed himself. 'What were that pair up to near you, Matthew?' he asked weakly. 'I could not see.'

Bartholomew suddenly realised that he had been the only one

able to see how the hoax was enacted. Cynric and Michael were outside, and Jonstan was too far away. They had been duped in the same way that the worshippers had. No wonder they were subdued.

'They were proving what you have always held, Michael,' he said, smiling. 'That the Devil's worst crimes are the handiwork of people.'

Jonstan slept on the pallet bed in Bartholomew's storeroom for the few remaining hours of the night and was helped home by his two beadles at first light.

'You must rest your foot for a few days,' Bartholomew advised. 'Do you have someone who can care for you?'

'My mother will attend to me,' said Jonstan, smiling weakly. 'Although she will tell me that it is my own fault for climbing around old buildings in the dark.'

Bartholomew watched him hobble out of the yard, and turned his thoughts to what they had learned. The high priest and his two helpers could not have been the same three Bartholomew had encountered in the orchard, because the man who had bitten him had been huge, and none of the three satanists were above average size. Could one of them be Sybilla's 'average man'? Bartholomew supposed that must be likely, since the high priest had forecast that another murder would occur before the new moon, and how else would he know unless he or one of his associates was planning to commit the crime?

Perhaps the high priest was Nicholas of York, newly returned from the dead to frighten the living daylights out of his coven. The more Bartholomew thought about it, and the other tricks used to keep the congregation in a state of terror, the more he became convinced it was plausible. What better trick than to rise from the grave? Especially since so many people had seen him dead.

'We must do something to stop another murder being committed,' said Bartholomew to Michael, who had poked his head around the door of Bartholomew's room.

'I agree,' said Michael, moving to sit on the bed. 'But what do you suggest? Shall we entertain the town's prostitutes in College to keep them off the streets for the next few nights?'

'No, but I know something we might do,' said Bartholomew, making for the door. Michael scrambled to follow, grumbling.

Bartholomew went to the kitchen and asked Agatha where he might find the Lady Matilde. The large laundress offered to show him, leaving through the back gate and cutting across the fields so that no one would ask why they were missing church. She took them to a small timber-framed house in the area near St John's Hospital known as The Jewry, dating from the time when it had been the home of Jewish merchants before their expulsion from England in 1290. Despite the fact that it was barely light, the town was already busy, and people ran here and there preparing for the day's business.

'Matilde,' Agatha yelled at the top of her voice, drawing the attention of several passers-by. 'Customers!'

Bartholomew cringed, while Michael looked furtive. Agatha gave them a knowing wink and marched into the house next door, calling loudly for yet another cousin. Bartholomew saw one or two people nudging each other at the sight of a physician and a monk outside the door of a well-known prostitute. Michael pulled his cowl over his head as if he imagined it might make him anonymous, and succeeded in making himself look more furtive than ever.

Matilde answered the door and ushered them inside, smiling at their obvious discomfort. She brought them cups of cool white wine and saw that they were comfortably seated before sitting herself. The room was impeccably clean, with fine wool rugs scattered about the floor, and tapestries on the walls. The furniture was exquisitely carved, and the chairs were adorned with embroidered cushions. A table with quills and parchment stood next to the window, suggesting that Lady Matilde could write as well as speak Court French.

'How may I help you?' she said. She gave Michael a sidelong glance that oozed mischief. 'I assume you have not come for my professional attentions?'

Michael, his composure regained now that he was away from public view, winked at her, and grinned.

'We have come to give you some information,' said Bartholomew quickly, before Michael could side-track them by flirting. 'We cannot reveal our sources, but we have reason to believe that there will be another murder in the town before the new moon.'

She looked at him intently, all humour gone from her face. 'The new moon is due in four days. When one is out at night, one knows these things,' she added, seeing Michael's surprise. She stood and went to look out of the small window, drumming her long, slender fingers on the sill as she thought.

Bartholomew watched her. She was indeed an attractive woman, with long, honey-coloured hair twisted into a braid that hung heavily down her back. She was tall, and carried herself with a grace that he had seen in few women other than Philippa, his betrothed. The thought of Philippa made him look away from Matilde guiltily: he had scarcely given her a thought since the business with the University chest had begun, and he realised he had not even remembered to write to her the day before – the first Sunday he had not sent her a letter since she had left for London two months previously.

'Thank you for telling me this,' said Matilde, turning to them, her voice breaking across Bartholomew's thoughts. 'I will ensure the word gets around to my sisters that they take extra care.'

'Sisters?' queried Michael, his green eyes dancing merrily.

'Fellow whores, Brother,' she said, with a gaze that would have discomfited most men.

Michael stared back unabashed, favouring her with what Bartholomew could only describe as a leer. 'Sisters mean something different to us holy men,' he said.

She smiled at him. 'Well, now you know what it means to us prostitutes,' she said.

Bartholomew had trouble dragging Michael away, and wondered yet again how someone with Michael's obvious interest in women could have chosen a vocation that demanded chastity. Bartholomew knew that Michael regularly broke other rules of his Order – he nearly always started eating before grace, he did not keep his offices, and his lifestyle was far from simple. Bartholomew wondered which other rules the large monk might bend or break.

They finally took their leave of Matilde, and walked home as early morning sun bathed the town. The High Street seethed with carts heading to the Fair, loaded way beyond safety limits with clothes, cheeses, meats, animals, furniture, and pots and pans. The drains at the side of the street were overflowing from the rain the night before, and great puddles of brown ooze forced Bartholomew and Michael to make some spectacular leaps to avoid them. In one, a sheep bleated pitifully as it stood up to its neck in mire, while a farmer tried to coax it out with a handful of grass.

Since they had missed breakfast, they bought hot oatcakes from a baker. Bartholomew winced as the coarse grain and particles of stone grated against his teeth. When he had finished, he was still hungry, but the few pennies in his pocket were not enough to buy one of the delicious pies carried on a baker's tray, nor the soft white bread carried in the basket of another. He saw some children jostle the man with the bread, and one of them escaped with a loaf. Two of the children were the tinker's daughters, and Bartholomew wondered if their younger brother were still alive.

Michael stopped off to report to de Wetherset, while Bartholomew walked back to Michaelhouse to test his students on the Galen that they were supposed to have read. He was not pleased to discover that they had become side-tracked before finishing the first paragraph.

'Brother Boniface says that predicting the outcome of a disease is tantamount to predicting the will of God, and that is heresy,' said Gray in explanation.

Bartholomew ran a hand through his hair in exasperation. Surely Boniface could not claim Galen's works were heretical? They had been standard, uncontroversial texts for physicians for hundreds of years. In fact, they were so old that newer discoveries were beginning to throw some of Galen's theories into question.

He picked up a cup from the table and held it in the air. 'Brother Boniface. If I allow this to fall from my hand, what will happen?'

Boniface eyed him warily. 'It will drop to the floor,' he said.

'And.if I drop a lighted candle into these dry rushes, what will happen?'

'They will burn.'

'You are making predictions about events. Why is predicting the outcome of a disease any different?'

'It is not heresy to predict the obvious,' said Boniface coldly. 'It is heresy to predict whether a man lives or dies.'

'But there are some injuries and wasting diseases from which it is clear a man will never recover, no matter what a physician might do,' said Bartholomew, frustrated. 'Is that knowledge heresy?'

'But those cases are obvious!' said Boniface, becoming angry.

'And at what point does the outcome become obvious, exactly?' said Bartholomew. 'And what is the difference between you deciding which cases are obvious and which are not, and predicting whether a patient lives or dies?'

Boniface glared at him, but was silent. Bartholomew could have taken the argument further, but he had made his point. He instructed that Gray was to read the passages from Galen that they should have read earlier with others from the *Tegni*. The students groaned. They would be busy until nightfall, but since they had already wasted time on meaningless debate, they had no choice if they wanted to pass their disputations.

'That was a neat argument,' said Michael, who had been listening. 'It put that beggarly Franciscan in his place. He is disruptive in my theology classes. I would not mind if he stimulated lively debate, but his arguments are based on ignorance and bigotry.'

Bartholomew frowned. 'Except for Deynman, the others will pass if Boniface lets them study. But I do not want to waste the day talking about Boniface. I have been invited to Gonville Hall for a debate on contagion with two physicians from Paris.'

He smiled enthusiastically, and ducked into his room for his bag. Michael waited outside. 'We have to go to see Sir Richard Tulyet,' he called.

'Tulyet?' said Bartholomew, looking out of his window at Michael. 'Is that not rather rash, considering what we saw yesterday?'

'We have been discreet for days, and it has got us nowhere,' said Michael. 'De Wetherset believes it is time for a more direct approach.'

'Easy for him to say, sitting safely next to his wretched chest,' grumbled Bartholomew.

Michael smiled grimly. 'De Wetherset wants us to go immediately.'

Bartholomew emerged from his room. 'Immediately? But what about my debate?'

'We will hurry. You will not miss much of it,' said Michael.

Bartholomew sighed. 'Damn this business!' he said. 'Come on, then. But no lagging on the way.'

The home of Richard Tulyet the elder was a gracious building near the Church of the Holy Sepulchre. It was half-timbered, rather than stone, but was sturdily built. There were expensive rugs on the polished floors, and the monotony of white walls was broken with fine tapestries. Bartholomew and Michael were shown into a sunny room overlooking a garden at the rear of the house.

Tulyet did not hurry to see them, and Bartholomew began to pace irritably. Even Michael, helping himself to several exotic pastries from a dish on the table, considered that Tulyet had exceeded the limit of courtesy for which visitors might be expected to wait. Eventually, Tulyet puffed into the room, spreading his hands in apology, although the expression on his face suggested anything but repentance. He was a small man with the same fluffy beige hair as his son.

'I have had a most busy morning,' he said, seating himself at the table and stretching his hand towards the pastry dish before realising that it was empty.

'We have not,' said Michael, pointedly.

Tulyet ignored his comment, and studied the monk over his steepled fingers. 'How might I help you?'

'How long have you been a member of the Guild of the Coming?' asked Michael bluntly.

Tulyet stared at him, the smile fading from his face. 'I do not know what you are talking about.'

'You were seen last night leaving All Saints' Church after a less than religious ceremony was conducted there,' said Michael. 'How is your wife, by the way?'

Bartholomew cringed. He realised that Michael was aiming to needle Tulyet into indiscretion, but suspected that this was not the way to gain the information they needed. Tulyet had been a burgess and Lord Mayor, and was unlikely to be goaded into revealing matters he wished to remain secret. Bartholomew stepped forward to intervene.

'Perhaps we might talk to Mistress Tulyet too,' he said politely.

'You may not,' Tulyet snapped. 'She is unwell. And before you tell me you are a physician, she has already seen one, and he advised her to rest after he finished bleeding her. Not that this is any of your affair. Good morning.'

He made to sweep past them. Bartholomew blocked his way. 'Who is it in the Guild of the Coming that you hold in such fear?' he asked softly.

Tulyet stopped abruptly and Bartholomew saw the uncertainty in his eyes.

'This must be stopped,' Bartholomew said gently. 'If you help us, we might be able to make an end to it.'

Hope flared on Tulyet's face, and he took a step forward.

'I do not believe my father wishes to talk to you.'

Bartholomew looked behind him and saw Tulyet's youngest son standing in the doorway with two of his sergeants from the Castle. 'We are trying to help,' said Bartholomew.

'You are trying to interfere, and succeeding very well,' snapped the Sheriff. 'My father's affairs are none of your business. Now, please leave our house.'

'Why will you not let your father answer for himself?' asked Michael.

'Get out!' yelled Tulyet the elder. 'I will not tolerate this in my own home. Leave now, or these men will throw you out.'

He spun on his heel and stormed out, all trace of his momentary weakness gone. Bartholomew was frustrated. The old man had almost told them what they needed to know, and he was clearly terrified by it. He had obviously sent to the Castle for his son while he kept him and Michael waiting, which meant that he must have felt he needed protection. Perhaps he had joined the Guild of the Coming for similar reasons to de Belem, and had become too deeply embroiled to back out.

The Sheriff leaned back against the door frame and sneered at them. 'You heard my father,' he said. 'Leave, or be thrown out by my men.'

'Are you not man enough to do it yourself?' asked Michael. 'The father unable to answer questions himself, and the son needing others to fight his battles. Come, Matt. This is no place for men.'

Bartholomew was impressed by Michael's nerve, but uncertain that such fieriness was prudent, and followed him out into the street half expecting to feel a knife between his shoulder-blades. Sheriff Tulyet followed.

'If I discover that either of you are interfering with my investigation again, or that you are intimidating my family, I will arrest you,' he said loudly. 'I will put you in the Castle prison, and your Chancellor and Bishop will not be able to do anything to help you. How could they in matters of treason?'

He slammed the door and stalked back towards the Castle, his men following.

'Treason?' said Michael, simultaneously startled and angry. 'On what grounds? This has nothing to do with treason!'

'It is not unknown for officers of the law to fabricate evidence to fit a case, or for them to force false confessions,' said Bartholomew drily, taking the monk's arm and leading him away from Tulyet's house. Justice was swift and harsh in England, and often men accused of crimes were not given time to prove their innocence. 'You should watch your tongue, Brother. It would not take much for Sheriff Tulyet to follow such a path. He seems unbalanced.'

'Me hanged for treason, and you burned for heresy,' said Michael with a flicker of a smile. 'What a pair the Chancellor has chosen for his agents.'

Bartholomew walked quickly from Tulyet's house down Milne Street to Gonville Hall, to which its Master of Medicine, Father Philius, had invited two physicians from Paris, Bono and Matthieu.

'Ah yes, Doctor Bartholomew,' said Bono, standing to bow

to him as he was shown into the conclave by a porter. 'I know your old master in Paris, Ibn Ibrahim.'

Bartholomew was delighted, but not surprised. Paris was not so large that a man of his master's standing could remain hidden. 'How does he fare?'

'Well enough,' said Bono, 'although I cannot imagine that he will remain so if he does not amend his beliefs. During the Death he suggested that the contagion was carried by animals! Can you credit such a foolish notion?'

'Animals?' queried Philius, startled. 'On what premise?'

'That he conducted certain tests to show it was not spread by the wind. He concluded that it must have been carried by animals.'

Bartholomew frowned. It was possible, he supposed, but he had not been in contact with animals during the dreadful winter months of 1348 and 1349, and he had been a victim of the plague. He wished Ibn Ibrahim was with them now that he might question him closer. The Arab usually had well-founded reasons for making such claims.

'The man is a heretic,' said Matthieu. 'I would keep your apprenticeship with him quiet if I were you. Do you know he practises more surgery than ever now?'

Bartholomew was silent. He too was using a greater number of surgical techniques, and the more he used them, the more he found them useful. He listened to the others discussing how surgery was an abomination that should be left to the inferior barber-surgeons. As the discussion evolved, Bartholomew began to feel a growing concern that his own teaching and beliefs would be considered as heretical as those of Ibn Ibrahim, and that he soon might have to answer for them.

The discussion moved from surgery to contagion, and Bartholomew found himself attacked again because of his insistence that a physician might spread contagion if he did not wash his hands. Bono shook his head in disbelief, while Matthieu merely laughed. Father Philius said nothing, for he and Bartholomew had debated this many times, and had never found common ground.

By the time the daylight began to fade and Gonville Hall's bell rang to announce the evening meal was ready, Bartholomew felt drained. He declined the invitation to stay to eat, and walked back along Milne Street towards Michaelhouse. As he reached the gates, the porter told him he was needed at the Castle. Wearily he set off, wondering why Tulyet should have summoned him so near the curfew, and whether he would have the strength to deal with the hostile Sheriff.

As he climbed Castle Hill, a sergeant hurried towards him with evident relief.

'You came!' he said, taking Bartholomew's arm and setting a vigorous pace towards the Castle. 'I thought you might not – under the circumstances.'

'What do you mean?' asked Bartholomew, disengaging his arm.

'The de Belem girl was a friend of yours, and the Sheriff is doing little to search out her killer,' he said, glancing around nervously. He added more firmly, 'He was a good Sheriff, but these last few weeks he has changed.'

'How?' asked Bartholomew.

The sergeant shrugged. 'Family problems, we think. But none of us know for certain. Here we are.'

They arrived at the gate-house, and Bartholomew was escorted inside. Torches hung in sconces along the walls so that the entire courtyard was filled with a dim, flickering light. The towers and crenellated curtain walls were great black masses against the darkening sky.

The soldier steered Bartholomew to the Great Hall against the north wall. In a small chamber off the stairs a man lay on a dirty straw pallet, groaning and swearing. Other soldiers stood around him, but moved aside as Bartholomew entered.

'A stupid accident,' said the sergeant in response to Bartholomew's unasked question. 'I told him to take down the archery targets, and Rufus here did not hear me shout that practice was over.'

Rufus slunk back into the shadows, aware that the eyes of all his colleagues were on him accusingly. 'It was an accident!' he insisted.

Bartholomew knelt and inspected the wound in the injured man's upper arm. The arrowhead that was embedded there was barbed, and Bartholomew hesitated. Two options were open to him: he could force the arrowhead through the arm and out the other side, or he could cut the flesh and pull the barbs free. The second option was clearly the better one for the injured man, since the arrowhead was not embedded sufficiently deeply to warrant forcing it through the arm. But it would involve surgery, and Bartholomew had just spent an entire day hearing how physicians that stooped to use methods suited to barbers were heretics. The injured man opened pleading eyes.

Bartholomew took one of the powerful sense-dulling potions he carried, mixed it into a cup of wine near the bed and gave it to the man to drink. When he saw the man begin to drowse, he indicated to the others that they should hold his patient down. He took a small knife and, ignoring the man's increasingly agonised screams, quickly cut the flesh away from the arrowhead and eased it out. The man slumped in relief as Bartholomew held the arrow for him to see. Bartholomew bound the arm with a poultice of healing herbs, gave him a sleeping potion, and said he would return later to ensure no infection had crept in.

Bartholomew was escorted to the gate by the sergeant.

'Thank you,' he said, handing Bartholomew an odd assortment of coins. 'Will he live, do you think? Will he keep the arm?'

Bartholomew was surprised by the question. 'It is not a very serious wound, and there seems to be no damage to the main blood-vessels. There should be no problem if it does not become infected.'

'Father Philius came this morning. He said he could do nothing, and that we needed Robin of Grantchester, the barber-surgeon. Robin offered to saw the arm off at the shoulder for five silver pennies payable in advance, but we could not raise one between us and he refused to give credit. We decided to ask you to come when the Sheriff left for the night.' He smiled suddenly, revealing an impressive collection of long, brown teeth. 'Agatha, your College laundress, is a cousin of mine, and she told me you are flexible about payments for your services.'

Bartholomew smiled back, and shook the sergeant's proffered hand before taking his leave. Agatha was right: although

Bartholomew kept careful records about the medicines he dispensed, he kept no notes of payments due, and more often than not, he forgot what he was owed. It was a bone of contention between Bartholomew and Gray, who argued that there were those who would take advantage of such carelessness. Master Kenyngham, however, saw that Bartholomew was popular among his patients, and encouraged Bartholomew's casual attitude towards remuneration on the grounds that it made for favourable relations between Michaelhouse and the town.

As he walked back to Michaelhouse, Bartholomew's doubts about his methods began to recede. Few patients who underwent amputations survived, especially amputations performed by the unsavoury Robin, who was so slow that many of his patients died from bleeding or shock before he had finished. He always demanded advance payments, because so few patients survived his ministrations and he had learned that it was difficult to extract payments from grieving relatives. In the young soldier's case, there had been no cause to amputate anyway, when all that was needed were a few careful incisions.

As he walked down Castle Hill, he was accosted by a breathless urchin.

'I was sent for you,' he gasped. 'There has been an accident. You are needed, Doctor. You must come with me!'

Bartholomew followed the lad, wondering what else would happen before he could go home. The boy trotted along the High Street and cut behind St Mary's Church. The first inclination Bartholomew had that something was not right was when the lad suddenly darted off to one side. Bartholomew watched in surprise as he disappeared between the bushes. Realising that he had been led into a trap, he turned and began to run back towards the main road.

A line of men emerged, cutting off his escape. Bartholomew put his head down and pounded towards them. They faltered, and for a moment he thought he would be able to force his way through them. Then he felt something akin to a brewer's cart slam into him and he went sprawling onto the wet grass. Something landed on top of him with such force that all the breath was driven from his body. He struggled frantically and uselessly.

Just as he was beginning to turn dizzy from lack of air, the weight lifted and he was dragged to his feet. As he leaned over, gasping for breath, he saw something large move through the undergrowth away from him, but when he looked a second time, there was nothing except two or three waving branches that indicated something had passed between them.

'Matthew Bartholomew! You go where you are uninvited and you run away from where you are welcome!' said Janetta, thick black hair falling like gauze around her face. She nodded to the two men holding him, and his arms were released. 'I thought you wanted to talk to me.'

Bartholomew, still trying to catch his breath, looked wildly around him. The men were withdrawing silently, although he knew they would reappear rapidly if she called for them. Within seconds, they were alone, although he knew they were being watched closely.

'Well?' she said, still smiling at him. 'What do you want?'

He thought of Matilde's words of warning, and tried to collect his confused thoughts.

'Master Tulyet told us that you were a witness to the murder of Froissart's wife,' he said. 'I wanted to ask you about that.'

'He told you what?' she said, her eyes opening wide with shock.

Bartholomew sat on a tombstone and watched Janetta suspiciously.

'I have never spoken to this Tulyet,' protested Janetta. 'I know of him by reputation, of course. But I have never spoken to him.'

'But why would he lie?' asked Bartholomew, his thoughts whirling.

Janetta sat on the tombstone next to him, although she was careful to maintain a good distance between them. 'I have no idea. I do not know how he would even know my name.'

'Did you know Froissart?'

'I know him,' she said. She shuddered suddenly. 'Do you know what people are saying? That Froissart is the one who is killing the whores.'

'Tulyet does not believe that,' said Bartholomew.

'That is because Tulyet almost had Froissart in his hands when he claimed sanctuary in the church, and his men allowed him to escape. What does that tell you about Tulyet?' Janetta spat.

'Do you believe Froissart is the killer?'

Janetta let out a deep breath and looked up at the darkening sky. 'I think that is likely.'

'On what grounds?'

Janetta turned to him with her slow smile. 'Questions! You are like the inquisition!' She leaned down, and picked a stem of grass that she began to chew. 'Froissart is a rough man who drinks heavily and is violent to his wife and sister. You are lucky he was not one of the ones who caught you in our alley last week.'

'Why did he flee to the church for sanctuary if there was no murder?' asked Bartholomew. In the darkening gloom, the scars on her jaw were almost invisible, and he wondered why she did not make an attempt to hide them with the powders she used on her cheeks.

'I did not say there was no murder. I said I did not witness it, and I did not speak to Tulyet. Marius Froissart's wife was murdered about two weeks ago.'

'So did Froissart kill her?' asked Bartholomew. This woman was worse than Boniface with her twisting and turning of words.

'I could not say. I did not witness it, as I have just said.'

Bartholomew was becoming exasperated. He forced himself not to show his impatience, knowing it would probably amuse her. He smiled. 'But what do you think?' he insisted as pleasantly as he could.

'I imagine he killed her,' she said, turning to face him.

'Where are the rest of his family?'

'They have fled the town because people believe Froissart is the killer. His family will not be safe here until Froissart is caught. People believed they were hiding him, and they left at my suggestion.'

'Where are they?' he asked.

'I do not know, and if I did, it would remain my secret,' she said, her smile not reaching her eyes. 'They have suffered enough.'

Bartholomew thought for a moment. 'Do you know a Father Lucius?'

Janetta looked amazed. 'A priest? Priests do not come to Primrose Alley!'

'What about high priests?' said Bartholomew, watching her carefully.

'High priests? You mean bishops?' she asked.

'I mean priests of satanism,' said Bartholomew, still eyeing her intently.

'Satanism?' She made an exasperated sound and flashed him a quick smile. 'You must think I am without wits: I keep repeating everything you say. Now, satanism. It is certainly practised in the town. But the poor only mumble the odd blasphemy and steal holy water to feed to their pigs. The rich summon great demons from hell. If you are wanting high priests, Doctor, do not look to our community, look to the merchants and the lawyers. And even the wealthier of the scholars.'

She mused for a moment. 'Why are you involved in all this? You are not a Proctor. Can you not see that this business is dangerous? Powerful men are involved who would kill you without a second thought. Leave this business for others to sort out.'

Bartholomew looked at her as she sat, her face shadowed. Another warning to stay away?

'Do you know where I might find the lay-brother who locked the church on the night of the friar's death?' he asked finally.

She sighed. 'So you will not heed my warning?'

Bartholomew did not reply, but waited for her to answer his question. She sighed again. 'The lay-brother you were chasing in our lane? No. That was the last any of us saw of him. You frightened him clean off the face of the earth.'

Bartholomew stood to leave. It was dark, and, although he would not have admitted it to Janetta, he did not feel safe with her in the churchyard. He wondered why she had picked this time and place to meet him, and felt uneasy. Was she watching his every move? Had she taken the arsenic from his bag and substituted it with white sugar? Was it Janetta who had left the goat's head on Michael's bed to warn him as she was warning Bartholomew now?

'You have been most helpful, Mistress Janetta,' he said. 'But please remember next time that it should not be necessary for your friends to sit on me to make me stay.'

A spark of anger glinted in her eyes so fast that Bartholomew thought he had imagined it, before it was masked by her enigmatic smile. He smiled, bowed, and walked purposefully away. His nerves tingled as he waited for figures looming out of the bushes that would block his escape. But there was nothing. He walked unmolested to the High Street and home to Michaelhouse.

When the sturdy gates of the College were barred behind him, he went straight to find Michael. The monk had just gone to bed, but was uncomplaining when Bartholomew dragged him from his sleep. They went to Bartholomew's room, where they would not disturb Michael's room-mates. Once Michael had settled himself comfortably on a stool, Bartholomew related the details of his meeting with Janetta.

'Oh Lord, Matt! I do not like that woman.'

He listened without further interruption until Bartholomew had finished his story and then sat thinking in silence.

'I think your other whore friend is right. I feel this Janetta is untrustworthy. Why did you not ask her about her scars?'

'That would not have been polite,' said Bartholomew. 'Why should I question her about a crime for which she had already paid?'

'You are too gentle,' said Michael. 'I suppose that and your curly black hair are the reasons you seem to have half the whores in Cambridge demanding your company. Janetta, Sybilla, "Lady" Matilde. What would the Franciscans say if they were to find out?'

'Michael, please,' said Bartholomew irritably. 'Think about what Janetta told me instead of troubling your monkish brain with unmonkish thoughts of prostitutes. Tulyet said Janetta was a witness to murder; she says she is not and has never spoken to him. It is black and white. They both cannot be right, so one of them is lying. Which? Is it Tulyet, who seems to be dragging his feet over the investigation, perhaps because of his family's involvement with the Guild of the Coming? Or is it Janetta, who holds sway over ruffians, and appears and disappears at will?'

'Or are they both lying?' asked Michael. 'Janetta saw the murder, but Tulyet never asked her. What about Froissart? You say you gave her no reason to assume that Froissart was dead? She has no idea he lies cold and stinking in St Mary's crypt?'

'Tulyet does not know of Froissart's death either. Janetta says the townspeople believe that Froissart is the killer and that Tulyet lost him. Tulyet says that Froissart does not have the intelligence to carry out the murders. Janetta says Froissart was violent.'

'They do not sound like the same man to me,' said Michael. 'Either Froissart was a clever and vicious killer or he did not have the intelligence to plan such things. Which Froissart was the real one?'

'I suppose it does not matter much,' said Bartholomew, leaning back with a yawn, 'since we know he is not in a position to do much about anything.'

Michael yawned too. 'I cannot make any sense out of this tonight. The Chancellor is burying Froissart and the woman tomorrow. Let us see what their funerals might bring to light.'

They both started suddenly, aware that someone else had entered the room and was standing silently in the shadows.

'Boniface!' said Bartholomew, leaning back against the wall again. 'You made me jump!'

'I am leaving, Master Bartholomew,' he said.

Bartholomew twisted around to look at him. 'Leaving? But your disputation is in two days. I have already told you that if you can put heresy to the back of your mind for a couple of hours, you should pass.'

'I do not want to become a physician,' said Boniface. He stood stiffly in the doorway. 'And I do not want to be a friar.'

'Boniface!' said Michael kindly. 'Think about what you are saying. You have taken vows. At least talk to Father William first.'

'I have,' said Boniface. 'He told me I should take some time to consider before I act.'

'That is good advice,' said Bartholomew gently. 'But do not consider tonight. It is late. Come to see me tomorrow and we will talk when our minds are fresh.'

Boniface was silent.

'Frances de Belem!' he blurted out suddenly. 'She was coming to see me the day she died. We usually met before dawn under the willows by the fish-ponds. I unbarred the gate and waited, but she did not come. All the time she was dying in the orchard.'

Bartholomew remembered Alban claiming that Frances had a lover, and even her father had known she was meeting someone at dawn. Poor Boniface! A murdered lover was hardly something for which a young friar could claim sympathy from his fellows.

'I thought you might have killed her,' he said, swallowing and looking at Bartholomew.

'Me?' said Bartholomew, appalled. 'What on earth could have given you that idea?'

'Well, you are often out of the College at night, and I thought you must have seen her and killed her to keep your comings and goings secret,' said Boniface, 'especially if you were involved in all this business with witchcraft that Brother Alban was telling us about.'

'Brother Alban is a dangerous old gossip,' said Michael firmly. 'And Matt is not the only one to slip in and out of College at night. I do, I have seen Hesselwell and Aidan do so, and now you say you did.'

'I know,' said Boniface, 'but I was distraught, and I had no one to tell. I did not know what to do. She told me she had something important to tell me, and I waited but she never came.'

Bartholomew could not meet his eyes. If Boniface was Frances's lover, then he must have been the father of her child. No wonder Frances had said that the father could not marry her. He decided nothing would be gained by telling Boniface that Frances was carrying his child when she died. The student was in enough turmoil already.

'She was almost hysterical,' Boniface reflected. 'I asked her to tell me then, but she said she needed to tell me privately. Against my better judgement, I agreed to meet her in the orchard.'

'Did you not wait at the gate for her?' asked Michael.

Boniface shot him a bitter look. 'I waited for her by the fish-ponds. I was afraid of being seen, and there are reeds and willows in which to hide around the ponds.'

Bartholomew could think of nothing to say. He tried to remember the times he had broken the rules to meet a woman in the night while a student in Oxford, but the memories were dim, and he could not recall his feelings. Boniface hurried on.

'When I heard she had been dying while I hid among the reeds, I felt wretched. I took the arsenic from your bag, and put the sugar in its place because I was going to swallow it. Then you gave your lecture on dosages and I realised there was not enough to kill me. Here.' He pushed a packet at Bartholomew.

'I never carry enough to kill in case anyone steals it, or it falls from my bag by accident,' said Bartholomew, staring at the small packet in his hands.

'I am glad you are cautious,' said Boniface with a faint smile. 'At least now I have not compounded one sin with another by committing suicide.' He stood to leave.

Bartholomew rummaged in his bag and handed him a twist of cloth. 'This is camomile,' he said. 'Mix it with some wine, and it will help you sleep. Tomorrow we can talk again.'

Boniface looked as if he would refuse, but then leaned forward and snatched it from him. He gave a sudden smile that lightened his sullen features and made him almost handsome. Michael sketched a benediction at him, and the friar disappeared. Bartholomew looked out of the window to make sure he returned to his own room. When he saw Boniface pour himself a drink and lie down on his bed through the open window opposite, he sat again.

'I wonder what she wanted to tell him,' said Michael.

'Nothing that is of import to us,' said Bartholomew.

'You know?' said the astute Michael immediately. 'She told you!' Bartholomew tried to change the subject, but Michael was tenacious. 'She carried his child!' he exclaimed, watching Bartholomew intently. 'They were lovers, and he made her pregnant! That is why you know and he does not. She must have asked you for a cure.'

'Michael . . .' began Bartholomew.

Michael raised his hands. 'No one will hear of this from me. I will say a mass for the child since no one else ever will, and there will be an end to it.' He paused. 'So that explains why she was in Michaelhouse. But not who killed her. Is it a scholar here, do you think?'

Bartholomew shook his head slowly. 'It is possible,' he said, 'but if Frances could get into Michaelhouse, so could another. Tulyet, perhaps, since his night patrols mean that he is sometimes out at night. Or Nicholas – dead, but seen alive at his own graveside. Or Buckley, who conveniently disappeared the night the friar died in the chest containing the controversial University history. Or perhaps even Boniface, to free himself from a romance that was destroying his peace of mind and threatening his vocation.'

Michael stretched. 'It is beyond me,' he said. 'Like Boniface, I need to sleep, and we will talk again in the morning.'

CHAPTER 9

THE FOLLOWING MORNING, BARTHOLOMEW FOUND THAT HIS students had managed to work their way through the first set of texts he had set the day before, but not the second. He instructed that they finish it that afternoon and attend Master Kenyngham's astronomy lectures in the morning. The students would be tested on their knowledge of astronomy, and hearing lectures would refresh their memories.

Boniface, looking more rested and relaxed than Bartholomew had ever seen him, approached Bartholomew shyly. He said he intended to spend the day praying in the church. Bartholomew gave him leave gladly, thinking uncharitably that his other students would be able to study better without him. Bartholomew decided to attend Kenyngham's lectures too, partly to ensure none of his students played truant, and partly because he found Kenyngham's knowledge fascinating, and liked to hear the enthusiasm in his voice as he spoke.

When the bell rang for dinner, Cynric was waiting to tell him that the Chancellor had arranged for Froissart and the unknown woman to be buried that afternoon. The ceremony would not be an open one, and Gilbert had told Cynric that the coffins had already been sealed to keep their contents from prying eyes.

Dinner was eaten in silence, apart from the voice of the Bible scholar who read a tract from Proverbs. His Latin was poor, and Bartholomew was not the only one of the Fellows to glance up at him in puzzlement when his pronunciation or missed lines made what he was saying incomprehensible. Beside him, Michael grumbled under his breath about the food, tossing a piece of pickled eel away in disgust when he found it rotten. Bartholomew felt little inclination to eat the fish and watery oatmeal, but he was hungry and ate it all. He noted that there was barely enough to go round, and many scholars left complaining they were still hungry.

'Damn the plague,' Michael muttered. 'The sickness has gone, but now we will starve to death.'

By mutual consent, Bartholomew and Michael resumed their discussion of the night before in the deserted conclave. The sun streamed through the windows, and Michael reclined drowsily among the cushions of the window seats. Bartholomew paced restlessly, trying to make sense of everything.

'I am certain that Janetta is involved in all this,' he said. 'Perhaps she killed the women.'

'Janetta?' said Michael in disbelief. 'That is not possible, Matt. She is not strong enough.'

'How strong do you need to be to cut someone's throat?' said Bartholomew. 'Perhaps she had help from one of those louts that always surround her. Perhaps it was her I saw in the orchard after Frances's murder.'

'But Sybilla saw the killer, and she said it was an average man, remember? There is no earthly chance that Janetta could be mistaken for an average man. Even wearing a man's clothes she would be too small.' He mused. 'But Nicholas is of average size.'

'So is Buckley. We have failed to find him, and it cannot be coincidence that he disappeared the night the friar died.'

'I think the killer might be Tulyet,' said Michael.

Bartholomew stopped pacing. 'He has good reason to be out at night while he keeps the Sheriff's peace, and he and his father are obviously involved with this Guild of the Coming.'

'If we knew the identity of the high priest, we would probably have the solution to all this in our hands,' said Michael. 'Did you see nothing at all that might give us a clue? A limp, a distinctive walk?'

Bartholomew shook his head. 'All I know is that he wore a similar mask to the one I saw on the man in the orchard. We should have raided All Saints' Church and had Jonstan arrest the lot of them.'

'That would have been outside Jonstan's power,' said Michael.

'He only has jurisdiction over University affairs, and there is not a shred of evidence that anyone from the University is involved. And we could hardly ask Tulyet to do it!'

Bartholomew rubbed his forehead, becoming exasperated with their lack of progress. He switched to another avenue of thought. 'So if you think Tulyet is the killer, it is likely that Tulyet is also the high priest, otherwise how would he be able to predict that there would be another victim before the new moon?'

Michael pulled at some stray whiskers at the side of his face. 'Yes,' he said slowly. 'Before the new moon, when it is especially dark.'

After a while, they realised that they were getting nowhere with their discussion. They could generate as many theories as they wanted, but progressed no further as long as they lacked the evidence to prove or disprove their ideas. Eventually, they left Michaelhouse to attend the funerals in St Mary's Church. The afternoon sun was blazing in a clear blue sky and the air buzzed with flies. They made their way to the crypt where Gilbert waited restlessly for de Wetherset and Father Cuthbert to arrive so that the ceremony could begin. There was a buzz of flies there, too, hovering over the coffin in which Froissart's remains were sealed.

Bartholomew wandered over to look at the coffins, and wondered how secret their presence could be. He saw that both had been securely nailed down, and frowned. He ran his fingers over the rough wood of the woman's coffin and leaned to inspect a join where the wood did not meet properly. Gilbert and Michael watched him in distaste.

'Who ordered the coffins sealed?' he asked Gilbert.

'No one,' said Gilbert. 'But I have been given the duty of ensuring that their presence is kept secret. I do not need to tell you how difficult that has been in this warm weather. I sealed them myself. If anyone had managed to gain entry to the crypt, a sealed coffin presents a far more formidable obstacle than an open one.'

Bartholomew looked up as de Wetherset arrived, ushering Cuthbert in front of him, and pulling the gate closed.

'I have four clerks to help,' he said, rubbing his hands together in a businesslike fashion to conceal his nervousness. 'They have been told we are burying two beggars. We will carry the coffins out of the crypt ourselves so that no one will detect how long they have been here.'

The others moved towards the coffins, but Bartholomew held back. 'This is perhaps an odd request,' he began, 'but they have been lying here for some time. I would like them opened to make certain that we know whom we are burying this time.'

De Wetherset looked at the coffins in distaste, while Gilbert was visibly angry. 'What for? Can we not just get this foul business over and done with? I am tired of all this death and corruption!'

The Chancellor patted the arm of his distraught clerk sympathetically. 'I am sorry, Gilbert. What I have asked you to do over the past week has been beyond your clerkly duties. I will see that you are well rewarded.'

Gilbert shook his head. 'You do not need to pay me for my loyalty. I want an end to this business with corpses and coffins. Let us just put these poor people in their graves and leave them in peace.'

De Wetherset nodded. 'You are right.' He bent to lift one of the coffins, and gestured to Bartholomew to pick up the other end.

Bartholomew stayed where he was. 'It will not take a moment,' he said. 'Wait outside if it distresses you, and I will do it alone.'

'What are your reasons for this?' asked de Wetherset, setting the coffin back down and eyeing Bartholomew with resignation.

Bartholomew pointed to the woman's coffin. 'When we exhumed the body of the lady, she was in an advanced state of decay. The coffin is flimsy, and the lid does not fit properly. If the woman was in there, Master de Wetherset, you would need more than a few bowls of incense to keep her presence from being known. She would be smelt from the porch.'

De Wetherset let out an exclamation of dismissal. 'Rubbish! The shock of the exhumation has addled your brain, and now you are suspicious of everything. Gilbert is right. Let us just get this done.'

Bartholomew looked at Michael for help. Michael raised his eyes to the ceiling, but rallied to his side. 'It will take only a few moments. What harm can it do?'

'Why can we not just let the poor souls rest in peace?' muttered Cuthbert. 'Both murdered, and now, even in death, they are not safe from desecration!'

De Wetherset was torn. He looked at Gilbert's pleading eyes and grey, exhausted face, and then back to Bartholomew. He sighed. 'In the interests of thoroughness, and to satisfy the Doctor's unpleasant curiosity, I suppose the coffins may be opened. Do it if you must.'

Gilbert backed out of the door. 'I want to see no more decaying corpses. I will wait in the church.'

'I will wait with you,' said de Wetherset. 'I too have had my fill of sights from beyond the grave.'

Cuthbert followed them out, his fat features set in a mask of sorrow.

When they had gone, Michael turned to Bartholomew irritably. 'Is this really necessary? De Wetherset will be furious if you are wrong, and poor Gilbert is at the end of his tether!'

'Then wait outside,' said Bartholomew, losing patience. 'It is for your Bishop that we are investigating this.'

Michael went to sit on the steps as Bartholomew took a knife from his bag and levered up the lid of the woman's coffin. The cheap wood splintered, but the lid came off easily. He stared in shock, unprepared for the sight that faced him. He took a deep breath and stood back.

'Well?' said Michael.

Wordlessly, Bartholomew went to perform the same operation on Froissart's coffin, while Michael went to look in the woman's. Michael stared down at the corpse in the coffin in mystification and, hesitantly, went to look at Froissart's too. Bartholomew shut it before he could see.

'Look if you will,' he said, 'but it is only Froissart, alone and unmolested.'

Michael gazed in horror at the woman's coffin. 'Where is she?' He began a fruitless search of the crypt, hunting for a body that was not there.

Bartholomew scratched his head. 'Who knows? We should tell de Wetherset.'

Michael went to fetch him while Bartholomew re-nailed Froissart's lid. De Wetherset peered cautiously into the woman's coffin.

'Nicholas of York!' he breathed. He raised a white face to Bartholomew. 'How?'

Bartholomew inspected Nicholas's body. There was some stiffness, but Bartholomew imagined he had not been dead for more than a day. Like Froissart, a deep purple mark on his neck indicated that he had been garrotted.

He told de Wetherset, who looked at him blankly. 'But how could this have happened? And where is the body of the woman?'

'Someone must have stolen her,' said Michael. 'But Gilbert said he had been guarding the crypt, and that it is always locked. How could anyone have gone in without him seeing?'

'Where is Gilbert?' said Bartholomew. The small clerk had not followed de Wetherset back into the crypt.

'He is unwell. I have told him to wait in the church with Father Cuthbert,' said de Wetherset. 'All this has proved too much for him. But how could anyone take a body from here while the gate was locked?'

'Perhaps the gate was not locked,' said Bartholomew quietly.

De Wetherset looked blank for a moment. 'What?' he said sharply. 'What are you saying? Gilbert has been my personal clerk for the past ten years. I trust him implicitly.'

'Gilbert always came with you and Buckley when you opened the University chest,' said Bartholomew slowly. 'He knew about Nicholas of York's book. He was with you when you found the friar, and he helped us remove Froissart from the tower. Now we find he is the person to have the only key to the crypt during the time the woman's body disappeared.'

'That is preposterous!' de Wetherset almost snarled. 'Gilbert is my trusted clerk. How do I know that one of you is not behind all this?'

'There is nothing to be gained from this line of thought,'

Michael intervened smoothly, giving Bartholomew a sharp glance. 'All we need to do is to talk to Gilbert. Come.'

He led the way out of the gloomy crypt and the others followed.

De Wetherset walked to the Lady Chapel where he had left Gilbert, but his clerk was not there, and neither was Cuthbert. The Chancellor walked outside.

'He has probably gone for some fresh air,' he said.

There was no sign of Gilbert outside either. De Wetherset hailed a lay-brother who was sweeping the path. The lay-brother strolled over to them.

'Poor Gilbert,' he said in response to de Wetherset's question. 'He came tearing out of the church as if it were on fire. Then he ran straight to the bushes there and disappeared. He ate at the Cardinal's Cap last night, and I have warned him about the food there.'

De Wetherset glared at Bartholomew. 'You have made him sick!' he exclaimed.

Bartholomew was looking over at the bushes where the lay-brother had pointed. 'Oh, I do not think so,' he said. He found the two tombstones and the tree he had used to calculate the entrance of the pathway to Primrose Alley from the church tower, ran through the angles and formulae in his mind, and headed for the spot where the entrance was concealed. De Wetherset and Michael watched him dubiously as he poked around the bushes before giving a triumphant shout.

They hurried over and he pointed out the path to them, almost invisible in the dense foliage, but an unmistakable pathway nevertheless.

'That proves nothing!' snapped de Wetherset. 'Gilbert? Are you there?'

He began to force his way through the undergrowth, while Michael followed. Bartholomew, recalling vividly the last time he had taken the path, grabbed at Michael's habit.

'Wait! We should fetch the Proctors,' he said urgently. He forced his way past Michael and seized de Wetherset. 'Wait!' he repeated.

There was a slight whistling sound followed by a thud, and de Wetherset gazed in disbelief at the arrow that trembled in the tree-trunk only inches from his head. Wordlessly, he turned and fled, thrusting Bartholomew out of the way in his haste to escape. Bartholomew followed more slowly. He knew that had Janetta's men meant to kill, the arrow would be in de Wetherset, and not in a tree. Perhaps Gilbert's loyalty to his Chancellor was worth something after all.

When he emerged into the sunshine, de Wetherset was white with fright, while Michael was bewildered.

'Gilbert might be dead in there,' de Wetherset gasped. 'He might be injured.'

'He might have set the archer there,' said Bartholomew.

De Wetherset strode over to him and grabbed him roughly by the shoulder. 'One more allegation like that, and you will be looking for a new teaching position!' he snapped angrily.

He thrust Bartholomew away from him with a glare, and strode back to the church, calling for a clerk to send for one of the Proctors. Michael watched de Wetherset go.

'Do you really think Gilbert is our man?' he asked.

Bartholomew shifted his bag into a more comfortable position. 'He is most certainly involved, would you not think? For a man who helped retrieve a corpse that had been nailed to a bellframe, he reacted very strongly over the mere opening of a coffin. Unless he already knew what we would find.'

'You are right,' said Michael, thinking carefully. 'I have been wondering whether one of the clerks has been acting as a spy. Who better than Gilbert, who is privy to all the Chancellor's secrets? That is why we have had so little success with our investigation. The perpetrators of these crimes have known exactly what we have been thinking and planning!'

Bartholomew rubbed his chin. 'Remember when we almost dug up Mistress Archer's grave because the marker Gilbert left was on the wrong tomb?'

Michael stared at him. 'Cuthbert said children must have moved it. But what if it had never been moved at all, and it was exactly where Gilbert had set it?'

'And he must have known precisely where to find the path,' said Bartholomew, looking back at where the bushes once again hid it from sight. 'He went there without hesitation. His arrival in Primrose Lane must have alerted them to the possibility of pursuit, and so the archer was set there.'

'I wonder what goes on in Primrose Lane that warrants such security?' mused Michael.

Bartholomew considered. Was that it? Did the seedy shacks and hovels behind the church hold the secret that would explain the deaths of the friar, Froissart, Nicholas, and the disappearance of Buckley?

'What can we do?' he said helplessly. 'We cannot ask Tulyet to raid it, because he is probably involved; it is beyond the Proctor's powers, because Gilbert disappearing down that path is insufficient to prove that it is University business; and if there are archers and crowds of ruffians on guard, we can do nothing ourselves.'

He turned as a large figure lurched out of the church. As Bartholomew and Michael waited for Cuthbert to reach them they saw tears glittering on his cheeks.

'Is it true?' he said. 'Does Nicholas lie dead in the crypt?'

Michael nodded, eyeing him suspiciously.

'He has been with me this past week. I confess it was a shock to see him out of his grave, but he told me he had needed to escape.'

'Escape what?' asked Bartholomew, bewildered.

Cuthbert shrugged, giving a huge sniff, and rubbing his face with his sleeve. 'He would not say, but he was clearly terrified. He said I would be safer not knowing.'

'Why did you not tell us?' cried Michael, exasperated.

'Because he said if I told anyone he was still alive, I would place him in mortal danger, and myself, too,' said Cuthbert, his voice rising. 'I am certain he told me the truth. I have never seen him so frightened or angry.' He looked up suddenly. 'That lay-brother who locked the church for me saw him once. He came to me and said he had seen Nicholas risen from the dead. I advised him to keep silent, and the next thing I knew was that he had fled the town.'

'Cuthbert!' exclaimed Bartholomew in disgust. 'Nicholas may have been the man who killed those women! How could you keep silent?'

'He was not!' cried Cuthbert vehemently. 'He would never kill,' he added more gently.

'But a dead woman was found in his coffin,' said Bartholomew. 'How can you explain that?'

'When we exhumed the grave, Nicholas had already come to me,' said Cuthbert. 'It was no surprise to me that he was not in the grave we dug up, but I was not expecting another corpse! When I returned home, I told him what we had found, and he became frantic with grief. He believed she was the woman he had been seeing before he escaped.'

'But why did you not tell us all this?' cried Michael in despair. 'Did you not recognise her?'

Cuthbert shook his head. 'She had thick black hair, and the woman in the coffin was bald. I told Nicholas it could not be his lover, but he said she had a disease whereby her hair fell out and she always wore a wig.'

'That is not proof that he did not kill her,' said Michael.

'He loved her,' said Cuthbert earnestly. 'I met her, and it is clear that they made each other very happy. He would not have harmed her. And we were members of the Guild of the Holy Trinity, a group dedicated to opposing sin. We do not kill!'

Bartholomew looked at him disbelievingly, while Michael walked with the distraught priest to his small house nearby. Bartholomew waited restlessly until Michael returned.

'Now what?' he said, exasperated. 'What a mess!'

'We must think,' said Michael, sitting down on the low wall surrounding the churchyard. 'Cuthbert claims that Nicholas returned a week ago in a state of terror.'

'We should start with his death,' said Bartholomew. 'He clearly feigned it, and if Cuthbert can be believed, he did so because he was afraid of something.'

'Yes,' said Michael. 'And what better way to escape danger than to pretend you are dead? Who ever hunts a corpse?'

'If the woman was Nicholas's lover, then she must have helped him feign his death, perhaps with potions and powders. Then she went to help him out of the coffin the night before he was due to be buried.'

'And then what?' asked Michael. 'We can prove nothing else. Did he kill her then to ensure her silence so that he would be safe? And why was she wearing that hideous mask?'

'Whatever happened, Nicholas fled, and then returned a week ago,' said Bartholomew. 'When Cuthbert told him that a bald woman was found in his coffin, he realised who it was, and took to roaming the streets.'

'But what could be so terrifying that he was forced to such measures?' mused Michael. 'It must be something to do with the book. Perhaps he was being threatened into revealing its contents.'

Bartholomew considered. 'You must be right,' he said. 'After Nicholas "died", whoever was terrifying him realised that alternative methods were needed to get at it. The friar was employed to steal the book, but was accidentally killed by the poisoned lock.'

'Which must mean that, as far as we know, whatever deadly secret led to all this is still there,' said Michael. 'Because de Wetherset seemed to have checked it all very carefully to ensure nothing was missing.'

'So did the person behind all this kill Nicholas?' asked Bartholomew.

Michael shrugged. 'It must be the same person who killed Froissart because they were both garrotted. It must be Gilbert.'

'Of course it must!' said Bartholomew suddenly. 'Gilbert has the only key to the crypt. It can only have been him who took the woman's body away and put Nicholas there.'

'It does not tell us why,' said Michael. 'But it does throw light on how the friar ended up inside the chest, dead, with the lid down. Gilbert must have used his keys to hide in the crypt, unbeknownst to the friar, before the lay-brother locked up, and emerged after the friar had gone to the tower to begin opening the chest. He probably had no intention other than to ensure his plan went smoothly. He must have become worried when the friar took so long, and went to see what had happened. He found the friar dead, and, in a panic, he pushed him into the chest and closed the lid.'

'De Wetherset said no pages were missing,' said Bartholomew.

'If Gilbert had gone to all this trouble, surely he must have stolen the part he wanted?'

Michael scratched his head thoughtfully. 'I am sure he did,' he said. 'When we lifted the friar from the chest, de Wetherset was only concerned about the book. He immediately went to check that certain sections were unmolested. The part Gilbert probably took must have been so unimportant to the Chancellor, he failed to notice it was missing. So there are at least two parts of this book that are important: the part that de Wetherset was so concerned with, and the part Gilbert took.'

Bartholomew thought again. 'Gilbert was not unduly worried about the friar's sudden death: after all, there was nothing to connect him with the dead man. He left the church, first removing the bar that the friar had put across the door for added security. One of the clerks mentioned to me later that the bar had been moved, proving that there had been two people in the church when the friar had died, not one.'

'Who was this Father Lucius who was allowed into the church by Froissart?' said Michael. 'Could that have been Gilbert?'

'No,' said Bartholomew. 'Froissart would have been a fool to allow anyone into the church. I suspect Gilbert, with his keys, hid himself in the crypt, and it was he who let this Father Lucius into the church, not Froissart. Froissart was probably already garrotted, and Father Lucius was necessary to help Gilbert haul his body into the belfry and secure it there.'

'Froissart garrotted, Nicholas garrotted,' said Michael. 'Gilbert must have killed them both. It almost fits, but we still do not know why all this happened.'

'And we never will so long as de Wetherset plays his own games and is less than honest with us about this book,' said Bartholomew.

Michael's shoulders sagged in defeat. 'Cynric is coming for you,' he said, seeing the small Welshman walking towards them. 'I will go to try to placate the Chancellor, and persuade him to send the Proctors after Gilbert.'

Bartholomew went to meet Cynric, who had a request that he visit the wounded soldier at the Castle. Cynric accompanied him, shyly confiding that he had an hour to spare before he was expected to meet Rachel Atkin at Stanmore's business premises.

The sergeant Bartholomew had met the night before was waiting for him, and he was conducted across the bailey to the hall. The small chamber was flooded with light, the window shutters thrown open, and it was thronging with men. They parted to let him through.

The injured soldier sat up in bed and held up his arm where he had removed the bandage Bartholomew had tied, showing a neat wound with no trace of infection.

Bartholomew bent to inspect it. 'It is healing well,' he said, as he tied another cloth around it. 'But you must give it time, or it will break open again.'

'It is a miracle!' proclaimed the soldier. 'Father Philius pronounced I would die, and Robin of Grantchester wanted to saw off my arm. But you came and I am healed!'

'It is no miracle,' said Bartholomew nervously. One thing he dreaded were rumours of miraculous cures. First, he would have half the country coming to him pleading for help, and, second, his colleagues would believe none of it, and he would likely find himself proclaimed a heretic.

The soldier smiled at him. 'Well, miraculous then,' he said. 'You saved my life, and you saved my arm. I will yet be as good an archer as my father.' He smiled up at the sergeant. Bartholomew, pleased at the young man's rapid recovery, left, with instructions not to overtax his strength too quickly. The sergeant followed him out across the courtyard.

'You looked sorrowful last night,' he said, 'and I thought you might like some happy news.' He seized Bartholomew firmly on the shoulders. 'You saved my son. I wish we could do something for you, and catch this killer.'

'Do you know anything that might help?' asked Bartholomew.

The sergeant shook his head. 'Nothing. And believe me, I would tell you if I knew. The Sheriff had discovered virtually nothing before he stopped investigating. He is not even looking into these stolen carts now.'

'Oswald Stanmore's carts?' asked Bartholomew.

The soldier inclined his head. 'There is a strange business. Those were not random attacks, but carefully planned manoeuvres. I know the work of soldiers when I see it, and there were soldiers involved in those robberies right enough. Good ones too.'

Bartholomew was startled. Did that mean that Tulyet was using part of his garrison to strike at the traders and steal their goods? Was that why he was failing to investigate the crimes in his town?

As they left, Bartholomew almost collided with Tulyet himself.

'You!' the Sheriff snarled. 'What do you want here?'

'I am just leaving, Master Tulyet,' Bartholomew replied politely, not wishing to become embroiled in an argument that might prompt Tulyet to arrest him.

'Then leave!' Tulyet shouted. 'And do not return here without my permission.'

Bartholomew studied him. Tulyet was younger than Bartholomew, but looked ten years older at that moment. His face was sallow and there were dark smears under his eyes. His eyes held a wild look that made Bartholomew wonder whether the man was losing his faculties. Was he the murderer, knowing he would have to commit another crime because he had been so ordered at the ceremony at All Saints'? As a physician, Bartholomew could see signs that the man was losing his sanity and reason.

Without a word, Bartholomew left, Cynric following. When they were out of the Castle, Cynric heaved a sigh of relief.

'I have heard around town that he is losing his mind. They say it is because he cannot catch Froissart. I thought he might order us locked up for some spurious reason. He has arrested several others and accused them of being Froissart.'

Bartholomew reflected for a moment. Perhaps they should tell Tulyet that Froissart was dead after all, to save innocent people from being arrested. But then, Bartholomew reasoned, what good would that do? And if Tulyet were the real killer, Bartholomew might be signing his own death warrant by telling him that Froissart was dead.

Engrossed in his thoughts, he jumped when Cynric seized his arm in excitement. He looked around. They were near All Saints' Church, which stood half-hidden by the tangle of bushes and low trees that were untended around it.

'Someone is in the church!' exclaimed Cynric.

Before Bartholomew could stop him, Cynric had disappeared

into the swathe of green. Bartholomew followed cautiously, making his way to the broken door and peering round it. Cynric was right. A person was there, bending to inspect the dark patches on the floor – a figure in a scholar's tabard like his own. Bartholomew looked around quickly. The man appeared to be alone, so he slipped through the door and made his way towards him, ducking from pillar to pillar up the aisle.

Was this the high priest, visiting the church to make certain he had left nothing, even after his careful removal of his accoutrements before he departed? He stopped as he trod on a piece of wood that had fallen from the roof, and a sharp crack echoed around the derelict church. The man looked up, startled at the loud noise.

'Hesselwell!' Bartholomew exclaimed.

On hearing his name, Hesselwell turned and fled, without waiting to see who had spoken. Bartholomew raced after him, throwing caution to the wind. Hesselwell reached the altar and stumbled as he reached the steps. Behind the altar was a large window and Hesselwell grabbed the sill with both hands to haul himself through. Bartholomew lunged at him as he was about to drop down the other side, and pulled as hard as he could. Both fell backwards, Hesselwell kicking and struggling like a madman.

Bartholomew gripped the flailing wrists and leaned down with all his weight. Pinned to the floor, Hesselwell was helpless.

'You!' he said to Bartholomew, his eyes wide with terror. 'It was you!'

Bartholomew was taken aback. Hesselwell began to struggle again, his face white with terror, but stopped when he saw Cynric come to stand over them, and sagged in resignation.

'What are you talking about?' said Bartholomew. 'What was me?'

'I should have guessed!'

'Guessed what?' Bartholomew was becoming exasperated. He released Hesselwell and watched as Cynric pulled the terrified scholar to his feet, keeping a firm grip on his arm. Hesselwell stood with his shoulders bowed and his tabard covered in dirt and flakes of rotten wood from the floor.

'What were you doing here?' asked Bartholomew, brushing off his own tabard. 'What were you looking for?'

Hesselwell tried to pull himself together, his eyes flicking over Bartholomew as though assessing whether he was armed. 'I wanted to know if the blood was real,' Hesselwell said. 'Or if it was dye.'

'You are a member of the Guild of the Coming?' asked Bartholomew, Hesselwell's actions suddenly making sense to him.

Hesselwell looked at him askance. 'You know I am,' he said.

'Why would I know?' asked Bartholomew, confused again. His flash of illumination was to be short-lived, it seemed.

'Because you are the high priest!' Hesselwell said, taking a deep breath and meeting Bartholomew's eyes. 'It makes sense to me now. You are always out at night; you dabble with poisons and potions; and your students say you are a heretic. You are the high priest,' he repeated. 'You gave me this,' he said, holding up a small glass phial. 'And even then I did not guess.'

Speechless, Bartholomew tore his gaze away from Hesselwell to look at the phial. It was, without question, one of the ones he used to dispense medicines, and it even had a small scrap of parchment wrapped around it with instructions for its use in his handwriting. Trying to bring his whirling thoughts into order, he reached out for the bottle.

Hesselwell misunderstood Bartholomew's expression of bewilderment for one of indecision, and the hand with the phial whipped behind his back. 'I could be of help to you,' he said slyly. 'No one else need know of this. After all, I have served you well, why should I not continue?'

'What are you talking about?' said Bartholomew, his skin beginning to crawl. If Hesselwell thought he was the high priest, did others too? Hesselwell leaned towards him and lowered his voice.

'I was successful in my warning of Brother Michael,' he said.

Bartholomew circled the altar to try to give himself time to bring his thoughts into order. So Hesselwell had put the goat's head on Michael's bed: it had been a Michaelhouse scholar all along. It explained how the intruder had known which room Michael slept in, and how he had known when the monk had returned from Ely. Michael was usually a light sleeper, but his long ride had probably tired him, which was why he had not woken when Hesselwell had entered his room.

He continued to edge around the altar as he tried to recall Hesselwell's reaction to Walter's poisoning. He had been standing with Father Aidan, and Bartholomew distinctly remembered their shocked faces. Unless he was possessed of an outstanding talent for deception, Hesselwell had been as horrified by Walter's brush with death as had the other Fellows.

'You almost killed the porter,' said Bartholomew carefully, watching him.

'That was not my fault,' said Hesselwell, his eyes desperate in his pale face. 'You left me the bottle of wine with instructions to give it to Walter without drawing suspicion to myself. You did not tell me it contained a virulent poison, only that it would make Walter sleep.'

'I am no high priest,' Bartholomew said to Hesselwell wearily. 'Your reasoning is flawed, Master Hesselwell. I am out at night usually because I am seeing patients; I dabble with poisons and potions because I am a physician and they are the tools of my trade; and some of my students think I am a heretic because they do not understand what I teach them. Not only that, but I know Walter sleeps on duty, and would have had no need to send him into a drugged slumber.'

Hesselwell gazed at him, nonplussed. 'Well, what are you then? Are you from the Guild of Purification?'

Bartholomew shook his head and Hesselwell sagged in Cynric's grip.

'What are you going to do? Who will you tell?' His eyes were pleading.

'I will tell the Master about your unholy alliance, and it will be up to him to decide what to do,' said Bartholomew.

'They will kill me!' cried Hesselwell. 'Please! You do not know their strength!' He looked so frightened that Bartholomew almost felt sorry for him. 'Will you tell him after sunset?' Hesselwell pleaded, wringing his hands together. Bartholomew squinted at the sky. Sunset was perhaps two hours away. 'It will give me a chance to collect my belongings, and hire a fast horse.'

He looked desperately from Bartholomew to Cynric. Bartholomew recalled the scholar's fright when he had first been apprehended in the church, and judged that he probably had very real grounds for his fear.

Bartholomew nodded after a moment's thought. 'But you must tell me all you know.'

Hesselwell looked wretched. 'They will kill me if I do.'

'They will kill you if I tell,' said Bartholomew. 'The choice is yours.'

Hesselwell glanced around him with furtive movements of his eyes. 'All right then,' he conceded wearily. 'But you will give me until sunset?'

Bartholomew nodded.

'How do I know I can trust you?' asked Hesselwell.

'You do not,' said Bartholomew. 'But you are not in a position to bargain.'

Hesselwell thought again, and then started to speak. 'I joined the Guild of the Coming when I first arrived in Cambridge. I was in a similar organisation in London because it brought me business – members of guilds tend to use the services of other members. I made enquiries, and was invited to join the Guild of the Coming.'

So that explained the lawyer's rich clothes, thought Bartholomew, when everyone else's gowns were either cheap, torn, old, or all three.

Hesselwell continued. 'All was well at first. There were occasional ceremonies and midnight meetings. Then, a month ago, our high priest disappeared, and another came to take his place. Things changed. There were more ceremonies, and they became frightening.'

'What can you tell me about this new high priest?'

Hesselwell shrugged. 'He, or one of his assistants, instructed me to perform certain duties for him, but I never saw his face. On one occasion, the smaller of his assistants told me to rub some mixture on the back gate of Michaelhouse so that it would burn. Another time, the high priest himself ordered me to keep watch for him while he went into our College the night after the de Belem girl died.'

He hit his head suddenly with an open palm. 'Of course you could not be the high priest. It was you he fought in the orchard, and who almost unmasked him! He told us not to intervene, no matter what happened, but when I saw he was about to be unmasked, I shot one of the fire arrows at the gate to allow him to escape. If he were unmasked, I felt certain he would betray me, and so it was imperative I helped him, regardless of his order.'

'Who was the other?' asked Cynric. 'The Devil?'

Hesselwell shrugged again. 'I have never seen him – or any of the high priest's assistants – without a mask, and I do not know who any of them are, or where they come from.'

'What else?' asked Bartholomew as Hesselwell lapsed into silence.

'I almost killed Walter, and it was me who left the goat's head on Michael's bed.'

'Why did he ask you to do that?' asked Cynric.

'I do not know. He merely gave orders, and I followed without question. He terrifies me. And I do not know what he had in mind with the back gate either, and that black sticky solution. I wish to God I had not become embroiled in all this evil!'

'What else did you do?' asked Bartholomew.

'Just two things,' said Hesselwell. 'He wanted me to prowl the streets at night to look for the whore killer. I thought the high priest was the killer because he predicted their deaths: I can only assume he was taking precautions to protect himself, so that he could say he was not the killer by virtue of the fact that he sent members of the coven to look for the real murderer.'

'And the second thing?' asked Bartholomew, recalling vividly how Hesselwell had almost fallen asleep in the church. He was not surprised Hesselwell was sleepy, if he were teaching all day, and out in the streets at night.

'With one of his assistants, I hid in the roof of the church and helped throw birds and bats down at the congregation. I had begun to be suspicious of some of the devices, and I think he decided to take me into his trust. He would know that once I was involved, I could never tell, for this makes me as guilty of the crimes as he is. And if I became a risk, he would simply kill me.'

'But why do you go along with all this if you know it is a hoax?' asked Bartholomew.

'Because I am afraid,' said Hesselwell. 'One member did question him, and was found a week later in the King's Ditch with his throat cut. And I believe the covens are not the ends in all this, but the means. They are aiming towards something bigger and more terrifying than I can imagine.'

Bartholomew was inclined to believe he was right, and that the elaborate hoax of the covens was simply a front for something infinitely more sinister. Some aspects of the affair had been made clearer by Hesselwell's information, and others less so. Bartholomew understood now what had happened on the night that Walter was poisoned: Hesselwell had merely been following orders, and had not known why the bottle was to be given to Walter. Bartholomew's reasoning that the poisoning had been carried out by an outsider was, in effect, true, since it had come from the high priest.

Hesselwell glanced up at the sun nervously.

'One last question,' said Bartholomew. 'Why did the high priest give you that phial of medicine?'

'I was nervous about opening the gate to him after Frances de Belem's death. I knew there were Proctors and beadles prowling. I was so nervous that he gave me the phial and said it would calm me and allow me to carry out his instructions. I was to give it back to him the same night, but in all the excitement, I forgot to give it, and he forgot to ask.' He smiled ruefully. 'And he was right to have given it to me, because I would not have had the presence of mind to shoot the fire arrow without its calming effects.'

'Is that all?' asked Bartholomew.

Hesselwell nodded. 'He asked about College gossip, but that is all. May I go?' Bartholomew nodded, and Hesselwell looked so relieved he reeled slightly.

'One more thing,' he said as he followed them out of the church. Bartholomew looked at him. 'When I first came, I heard there were two guilds which were covens. No matter how hard I tried, I have never been able to find out about the Guild of Purification. People told me rumours about it – how it was powerful, and a rival to the Guild of the Coming – but I have never met a member of it, and to be honest, I am uncertain that it exists at all.'

Cynric was disapproving that Bartholomew had allowed Hesselwell to make good his escape, and so was Michael when they told him.

'He might come back and wreak all manner of havoc,' said the monk crossly. 'A self-confessed satanist and you let him go!'

'He was terrified, Brother, and his escape will make no difference. What if he had been right and he was murdered? How would you feel then?'

'He might have been able to tell us more about this high priest,' said Michael. 'He might have known what he was looking for in the orchard!'

'He told us all he knew,' said Bartholomew wearily, scrubbing at his face. 'He was used by the high priest, and told virtually nothing in return.'

'But he left that thing on my bed and you allowed him to go just like that!' said Michael, bristling with the injustice of the situation. 'He tried to murder Walter!'

'He did not know the bottle was poisoned. He was told it contained a sleeping draught,' said Bartholomew. He held up the phial Hesselwell had given him. 'This is perhaps the most important clue we have. When we know what it is, I will know to which of my patients I gave it, and we will know the high priest.'

Michael eyed it dubiously. 'But what if it is one of those common concoctions you give out to dozens of people, like betony and ginger oil?'

Bartholomew shook his head. 'I use these phials for more powerful potions.' He took out the stopper and sniffed cautiously. He recognised the compound immediately: there was only one patient to whom he had recently prescribed this medicine! Stunned, he turned to Michael.

'Master Buckley!' he exclaimed. 'He needs this strong draught when the hot weather makes his skin condition unbearable!'

'Buckley the high priest?' said Michael, frowning in concentration. 'It is beginning to come together. But it is well past sunset. Go and tell the Master about Hesselwell and his evil doings. Do not give him more time than you have already promised to make good his escape.'

Bartholomew began to walk across the courtyard to the Master's room when a man walked through the gate. He stopped dead in his tracks as Richard Tulyet the elder strode purposefully towards him. Bartholomew glanced up at the darkening sky as he did so. It seemed Hesselwell was to have more time still.

'Doctor,' said Tulyet quietly. 'Is there somewhere I can talk with you and Brother Michael alone?'

Cynric led the way to the conclave, and lit some candles, stolen from Alcote's personal supply that was secreted behind one of the wall hangings. Tulyet would say nothing until the Welshman had left, closing the door behind him.

'I should have come to see you before now,' said Tulyet, facing Bartholomew and Michael in the flickering light, 'but I did not know whom I could trust.'

Bartholomew knew exactly how he felt, but said nothing.

'You were right when you said I was a member of the Guild of the Coming, and you were right when you said I had been at All Saints' Church two nights ago.' He shuddered. 'I joined the Guild because the Death took my three daughters and all my grandchildren. The Church said that only those who sinned would die, but I lived and the children died. I realised the Church had lied to me, and I wanted nothing more to do with it. The Guild of the Coming offered answers that made much more sense than the mumblings of drunken priests safe in their pulpits. Sorry, Brother, but that is how it seemed.'

His story was similar to de Belem's, and it seemed that the fears the Bishop had voiced to Bartholomew before the plague were realised: that the people would turn from the Church after the Death struck, and there would be insufficient priests and friars to prevent it. Tulyet continued.

'All was well at first, and I even introduced my family to the guild. But a month ago things began to change. A new high priest came to us, very different from Nicholas.'

'Nicholas?' said Michael in astonishment. 'Nicholas of York, the clerk at St Mary's?'

Tulyet nodded. 'Only I knew his identity, but he died this last month, and it cannot matter that I tell you now. After he died, we thought to elect one of our members as our leader, but even as we raised our hands to vote, the new high priest arrived in a puff of thick black smoke. He said he had been sent by the Devil to lead us.'

Thick black smoke, thought Bartholomew. Smouldering grass mixed with tar, perhaps, and blown around the high priest by bellows operated by his accomplices?

'Then the guild changed. Our ceremonies became frightening, full of blood and evil conjurings. I wanted to take my family away, but I was told that if I did, they would die. The high priest said the murders in the town were the Devil claiming his own. My wife is old, and I sometimes visited a certain young lady. Fritha. She was the second girl to die.'

He put his head in his hands while Michael and Bartholomew exchanged glances.

'The new high priest asked questions, too,' Tulyet continued. 'He wanted to know about town politics, my business as a tailor, and with whom I traded.'

The high priest had questioned Hesselwell too, thought Bartholomew, about Michaelhouse.

'Do you know who the high priest is?' asked Bartholomew gently.

Tulyet raised his head, his eyes haunted. 'No. None of us do. But I have a terrible fear of who it might be.'

'Is that why you have come?' asked Bartholomew. 'To tell us who you think it is?'

Tulyet nodded. 'I do not know who else I can tell, and I must do something. He is going to claim another victim!' He took a deep breath. 'The high priest is Sir Reginald de Belem.'

'De Belem!' exclaimed Michael. 'But that cannot be. Frances was his daughter. He would not have killed his own daughter!' Or Isobel, the woman who visited him on certain nights, was his clearly unspoken thought.

And de Belem was the high priest of the Guild of Purification anyway, Bartholomew thought, or so he claimed. Hesselwell had

246

said he did not believe the Guild of Purification existed – but it would have been an easy matter to put about rumours of meetings, and to splash blood on the altar of St John Zachary's Church occasionally. And Stanmore had said there were only five people at the last meeting – perhaps the high priest of the Guild of the Coming and a few trusted helpers attending a meeting, the only purpose of which was to maintain the illusion that the Guild of Purification existed.

Bartholomew rubbed a hand through his hair. But they had already surmised that it was Gilbert who had killed Nicholas, so how did all this tie together? And the medicine the high priest gave to Hesselwell belonged to Buckley. Was there more than one high priest in all this business, just as there might be more than one killer of the women? Was it Buckley, Gilbert, or de Belem in the orchard with Hesselwell and the big man? Who was in the roof with Hesselwell, throwing birds and bats down at the coven? And why had de Belem told Bartholomew he was grand master of the Guild of Purification if no such organisation existed?

Tulyet gnawed at his lip. 'I have been over this again and again, but all the evidence points to de Belem. I am certain he is the high priest.'

'We thought it might be your son,' said Michael bluntly.

'Richard?' said Tulyet, aghast. 'Why would you think that?'

'Because he has made no attempt to catch the killer of these women, and because he has thwarted the efforts of others to do so,' said Michael.

Tulyet leaned back in his chair wearily. 'My son is not in a position to do anything,' he said.

'Why not?' said Michael. 'He is the Sheriff.'

'Because de Belem has Richard's son,' said Tulyet, putting his head in his hands. 'If he makes any moves against the guild, de Belem will kill him.'

'You mean his baby?' asked Bartholomew, horrified. 'The one born last year?'

Tulyet nodded. 'My only grandchild born after the Death. The only child Richard will ever have, as you told him yourself, Doctor.'

'But how do you know it is de Belem?' insisted Michael.

Tulyet took a deep breath, and composed himself before starting. 'Shortly after Richard's baby was snatched, he had a note warning him that his son would be killed if his investigations into the guilds did not cease immediately. Because Richard thought the guilds were connected with the killer of the women, he had to stop looking into that too. Richard is the only member of my family who refused to join the Guild of the Coming, because he did not want to be put in a position where his loyalty to members of the guild might conflict with his office as Sheriff.'

So that explained Tulyet's behaviour, thought Bartholomew, and why he was so vocal in threatening him and Michael. He was not threatening them so much as telling the spies of the high priest that he was not co-operating. It also explained his increasing agitation.

'Does Richard believe de Belem is committing these murders?' asked Bartholomew.

Tulyet nodded. 'He told me that the victims had circles on the soles of their feet. He assumed it was the killer claiming that the murders were committed by members of the Guild of Purification. When he began to investigate, his baby was snatched.'

Bartholomew frowned. But if de Belem were the killer, why did he encourage Bartholomew to investigate the death of Frances? He shook his head impatiently. It made no sense.

'The only clue Richard had as to his son's kidnappers was the note,' continued Tulyet. 'He noticed there were traces of yellow dye on the parchment.'

'And because de Belem is a dyer, you think he wrote it?' asked Michael incredulously. 'There are other dyers in the town, too!'

'No, there are not,' said Bartholomew. Stanmore had become tedious on the subject since the plague: de Belem held a monopoly on dyes. He was not only the sole dyer in the town, he was the only one for miles.

'But that is not sufficient evidence,' said Michael, shrugging his shoulders.

'I have not finished,' said Tulyet, tiredness in his voice. 'The day before her death, Isobel Watkins came to see Richard. She was de Belem's whore, and she told Richard that she had wandered where she should not have in de Belem's house and had discovered a dead goat and caged birds and bats. But what frightened her most was that she thought she had heard the cry of a baby.'

'Birds and bats?' said Bartholomew, thinking about the ceremony in All Saints'.

Tulyet met his eyes. 'Crows and big black bats, she said. And a dead goat. As you know, the goat is the symbol of our guild. Two nights ago at the ceremony you appear to have observed, birds, bats, and a dead goat made their appearance. I did not connect the contents of de Belem's house with the horrible ceremony in All Saints' until yesterday. It terrified me to the point where I simply forced it from my mind, and I did not think properly.'

'But why did Richard not demand to search de Belem's house for his baby?' asked Bartholomew. 'Once he had his son back, de Belem would be powerless to blackmail him, and Richard could pursue his investigation of the murderer and the guilds.'

'I said he should, but his wife was against it. She was afraid the baby would be killed as soon as Richard entered the house,' said Tulyet. 'Richard delayed, Isobel died, and, despite the fact that Richard has been watching the house, no baby has been heard since.'

Bartholomew leaned back against the wall and rubbed his chin. De Belem was a dyer, which meant that he would have ready access to certain chemicals, and would know which ones would explode, burn, or give off smoke. Added to the bats and birds, the evidence was powerful. He thought of the high priest's performance in All Saints'. He had been of a height and build similar to de Belem's. It could have been a good many other people too, however. But what about Frances? Bartholomew recalled his grief when he had broken the news of her death. Surely he had not killed her himself? What had she said on the night she died? That it was 'not a man'. Was it because de Belem had been wearing his red mask as he had in the church, perhaps the same red mask that Bartholomew had seen in the Michaelhouse orchard?

'So what do we do now?' Michael asked Tulyet.

Tulyet's face fell. 'I hoped you would know,' he said. He looked out of the window. 'It is getting dark and the high priest promised another murder. Richard's anguish has made him increasingly unstable over the last few days. I cannot allow him to be involved any further until he has the baby back. You are my last hope,' he said with sudden despair.

'How long has the baby been gone?' asked Bartholomew.

'Almost four weeks,' said Tulyet. 'He is a bonny babe, strong and healthy. Not like the yellow weakling you saw when he was born. But he still needs his mother.'

Bartholomew mused. About a month. The same time that Nicholas feigned his death, and the woman had been placed in his coffin; the same time that de Belem had made himself the new high priest of the Guild of the Coming; and about the same time that Janetta had been in town.

'We should question de Belem,' said Michael. 'Discreetly.'

'But if you go to de Belem, and he has even the slightest inkling of what you know, he might harm my grandchild,' said Tulyet.

'He asked us if we would investigate the death of his daughter,' said Bartholomew reasonably. 'He cannot be suspicious of us. We will go to him tonight. The longer we wait, the more likely it is that the child will come to harm.'

'But what of the risk?' cried Tulyet. 'What if you make a mistake?'

'What if the child dies because he is in the care of a man who does not know about children?' asked Bartholomew.

'Do you think he might die from neglect?' asked Tulyet anxiously.

Bartholomew raised his hands. 'It is in de Belem's interest to keep the child alive, but he will not be as well cared for as if he were at home.'

Tulyet sat in an agony of indecision, looking from Michael to Bartholomew with a stricken expression.

'This cannot go on,' said Michael gently. 'A child needs its mother. And we cannot allow another murder to happen when we know what we do. Think of Fritha.'

Tulyet nodded miserably. 'But please be careful for the child,' he said. 'Many people are guilty of vile crimes in this business, but he is wholly innocent.'

Tulyet stood, white faced, and Michael clapped him reassuringly on the shoulder. 'Do not go home. Your anxiety might alert your son, and he may interfere and do harm. Wait with Master Kenyngham until we return. Tell him what you have told us, and we will inform you of what we have learned as soon as we can.'

Tulyet nodded again. Bartholomew called for Cynric to escort the merchant to Kenyngham's room.

'What made you come to us now?' asked Michael as he left.

Tulyet gave a weak smile. 'The town has failed since the Sheriff is helpless, and my own information has revealed nothing. The Church will not help me now I have sold my soul to the Devil. What else is there but the University? I came close to telling you the other day. Now I feel you are our only hope.'

They watched him walk across the yard, his shoulders stooped.

'What shall we do first?' asked Michael.

'I have an idea,' said Bartholomew.

CHAPTER 10

ICHAEL PUFFED ALONG NEXT TO BARTHOLOMEW ON their way to Milne Street, while on his other side, Cynric glided through the shadows like a cat.

Bartholomew hoped Stanmore had not already gone home, and he was relieved when he saw lights burning in one of the storerooms. He led the way through Stanmore's yard, and found his brother-in-law supervising two exhausted labourers with the last bales of cloth from a consignment that had arrived from the Low Countries. Stanmore smiled at his unexpected visitors, waved his men home for the night, and wiped his hands on his gown.

'Dyed cloth from Flanders,' he said, patting one of the bales in satisfaction. 'Excellent quality. It goes to show that it is better to use the barges than the roads these days.'

'Do you have anything in black?' asked Bartholomew, looking around.

'I have black wool. What do you want it for?' asked Stanmore.

'A Benedictine habit,' said Bartholomew.

Stanmore frowned and looked at Michael's habit. 'I have nothing in stock that would be appropriate. I would need to have something dyed. When do you need it?'

'Two days,' said Bartholomew. Michael looked from one to the other in confusion.

'I do not need another habit,' he said. 'I have two already.'

Bartholomew wandered to where Stanmore kept his tools and a small bucket of red dye used for marking bales of cloth as they arrived. He took a brush from the bucket and flicked it at Michael, who gazed in disbelief at the trail of red drops down the front of his black robe. Stanmore looked at Bartholomew as if he had gone mad, and edged nearer the door.

'Now you have only one,' said Bartholomew. 'But it is not good enough for you to attend your students' disputations in two days' time. The Bishop will be there, and you know how vain Benedictines like to look their best. It is a shame you were careless in Oswald's workshop when he had just told you he had no black cloth in stock.'

Michael looked up slowly, his green eyes gleaming as he understood Bartholomew's plan. 'It is essential we get the cloth tonight,' he said, 'or the habit will not be ready in time.'

It was Stanmore's turn to look from one to the other in bewilderment. 'I can buy some from Reginald de Belem,' he said. 'He always has plenty of black cloth dyed ready to sell me.'

'I bet he does,' said Bartholomew, drily. 'What do you think he would do if we wanted him to give us some tonight?'

'Like any good merchant, I imagine he would try to accommodate a customer.' Stanmore looked at him suspiciously. 'This is about the guild business, isn't it?' he said.

Bartholomew nodded. 'De Belem appears to be playing a bigger part in this than we thought. We need to enter his house. Once in, we will distract him while Cynric looks around.'

Cynric's dark face was alight with excitement, but Bartholomew felt a twinge of guilt for once again involving his book-bearer in something dangerous. He hoped Tulyet's information was accurate. It was only Isobel's claim that she had heard a baby that drove him on – since Isobel had been killed only a few days ago, the baby might yet be alive. That he had not been heard since might merely mean that he had been moved to a different room in de Belem's sizeable house. But at the back of his mind doubts nagged where facts did not fit together: de Belem's daughter had been murdered; the nerve-calming medicine the high priest of the Guild of the Coming had given to Hesselwell was Buckley's; and de Belem had been desperate that Bartholomew should investigate the murders. Yet other facts pointed clearly to de Belem's guilt: the birds and bats in his home; Isobel murdered after she had discovered them, albeit too late to ensure her silence; the baby crying in his house; and the dye staining the blackmail note. It was clear de Belem had some role in the affair, but Bartholomew remained uncertain whether it was that of high priest.

'This is not illegal, is it?' said Stanmore nervously.

'De Belem has already broken the law,' said Michael. 'We are trying to ensure that he does not do so again.'

He explained briefly what they had learned from Tulyet, and added one or two speculations of his own. Stanmore picked up his cloak from where it lay on a bale of cloth. 'Well, let us see if Master de Belem will sell us what we need,' he said. He saw Bartholomew hesitate. 'Your excuse will appear more convincing if I am there also. And another man present will do no harm.'

They left Stanmore's premises and knocked at the door of de Belem's house. The house was in silent darkness, and all the window shutters were closed. For a moment, Bartholomew thought he may have ruined Michael's habit for nothing and that de Belem was not home, but eventually there were footsteps and de Belem himself opened the door. When he saw Bartholomew, Michael, and Stanmore, hope flared in his eyes.

'You know?' he said. 'You know who killed Frances?'

Stanmore shook his head. 'Not yet,' he said. 'We have come on another matter.'

He stood back to indicate Michael with his hand. De Belem's puzzled frown faded into a smile when he saw the red stains on the front of Michael's habit.

He leaned forward and inspected it. 'I can re-dye this and those marks will not show,' he said. 'That way, you can avoid buying new cloth from Master Stanmore and the cost of a tailor to sew it. Bring it to me tomorrow.' He ignored Stanmore's indignant look, and prepared to close the door.

'I need it dyed tonight,' said Michael quickly. 'This is my best habit and I want to wear it to my students' disputations.'

'I cannot dye it tonight, Brother,' said de Belem reasonably. 'All the apprentices have gone home, and the fires under the dyeing vats have been doused. Come back tomorrow at dawn. I will make it my first priority.'

'I will light the fires myself,' said Michael, inserting a foot into the door, 'if you dye it tonight.'

De Belem, despite his reluctance to refuse a customer, was beginning to lose patience. 'Sir Oswald, tell the Brother that it is not an easy matter to light the fires under the vats, and that if we were to start the process now, we would be here all night. I cannot help you, Brother.'

'Do you have any black cloth, then?' asked Michael.

Bartholomew was impressed at the monk's tenacity. De Belem sighed in resignation. 'Yes. I have black cloth dyed for the abbey at Ely. It will be a more expensive option for you, but if it will satisfy your desire to have something done tonight, I will sell you some now.'

They followed him into his house.

'He is exceeding himself in this!' Stanmore hissed to Bartholomew. 'He is not authorised to sell cloth, only to dye it. And he even has the gall to sell it with me present!'

Bartholomew shrugged off his arm impatiently and followed Michael inside, careful not to shut the door so that Cynric could slip in. Stanmore followed, still grumbling.

'If there were other dyers in the town this would never happen. The man thinks he can do what he likes now he has this monopoly. No wonder the cloth trade is poor if we are constantly being undercut by de Belem.'

Bartholomew silenced him with a glance, and Stanmore, still bristling with indignation, said no more. They followed de Belem down a long corridor where a door led directly into the yard. Two wooden buildings had been raised there. The smaller one, judging from the smell and the stained ground outside, was the dyeing shed, while the other was for drying and storage. De Belem took some keys from his belt and unlocked the door to the storeroom. A torch stood ready near the door, and he kindled it so he could find the correct cloth. The room smelled so strongly of the plants and compounds used for dyes that it was overpowering.

Bartholomew stayed outside, looking over at the house on the other side of the yard. It was in darkness except for lights flickering at one window, and Bartholomew saw a figure walk across it. He wondered who it might be. De Belem lived alone now his daughter was dead. Perhaps de Belem had found himself another prostitute. He felt his stomach churn. He hoped not, for that might mean that she was in very serious danger.

Bartholomew edged away from the storeroom when he heard Stanmore begin an argument with de Belem, first about the price and then about which cloth was best for the purpose. De Belem was becoming exasperated with his late customers and Bartholomew knew he would not tolerate them much longer. He had a sudden fear that they would not be able to distract him long enough for Cynric to conduct his search of the house, or worse, that Cynric would still be inside when they left.

Taking a hasty decision, he ran back across the courtyard to the house and began to climb up some large crates that were piled up against the outside wall. The house was not as well built at the back as it was in the front, and he was able to climb higher on ill-fitting timbers that jutted from the plaster. He made his way towards the lighted window, wincing as his feet slipped and scraped against the wall. Grasping the window-sill, he hauled himself up and peered through the open window just as Janetta of Lincoln looked out to see what had made the noise.

For a second, they regarded each other in silence, and then Janetta tipped her head back and yelled as loudly as she could. Someone who had been sitting with his back to the window leapt to his feet and spun around, and Bartholomew had his second shock as he recognised the missing Evrard Buckley. Bartholomew heard a shout from the storeroom and glanced back to see de Belem race out, pulling the door closed behind him. Something crashed against it from the other side just as de Belem got a stout bar into place.

De Belem saw Bartholomew and began to run towards him. Bartholomew cursed in frustration. How had Michael and Stanmore managed to let de Belem lock them in the storeroom? Janetta tried to prise his fingers from the window-frame, and at the same time, he felt de Belem make a grab for his feet.

'Michael!' he yelled, kicking out so hard he almost dislodged himself from the wall. Janetta picked up a heavy jug from the table and began clumsily to swing it at Bartholomew's head. As Bartholomew ducked, and tried to keep his feet out of de Belem's reach, he was vaguely aware of Buckley grabbing something from the bed. He heard a small whimper and knew

Buckley had Tulyet's baby. Janetta gave a yell of anger and hurled the jug at Bartholomew, spinning round to follow Buckley to the door. Even as Buckley reached for the lock, the door flew open, and Cynric stood there, breathing hard.

'Cynric! The baby!' Bartholomew gasped.

De Belem had a good grip on Bartholomew's leg and was pulling with all his might, and Bartholomew found he could hold on no longer. As his fingers began to slip, he saw Janetta and Cynric engaged in their own furious struggle. And then he finally lost his grip on the window-sill, and was tumbling through the air.

His fall was broken by de Belem. For a moment, they both lay dazed until Janetta cried out, 'They have the baby!'

Abandoning Bartholomew, de Belem struggled to his feet and began to run towards the door of the house. Bartholomew dived after him and, grabbing him around the knees, brought him down again. De Belem twisted onto his back and lashed out, catching Bartholomew hard on the side of the head with his clenched fist. Stunned, Bartholomew released him, and heard de Belem scramble away. Vaguely he heard Stanmore and Michael shouting in the storeroom and de Belem yelling orders. He tried to stand to release Michael and Stanmore, but he was dizzy, and his legs would not hold him up.

The clatter of hooves brought him to his senses, and he saw horses being taken from the stable. He pulled himself into a sitting position and saw de Belem haul open the gates, leap onto a horse, and urge it into the street. Janetta followed and Bartholomew heard the thudding of hooves fading away. Someone slumped down beside him, and Bartholomew saw it was Buckley, awkwardly holding Tulyet's baby.

'Thank God!' Buckley said unsteadily. As Bartholomew took the baby from him, he saw the Vice-Chancellor's gloved hands were tied in front of him. 'I thought it would never end.'

Bartholomew turned his attention to the baby. It was feverish, but alive. He suspected it had not been given enough to drink and it was weak. That probably explained why it had not been heard crying. It was dirty too. He felt it carefully to ascertain that it was not more seriously hurt, while Cynric emerged from the house unsteadily and made his way to the storeroom. He heaved the bar up, and Michael and Stanmore exploded into the yard, looking about them.

'Master Buckley!' exclaimed Michael, hurrying across to them. 'And you have the baby!'

Cynric took a knife and sawed through the ropes on Buckley's hands.

'He had my cloth!' shouted Stanmore, beside himself with anger. 'Those were no random attacks on my cart. It was de Belem! He must have wanted to discourage me from sending cloth elsewhere to be dyed, and so he arranged to steal it from my carts! He must have killed Will, too!'

'To buy more time, I pretended to stumble and knock some bales down,' explained Michael. 'Hidden behind them was Oswald's stolen cloth. While we were witless with surprise, he dashed out and locked us in.'

'They have fled,' said Bartholomew, his voice jangling in his aching head. 'They took horses and left.'

Stanmore looked at the open gates. 'We might still catch them,' he said. 'Michael, Cynric! Help me with the horses!'

As they ran from the yard, Bartholomew turned to Buckley. 'Are you hurt?' he asked.

Buckley shook his head, his face grey with strain. 'They cut my arm when they came for me in the middle of the night. But that is healing. And they took my medicine. But that was perhaps as well since I did not want to sleep too deeply with de Belem and that woman prowling around. And there was that poor whimpering child that needed me.'

So that explained the blood they had seen on the ground outside his window at King's Hall. 'What happened?' Bartholomew asked.

'A noise awoke me one night, and the next thing I knew was that de Belem was in my room with some of his hired thugs. They made me climb out of the window and wait in a cart while they took everything from my room. I later assumed he meant he wanted it to look as if I had done something dreadful and fled with all my belongings.'

The baby gave a strangled cry, and Bartholomew rocked it.

Buckley swallowed hard. 'Will the child live? I have been trying to look after him, but he was becoming weaker. They told me he is Richard Tulyet's child, and that Tulyet would never come to rescue me as long as the baby was here. They were going to kill him if Tulyet so much as set foot in the yard.'

'I think he will recover once he is fed properly. Is there anything you can tell us that might help us catch de Belem and Janetta?' Bartholomew asked.

Buckley shook his head slowly. 'Only that the woman is here rarely, and that de Belem's men are mercenaries who are beginning to waver in their loyalties. I heard a savage argument last night between de Belem and one of the sergeants. Some have already gone. He had about thirty, half were garrisoned in Primrose Alley and half are elsewhere. Of the ones in Primrose Alley, he probably has fewer than five left. There are other things, too, but they are supposition, and I have little to substantiate them.'

He continued talking quickly, while Bartholomew listened, pieces of the puzzle falling into place with the scraps of information he had already gathered. He was still sitting on the ground, holding the baby, and listening to Buckley, when Michael and Stanmore returned with Cynric and two of Stanmore's men, all mounted and armed. Behind Cynric were Rachel Atkin and Sybilla.

'Matt! Come on, we must catch them!' said Michael, leaning down and grabbing at Bartholomew's tabard. Bartholomew climbed unsteadily to his feet and handed the baby to Rachel.

'Take him to Richard Tulyet's wife,' he said. 'You must tell her to feed him immediately. He is unharmed, but weak.'

'Matt, come on, or we will lose them!' cried Stanmore, already mounted.

'Tell her if she cannot feed him herself she must find a wet-nurse at once,' Bartholomew continued, glancing at Stanmore irritably.

Rachel nodded and wrapped the baby more warmly in her own cloak.

'Matt!' yelled Michael, wheeling round on his impatient horse.

'He is to be fed in small amounts. Too much at once and he will get colic. Master Buckley, will you go to the Sheriff?

If you are too weak, call at Michaelhouse and they will send a student.' He gave one last look at the baby, and ran to the horse Stanmore was holding for him.

He climbed clumsily into the saddle, and closed his eyes as the ground appeared to tip and sway beneath him. The feeling passed, and he grabbed at the horse's reins in an attempt to stop it from skittering.

'They took the Trumpington Road,' said Stanmore. 'I heard them.'

Bartholomew jabbed his heels into the horse's side and followed the others as they clattered out of the yard, along Milne Street, and towards the High Street. They slowed as they neared the Trumpington Gate, and he saw the guards milling around. One of them was sitting on the ground holding a hand to his head.

'They ran him down!' the sergeant from the Castle shouted indignantly to Stanmore. 'There were two of them. Rufus stood to stop them and they just ran him down.'

Bartholomew moved to dismount to attend to the man, but the sergeant stopped him. 'Rufus will be fine, Doctor. They took the Trumpington Road, probably off to London. Go after them and bring them back to me. I will send to the Castle.'

'If Tulyet does not know yet, tell him his baby is safe,' Bartholomew yelled back at him as his horse, fired with the chase in the night, began to gallop after the others with no encouragement from him. 'You will find him more than willing to take action this time.'

The night was cloudy and dark. The new moon was not due for two nights and so there was nothing to light their way. They were forced to reduce their speed for fear of being thrown, since the Trumpington Road was, as usual, deeply rutted with cart tracks and pot-holes so deep that Bartholomew had seen a drowned sheep in one during the spring.

They reached Trumpington and Stanmore slowed, yelling at the top of his voice. Several people emerged from their dark cottages and told him that other horses had passed moments earlier and had taken the path to Saffron Walden.

'Good thing we stopped,' Michael muttered, turning his horse down the smaller of the two roads. 'I would have bet my dinner they would make for London.'

'Wait for the Sheriff's men,' Stanmore shouted to the villagers. 'Tell them which way we have gone.'

He wheeled his horse round and started off down the Saffron Walden road, the others streaming behind him. Another piece of the jigsaw clicked into place in Bartholomew's mind. Saffron Walden. He thought about the two people he had seen in the roof of All Saints': one small and sure-footed, the other larger and less adept, but stronger. Janetta and Hesselwell, the high priest's assistants, throwing the birds and bats down into the church to frighten the congregation, with Hesselwell not knowing the identity of the other.

His horse stumbled, and Bartholomew was forced to abandon his analysis and concentrate on riding. He was not a good horseman, and was finding it difficult to stay in the saddle, let alone direct the horse. He was grateful Stanmore had thought to give him one that seemed able to look after itself. Michael was an excellent rider, having learned on the fine mounts kept in the Bishop's stables, while Cynric was inelegant, but efficient.

He strained his eyes, trying to see if he could detect any movement that they were drawing closer to their quarry, but could see nothing. He swore as a dangling twig clawed at his face, and leaned further down against his horse's neck. The beast was beginning to glisten with sweat and Bartholomew could see foam oozing from its mouth. Behind him, he heard Michael curse loudly as his own mount staggered, and only his skill kept him in the saddle.

'Slow down!' Michael yelled to Stanmore. 'You will ruin the horses!'

The pace dropped, and then was forced to drop further still when the road degenerated into a morass of thick cloying mud and great puddles. Spray flew and Bartholomew blinked muddy water from his eyes.

'There!' he yelled, glimpsing two shadowy figures far ahead, silhouetted against the skyline.

Stanmore stood in his stirrups and peered forward. He began to urge his huge piebald forward again, faster than before. Bartholomew clung on for dear life, feeling his legs begin to ache, and hoped they would catch de Belem soon. Saffron Walden was perhaps fifteen miles on the winding track from Cambridge, and they had travelled at least two thirds of that already. The track became better as they neared the small settlement at Great Chesterford and they thundered forward. Janetta and de Belem had also made good time through the village, and when they emerged at the other end, they were out of sight.

The road split again after Great Chesterford. A man materialised out of the darkness and pointed to the right fork.

'Horsemen went that way,' he said. 'The road is a better and faster route to London than the road from Trumpington at the moment.'

'No! They went left,' cried Bartholomew, clinging on to his horse as it skittered restlessly.

Stanmore hesitated, so Bartholomew urged his mount down the road on the left to lead the way. The horses were beginning to tire, and as soon as the track degenerated again, they were forced to slow to a trot. Michael swore and muttered, leaning forward to squint into the darkness to see if he could spot de Belem again. At a wider part, he drew level with Bartholomew, while Stanmore pushed past them.

'I do not understand this,' he said breathlessly. 'Why Saffron Walden? Why not London where they could easily disappear?'

'De Belem is a dyer,' said Bartholomew.

Michael looked blankly at him. 'So?'

'Saffron Walden is where crocuses are grown for saffron.' Bartholomew was surprised at Michael's slowness. 'Saffron is used for dye. De Belem is a dyer. He probably owns fields there. The plague left land vacant all over the country, and I am sure that the crocus fields could be bought relatively cheaply. I cannot imagine that an astute merchant like de Belem would miss an opportunity for that kind of business investment.'

'Stanmore's carts!' said Michael, urging his horse round a deep puddle. 'They were attacked at Saffron Walden, and Will was killed near there!'

'And de Belem was planning to marry Frances to some lord of the manor there,' said Bartholomew.

The track became narrow again, and Bartholomew was forced

to drop back so Michael could ride ahead. Stanmore, now in the lead, saw a flash of movement ahead and urged them on.

'What do they think will happen when they reach Saffron Walden?' Michael yelled. 'We are still in pursuit.'

'They must have somewhere to hide,' Stanmore yelled back.

Bartholomew thought about Buckley's information. Fifteen mercenaries elsewhere. De Belem and Janetta would not ride so wildly just to be taken at Saffron Walden, hiding place or no. They must have had a plan!

'Stop!' he shouted. 'Wait!'

But Michael and Stanmore did not hear him. He kicked at his horse to try to catch up with them. As they reached the brow of a hill, he could see the dark regular shapes of buildings in the hollow below. They were almost there.

'Michael!' he yelled at the top of his voice, but the monk did not hear.

The track narrowed further so that trees slapped past the horses on both sides. Bartholomew's horse reared suddenly, panicked by some shadow that flicked across the path. Bartholomew fought to control it, drawing the reins tight and clinging with his knees to prevent himself from falling off. Branches tore at him, forcing him to raise one arm to protect his face against being blinded. His horse snorted with fear and thrashed with its hooves, and Bartholomew felt himself begin to slide off.

Stanmore's men, who had been behind, were past him before he could stop them, further panicking his horse. It turned and tried to bolt, but stumbled in the rutted track. Horse and rider fell together into the undergrowth. The horse staggered to its feet and was away, crashing blindly along the path the way it had come. Bartholomew heard its hooves drumming off into the distance and then there was silence.

The thick undergrowth had broken his fall, and Bartholomew was unharmed. Cautiously he began to inch his way along the track towards the small settlement of Saffron Walden. He became aware of shouts ahead and slowed, wishing he could move as silently as Cynric. Peering through the undergrowth, he watched in horror as he saw Stanmore and Michael engaged in a violent skirmish with several rough-looking men wearing boiled-leather jerkins. Bartholomew had seen men dressed like this before: twice, when he had spoken to Janetta. These were the other half of de Belem's mercenaries, men who had fought with the King at the glorious victory at Crécy, but came back to roam restlessly around the country waiting for another war and selling their services to the highest bidder.

The highest bidder was apparently de Belem, who advanced as the skirmish ended, watching Stanmore and the others drop their weapons in surrender. Bartholomew was furious at himself. It had been obvious that de Belem was riding at such a pace for a reason, and they had fallen right into his trap.

'The Sheriff's men will be here soon,' said Stanmore boldly. 'You will only make matters worse for yourself if you do not surrender.'

De Belem laughed and his men joined in. 'The Sheriff's men will find nothing here,' he said. 'They will be told you must have taken the London road at Great Chesterford, for no horsemen came this way tonight.'

'You did not fool us. Why would you fool them?' asked Michael.

'My man at Great Chesterford will do a better job next time,' said de Belem. 'Because he knows what will happen to him if he does not.'

'Tulyet will hunt you down now that you no longer have his child,' said Michael.

De Belem sighed. 'There are many ways to skin a cat; I will think of something else.'

He motioned with his hand that they were to dismount and rounded them into a small group to be escorted into the village. Janetta suddenly appeared.

'Where is Bartholomew?' she said, looking around. 'Search for him,' she ordered two of the mercenaries.

'He stayed with the baby,' said Michael. 'We came without him.'

'Search for him,' said Janetta again, casting a disdainful look at Michael. 'Do not let him escape.'

Bartholomew fought down panic as the two mercenaries began to move towards him. He ducked back into the undergrowth, and wondered if he should try to run or try to stay hidden. One of the mercenaries carried a crossbow, already wound. Bartholomew crouched on the ground covering his face with his arms. If he stayed perfectly still, wrapped in his dark cloak, he might yet escape detection. He did not know the area well enough to escape through the woods, and would probably run into thicker undergrowth and make an easy target for the mercenaries.

He almost leapt up as he heard crashing behind him. He saw a figure dart across the path and plunge into the woods on the opposite side of the track. With howls of success, the mercenaries dived after him. Cynric, Bartholomew thought, unsurprised. He had obviously anticipated the ambush, even if the others had not.

Bartholomew stayed where he was until the sounds of Cynric leading the men away from him had faded. Looking both ways, he set off down the track towards the village, stopping frequently to listen as he had seen Cynric do on occasions. The village comprised parallel rows of houses, most of them simple wooden frames packed with dried mud and straw. One or two gleamed with limewash, but most were plain. The dark mass of the castle crouched at the far end, looming over the village with empty malice since it had not been garrisoned since the plague. The large church, built on profits from the saffron trade, stood at the other end of the village.

He paused at the outskirts and listened. He heard de Belem speaking. Keeping to the shadows, he slunk along one side of the street towards the church, where Michael and the others had apparently been taken. He crept over grassy graves, and climbed on a tombstone to look through one of the windows.

De Belem was wearing his red mask, and white-faced villagers were trickling into the church, drawn by the noise and the torches that lit the inside of the church. Michael, Stanmore and his men were clustered together near the altar, under the guard of several heavily-armed mercenaries. More villagers began to arrive as someone rang the church bell, and a figure swathed in a black robe, that Bartholomew knew was Janetta, began to organise the church in preparation for a ceremony. She took a long knife from one of the mercenaries and laid it reverently on the altar in front of de Belem, and rearranged the torches so that most of the church was in shadow.

Bartholomew felt sick and crouched down on the tombstone so he would not have to watch. De Belem was about to perform some dreadful ceremony in which Michael and Stanmore would be murdered in front of the entire village. The sight of what would happen to those who did not comply with his wishes would doubtless be enough to ensure their co-operation for whatever other nasty plans de Belem had in mind. Bartholomew stood shakily and looked at the villagers. They were sullen and frightened; and some wore a dazed expression that suggested no such ceremony would be necessary to terrify them further. De Belem was holding an entire village to ransom.

He spun round as he heard a noise behind him and found himself staring down at a priest. He braced himself. He could not be caught now, not when he was the only one who could help his friends! Although the priest was tall, he was thin and looked frail. Bartholomew's only hope was that the priest would not cry out a warning when Bartholomew launched himself at him. As Bartholomew prepared to dive, the priest raised both hands to show that he was unarmed, and then very deliberately drew a cross in the air in front of him. Bartholomew watched in confusion. The priest put his fingers to his lips and motioned that Bartholomew should follow.

Bartholomew looked around him desperately. What should he do? The priest seemed to be telling him he was not a part of de Belem's satanic following by drawing the cross in the air. Perhaps he could persuade him to help. With a last agonised glance through the window, he jumped from the tomb and followed the priest.

'I am Father Lucius,' the man said when they were a safe distance from the church.

Bartholomew leapt away from him. He had been tricked! It was the man who had last been seen visiting Froissart before he died! But the soldiers said that Father Lucius was a Franciscan, and this man was wearing the habit of a Dominican friar. Holding his breath, every fibre in his body tense, Bartholomew waited.

'These people have taken my church and I can do nothing about it. They say they will kill five of my parishioners if I send to the Bishop for help, and that I will be unable to prove anything anyway. I saw the horsemen being taken into the church. Are they your friends?'

Bartholomew nodded, still not trusting the man.

Lucius sighed. 'The high priest will kill them. He has done so before.' He shook his head in despair. 'More blood in my church.'

'Well, we have to stop him,' said Bartholomew. He chewed on his lip, scarcely able to think, let alone come up with a plan. He took a deep breath and forced himself to calm down. 'What is de Belem's business here?'

Lucius shrugged. 'Saffron. That is all we have here, and he owns all of it now.'

'All of it?' Bartholomew was amazed. Saffron was a valuable commodity. It could be used for medicine and in cooking as well as a high-quality dye for delicate fabrics like silk. Thousands of flowers were needed to produce even small amounts of the yellow-orange spice, and so it was expensive to buy. Anyone with a monopoly over saffron would be a rich man indeed. More pieces of the mystery fell into place in Bartholomew's mind, but he ignored them. Now was not the time for logical analysis. He needed to do something to help Michael and Stanmore.

'Is the saffron picked yet?' he asked, the germ of an idea beginning to unfold in his mind.

Lucius looked at him. 'The crocuses are picked, yes. The high priest has been withholding the saffron from the market to force up the price. It is stored in his warehouses.'

Bartholomew pushed him forward. 'Show me,' he said. 'Quickly.'

'They will be guarded,' said Lucius. 'They always are.'

He led the way through the churchyard to where two thatched wooden buildings stood just off the main street. Several men could be seen prowling back and forth. De Belem was obviously taking no chances with his precious saffron. Bartholomew tried to think. He would not be able to reach the storehouses without being seen by the guards. And even if he did reach them, he would be an easy target for the bows they carried: the same great longbows that had been used to devastate the French at the battle of Crécy.

He thought quickly. 'I need a bow,' he muttered to Lucius.

He began to assess which of the guards he might be able to overpower without the others seeing.

'Will you shoot them?' Lucius asked fearfully. 'More killing?'

Bartholomew shook his head and clenched his fists to stop his hands from shaking. He could hear de Belem's voice raving from the church. He was running out of time.

'I will get you one,' said Lucius, suddenly decisive. He rose from where he had been crouching and slipped away.

Bartholomew took a flint from his bag and began to kindle a fire from some dry grass. He took rolled bandages and began to soak them with the concentrated spirits he used to treat corns and calluses. When Lucius returned, Bartholomew wrapped the bandages around the pointed ends of the arrows and packed it all with more grass. That should burn, he thought. Clumsily, he tried to fit the arrow to the bow, but it had been many years since Stanmore had taught him how to use the weapon, and he had not been good at it even then.

He almost jumped out of his skin as a hand fell on his shoulder. It was Cynric. 'Those men were difficult to lose,' he said. Bartholomew closed his eyes in relief.

'Michael and the others are captive in the church,' he said. 'We need to create a diversion. If de Belem sees his saffron burning, he will try to save it and we might be able to rescue them.'

Cynric nodded, and calmly took the bow from Bartholomew's shaking hands. 'A Welshman is better for this, boy.'

'When the arrow begins to burn, shoot it where you think it will catch light,' said Bartholomew.

Cynric, understanding, looked across at the storehouses. 'They thought to frighten us by making our College gate explode into flames as if by magic, and now we use their idea to burn the saffron!' he said in satisfaction.

Bartholomew nodded, knowing he would never have thought to use fire arrows on the saffron stores had he not seen them used on the gate a few nights earlier.

Cynric touched the arrow to the fire, and Bartholomew and Lucius ducked back as it exploded into flames. Cynric put it to the bow and aimed. They watched it soar through the air like a shooting star and land with a thump on one of the thatched roofs. Without waiting to see what happened, Bartholomew began preparing another. Their only hope of success was to loose as many arrows as possible before they were discovered. He gave Cynric a second, and then a third. He glanced up, his body aching with tension. He could see no flames leaping into the air, hear no cries of alarm from the guards.

'It's not working,' he said, his voice cracking in desperation.

'Give it time,' said Lucius calmly. 'It has been raining a good deal lately. The thatching is probably damp. Try another.'

Bartholomew used the last of the alcohol and handed another arrow to Cynric. They watched it sail clean through a gap between the roof and the wall, leaving a fiery trail behind it. Nothing happened. Bartholomew put his head in his hands in despair. What else could he do? He could do nothing with only Cynric against a band of mercenaries and an entire village. He took a deep breath. He would grab a handful of burning grass and run towards the storehouses with it himself. If he reached them and set them alight before the guards realised what was happening, the diversion would be caused; if they shot him, then that would also cause a diversion. Michael and Oswald would have to use it to fend for themselves.

'Look!' whispered Lucius in excitement. 'There is a fire inside!'

As Bartholomew looked up, he saw yellow flames leaping up inside the nearest of the storehouses, while the other began to ooze smoke from its roof.

'The dry saffron is going up like firewood!' said Lucius, his eyes gleaming. 'Do you have any more of that stuff that burns?'

Bartholomew shook his head, but made two more fire arrows from bandages and grass alone. They did not burn as well, but there was no harm in trying.

There was a shout as one of the guards saw the flames and ran towards the building. He grasped at the door and pulled it open. As air flooded in, there was a dull roar, and the entire building was suddenly engulfed in flames. Of the guard there was no sign. The flames began to lick towards the other storehouse.

'Back to the church,' Bartholomew said urgently to Lucius. 'You must raise the alarm.'

Lucius nodded and they ran back to the main road. He began yelling as they reached the church, flinging open the doors to rush inside. The frightened villagers looked at their priest in confusion, while de Belem hesitated at the altar. Bartholomew and Cynric slipped into the church while attention was fixed on the apparently gibbering Lucius, and hid behind a stack of benches.

Bartholomew saw with relief that Stanmore and his men were unharmed. De Belem, however, had Michael in front of him, held securely by two of the mercenaries. The knife de Belem waved glittered in the torchlight.

Janetta stepped forward. 'Why do you disturb us, priest?'

'Fire!' shrieked Lucius. 'Fire in the saffron! Run to see to your houses, my children! Save what you can before the fire spreads!'

Bartholomew saw de Belem's jaw drop as he heard his precious saffron was burning, and he exchanged a look of horror with Janetta. Lucius, meanwhile, was exhorting his people to save their homes. Lucius was clever, Bartholomew thought, for if the villagers were scattered to see to their own property, they could not quickly be organised into groups to fight the fire in the saffron stores. In twos and threes, the people began to run away, the fear of losing what little they had greater than de Belem's hold over them.

Bartholomew expected that de Belem would drop everything and run to save his saffron, but the flickering light of the fires could be seen through the windows, and de Belem obviously knew that there was little he could do. In the turmoil, he turned his attention back to Michael, and Bartholomew saw the raised knife silhouetted against the wall behind. He closed his eyes in despair, before snapping them open again. Silhouetted!

He edged round the pillar, and raised his hands near the torch burning on a bracket. They were enormous on the blank wall opposite. He moved them around until he got them into something vaguely resembling an animal with two horns and waggled it about on the wall.

'*Caper* is here!' he yelled at the top of his voice, hoping de Belem would be taken off guard for the instant that might enable Michael to wriggle free. At the same time, Cynric unleashed one of his bloodcurdling Welsh battle-screams that ripped through the church like something from hell itself.

The few remaining villagers fled in terror, led by Father Lucius. Several of the mercenaries followed, while de Belem and Janetta looked at the shadow in horror. Janetta glanced at de Belem once and followed the mercenaries. As she ran past, Bartholomew dived from his pillar and caught her, wrapping his arms firmly around her so she could not move. Meanwhile, Michael had seized his chance, and the two mercenaries lay stunned on the ground, their heads cracked together. Stanmore and his men appeared as dazed as the mercenaries, but a furious shout from Michael brought them to their senses.

'Any man who works for me will be paid twice what de Belem pays,' said Stanmore quickly, addressing the bewildered mercenaries. He plucked a purse from his belt and tossed it to one of them. 'Down payment. And I promise you will not have to do anything that is against the law or against God. The brave heroes of Crécy deserve better than this,' he cried, waving his hand at de Belem's satanic regalia.

For a moment, Bartholomew thought his speech had not had its desired effect, since the men merely stood and watched. Eventually, one of the men gestured impatiently at Stanmore. 'So what are your orders?' he asked.

'No,' yelled de Belem. 'I have power over you. You saw what I can bring into this world!' He pointed towards the wall where Bartholomew's goat silhouette had been.

Michael raised one of the hands and made the shape of a duck on the wall behind him.

'Children's tricks!' he said. 'Is that not so, Matt?'

De Belem looked in disbelief at Michael's duck and then down the church to where Bartholomew was holding a struggling Janetta, and sagged in defeat.

CHAPTER 11

AS DAWN BROKE, ALL THAT WAS LEFT OF DE BELEM'S STORE-houses was a smouldering heap of wood. Bartholomew turned to Father Lucius.

'What will happen to the people?' he said. 'How will they live without the saffron?'

Lucius smiled. 'I have some tucked away that I stole as we laboured in the fields. We will be able to sell it at the inflated price forced by de Belem. I hear the labourers can earn high wages these days for their toil, and now that we are free, some may well look elsewhere for work.'

'Were you at St Mary's Church about two weeks ago?' Bartholomew asked, wanting to get certain things clear in his mind.

The priest looked surprised. 'No. I have never been to Cambridge. I have heard it smells like a sewer in the hot months and have no wish to go there.'

'How long has de Belem been here?'

'He was buying land here before the Death, but I was foolish enough not to guess that it was he who came in the guise of this high priest later. After the Death took so many, it was easy for him to buy, or simply take, all the remaining stocks, and the few who resisted selling were threatened with demonic devices until they sold too.'

'Demonic devices?' asked Bartholomew.

'Goats' hooves left in their houses, black birds flying around at night. All things with a rational explanation,' said Lucius. He turned to Bartholomew. 'Not like that thing he called up in my church,' he added, shuddering.

Bartholomew smiled. 'I did that,' he said, and, seeing the

priest's expression of horror, added quickly, 'with my hands against the light, like this.'

Lucius looked blankly at him for a moment and then roared with laughter. 'Is that what it was?' he said. 'Are you telling me that de Belem, who had fooled so many with tricks, was fooled by one himself?'

Bartholomew nodded and watched Lucius, still laughing, stride off to tell his parishioners. He went to join the group of soldiers who had Janetta, de Belem, and several others carefully guarded. Tulyet had arrived when all was still confusion. De Belem had underestimated him, and the Sheriff had not trusted the words of a conveniently alert villager to send him down the London road.

'I owe you an apology,' said Tulyet. 'But they had my son. After you came to see me, Brother, they sent me some of his hair, and said if I spoke to you again, they would send me one of his fingers. I had to be seen to be following their demands, which is why I threatened you so vociferously. One of the soldiers was watching my every move and reporting to de Belem.' He smiled grimly. 'He is now in the Castle prison awaiting the arrival of his high priest.'

'Did you have any idea de Belem was involved in all this?' asked Michael, waving a hand at the smouldering storehouses.

Tulyet shook his head. 'I had only begun to suspect that the high priest was de Belem recently. After his daughter was killed, he told me that he had been the high priest of the Guild of Purification, but that he had given that up in grief. I now realise that there was never a Guild of Purification, that it was simply a ruse set up by de Belem to keep his other coven in fear.'

'That cannot be,' said Michael. 'Hesselwell and your father told us the new priest arrived only a month ago after Nicholas died.'

'But he had spies in the Guild of the Coming,' said Tulyet, 'right from the start. Nicholas's death was simply an opportune moment for de Belem to step in and control directly what he had been controlling indirectly for some time.'

'But why bother with the covens at all?' asked Stanmore. 'It all seems rather elaborate.'

'Because it gave him power over people,' said Bartholomew. 'Everyone who had become embroiled was terrified – like old Richard Tulyet and Piers Hesselwell. Once they were in, it was impossible to leave, and tricks, like the ones we saw used in All Saints', were employed to keep them frightened. The murders in the town, too, aided his purpose. He claimed they were committed by his satanic familiar, showing his presence to his followers.'

'But why did he need this power over people?' persisted Stanmore.

'Because all over the country, labourers are leaving their homes to seek better-paid work elsewhere. De Belem had no intention of paying high wages to the villagers here, although he needed their labour. He realised that he could use tricks to make them too terrified to do anything other than bend to his will.'

'I had worked that out myself,' said Stanmore impatiently. 'But why bother with the likes of old Tulyet and Hesselwell? They did not labour for him.'

'In Hesselwell's case, de Belem wanted a contact in Michaelhouse where Michael and I were working for the Chancellor. Hesselwell said the high priest asked him many questions.'

'And my father?' asked Tulyet.

'De Belem had a monopoly on saffron and was the only dyer in the town. As Oswald will attest, he was sufficiently confident of his monopoly that he was even beginning to sell cloth, the prerogative of drapers, not dyers. De Belem would want to know of plans by cloth merchants and tailors to attempt to buy dyeing services from anyone else. Oswald arranged to buy coloured cloth from London, but his carts were attacked and the cloth stolen. That was because Oswald had mentioned it to your father, and your father told his high priest: de Belem.'

Stanmore nodded. 'The stolen cloth is in de Belem's storerooms in Milne Street if you have any doubts,' he said.

Tulyet sighed and looked at where his men were guarding de Belem and his helpers, waiting for full daylight. Tulyet was taking no chances by travelling too early, and running the risk of being attacked by outlaws.

'So that was it,' he said. 'The note I received said my son had been taken to ensure I did not investigate the guilds, but what I was really being stopped from looking into were de Belem's business dealings. I should have thought harder: my son was taken when I began to investigate the theft of Sir Oswald's cloth. To me, the theft was far less important than the whore murders, but to de Belem, it was obviously paramount. Well, we have him now.'

Stanmore gazed about him. 'I am astonished this is all so well organised,' he said. 'You say Buckley overheard that half the mercenaries were garrisoned here and half in Primrose Alley?'

'Primrose Alley?' said Tulyet sharply. 'Where Froissart lived?'

'Froissart and his family were among the few people who survived the plague in Primrose Alley,' said Bartholomew. 'Because there were so many empty houses, and because no one wanted to live there if they could be somewhere better, de Belem used it to garrison his mercenaries. Poor Froissart probably discovered something incriminating. He ran to the church for sanctuary not for killing his wife, but to escape de Belem. That night, Gilbert hid in the crypt, to which he has the only set of keys, while the church was locked. He emerged from his hiding place, garrotted Froissart, and waited for "Father Lucius" to come to help him hide the body where it would not be found. Father Lucius, was, of course, de Belem, and he was let into the church by Gilbert, and not by Froissart, as the guards believed.'

'The guards saw de Belem, and described him as mean-looking with a big nose,' elaborated Michael. 'For de Belem, used to dealing with the trappings of witchcraft, it would not have been difficult to make himself unrecognisable to guards more interested in dice than in watching the church, especially a man wearing the hooded robe of a friar.'

'Gilbert is involved in all this?' asked Tulyet, amazed. 'The Chancellor's clerk? I will send a man for him before he realises something is amiss and escapes.'

'That is not necessary,' said Bartholomew. 'Have you noticed that you never see Janetta and Gilbert together? That is because they are one and the same.'

'What?' exclaimed Michael, Tulyet, and Stanmore simultaneously. Michael continued, 'That is outrageous, Matt! Gilbert has a beard for a start, and Janetta is a woman! That fall you had at de Belem's has addled your wits!'

'Go and see,' said Bartholomew. 'You will find that splendid head of hair will come clean off if you give it a tug.'

'You do it,' said Michael primly. 'Monks do not pull women's hair!'

Bartholomew went to where Janetta was being guarded with de Belem in the back of a small cart, followed closely by the others. Janetta smiled falsely at Bartholomew, and he smiled back as he reached out a hand towards her hair. Her smile faded, and she tried to move away.

'No! What are you doing?'

Bartholomew grabbed some of the hair and Janetta screamed. It was held in place firmly, so he pulled harder. Then the wig was off, and Gilbert's thin, fair hair emerged, plastered to his head. De Belem watched impassively, while Gilbert, barely recognisable without his beard, spat and struggled.

'How did you know?' asked Tulyet in astonishment.

'Because the wig may have fooled us, but it did not fool the town prostitutes,' said Bartholomew. 'Matilde told me the hair was a wig. I looked closely when I met Janetta in St Mary's churchyard, and I saw that she was right. And I was puzzled that a woman, obviously concerned with her appearance, would not take pains to hide her scarred face with the thick powders she wore on her cheeks on occasions.'

'That would not be easy to do,' mused Tulyet thoughtfully. 'My wife has a mark on her neck that she does not like to be seen. When she cannot cover it with her clothing, she applies powders. The whole business is very time-consuming. If Janetta had needed to make a sudden appearance, there would not be time to start such a lengthy process. Better to be open about the scars from the start than try to hide them and have them exposed at a point that might be inconvenient.'

'I also noticed that Janetta's hair partly hid her face when she spoke to me, but not when she spoke to the men. That was because I knew Gilbert, and he was taking precautions against being recognised. I was certain, however, when I grabbed him in the church earlier. It did not take a physician to know that the person I held was no woman!'

Michael continued. 'Cuthbert drew attention to the fact that the woman in Nicholas's grave had sparse hair. She died a month ago, at the precise time Janetta made her appearance with her luxurious black hair.'

'Nicholas's lover,' said Stanmore. 'Was she killed for her wigs, then?'

Bartholomew was stumped. It was a possibility he had not considered.

Michael answered instead. 'No, she was killed for something far more serious. The woman had thin, fair hair just like Gilbert's.'

He looked at Gilbert, who refused to look back. Bartholomew gave an exclamation as Janetta's relationship with Gilbert suddenly became clear.

'She was his sister!' he said. 'She was small like him, too. Tiny, in fact.'

'Yes, his sister,' said Michael, still looking at Gilbert. 'Janetta of Lincoln was no fictitious character, was she? She was your sister who was summoned from Lincoln to help with de Belem's plan. You knew Nicholas was working on a book, and that it might contain information dangerous or detrimental to you. Janetta came to insinuate herself into Nicholas's affections in order to discover exactly what he had learned. Cuthbert told us Nicholas was deeply in love, and that the woman seemed to reciprocate these feelings, so perhaps her affection turned her from her true purpose, and that was why she was murdered.'

'And why Gilbert stole her body away from the crypt,' said Bartholomew. 'I hope she lies somewhere peaceful now, without the desecration of that foul mask.'

Gilbert gave a half-smile. 'You will never prove anything other than the fact that I occasionally assumed another identity,' he said.

Tulyet shrugged. 'It does not matter. There is evidence enough to hang you already. Anything we learn now will make no difference to the outcome. We can prove two cases of kidnapping and the practice of witchcraft.'

'We have never practised witchcraft,' said de Belem. 'Everything we did had a rational explanation, and was only harmless fun. A joke. It is not my fault that people were afraid. We have killed no one, and all my property came to me perfectly legally. My lawyer, Piers Hesselwell, will attest to that. You have no proof, just a series of unfounded suppositions. I have powerful friends in the town and in Court. You will not hang me.'

Bartholomew had a cold feeling in the pit of his stomach that de Belem might well be right. They had strong evidence – Tulyet's baby in de Belem's house, Buckley's kidnapping, and Stanmore's stolen cloth – but it was so complex that he imagined a good lawyer could easily find alternative explanations that de Belem's powerful friends would choose to believe as the truth. He walked away, finding de Belem's confident gloating unbearable. He ached all over from his hard ride, and his head was beginning to throb from the hours of tension.

A small stream trickled behind one of the rows of houses, and he crouched at the edge of it to scoop handfuls of water over his face. He heard a sound behind him and spun round, thinking it might be one of de Belem's men still lurking free, but relaxed when he saw it was only Michael.

'Father Lucius has some potage for us,' he said. 'Come. We need something warm inside us if we are to face the rest of the day.'

Bartholomew followed him to the small priest's house next to the church. It was little more than a single room with a lean-to shack at the back for animals. But the rushes on the floor were clean and the crude wooden table in the middle of the room had been scrubbed almost white. Bartholomew sat on a bench with Michael next to him. Stanmore was already there, sipping broth from a blue-glazed bowl. Lucius set other bowls on the table, and Bartholomew closed his cold fingers around one, grateful for the warmth after the chill of the stream.

'De Belem is right, you know,' he said to the others. 'A good lawyer will be able to overturn the evidence we have, especially if the court is full of his powerful friends.'

Stanmore shook his head. 'There is no lawyer that good,' he said. 'And I too will hire one. It was my cloth he stole, and my man he murdered for it. For Will's sake, I will see he does not go free.'

'But we cannot prove he killed the prostitutes,' said Bartholomew. 'De Belem will claim he would not kill his own daughter, nor his woman.'

'But we know they killed Janetta,' said Michael. 'And all the women died of wounds to the throat, like she did. It is too much coincidence not to be true.'

'But the others had that circle on their feet, and we cannot show Janetta had one,' said Bartholomew. 'And we cannot really prove they killed Janetta. We have no witness, no firm, undeniable proof.'

'I am still confused by much of this,' said Stanmore. 'Pieces fit together, but I have a problem with the whole.'

'We should clarify it,' said Michael. 'We have deduced so much that has been proven wrong over the last week, that we need to see whether we agree now.'

Bartholomew grimaced. He was tired, and, like Stanmore, the complete picture still eluded him. There were pieces that still did not fit together, and he was not sure whether his mind was sharp enough to analyse them properly. He took a sip of the potage and almost choked as Michael slapped him encouragingly on the back.

'Let us begin at the beginning,' he said heartily, and Bartholomew wondered where the fat monk's energy came from. 'We need to go back a long way, before all this business started, to Lincoln from whence Gilbert and his kin hail. In Lincoln there was a judge who punished petty criminals by disfiguring their faces. Gilbert must have been punished, rightly or wrongly, for some crime while visiting his family.'

He paused, and Bartholomew recalled what Buckley had said to him as they sat in de Belem's yard waiting for Stanmore to come with the horses. 'Buckley remembered Gilbert's returning from Lincoln with the beard, because he wondered whether he might be able to grow one to hide the sores on his face. Buckley grew a beard, but was impressed that Gilbert's was so much fuller, while his own remained straggly. But Gilbert's scarred face could never sprout such luxurious growth, and the beard was false. He has worn it ever since, to hide the scars that betray him as a criminal.'

'Well, no one would suspect he and Janetta were one and the same, as long as Gilbert wore a beard,' said Stanmore.

'Then we come to the book,' said Michael, holding out his bowl to Lucius for more potage. 'Nicholas had been employed by the Chancellor to write a history of events concerning the University, so that there would be a record for future scholars. As the Chancellor told us, it contained information that could prove embarrassing in some quarters. It not only involved members of the University, but people from the town with whom scholars had had dealings. Nicholas appeared to have taken his task seriously. He joined the Guild of the Coming in order to see what he could learn, and was even elected their leader.'

Bartholomew took up the tale. 'When de Belem learned from Gilbert that Nicholas was writing the book, he became nervous. Gilbert's sister was drafted in from Lincoln to worm her way into his affections to discover what he had learned.'

'But Cuthbert thought that Janetta and Nicholas seemed happy together,' said Michael. 'She failed to tell de Belem and Gilbert what they wanted to know, and possibly even gave Nicholas information about them. And now we are stuck. What happened next?'

Bartholomew pondered, smiling up at Lucius as he filled his bowl again. Stanmore looked from one to the other in anticipation.

'Well, what *do* we know?' said Bartholomew. 'Cuthbert said that Nicholas felt he was in fear of his life, so he feigned his death. De Belem must have threatened him in some way. Nicholas, apparently, felt the only way he could be safe was if he were presumed dead. If he and Janetta were as fond of each other as Cuthbert believes, then the chances are that she helped him execute the plan.'

'And of course we know how!' exclaimed Michael suddenly. 'Gilbert was able to switch Nicholas's body for Janetta's in the crypt yesterday because he is the only one with the keys. Janetta, who doubtless shared Gilbert's house, must have stolen his keys when Nicholas was sealed in his coffin and locked in the church for the night, and gone to let him out. How else would he have escaped the church and still kept secret the fact that he was alive?'

'Gilbert must have suspected, or perhaps he woke to see the keys gone,' mused Bartholomew. 'He followed her to the church and saw Nicholas alive.'

'But then what?' said Stanmore. 'A small man like Gilbert could not hope to overpower two people.'

'He must have fetched de Belem,' said Michael. 'Nicholas and Janetta had to make the coffin look as though there were still a body inside, and that would take a while. Gilbert would have had time. Then there must have been a skirmish in which Janetta was killed and Nicholas escaped.'

'And why the mask?' asked Stanmore. 'Why would Gilbert bury his sister with that?'

'Perhaps she had worn it to hide her face when she went to release Nicholas,' said Michael.

'No,' said Bartholomew slowly. 'I think de Belem probably wore it to frighten Nicholas when Gilbert fetched him. He probably meant to terrify Nicholas into revealing what was in the book before they killed him. The mask was huge, and perhaps dawn was coming by the time Janetta was killed and Nicholas had escaped. It was probably placed on Janetta merely to get rid of it so that de Belem would not have to carry it home through the streets, and Gilbert would not have to hide it in the church.'

Michael nodded. 'And de Belem must have gained some information from Nicholas before he fled, because he knew there was something important in the book. De Belem then hired a professional thief to come to steal it for him. Gilbert could not steal it, because he had the keys to the church but not to the chest. And we know what happened to the friar.'

'I see,' said Stanmore. 'But why bother with poor old Buckley?'

'We know de Belem and some of the mercenaries went to kidnap Buckley at the same time that the friar went to steal the book,' said Bartholomew. 'They took everything from his room to make it look as if he had fled the town after some guilty deed – the theft of the book. But the plan misfired when the friar scratched his thumb on the lock and died.'

'We suspect Gilbert went to check on the friar, found him dead, and tipped him into the chest in a panic,' said Michael. 'The friar had been told to steal the whole book, because not only did de Belem want the information about himself, he liked to know the secrets of others. We know he asked questions of old Tulyet and Hesselwell: de Belem liked to gather information so that he could use it against others.

'Gilbert, panic-ridden because the plan had gone awry, did not steal the whole book as the friar would have done, he stole only the parts that involved him and de Belem. The Chancellor obviously did not deem these parts important because he did not miss them. But de Wetherset later removed sections he *did* deem important, thus muddying the evidence. Because Gilbert had taken the part that concerned de Belem, there was nothing left to shed light on the affair. Thus it seemed to us that Buckley lacked a motive for fleeing and taking all his belongings.'

'Buckley told me he thought something had gone wrong, and he was a problem to de Belem,' said Bartholomew. 'De Belem was keeping him prisoner until the opportunity arose to use him, or his death, to further his plans.'

'Now,' said Michael, leaning across to peer into Bartholomew's bowl to see if he had left any food. 'Janetta died from a throat injury, Froissart was garrotted, and Nicholas was garrotted. This is not a common method of execution, and we are sure all were killed by one and the same. We know Gilbert killed Froissart because he had the keys to the crypt and could hide there unseen while the church was locked.'

'Froissart's wife was garrotted,' said Stanmore. 'One of my men told me.'

The four men were silent, Lucius looking from one to the other in horror at such convoluted evil.

'So Gilbert killed his sister when he found out she was planning to run away with Nicholas; he killed Froissart when he discovered something amiss in Primrose Alley; he killed Froissart's wife to make it appear as if Froissart had fled into sanctuary for her murder; and he killed Nicholas when he mustered the courage to return to Cambridge to look for Janetta,' said Bartholomew.

'Gilbert must also be the killer of the whores,' said Stanmore. 'Because their throats were slashed.'

'Frances was not a whore,' said Bartholomew. 'Her last words that her killer was not a man must mean that it was Janetta. It was not a man in a mask at all, but the mysterious woman she had perhaps seen in and out of her father's house in the night. Oh, Lord!'

'What?' said Michael. 'What have you thought of?'

'Boniface,' said Bartholomew. The others looked at him uncomprehendingly. 'Frances asked Boniface to meet her in the orchard because she had something to tell him. He waited but she never arrived. I thought she was going to tell him something personal, but she must have been going to tell him about strange happenings at her father's house – the baby crying in the night, birds and bats in his attics, a room always locked where Buckley was captive. I imagine she thought that, as a friar, he might be able to secure the help of the other Franciscans and investigate. Perhaps she knew of her father's involvement with the guilds and considered he had become too deeply caught for his own safety. Gilbert guessed what she was about to do, followed her disguised as Janetta, and killed her in Michaelhouse.'

'That makes sense,' said Michael. 'Her father's involvement with the coven was probably something that became an increasing worry to her as time went on. Perhaps she reached the end of her tether with her other problem.'

'What problem?' asked Stanmore, interested.

'Nothing that will concern her now,' answered Michael quickly, catching Bartholomew's eye and wincing at his own near-indiscretion.

'The wounds on Janetta, Frances, Isobel, and Fritha were not the same,' said Bartholomew thoughtfully. 'Isobel's and Fritha's throats were slit; the others' were hacked.'

Stanmore looked at him distastefully. 'It is all much the same,' he said. 'And anyway, they all had bloody circles on their feet. It stands to reason de Belem would not kill his own daughter and whore. I wonder if he knows Gilbert is their killer.'

'He cannot,' said Bartholomew, 'or he would not have asked us to investigate. It was Gilbert as Janetta that warned us away from investigating – once in Primrose Alley and once in the churchyard; it was Gilbert who instructed Hesselwell to leave the head in Michael's room claiming it was the will of the high priest; and it was Gilbert who ordered Hesselwell to prepare the back gate of Michaelhouse with a substance that would burn. He knew we used the gate at night, and planned to set it alight as we emerged. Even if we were not killed or injured, we would have received another warning. Meanwhile, de Belem discouraged us from looking into the guilds, but encouraged us to look elsewhere. He must believe the murders have nothing to do with his business.'

'But he is the high priest who said there would be another killing,' said Michael. 'He must know!'

Bartholomew was silent, trying to impose reason onto the muddle of facts. 'Well,' he began uncertainly, 'he knew Tulyet would not investigate Frances's death, because he was bound by de Belem's own blackmail note. If he wanted her killer found, he would have to ask others to investigate. He had Hesselwell walking the streets at night. He urged us to investigate, and then, at the meeting of the Guild of the Coming that night, he called on the murderer to strike again, hoping to draw him into the open. He received no note from the killer purporting to be from the Guild of the Holy Trinity. That was a ruse to encourage us to help him, but to ensure we did not start by looking into the covens.'

'Perhaps he really does believe the killer is from the Guild of the Holy Trinity,' said Michael. 'If Gilbert had any sense he would encourage that belief to protect himself.' He shook himself. 'I am glad Gilbert and de Belem were lying to each other and misleading each other as they did to others,' he added.

Lucius scratched his head. 'All this makes sense, except for why Gilbert should assume his sister's identity.'

Bartholomew frowned. 'Buckley said de Belem was beginning to lose control of his mercenaries. He needed help. Gilbert could not risk entering Primrose Alley as himself, but he could control the mercenaries as Janetta, the mysterious woman who was the subject of so much speculation among the town's prostitutes.'

'And all so that de Belem could continue to maintain a

monopoly over the dyeing business!' said Lucius, shaking his head.

Stanmore pursed his lips. 'That would be a most lucrative position to hold. He would have held sway over a vast region.' He twisted round to look out of the window. 'The sun shines,' he said, 'and we should be away before the day is gone.'

They thanked Lucius for his hospitality and went to where Tulyet was organising a convoy with the cart of prisoners in the middle. De Belem regarded them with a triumphant sneer, while Gilbert huddled in a corner looking frightened. Michael strode over to them.

'We have it reasoned out,' he said. 'We know Gilbert murdered his sister, then Froissart and his wife, and then Nicholas. We know that you hired the friar to steal the book. And we know that the covens were merely a front to hide the size of your business empire from prying eyes, and to ensure these poor people continued to work for you for pitiful wages.'

De Belem shrugged. 'You can think what you like, but you can prove nothing.'

'Taxes!' said Stanmore all of a sudden. 'Part of the reason you have kept the size of your business secret is that you are swindling the King out of his taxes!'

De Belem paled a little, but said nothing. Stanmore rubbed his hands together. 'Old Richard Tulyet has an eye for figures. We will petition the King that we be allowed to assess how much you have cheated him. I am sure he will be willing to let us look. Then the Sheriff will charge you with treason!'

'Why did you kill your sister, Gilbert?' asked Bartholomew gently, hoping to coax with kindness what they might never learn by force.

'Do not deign to answer,' said de Belem harshly. 'They can prove nothing.'

'We can prove Gilbert killed Froissart,' said Michael. 'And he will hang. Is that what you wish, Gilbert, for you to hang while de Belem goes free?'

'She betrayed me,' said Gilbert in a small voice. De Belem made a lunge for him, but was held by two of Tulyet's men.

'Say nothing, you fool! I can hire lawyers who will make a mockery of their feeble reasonings.'

'Now you have no saffron, you have nothing. Tricks and lies will not work now.'

De Belem tried to struggle to his feet, but was held firmly by the soldiers. Gilbert ignored him and continued.

'I did not mean to kill her. The knife was in my hand. I was angrier than I have ever been before, and the next thing I knew was that she was lying at my feet. I regret it bitterly. Nicholas seized his opportunity and escaped.'

He gave Bartholomew a weak smile. 'I heard you say to Master de Wetherset that Nicholas's coffin had been desecrated because it was meant to be found. You could not have been more wrong. It was never intended to be found. I tried hard to dissuade the Chancellor from excavating the grave, and moved the marker so that you would dig up another. But all failed, and she was exposed to prying eyes in the end. I did not want her to be reburied where she had been so defiled by that mask,' he said, casting a defiant look at de Belem. 'I buried her elsewhere. I will never tell you where because I do not want her disturbed again.'

Bartholomew hoped no one would ask. He had no wish to conduct more exhumations.

'And Froissart and Nicholas?'

Gilbert nodded. 'Marius Froissart came barging into my house when I was removing my beard. It was obvious from his face he knew who I was. He fled to the church. I followed and told him I would kill his family unless he kept silent. I killed his wife, put about Froissart had murdered her, and killed him later that night. Nicholas was easier. He came to look at Janetta's body in the crypt, and I killed him there.'

'And why did you kill Frances?' Bartholomew asked.

'Frances?' whispered de Belem, the colour fleeing from his face.

'She knew too much,' said Gilbert. 'She was on her way to reveal all when I killed her.'

'You killed Frances?' whispered de Belem. 'My daughter?'

'Yes!' said Gilbert loudly. 'I killed her. I did it for the sake of the saffron. Believe me, Reginald, once that fox-faced friar knew about it, it would not have been a secret for long, and we would have lost everything.'

'How could you?' whispered de Belem. 'Why did you not tell me what she was doing? I could have spoken with her. She loved me!'

'Like Isobel?' asked Michael casually.

'Did you kill her too?' asked de Belem, his face grey.

'I did not,' said Gilbert. 'Although doubtless I will be accused of it. I did not touch the whores.'

'But you have already told us you killed Janetta and Frances!' said Stanmore.

Gilbert raised his manacled hands. 'But I did not kill the others. Perhaps de Belem did. It was he, who as high priest, called for another murder. How would he know if he were not the killer?'

De Belem looked away. 'Not I,' he said.

'Rubbish!' said Michael. 'Gilbert deliberately started the rumours that Froissart was the killer because the killer was him! He confessed to killing Frances, and she, like the others, had a circle on her foot.'

'I saw that mark on the others,' said Gilbert. 'I copied it. It was the high priest who killed the others.'

De Belem eyed him coldly. 'What anyone thinks matters nothing now that I know my daughter's murderer will hang.' He gave a soft laugh. 'I really thought it was the Guild of the Holy Trinity punishing me for my involvement with the covens. I did not imagine it would be a colleague! The reason I predicted another death was because it is time. Excluding Janetta, whom Gilbert killed, there has been a murder every ten days or so. The ten days since Isobel are almost up.'

'It does not matter which of you is the killer, you will both hang,' said Tulyet impatiently, and called to his men to start the journey back to the town. It was light, and time spent talking now was time wasted.

Bartholomew and Michael watched them go. 'Do you believe him?' asked Bartholomew.

Michael shook his head. 'I do not. De Belem is merely trying to confuse us. He lied to us in the garden of the Brazen George, so why should he not lie to us again? And Gilbert has confessed to killing Janetta and Frances. We know why the friar died and how; we have discovered who killed Froissart and Nicholas; and we have rescued Buckley. We have done all that de Wetherset has asked of us.' He rubbed his eyes tiredly. 'It is over for us, Matt.'

'You are wrong, Brother,' said Bartholomew softly. 'This business is not over yet.'

chapter 12

TANMORE INSISTED THAT BARTHOLOMEW AND MICHAEL stop at Trumpington for breakfast. Tulyet and his men, aided by Stanmore's new recruits, rode on to Cambridge. Tulyet had a busy day ahead of him. He would need to interview all his prisoners, round up any others who were implicated, and begin the documentation of the case. As they parted, Tulyet made arrangements to call at Michaelhouse later to go over the details once more. Cynric wanted to see Rachel Atkin to let her know he was safe, and said he would take word to de Wetherset.

'Shall I tell him that his clerk spent his spare time as a woman?' Cynric asked guilelessly.

'Not unless you want to spend the rest of the day in the custody of the Proctors,' said Bartholomew mildly. Cynric grinned and sped off after Tulyet's cavalcade.

Michael leaned back in one of Stanmore's best chairs and stretched his feet towards the fire Edith was stoking up. Stanmore sat opposite him, sipping some wine. Michael's habit was still splashed with the paint Bartholomew had flicked at him the night before. Bartholomew wondered who would dye it now de Belem was gone.

They discussed details of the night's work. Edith sniffed dismissively when they told her how Gilbert had disguised himself, and claimed a woman would have been able to tell the difference.

'You are probably right,' said Bartholomew. 'Once I knew, it was very obvious. His walk was masculine and his cheeks were sometimes thickly coated in powders.'

'That would be to hide his whiskers,' said Edith. 'He would

need to shave constantly, even though his beard was not adequate to hide the scars on his face.'

'No wonder Janetta was difficult to track down,' said Michael. 'And Gilbert fooled Tulyet, too. He went to interview "Janetta" when Froissart first claimed sanctuary, and she even told him she had witnessed the murder she had committed herself!'

'And then she denied ever meeting Tulyet to add to our growing concerns over Tulyet's involvement,' said Bartholomew. He thought for a moment, staring pensively at the wine in his cup. 'But I am still concerned about their claim that they did not kill the other women.'

'They are lying to confuse us,' said Stanmore. 'It was them. Gilbert confessed to killing Janetta and Frances. How much more evidence do you need? Think about Sybilla's description, Frances's last words, and the circles on their feet.'

'Sybilla gave no kind of description at all,' said Bartholomew impatiently. 'It could fit just about anyone. And, as you pointed out, they will hang anyway, so why bother to lie?'

'Because they have spent the last several months doing little else,' said Stanmore. 'They have perpetrated the most frightful fraud, terrifying people with false witchcraft, and pretending to be those they are not. Their whole lives have been a lie.' He reached for the jug of wine. 'It is over. We should look to the future, and I must decide whether I should employ a dyer until another comes to take de Belem's place.'

'What will you do with your private army?' asked Michael, beginning to laugh.

Stanmore regarded him coolly. 'I do not see why you find that prospect amusing,' he said. 'If there had been men like these with us tonight, we would not have been ambushed. We live in dangerous times, Brother. These men will guard my goods, and I will be able to trade much further afield.' He rubbed his hands. 'Ely is lacking in good drapers.'

Michael rubbed his eyes. 'I will have nightmares about this for weeks,' he said. 'I hate to confess this to you, Matt, but when I saw that shadow figure and heard that awful screech, I thought de Belem really had conjured something from hell. It was something to do with the atmosphere of that place, with the chanting and the torchlight. I can understand how de Belem was able to use people's imaginations to increase their fear.'

Bartholomew stretched, feeling his muscles stiffening from his unaccustomed ride. 'I did not imagine de Belem would give it a second glance, but I was desperate. I certainly did not think you would be fooled by it, especially in view of the fright you gave me last week.'

'But mine was only a goat!' said Michael, his eyes round. 'Lord knows what yours was meant to be, but it looked like a demon from hell! It was horrible: all gnarled and twisted!'

'It was meant to be a goat. And I am sure you will appreciate there was little time for practice under the circumstances,' Bartholomew added drily.

Michael gave a reluctant smile. They took their leave of the Stanmores and walked back to Michaelhouse. De Wetherset had posted a clerk at the Trumpington Gate to bring them to him when they arrived. He was waiting in his office with Buckley and Harling at his side.

Bartholomew smiled at the grammar master, pleased to see that he had regained some colour in his face, and his eyes had lost the dull, witless look they had had the night before. De Wetherset, however, looked grey with shock.

'I am sorry,' he said. He must be shaken indeed, thought Bartholomew, to admit being wrong. 'When did you begin to suspect Gilbert?'

'Only yesterday,' said Michael, 'although the clues to Gilbert's other identity were there all along. It is ironic that Gilbert heard us discussing the probability that Master Buckley was the culprit, while all along, it was he.'

De Wetherset put his face in his hands, while Buckley patted him on the shoulder consolingly. Bartholomew wondered how he could ever have considered the possibility that this bumbling, gentle old man would have hidden bodies in chests and stolen from the University.

He stole a quick glance at Harling. He stood behind de Wetherset, his face impassive, although his fingers picked constantly at a loose thread on his gown. Now Buckley was back, he would have to relinquish his position as Vice-Chancellor.

Michael tried to encourage the dejected Chancellor. 'It is

over now. No one stole the book, so the University's secrets are safe. Even from me,' he added guilelessly, making de Wetherset favour him with a guilty glance. 'I must say that it has caused me to wonder whether such a book should exist at all, given that it could become a powerful tool in the hands of wicked men.'

De Wetherset pointed at a pile of grey ashes in the hearth, twitching gently in the draught from the door. 'There is Nicholas's book. You are right, Brother. Master Buckley and I decided that if the book were gone, no one will be able to use it for evil ends. But I am afraid you are wrong when you say it is over. There was another murder last night. A woman was killed near the Barnwell Gate.'

Bartholomew looked sharply at Harling, but his face betrayed nothing.

'But that is not possible!' said Michael. 'We knew where de Belem and Gilbert were all of last night.'

'De Belem and Gilbert do not know the identity of the killer,' said Buckley. 'I heard them talking about it.'

'Well, who is it then?' exploded Michael.

Bartholomew watched Harling intently.

'And of which guild were you a member, Master Harling?' he asked quietly.

Harling gazed at him in shock before he was able to answer. 'Guild? Membership of such organisations is not permitted by the University!'

'No more lies, Richard,' said de Wetherset wearily. 'Brother Michael and Doctor Bartholomew have served me well in this business. I will not have them deceived any longer.'

Harling pursed his lips in a thin, white line and looked away, so de Wetherset answered.

'Master Harling became a member of the Guild of the Coming when he took over as my deputy. I am ashamed to say that a Physwick Hostel scholar was a member, and Richard persuaded him to take him to one of the meetings. He joined to gather information to help you.'

Bartholomew looked sceptical, and Harling's eyes glittered in anger. 'My motives were purely honourable,' he said in a tight voice. 'As Vice-Chancellor, it was only a question of time before I took over from Master de Wetherset. I did not want to inherit a University riddled with corruption and wickedness, so I undertook to join the coven so that any University involvement in this business could be stamped out.'

'Only I knew of Harling's membership,' said de Wetherset. 'I considered it too dangerous even for Gilbert to know.'

'So what did you discover?' asked Bartholomew, looking at the still-angry Harling.

'Very little,' he said. 'Only that the high priest often had an enormous man with him, and there was the woman, whom I now understand was Gilbert.'

'Yes, I saw him at de Belem's house!' said Buckley. 'A great lumbering fellow that shuffled when he walked, and whose face was always covered by a mask.'

'There was something odd about him,' Harling continued. 'His movements were peculiar – uncoordinated – but at the same time immensely strong. Frankly, he frightened me.'

'Are you suggesting that this man might be the killer?' asked Michael.

Bartholomew's mind raced. He remembered the huge man whom he had struggled with in the orchard, and who had probably knocked him off his feet in St Mary's churchyard when Janetta had wanted to speak with him. Hesselwell had mentioned a large man, too.

Harling shrugged. 'I can think of no other, now that it appears that Gilbert and de Belem cannot be responsible.'

Bartholomew and Michael took their leave and walked to the Barnwell Gate.

'Damn!' said Michael, banging his fist into his palm. 'The high priest claimed that another victim would be taken before new moon, and we were so convinced that it was de Belem that we did not consider the possibility of another.'

Bartholomew rubbed tiredly at his mud-splattered hair. 'We have been stupid,' he said. 'Logically, neither de Belem nor Gilbert could have killed Isobel. Gilbert was in the church waiting for the friar, and de Belem was off kidnapping Buckley. Of course this large man could be a ruse of Harling's to deflect suspicion from him.'

'What?' said Michael. 'Do you think Harling is the killer?'

Bartholomew spread his hands. 'Why not? We have little

enough evidence, but it can be made to fit to him. First, he is a self-confessed member of a coven, whatever his motive for joining. Second, he would have had a good deal to gain if Buckley had not returned to reclaim his position, so why should he not be in league with de Belem to keep Buckley out of the way? Third, I do not like him!'

'Oh, Matt!' said Michael, exasperated. 'That is no evidence at all! I do not like him either, but he says he joined the guild after Buckley's disappearance, and I hardly think de Belem would be so foolish as to trust him immediately with the information that he had the previous Vice-Chancellor as prisoner in his house!'

They walked in silence until Bartholomew saw the large figure of Father Cuthbert puffing towards them. Although the day was not yet hot, Cuthbert's face was glistening with sweat and dark patches stained his gown from his exertions.

'Good morning,' said Cuthbert breathlessly, drawing up for a welcome pause. 'I have been out visiting before the sun gets too hot. Have you heard the news? Another murder at the Barnwell Gate, the same as the others.'

'How do you know it was the same as the others?' asked Bartholomew. He saw Michael's glance of disbelief and tried to pull himself together. Now he was suspecting everyone! There was no way the cumbersome Father Cuthbert would be able to catch a nimble prostitute.

'Master Jonstan told me,' said Cuthbert. 'I have been to visit him. He has not been himself since the death of his mother.'

'His mother died?' said Bartholomew. 'We had not heard. I am sorry to hear that. He talked about her a lot.'

'Yes, they were close,' said Cuthbert. 'But it was as well she died. She was bed-ridden for many years.'

He ambled off, waving cheerily, and Bartholomew turned to watch him as he stopped to talk to a group of dirty children playing with an ancient hoop from a barrel.

'No,' said Michael, firmly taking his arm and pulling at him to resume walking. 'Not Father Cuthbert. He is too old and too fat, and you are clutching at straws.'

Bartholomew stopped abruptly and took a fistful of Michael's habit. 'Not Father Cuthbert,' he said, his mind whirling. 'Alric Jonstan.'

Michael stared at him, eyes narrowed, and pulled absently at a stray strand of hair. 'Jonstan told Cuthbert the murder was the same as the others, but how would he know?' he began slowly. He shook Bartholomew's hand from his robe impatiently. 'It does not fit, Matt! Jonstan lives near the Barnwell Gate and probably heard the alarm when the body was found and went to see. As Proctor, he probably saw the other victims.'

'His mother!' exclaimed Bartholomew suddenly. 'When Jonstan sprained his ankle, he said his mother would look after him. Cuthbert just said she was bed-ridden.'

'He probably said that so you would not worry about him,' said Michael.

'Father?' yelled Bartholomew, running after the fat priest. 'When did Master Jonstan's mother die?'

Cuthbert turned, surprised at Bartholomew's tense face and the question out of the blue. He scratched one of his chins and thought. 'Mistress Jonstan passed away . . . four, perhaps five weeks ago . . .'

Bartholomew sped back to Michael. 'Come on!' he cried.

Michael lunged at him. 'His mother died four weeks ago? So what?'

Bartholomew struggled to free his tabard from Michael's grip. 'He was talking about her as if she were still alive last week. The man is unhinged.'

'Grief does things to people other than make them into murderers,' said Michael, gently maintaining his hold on his friend's clothes. 'Matt, you cannot go charging into Jonstan's home and accuse him of committing these foul crimes with the evidence you have. It is all circumstantial.'

'Think!' said Bartholomew, exasperated. 'Tulyet's men patrolled the streets and so did the Proctors and their beadles. Jonstan was out in the dark quite legitimately about University business. He would become familiar with others who regularly stole around in the night – the prostitutes, over whom he had no jurisdiction because they are not members of the University. I am willing to wager anything that the murders were committed on days when it was Jonstan's turn to do night patrol. For heaven's sake, Michael!' he yelled, 'Sybilla saw the Proctor and his men the night of Isobel's murder.'

Michael began to waver. 'But what about the Guild of the Holy Trinity . . . ?'

Bartholomew shook his head dismissively. 'That is irrelevant. All the other murders were committed in churchyards of the High Street, and now this one is committed at the Barnwell Gate, near Jonstan's home, from which he cannot move because he has a sprained ankle.'

Michael relinquished his hold of Bartholomew's gown with a flourish. 'Have it your way. I remain sceptical. We will visit Master Jonstan. You can say you came to look at his foot, and that way, if we find you are wrong, we will at least have an excuse for being there.'

They walked the short distance to the Barnwell Gate. Tulyet was still there, looking exhausted. He indicated a sheeted body in despair.

'I thought we had it all worked out,' he said. 'And now this. Is there no bottom to this pit of wickedness?'

'Have you rounded up any more of de Belem's followers?' asked Michael.

'Oh, yes,' said Tulyet. 'My men started the moment we arrived. Primrose Alley had been used to garrison de Belem's mercenaries, and we discovered Gilbert's clothes and beard and a spare wig in one of the houses. There were red masks, too, and more black cloaks than you would believe. We also found him.'

They looked to where he pointed. Against the wall of a house, an enormous man sat smiling up at the sun with a vacant grin, guarded by one of Tulyet's soldiers. He saw a black cat slink past and gurgled at it. Bartholomew went over to him and knelt down. The man beamed at him with an open mouth of poorly-formed teeth and then began to prod at a spot of mud on Bartholomew's tabard.

'What's your name?' he asked.

The man continued to prod at Bartholomew's tabard.

'Be careful,' Tulyet warned. 'He is dangerous.'

Bartholomew snapped his fingers near the man's ear, but there was no reaction. He put a hand under his chin and gently tipped his head back so he could look at his face. It was flat, and his tongue was too large for his mouth and lolled out. Bartholomew looked at the faint marks still on his hand from when he had been bitten in the orchard, and saw that they matched the man's asymmetrical teeth. He had unquestionably found his attacker. The man gurgled in panic, and Bartholomew let him go.

'I think he is deaf, and I doubt he can speak. The poor man has the mind of a child. He was at Michaelhouse the night the gate burned, but I do not think he had the slightest idea what he was doing. Give him to the Austin Canons at the hospital, Master Tulyet. Perhaps they can find some simple tasks for him to do until he becomes too weak.'

'Weak?' said Tulyet. 'He is as strong as an ox, as my men can attest!'

'He is dying,' said Bartholomew. 'Listen to his breathing. I have seen this before in these people. Their chests do not develop normally and they are prone to infections. Perhaps he will recover this time, but I doubt he will the next. Let him go: he is a child.'

Tulyet grimaced, but gave a curt order to the guard to escort the man to St John's Hospital. 'When we found him, he was tethered to a door frame with a simple knot that any five-year-old could have untied. You are doubtless right in that he was unaware of what he was doing. But I hope he is not dangerous.'

Bartholomew shook his head. 'If he was violent to your men it was probably because they frightened him. Mistress Starre had such a son, but I assumed he had died when she did during the plague. He was probably cared for in Primrose Alley by neighbours, until de Belem and Gilbert came and used him for their own purposes.'

'Who was the victim?' asked Michael, nodding at the sheeted figure being loaded onto a cart.

'Sybilla, the ditcher's daughter,' said Tulyet. 'She was identified by that woman over there.'

Bartholomew stared in disbelief, and felt the blood pound in his head. He looked to where Matilde sat on the grass at the side of the road with her back to him. He walked over to her, feeling his legs turn weak from the shock, and sank down on the grass.

'Why?' he asked.

She turned a tear-stained face. 'She saw you ride off after de Belem and Janetta last night and heard Master Buckley telling the Sheriff's men that de Belem was the high priest. She thought she was safe. She said she was going to the Sheriff's house to tell him what she had seen so that she could be a witness for him. She was killed on her way there.'

Bartholomew rubbed a hand across his face and stared at the cart containing Sybilla's body. She had jumped to the same conclusions that he had done, but for her they had proved fatal. He suddenly felt sick, as the exertions of the previous night's activities caught up with him.

Matilde rested a hand on his arm. 'There was nothing you could do, Doctor. You were kind to her and I will never forget that.'

As he looked from Sybilla's body to Matilde's grieving face, Bartholomew's despair began to turn to anger. He stood slowly.

'Do you know which house belongs to Master Jonstan, the Proctor?' he asked softly.

Matilde stood with him. 'Yes. It is a two-storey house with a green door on Shoemaker Row. Why do you want to see him? He will not help you for our sakes. He was always calling us whores and bawds. Each morning, he would prop his bed-ridden mother near the window so that she could yell abuse at us as we walked past her house.'

'They did not like prostitutes?' asked Bartholomew. He thought of when they had drunk ale with Jonstan at the Fair and he had told them his belief that the plague would return if people did not amend their sinful ways.

'Few people do,' said Matilde. 'At least not openly. But Master Jonstan is perhaps one of our most hostile opponents.'

Bartholomew waited to hear no more. Leaving Matilde staring after him, startled, he raced across the road and made for Shoemaker Row. He ignored the shouts of Michael and Tulyet behind him and ran harder, almost falling as he collided with a cart carrying vegetables to the Fair. He leapt over the fence surrounding Holy Trinity Church and tore across the churchyard, bounding over tombstones and knocking over a pardoner selling his wares on the church steps. When he emerged in Shoemaker Row, he pulled up, shaking off the angry hands of the pardoner who had followed him.

Then he saw the house, near the lower end of the street. He set off again at a run and pounded on the door of Jonstan's house. There was no answer and the shutters were firmly closed. Bartholomew grabbed one and shook it as hard as he could, drawing the attention of several passers-by, who stopped to watch what he was doing.

'Try the back door, love,' said an elderly woman kindly. 'He never uses the front door now his mother has gone.'

Bartholomew muttered his thanks and shot around the side of the house to where a wooden gate led into a small yard. Finding the gate locked, Bartholomew stood back and gave it a solid kick that almost took it off its hinges. He heard shouting in the lane and guessed that Michael and Tulyet had followed him.

The yard was deserted so Bartholomew went to the door at the back of the house. He grabbed the handle and pushed hard with his shoulder, expecting that to be locked too, and was surprised to find himself hurtle through it into Jonstan's kitchen. The Proctor was there, sitting at the table eating some oatmeal, his injured foot propped in front of him. He looked taken aback at Bartholomew's sudden entry, his blue eyes even more saucer-like than usual.

Behind Bartholomew, Michael elbowed his way in, his large face red with exertion and his breath coming in great gasps.

'Matt has come to see to your foot,' he said, his chest heaving.

'I have not!' retorted Bartholomew. He was across the kitchen in a single stride. 'So, you could not walk to the High Street last night!' he said, seizing the front of Jonstan's tabard and wrenching him from the chair. 'And you had to kill Sybilla here, where it was not so far for you to go. You were lucky, were you not, Jonstan? Most of the prostitutes have been off the streets for the past two days, but then Sybilla appeared.'

'I have no idea what you are talking about,' said Jonstan. He appealed to Michael with Tulyet behind him. 'He has gone insane!'

Bartholomew dropped Jonstan back into his chair.

'Where are your bloodstained clothes, Jonstan?' he said. He began to look around the kitchen. 'I have seen the bodies of your victims. You must have been covered in blood when you came home. What were you wearing?' He grabbed a bucket and upended its contents onto the floor, and then began to open the doors to the cupboards.

Jonstan rose unsteadily to his feet, favouring his injured ankle. 'Stop him!' he said to Tulyet. 'He cannot barge into my home and start going through my possessions! Arrest him! Brother, he is your friend. Stop him before I decide to press charges!'

Tulyet took hold of Bartholomew's shoulder, but was shaken off angrily. Michael made a half-hearted attempt to stop his friend as he went towards the small scullery.

Jonstan limped across the floor after Bartholomew.

'Stop!' he almost screamed. 'You have no right!'

Bartholomew grabbed something and pushed it into Jonstan's face. It was a bloodstained hose. 'What is this?' he snarled.

Jonstan's face was an unhealthy colour. 'I cut myself,' he said. 'I was going to wash that this afternoon.'

'Show me where you cut yourself, Master Jonstan,' said Bartholomew, clenching his fists to stop them from grabbing the Proctor by the throat.

'I will do no such thing. I am a Proctor of the University and you are under my jurisdiction. Brother, take your colleague back to his College and lock him away where he can do no more harm,' said Jonstan, pushing Michael towards Bartholomew.

Bartholomew wrenched the doors open on another cupboard and rummaged inside. He held up an assortment of women's shoes. The victims Bartholomew had seen had their shoes removed so that the little circle could be painted on their feet.

'Where did you get these?' he demanded, hurling one at Jonstan.

'They belong to my mother, not that it is any of your business,' said Jonstan.

Bartholomew continued his prowling and bent to retrieve

another article of clothing from where it had been hurled into a corner. He held it up so that Michael and Tulyet could see the huge dark blotches that stained Jonstan's tabard.

'I told you I cut myself,' said Jonstan. 'You go too far, Doctor. Leave my house at once!'

'Show me the cut that produced this much blood, and I will leave,' said Bartholomew.

Tulyet looked from the bloodstained tabard to Jonstan and began to move towards him. Jonstan made a sudden dive into the scullery, slamming the door closed, locking Michael and Tulyet in the kitchen. He turned to Bartholomew and brandished a knife coated thickly with clotting blood. He lunged towards Bartholomew, who countered his blow with a small stool he had grabbed. One of the legs bounced to the floor and Bartholomew began to back away.

'Harlot-lover!' Jonstan hissed. 'I know how you visit that filthy Matilde, and I know how you secreted the ditcher's daughter away, thinking to keep her from me!'

A great crash shook the kitchen door as Michael and Tulyet began to batter it down. Jonstan ignored it.

'My mother warned me about men who go with whores,' he said, limping closer to Bartholomew. 'And she told me the Death would come again as long as we did not learn from our sins and continued to allow the whores to roam.'

There was another crash from the kitchen door. Jonstan darted forward and made a feint to his right with the knife. Bartholomew swung wildly with the stool, and remembered that Jonstan was well trained in hand-to-hand fighting. He was not a Proctor, prowling the streets at night for miscreant scholars, for nothing. He had doubtless wrestled many a reluctant student back to his lodgings. Before he realised what was happening, Bartholomew felt one arm bent painfully behind him and saw the knife flash at the same time that there was a third crash from the locked door. He saw the hinges begin to give, as he squirmed sideways using every ounce of his strength. Jonstan's knife stabbed harmlessly into his bag. Jonstan wrenched it free but did not relinquish his hold on Bartholomew's arm.

As the door flung open, Jonstan calmly held the knife to Bartholomew's throat and smiled at Michael and Tulyet. They stopped dead. Bartholomew began to struggle, but Jonstan merely pressed the knife more firmly to his throat.

'This is a sharp knife, gentlemen,' he said. 'I have reason to know.'

'Let him go, Alric,' said Michael softly. 'You cannot escape now.'

'He is a lover of whores,' said Jonstan again. 'And that is not appropriate behaviour for a scholar. I am a Proctor and it is my duty to see that he does not do it again. My mother would not be pleased to hear that I had let him escape.'

'Your mother is dead,' said Michael. He began to move towards Jonstan, but stopped as he lifted the knife, preparing to strike.

'Stay back! My mother is upstairs. She will come down soon to see what all this noise is about. She will not be pleased to see what you have done to her door.'

Bartholomew felt Jonstan grip him tighter still. He saw that Jonstan was sufficiently unbalanced that if Michael or Tulyet made a move towards him, he would not hesitate to kill. Gritting his teeth against the ache in his arm, Bartholomew began to undo the strap on his medical bag.

'Why did you kill all those women?' asked Tulyet, seeing what Bartholomew was doing and trying to buy him time.

'My mother told me to,' Jonstan replied.

'That is not possible,' said Tulyet. 'Your mother died before the first of your victims was killed.'

'I told you, she is upstairs,' said Jonstan with exaggerated patience.

Bartholomew had his hand inside the bag and began to feel around.

'Were you a member of one of the guilds?' asked Michael, keeping his eyes firmly fixed on Jonstan's face so he would not betray what Bartholomew was doing.

'It is against the University regulations to be in a guild,' said Jonstan. 'And I most certainly was not a member of a coven.'

'But what about the Guild of the Holy Trinity?' asked Michael. 'Men like Richard Harling believe as you do that continued sin will bring about a return of the Death.'

Bartholomew had what he wanted and was struggling to open

the packet without making it rustle. Jonstan made a dismissive gesture at Michael, who licked dry lips.

'If you were not a member of the covens, why did you kill Sybilla before new moon as the high priest demanded?' he asked.

'I did nothing of the kind,' said Jonstan. 'It was time for another whore to die – one every ten days so they will all be gone before Christmas – and that is why she died, not because that raving maniac in the mask told me to do it.' He took the knife away from Bartholomew's throat but put it back again when Tulyet made a move forward.

Jonstan continued matter-of-factly. 'I killed them because my mother did not like whores patrolling the streets outside her home. You must appreciate that the Death will return if we do not take steps to eradicate evil from our land. We have been warned, and God will send another plague to destroy us if we continue to sin.'

'Why did you draw a circle on the feet of the victims?' asked Tulyet, seeing beads of sweat breaking out on Jonstan's face, and desperately trying to keep him talking.

'Because that was the sign one of the guilds used: a fallen halo. A sign that represented evil seemed an appropriate mark for evil women,' said Jonstan. He gave a short chuckle and began to move the knife.

'Matt!' yelled Michael, leaping forward. Bartholomew hurled the contents of his hand backwards into Jonstan's face, and struggled free as the Proctor fell back, choking and flailing wildly. As the powder began to burn Jonstan's eyes, he dropped the knife and began to cry out, covering his face with his hands. Bartholomew staggered back, while Tulyet kicked the knife out of reach and pushed Jonstan up against the wall.

'I cannot see!' Jonstan cried, struggling to wrench his arms from Tulyet to rub at his eyes.

'Neither can Sybilla!' said Bartholomew quietly, as he left the house.

Later that day, after they had spoken again to de Wetherset and had made formal statements to Tulyet, Bartholomew and Michael sat on the fallen tree next to the wall of the orchard, watching the sun sink down behind the trees. There was a haze of insects in the air, but it was quiet in the orchard, and Bartholomew did not want to answer any more questions that day.

He stretched his legs out in front of him and folded his arms across his chest. Next to him Michael fidgeted to get comfortable as he leaned back.

'So,' Michael said. 'Jonstan acted alone in the murder of the women. He claimed his first victim the day that his mother died, selected a prostitute randomly every ten days or so, and intended to continue so that the town would be free of them by Christmas. He was wholly unconnected with the guilds and selected one of their symbols only because it represented evil to him, in much the same way that the poor prostitutes did.'

Bartholomew was silent. Jonstan's mad claims had so unsettled him that he had asked Michael to return to Jonstan's house, just to make certain that there were no ancient mother still living upstairs as Jonstan had maintained. Michael had found no mother, but had found her room laid out as though she would return at any moment to use it.

He watched a blackbird hopping through the grass, eyeing them cautiously with beady, yellow-rimmed eyes. Michael cracked his knuckles and stretched his arms.

'So, we were called to investigate the possible death of a friar in the University chest, and we discover that the friar died because the Chancellor did not maintain his locks; that a man was killed and hidden in the bell tower because he saw the Chancellor's clerk changing his identity; that one of the town's best-known merchants was using witchcraft and kidnapping to terrify people into helping him gain a monopoly over the dyeing trade; and that the Senior Proctor was insane and was killing the town's prostitutes. Quite a feat of investigation considering how little we had to go on,' he said.

They sat for a while longer, watching the red fade from the sky as it grew dark and silent; black bats flitted between the trees. Bartholomew was tired, but did not want to move. The air was cool and pleasant after the long, hot day. His students' disputations were the next morning, and he did not want them pestering him trying to find out what questions they might be asked.

'What did you throw at Jonstan?' asked Michael after a while.

'Pepper,' said Bartholomew. He smiled suddenly. 'It is not a usual component of my medical supplies, but I was rash enough to ask Deynman to refill some of the bottles and packets that I wanted to replace after my bag was stolen in Primrose Alley. It is not a difficult task, and they are all clearly marked. I use ground mustard seeds for some treatments, but Deynman could not find any because it had all been used to make Walter sick. He gave me pepper instead. I meant to take it out and get the mustard, but never got around to it.'

'Would mustard have worked?'

Bartholomew shook his head. 'Not nearly as well as pepper.'

A shadow fell across them and Bartholomew looked up to see Boniface. In place of his habit he wore baggy homespun leggings and a dark green tunic. He sat next to them on the fallen tree and looked up to where the bats were feasting on the thousands of insects that hovered in the air.

'I assume you have decided what you wish to do,' said Bartholomew.

Boniface nodded. 'I made my confession to Master Kenyngham, and he agreed that I should go home. He said I need time to consider, and that I will be a better friar if I return than if I stay.'

'Wise advice,' said Bartholomew. 'And I imagine you do not wish to be a physician either?'

Boniface grimaced. 'Never!' he said. 'I only agreed to study medicine to follow in my father's footsteps.'

'Your father is a physician?' said Bartholomew in disbelief. How had a physician managed to sire the surly Boniface, with his rigid ideas about bleeding and treatments?

Boniface nodded. 'We seldom see eye to eye,' he added with a wry grin at Bartholomew. 'Perhaps we might do better now.'

'You live in Durham, I recall?' said Bartholomew. Boniface nodded. 'Do you have enough money to travel?'

Boniface shook his head. 'I gave it all to Master Kenyngham for my College bill, but I will manage.'

'Take this,' said Bartholomew, rummaging in his bag and handing Boniface a package.

'What is it?' he asked, taking it warily.

'Saffron,' said Bartholomew. 'Friar Lucius gave it to me. You should be able to sell it for a high price, since it is apparently almost impossible to obtain these days. It should give you enough to get home.'

'Saffron!' exclaimed Boniface, turning the package over in his hands. 'I have not seen saffron since before the Death.' He thrust it back. 'I cannot take this from you.'

'You can,' said Bartholomew. 'And if you will not take a gift, you can send the money later. Go, Boniface, before Father William realises you are missing.'

The student turned to leave, and then came back.

'The Master was right,' he said, with a sudden smile that made him look young. 'You are a good man for a heretic!'

He sped off through the trees and they heard the gate slam behind him as he left.

'Father Lucius gave me some saffron too,' said Michael, standing stiffly and stretching.

'And what did you do with yours, Brother?' asked Bartholomew, rising and looping his battered bag over his shoulder.

'I gave half to Agatha and half to Lady Matilde,' said Michael. 'Agatha will now let me into the kitchen again, while Matilde has promised me a fine meal.'

Since it was a pleasant evening to be out, they decided to walk along the river and then cut back to Michaelhouse along the High Street. The paths and streets were full of people returning home after a day at the Fair. Bartholomew saw Stanmore's apprentices pulling a cart, and realised that his brother-in-law's already considerable fortune was still being made even when he was away chasing murderers and tricksters. Bartholomew stopped to buy some over-ripe pears from a scruffy child, and shared them with Michael as they walked. As they turned down St Michael's Lane, they met Master Kenyngham going in the opposite direction.

'The Chancellor told me he is very grateful for your help over these last few days,' he said, beaming benignly at them. 'He has asked me to read over his account of it to ensure that it is accurate.'

'His account? Why would he write an account?' said Bartholomew.

'For the book of the University history,' said the Master, surprised at his question.

'But de Wetherset burned the book,' said Michael. 'He showed us.'

'He burned the one in the University chest,' said Kenyngham, 'but there is a complete copy in the chest at the Carmelite Friary – one that is not missing the pages that Gilbert stole. Of course, there are duplicates of most documents there.'

'And he is keeping that book up to date?' asked Michael incredulously.

'Well, of course,' said Kenyngham. 'It would be of no use to anyone incomplete.' He suddenly stood back, putting his hands over his mouth like a child. 'I do hope I have not been indiscreet. The Chancellor told me to keep its presence secret, but I assumed you would know, since you have been involved with the affair during the last two weeks. Oh, dear!'

'The Bishop told me there was a second chest,' said Michael. 'You have not told us anything we did not already guess.'

Kenyngham looked relieved, and his habitual gentle smile returned. He patted Michael on the arm and went on his way. When he had turned the corner, Bartholomew started to laugh.

'What is so funny?' said Michael. 'We have just learned that the Chancellor has deceived us yet again. He withheld important facts from us about members of the University; he hid vital pages when I was trying to discover a motive for the friar's death; and now he has claimed to have burned the book while all the time there is another!'

'Yes,' said Bartholomew. 'But how can you fail to admire his guile? He not only misleads us into believing that he had burned the only copy of the book, but he is using our own Master to check his facts!'

Michael laughed too, and took his arm. 'Come on, Matt. Let's go home.'

hISTORICAL NOTE

In 1350 Cambridge, like the rest of England, was still reeling under the impact of the Black Death. It is not known how many people died: social historians estimate that between one third and one half of the population of Europe perished between 1348 and 1350. The consequences of this high mortality rate have been argued for many years – some historians have suggested that the full impact of the massive population drop was not fully felt until the subsequent plagues in the 1360s and 1370s, while others argue that the effect was devastating and immediate.

Neither the University of Oxford nor the University of Cambridge left contemporary accounts of the Black Death, and so we cannot be certain how the academic communities dealt with the catastrophe and its aftermath.

Contemporary records tell that in Cambridge all members of the Dominican Friary died, while the monks at Barnwell Priory lost half their number. This abrupt decline in the number of clergy meant that there was a serious shortage of priests willing and able to work in the community. In 1349 the Bishop of Bath and Wells wrote to the clergy of his diocese to instruct them that confessions might be made to a layman if a priest was unavailable. In the same year the Archbishop of York wrote to his brother and bemoaned a lack of secular priests. Churches fell into disuse and were decommissioned, or closed up to await the time when they had a congregation again. And a few people, bereft of clergy, began to turn to other forms of worship.

In 1350 Thomas Kenyngham was the Master of Michaelhouse; Richard de Wetherset was Chancellor of the University of Cambridge (Richard Harling succeeded him in 1351); and Richard Tulyet was Mayor of Cambridge six times between

1337 and 1346. Guilds were an important part of medieval life, some taking the form of trade associations, while others were predominantly religious. The Guild of the Holy Trinity and the Guild of Purification existed in medieval Cambridge.

Important documents were kept in the tower of St Mary's Church until 1400. After 1400 Colleges began to build their own towers, and took responsibility for their own muniments. Some of these can still be seen today in Christ's College, where a narrow staircase leads to a chamber in the gate tower, where precious documents are still stored in heavy oak, iron-bound chests. The great chest at St Mary's was seized by rioting townspeople in 1381, and all the documents burned. A similar chest at the Carmelite Friary was also destroyed. Today, general University funding is still referred to as 'the University Chest', recalling a time when valuables really were kept in a strong-box.

Michaelhouse was founded in 1324 by Hervey de Stanton, who was Edward II's Chancellor of the Exchequer. King's Hall was endowed in 1337, and was a powerful institution with 32 Fellows. Physwick Hostel was a small institution which was a dependency of Gonville Hall. In 1546, Henry VIII founded Trinity College, and the buildings and lands of Michaelhouse, King's Hall, and Physwick Hostel went to make up the new institution. No parts of Michaelhouse survive, but Trinity's Great Gate dates from 1520, and was part of King's Hall.

Finally, the Stourbridge Fair was one of the most important trade gatherings in medieval England, taking place each year between August and September. The licence to hold the Fair was granted by King John to the leper hospital of St Mary Magdalene. Although the hospital ceased to exist in 1279, the Fair continued to grow and is Bunyon's 'Vanity Fair' in *Pilgrim's Progress.* It began to decline at the end of the 19th century, and finally died away in the early 1930s.

'That cough of Heppel's,' said Bartholomew, frowning as he changed the conversation to matters medical. 'It reminds me of the chest infection some of the plague victims contracted. It—'

Michael leapt to his feet in sudden horror, startling a blackbird that had been exploring the long grass under a nearby plum tree. It flapped away quickly, wings slapping at the undergrowth. 'Not the Death, Matt! Not again! Not so soon!'

Bartholomew shook his head quickly, motioning for his friend to relax. 'Of course not! Do you think I would be sitting here chatting with you if I thought the plague had returned? No, Brother, I was just remarking that Heppel's chest complaint is similar to one of the symptoms some plague victims suffered – a hacking, dry cough that resists all attempts to soothe it. I suppose I could try an infusion of angelica . . .'

As Bartholomew pondered the herbs that he might use to ease his patient's complaint, Michael flopped back down on the tree trunk clutching at his chest.

'Even after four years the memory of those evil days haunts me. God forbid we should ever see the like of that again.'

Bartholomew regarded him sombrely. 'And if it does, we physicians will be no better prepared to deal with it than we were the first time. We discovered early on that incising the buboes only worked in certain cases, and we never learned how to cure victims who contracted the disease in the lungs.'

'What was he like, this martyr, Simon d'Ambrey?' interrupted Michael abruptly, not wanting to engage in a lengthy discussion about the plague so close to bedtime. Firmly, he forced from his mind the harrowing recollections of himself and Bartholomew trailing around the town to watch people die, knowing that if he dwelt on it too long, he would dream about it. Bartholomew was not the only one who had been shocked and frustrated by his inability to do anything to combat the wave of death that had rolled slowly through the town. The monk flexed his fingers, cracking his knuckles with nasty popping sounds, and settled himself back on the tree trunk. 'I have heard a lot about Simon d'Ambrey, but I cannot tell what is truth and what is legend.'

Bartholomew considered for a moment, reluctantly forcing medical thoughts from his mind, and heartily wishing that there was another physician in Cambridge with whom he could discuss his cases – the unsavoury Robin of Grantchester was more butcher than surgeon, while the other two University physicians regarded Bartholomew's practices and opinions with as much distrust and scepticism with which he viewed theirs.

'Simon d'Ambrey was a kindly man, and helped the poor by providing food and fuel,' he said. 'The stories that he was able to cure disease by his touch are not true – as far as I can remember these stories surfaced after his death. He was not a rich man himself, but he was possessed of a remarkable talent for persuading the wealthy to part with money to finance his good works.'

Michael nodded in the gathering dusk. 'I heard that members of his household were seen wearing jewellery that had been donated to use for the poor. Personally, I cannot see the harm in rewarding his helpers. Working with the poor is often most unpalatable.'

Bartholomew laughed. 'Spoken like a true Benedictine! Collect from the rich to help the poor, but keep the best for the abbey.'

'Now, now,' said Michael, unruffled. 'My point was merely that d'Ambrey's fall from grace seems to have been an over-reaction on the part of the town. He made one mistake, and years of charity were instantly forgotten. No wonder the townspeople believe him to be a saint! It is to ease their guilty consciences!'

'There may be something in that,' said Bartholomew. He paused, trying to recall events that had occurred twenty-five years before. 'On the day that he died, rumours had been circulating that he had stolen from the poor fund, and then, at sunset, he came tearing into town chased by soldiers. He always wore a green cloak with a gold cross on the back and he had bright copper-coloured hair, so everyone knew him at once. As the soldiers gained on him, he drew a dagger and turned to face them. I saw an archer shoot an arrow, and d'Ambrey fell backwards into the Ditch.'

'It is very convenient for Thorpe that his body was never found,' observed Michael.

Bartholomew nodded. 'A search was made, of course, but the Ditch was in full flood and was flowing dangerously fast. There were stories that he did not die, and that he was later seen around the town. But I have seen similar throat wounds since then on battlefields in France, and every one proved fatal.'

'I still feel the town treated d'Ambrey shamefully,' mused Michael. 'Even if he were less than honest, the poor still received a lot more than they would have done without him.'

'I agree,' said Bartholomew, with a shrug. 'And, as far as I know, it was never proven that he was responsible for the thefts. Just because his relatives and servants stole from the poor fund did not mean that d'Ambrey condoned it, or even that he knew. After his death, his whole household fled – brother, sister, servants and all – although not before they had stripped the house of everything moveable.'

'Well, there you are then!' said Michael triumphantly. 'His family and servants fled taking everything saleable with them. Surely that is a sign of their guilt? Perhaps d'Ambrey was innocent after all. Who can say?'

Bartholomew shrugged again, poking at a rotten apple with a twig. 'The mood of the townspeople that night was ugly. D'Ambrey's family would have been foolish to have stayed to face them. Even if they had managed to avoid being torn apart by a mob, the merchants and landowners who had parted with money to finance d'Ambrey's good works were demanding vengeance. D'Ambrey's household would have been forced to compensate them for the thefts regardless of whether they were guilty or not.'

'So d'Ambrey paid the ultimate price, but his partners in crime went free,' said Michael. 'A most unfair, but not in the least surprising, conclusion to this miserable tale. Poor d'Ambrey!'

'No one went free,' said Bartholomew, sitting and leaning backwards against the wall. 'The town nominated three of its most respected burgesses to pursue d'Ambrey's family and bring them back for trial. Although the d'Ambreys had gone to some trouble to conceal the route they had taken, they were forced to sell pieces of jewellery to pay their way. These were identified by the burgesses, who traced the family to a house in Dover. But the evening before the burgesses planned their confrontation with the fugitives, there was a fire in that part of the town, and everyone died in it.'

'Really?' asked Michael, fascinated. 'What a remarkable coincidence! And none of the fugitives survived, I am sure?'

Bartholomew shook his head. 'The town erupted into an inferno by all accounts, and dozens of people died in the blaze.'

'And I suppose the bodies were too badly charred for identification,' said Michael with heavy sarcasm. 'But the requisite number were found in the d'Ambrey lodgings, and the burgesses simply assumed that the culprits were all dead. D'Ambrey's family must have laughed for years about how they tricked these "most respected burgesses"!'

'Oh no, Brother,' said Bartholomew earnestly. 'On the contrary. D'Ambrey's household died of asphyxiation and not burning. None of the bodies were burned at all as I recall. D'Ambrey's brother and sister had wounds consistent with crushing as the house collapsed from the heat, but none of their faces were damaged. The bodies were brought back to Cambridge, and displayed in the Market Square. No member of d'Ambrey's household escaped the fire, and there was no question regarding the identities of any of them.'

'I see,' said Michael, puzzled. 'This body-displaying is an addendum to the tale that is not usually forthcoming from the worthy citizens of Cambridge. Do you not consider these deaths something of a coincidence? All die most conveniently in a fire, thus achieving the twofold objective of punishing the guilty parties most horribly, and of sparing the town the bother and cost of a trial.'

Bartholomew flapped impatiently at the insects that sang their high-pitched hum in his ears. 'That was a question raised at the time,' he said, 'although certainly not openly. I eavesdropped on meetings held at my brother-in-law's house, and it seemed that none of the burgesses had unshakeable alibis on the night of the fire.'

'What a dreadful story,' said Michael in disgust. 'Did any of these burgesses ever admit to starting the fire?'

'Not that I know of,' said Bartholomew, standing abruptly in a futile attempt to try to rid himself of the insects. 'They all died years ago – none were young men when they became burgesses – but I have never heard that any of them claimed responsibility for the fire.'

'So, dozens of Dover's citizens died just to repay a few light-fingered philanthropists for making fools of the town's rich,' said Michael, shaking his head. 'How unpleasant people can be on occasions.'

'We do not know the burgesses started the fire,' said Bartholomew reasonably. 'Nothing was ever proven. It might have been exactly what they claimed – a fortuitous accident, or an act of God against wrongdoers.'

'You do not believe that, Matt!' snorted Michael in amused disbelief. 'I know you better than that! You suspect the burgesses were to blame.'

'Perhaps they were,' said Bartholomew. 'But it hardly matters now. It was a long time ago, and everyone who played any role in the affair died years ago.' He sat again, fiddling restlessly with the laces on his shirt. 'But all this is not helping with our skeleton. Did you have any luck with the Sheriff this afternoon, regarding to whom these bones might belong?'

'Do bones belong to someone, or are they someone?' mused Michael, rubbing at his flabby chins. 'We should debate that question sometime, Matt. The answer to your question is no, unfortunately. There are no missing persons that fit with your findings. Are you sure about the identification you made? The age of the skeleton?'

Bartholomew nodded slowly. 'After you had gone to the Chancellor, I helped Will dredge up the rest of the bones and the skull. I am certain, from the development of the teeth and the size and shape of other bones, that the skeleton is that of a child of perhaps twelve or fourteen years. I cannot say whether it was a boy or a girl – I do not have that sort of expertise. There were no clothes left, but tendrils of cloth suggest that the child was clothed when it was put, or fell, into the Ditch.'

'Could you tell how long it had been there?' said Michael. 'How long dead?'

Bartholomew spread his hands. 'I told you, I do not have the expertise to judge such things. At least five years, although, between ourselves, I would guess a good deal longer. But you should not tell anyone else, because the evidence is doubtful.'

'Then why do you suggest it?' asked Michael. He leaned

forward to select an apple on the ground that was not infested with wasps, and began to chew on it, grimacing at its sourness.

The blackbird he had startled earlier swooped across the grass in front of them, twittering furiously. Bartholomew reflected for a moment, trying to remember what his Arab master had taught him about the decomposition of bodies. He had not been particularly interested in the lesson, preferring to concentrate his energies on the living than learning about cases far beyond any help he could give.

'All bones do not degenerate in the same way once they are in the ground, or in the case of this child, in mud. Much depends on the type of material that surrounds them, and the amount of water present. These bones had been immersed in the thick, clay-like mud at the bottom of the Ditch, and so are in a better condition than if they had been in peat, which tends to preserve skin, but rot bone. But despite this, the bones are fragile and crumbly, and deeply stained. I would not be surprised if they had been lying in the Ditch for twenty or thirty years.'

'So, we might be looking for a child of fourteen who died thirty years ago?' asked Michael in astonishment. 'Lord, Matt! Had he lived, that would make him older than us!'

'I could be wrong,' said Bartholomew. He stood and stretched, giving such a huge yawn that Michael was compelled to join him.

Michael tossed his apple core into the grass. 'Simon d'Ambrey died twenty-five years ago,' he said thoughtfully. 'Perhaps even at the same time as this child. Can you tell how this child met its death?'

'Again, I cannot be certain,' said Bartholomew, rubbing his eyes tiredly. 'But there is a deep dent on the back of the skull that would have compressed the brain underneath. Had the child been alive when that wound was delivered, it would have killed him – or her – without doubt. However, if the body has lain in the King's Ditch for thirty years, the damage may have been done at any time since by something falling on it. So, this child may have been knocked on the head and disposed of in the Ditch; he may have fallen and hit his head; or he may have died of some disease and his body disposed of in the Ditch and the skull damaged later.'

Michael disagreed. 'Not the latter. Why would anyone need

to hide a corpse of someone who had died in a legitimate manner? And surely someone would miss a child if it had had an accident and fallen in the river? The only likely solution, I am sorry to say, is the first one. That the poor thing was killed and the body hidden in the Ditch.'

Bartholomew shook his head, smiling, and slapped his friend on the shoulders. 'You have become far too involved in murder these last few years,' he said. 'Now you look for it where there may be none. How do you know the child was not an orphan, or that his parents simply did not report him missing? You know very well that a death in a large, poor family is sometimes seen as more of a relief than a cause for grief, in that it is one less mouth to feed – especially with girls. Or perhaps he was one of a group of travellers, who had passed out of Cambridge before he was missed? Or perhaps he was a runaway from—'

'All right, all right,' grumbled Michael good-humouredly. 'Point taken. But you were in Cambridge as a child. Did any of your playmates go missing with no explanation?'

Bartholomew leaned down to pick up his medicine bag. 'Not that I recall. It was a long time ago.'

'Oh, come now, Matt!' exclaimed Michael. 'You are not an old man yet! If you are right in your hunch about the time of this child's death, he may well have been a playmate of yours. Older than you, perhaps, but you would have been children together.'

Bartholomew yawned again. 'I can think of none, and I did not play with girls, anyway, which means I only have knowledge of half of the juvenile population. You should ask someone else. And now it is late, and so I will wish you good night.'

He turned to walk back through the orchard to the College, leaving Michael to his musing. He cut through the kitchens, his leather-soled shoes skidding on the grease that formed an ever-present film over the stone-flagged floor. The great cooking fires were banked for the night, and the kitchens were deserted. A door, concealed behind a painted wooden screen, led from the kitchen to the porch where Michaelhouse's guests were received before being ushered to the hall and conclave above. Bartholomew walked through the porch, and across the beaten earth of the courtyard to his room in the north wing.

The last rays of the sun were fading, and the honey-coloured stone of Michaelhouse's walls was a dark amber. Bartholomew paused, and glanced around at the College, admiring, as he always did, the delicate tracery on the windows of the north and south wings where the scholars slept. The dying sunlight still caught the bright colours of the College founder's coat of arms over the porch, a cacophony of reds, blues and golds. He yawned yet again, and gave up the notion of reading for an hour by the light of a candle before he slept – all that would happen would be that he would fall asleep at the table and candles were far too expensive a commodity to waste, not to mention the possibility that an unattended candle might fall and set the whole College alight.

His mind wandered back to the grisly display of asphyxiated corpses in the Market Square some twenty-five years ago, the result of another careless candle if the burgesses were to be believed. Then, he pushed thoughts of murder and mayhem to the back of his mind, opening the door to his small, neat room. He lay on the bed, intending to rest for a few moments before rising again to wash and fold his clothes, but he was almost immediately asleep, oblivious even to the sharp squeal of a mouse that the College cat killed under his bed.

Alone in the orchard, Michael chewed his lip thoughtfully. Bartholomew had a sister who lived nearby, whose husband was one of the richest and most influential merchants in the town. Edith was some years older than her brother. She had married young, and Bartholomew had lived with her and her new husband until he went to the school at the Benedictine Abbey in the city of Peterborough to the north. Perhaps Edith, or her husband, Sir Oswald Stanmore, might remember something about a missing child.

Michael saw the Stanmores the following day on his way back from church. It was a fine Sunday afternoon, and the streets thronged with people. Gangs of black-gowned students sang and shouted, eyed disapprovingly by the merchants and tradesmen dressed in their Sunday finery. Edith and her husband looked happy and prosperous, walking arm-in-arm down Milne Street to the large house where Stanmore had his business premises. Although Stanmore worked in Cambridge, he preferred to live at his manor in Trumpington, a tiny village two miles south of the town. It was unusual to see him and his wife in Cambridge on a Sunday, and Michael strongly suspected that the merchant had been conducting some covert business arrangement when he should have been paying attention to the words of the priest at mass. Edith, a lively soul who enjoyed the occasional excursion into the town from the village, would not have noticed what her husband was doing, and would have been more interested in catching up with the local gossip from the other merchants' wives.

Edith had the same distinctive black hair and pale complexion of her brother, a stark contrast to Stanmore's slate-grey hair and beard. She wore a dress of deep crimson, and she carried a blue cloak over one arm, one corner of it trailing unheeded along the dusty road. With a smile, the monk recognised that she apparently had the same careless disregard for clothes as her brother, whose shirts and hose were always patched and frayed. He headed towards her, dodging past a procession of Carmelite friars heading towards St Mary's Church, and jostling aside a pardoner with unnecessary force. Michael did not like pardoners.

Edith hugged Michael affectionately, making the usually sardonic, and occasionally lecherous, monk blush. Oswald Stanmore admonished her for her undignified behaviour in the street, but his words lacked conviction, and they all knew she would do exactly the same when she next met Brother Michael.

Stanmore, ever aware of the latest happenings in the town from his extensive network of informants, asked Michael about the skeleton that had been found. Michael told them briefly, and asked whether they were aware of any missing children during the last twenty or thirty years.

'Thirty years!' exclaimed Edith. 'Has this body lain in the Ditch so long?'

Michael shrugged indifferently. 'No, no. I am just keen to ensure we do not confine ourselves to looking recently, when the child may have died much earlier.'

Stanmore scratched his chin as he wracked his brains. 'There was old Mistress Wilkins' daughter,' he said uncertainly.

Edith shook her head. 'Reliable witnesses saw her alive and married to a farm lad over in Haslingfield village a few weeks after she disappeared. What about the tinker's boy? The one who was said to have drowned near the King's Mill?'

Now Stanmore shook his head. 'His body was found a year later. And anyway, he was too young – four or five years old. There was that dirty lad whom Matt befriended, who told us he was a travelling musician, and led the local boys astray for a few weeks.' He turned to Edith. 'It may well be him; he would have been about twelve. He set the tithe barn alight and then ran away. What was his name?'

'Norbert,' said Edith, promptly and rather primly, her mouth turning down at the corners in disapproval. 'I remember him well. We had only just arrived in Trumpington, and Matt immediately struck up a friendship with that horrible boy. It hardly created a good impression with my new neighbours.'

Stanmore gave her hand an affectionate squeeze, and spoke to Michael. 'After the barn fire, we locked this Norbert in our house, so that the Sheriff could talk to him about it the next day. But somehow he escaped during the night.'

'Poor Norbert!' said Bartholomew, coming up silently behind them, making them all jump. 'Still blamed for burning the tithe barn, even though he had nothing to do with it.'

'So you insisted at the time. But he fled the scene of the crime, and that was tantamount to admitting his guilt,' said Stanmore, recovering his composure quickly.

'He fled because he knew that no one would believe his innocence,' said Bartholomew. 'And because I let him go.'

There was a short silence as his words sank in. Michael smothered a grin, and folded his arms to watch what promised to be an entertaining scene.

'Matt!' exclaimed Edith, shocked. 'What dreadful secrets have you been harbouring all this time?'

Bartholomew did not reply immediately, frowning slightly as he tried to recall events from years before. 'I had all but forgotten Norbert's alleged crime.'

'Alleged?' spluttered Stanmore. 'The boy was as guilty as sin!'

'That was what everyone was quick to assume,' said Bartholomew. 'No one bothered to ask his side of the story and then make a balanced judgement. That was why I helped him to escape.'

'But we locked the priest with him in the solar!' said Stanmore, regarding Bartholomew with patent disbelief. He turned to Michael, who quickly assumed an air of gravity to hide his amusement. 'Norbert was only a child, and even though he had committed a grave crime, we did not want to frighten him out of his wits. We also thought the priest might wring a confession from him.' He swung back to Bartholomew, still uncertain whether to believe his brother-in-law's claim. 'How could you let him out without the priest seeing you?'

'The priest was drunk,' said Bartholomew, smiling. 'So much so, that the cracked bells of Trumpington Church and their unholy din could not have roused him. I waited until everyone was asleep, took the solar key from the shelf outside, and let Norbert out. After, I relocked the door, and Norbert disappeared into the night to go to his sister, who was a kitchen maid at Dover Castle.'

'But this is outrageous!' said Stanmore, aghast. 'How could you do such a thing? You abused my trust in you! And those bells are not cracked, I can assure you. They just need tuning.'

Edith suddenly roared with laughter, and some of the outrage went out of her husband. 'All these years and you kept your secret!' she said. She reached up and ruffled her brother's hair as she had done when he was young. 'Whatever possessed you to risk making my husband look foolish in front of his neighbours?'

Bartholomew looked at Stanmore thoughtfully for a moment before answering. 'I am not the only one who knows Norbert was innocent. I suppose I still should not tell, but it was such a long time ago that it cannot matter any more. It was not Norbert who fired the tithe barn: it was Thomas Lydgate.'

'Thomas Lydgate? The Principal of Godwinsson Hostel?' said Michael, halfway between merriment and horror.

Bartholomew nodded, smiling at the monk's reaction. 'I suspect he did not set the building alight deliberately, but you know how fast dry wood burns. I suppose he had no wish to own up to a crime that might make him a marked man for the rest of his life, and Norbert was an ideal candidate to take the blame, since he was an outsider, and had no one to speak for him.'

'But how do you know this?' asked Stanmore, still indignant about the wrong that had been perpetrated against him in his own house. 'Why are you so certain that Norbert did not commit the crime and Lydgate did?'

'Because Norbert and I saw Lydgate enter the barn when we were swimming nearby; we saw smoke billowing from it a few moments later and someone came tearing out. Naturally curious, we crept through the trees to see who it was. We came across Lydgate, complete with singed shirt, breathing heavily after his run, and looking as though he had seen the Devil himself. If you recall, it was Lydgate who raised the alarm, and Lydgate who first blamed Norbert.'

'But what if Lydgate followed Norbert and killed him to ensure he would never tell what he had seen?' mused Michael, suddenly serious. 'It is perfectly possible that the bones in the Ditch belong to your Norbert. From what you say, he was the right age, and all this appears to have happened about twenty-five years ago.'

'Impossible!' said Bartholomew. 'I received letters from Norbert in Dover a few weeks later to tell me that he had joined his sister, and he wrote to me several times after that, until I went to study in Paris. He has made a success of his life, which is more than could be said had the Trumpington witch-hunters laid their vindictive hands on him.'

'And how could you receive letters without my knowledge?' demanded Stanmore imperiously. 'This is nonsense! How could you have paid whoever brought these messages, and how is it that my steward never mentioned mysterious missives from Dover? Not much slips past his eagle eyes!'

Edith shuffled her feet, and looked uncomfortable. 'Letters from Dover, you say?' she asked. 'From someone called Celinia?'

Stanmore rounded on her. 'Edith! Do not tell me you were a party to all this trickery, too!'

'Not exactly,' said Edith guiltily, looking from her husband to her brother.

'Not at all,' said Bartholomew firmly. 'Norbert's sister was called Celinia. I imagine she wrote the letters, since Norbert was illiterate, and she signed her own name so that no one would know the letters were from him. Celinia is an unusual name, and Norbert knew I would guess that the letters were from him if she signed them. Edith simply assumed I had found myself a young lady. She did not ask me about it, so I did not tell her.'

'Extraordinary!' said Michael gleefully. 'All this subterfuge in such a respectable household!'

'Really!' said Stanmore, still annoyed. 'And in my own house! The villagers were not pleased that Norbert had evaded justice while in my safekeeping, and neither was the Sheriff when he found he had made the journey for nothing. Thank God Norbert was not caught later to reveal your part in his escape, Matt!'

'Well I never!' drawled Michael facetiously, nudging Bartholomew in the ribs. 'You interfering with the course of justice, and Lydgate an arsonist! Did you confront him with what you had seen?'

'Are you serious?' queried Bartholomew. 'Since Lydgate was not above allowing a child to take the blame for his crime – for which Norbert might well have been hanged – it would have been extremely foolish for me to have let him know that I had witnessed his guilty act. No, Brother. I have carried Lydgate's secret for twenty-five years and none have known it until now except Norbert.'

'I still cannot believe you took the law into your own hands in my house in such a way,' said Stanmore, eyeing his brother-in-law dubiously. 'What else have you done that will shock me?'

Bartholomew laughed. 'Nothing, Oswald. It was the only serious misdemeanour I committed while under your roof . . . that I can remember.'

Stanmore regarded Bartholomew with such rank suspicion that the physician laughed again. He was about to tease Stanmore further, when he saw the Junior Proctor, Guy Heppel, hurrying along the street towards them, his weasel-like face creased with concern.

When Heppel reached them, he was breathless, and there was an unhealthy sheen of sweat on his face. He rubbed his hands down the sides of his gown nervously.

'There is another,' he gasped. 'Another body has been found in the King's Ditch next to Valence Marie!'

On a chilly January evening in 56 B.C., an Egyptian ambassador and a eunuch priest seek out Gordianus the Finder. But the ambassador, a philosopher named Dio, has come to ask for something Gordianus cannot give—help in staying alive. Before the night is out, he will be murdered.

Hired to investigate Dio's death by a beautiful woman with a scandalous reputation, Gordianus will follow a trail of political intrigue into the highest circles of power and the city's most hidden arenas of debauchery. There he will learn nothing is as it seems—not the damning evidence he uncovers, not the suspect he sends to trial, not even the real truth behind Dio's death which lies in secrets—not of state, but of the heart.

THE VENUS THROW

Steven Saylor

The Owen Archer historical mysteries of

Candace M. Robb

from
ST. MARTIN'S DEAD LETTER MYSTERIES

The Apothecary Rose

Christmastide, 1363—and, at an abbey in York, two pilgrims lie dead of an herbal remedy. Suspicious, the Archbishop has Owen Archer masquerade as an apprentice at the shop that dispensed the fatal potion.
_____ 95360-7 $5.99 U.S./$7.99 Can.

The Lady Chapel

During a summertime feast, a prominent wool merchant is murdered in the shadow of York's great Minster. Owen Archer must unravel threads of greed, treachery and passion that run all the way to the royal court...
_____ 95460-3 $5.50 U.S./$6.50 Can.

The Nun's Tale

A ghostly pale woman claims to be the resurrected Joanna Calverley, a nun who died of a fever some months before. Owen Archer is called to investigate the murders that seem to follow in her wake.
_____ 95982-6 $5.99 U.S./$7.99 Can.